Praise for *The Good Pa*

"Underwritten by a wealth of human understa............ ....
characters toward each other against the forces of nature. The results are as
powerful as they are unsettling."
—*The Sydney Morning Herald*

"An exquisite piece of writing, carefully and deliberately told."
—*Herald Sun* (Australia)

"From the first word, London is in control, unfolding the surprises
tantalizingly, little by little. . . . The quality of observation, close-focus and
long-range, is so sharp you'll jab Post-It notes on every page. . . . A lifetime's
close scrutiny has been made sense of and placed in this book."
—*The Australian*

"A novel you read slowly, with steadily increasing pleasure and interest,
getting to know the widely varied and vividly realized characters, savoring the
experience of so thoroughly inhabiting someone else's world and taking it
away with you at the end."
—*The Advertiser* (Australia)

Praise for *Gilgamesh:*

"Streamlined, strong, and remarkably lovely . . . Reading [it] is like watching a
magician who can do many things rapidly, expertly, and all at once."
—Francine Prose, *The New York Times Book Review*

"Bold and beautiful . . . [An] astonishing saga . . . A woman as epic hero? It's
high time."
—*O: The Oprah Magazine*

"London is such a pleasure to read, her prose a seamlessly shifting blend of
poetry, pathos, and humor."
—*The Washington Post*

"[A] compelling debut novel . . . The epic scope of the novel is
complemented by an extraordinary sensitivity to detail. . . . The settings glow
with a dreamlike intensity, evoking both the allure of adventure and the
ambivalent embrace of home."
—*The Boston Globe*

"A story of personal odyssey with mythic reverberations . . . A quiet stunner
of a book about growing up, leaving home, and finding our way back."
—Colleen Kelly Warren, *St. Louis Post-Dispatch*

The Good Parents

The Good Parents

Parents

JOAN LONDON

BLACK CAT
New York
a paperback original imprint of Grove/Atlantic, Inc.

Published simultaneously in Canada
Printed in the United States of America

First published in 2008 in Australia by Vintage an imprint of
Random House Australia Pty Ltd.

ISBN-10: 0-8021-7057-9
ISBN-13: 978-0-8021-7057-6

Black Cat
a paperback original imprint of Grove/Atlantic, Inc.
841 Broadway
New York, NY 10003

Distributed by Publishers Group West

www.groveatlantic.com

09 10 11 12   10 9 8 7 6 5 4 3 2 1

For my family

1
The Office

The best time was always afterwards, alone, in the Ladies' Restroom on the first floor. It had high frosted-glass windows that at this hour, before the frail winter sun had found its way between the buildings of the city, shed a dim grainy light like old footage in a documentary film.

How long since this room had been modernised? There was a quicklime incinerator for tampons and a yellowed notice about a women's refuge, *contact Terri*, which might have been there since the seventies. It was the sort of place she was always trying to describe in the on-going letter in her head. But who was this letter to? Who wants to read about the toilets at your place of work? The rotating chrome soap dispensers, the mint-green handbasins on their pedestals, the big wire basket for paper towels – the sense of living in another generation's film?

Her father of course would be hanging out for this sort of news, but she wasn't going to ponder to his romanticism. And Jason Kay – if a letter ever reached him – would read anything from her with painstaking attention, but she didn't want to think about Jason. In fact she hadn't sent a single letter home since she'd come to Melbourne, though she'd started several on the office computer in the afternoons.

She had this room to herself. The other women in the building, the beauticians from Beauty by Mimi on the ground floor, didn't start work till nine. It was pristine, like a beach first thing in the morning. She didn't switch on the fluoro, but stayed in the gray light. All the contents of the little bag she kept in her desk were laid out on the broad sill of the handbasin. She washed and dried herself with paper towels, fixed her hair, put on deodorant and mascara. The antique plumbing hummed as she ran the taps. She felt safe here, performing these classic female rituals. Every morning at this mirror she thought for a moment of her mother and the compulsive little pout she made when she looked at herself, like an old-fashioned model.

When do you stop being haunted by your parents? The face that looked back at her was not a face that they had ever seen, the eyes darkened and reckless, the skin luminous. It made her shy, she turned away and then could not resist another peek. She knew this transformation wouldn't last for long.

It was time to go back upstairs. She liked the washed lightness of her body as she moved to the door. She liked the silver flecks in the faded terrazzo floor. But then of course she liked everything, everything seemed to have significance, for a short while, afterwards.

Global Imports occupied the whole top floor of the narrow old building, above Jonathan Fung Barristers. Its corridor ended in a door out to the rusty metal landing of the fire escape, where on a fine day, amongst the roar of air-con vents, you could sit and eat your lunch and look out over the roofs along the back laneway. Someone had once slung a little washing line out there and tried to grow basil in a pot. It was like being in Naples or New York.

The office consisted of one large bare-walled room, high-ceilinged like all the rooms in this building, with two tall front windows facing the street. A head-high partition of varnished ply and frosted glass made a waiting space by the door. Here there were two cane armchairs and a low glass table on which sat a Cinzano ashtray – some of the clients came from countries where it was still OK to smoke at business deals – and a neat pile of magazines, *Time*, *Fortune*, *BRW*. It was part of her duties to keep these up to date and to water the rubber plant in its bamboo stand.

As soon as she opened the door she knew he wasn't there. She could sense his absence even before she saw that his black coat had gone from beside her sheepskin jacket on the hooks behind the door. Inside the office the answering machine's red light was flickering on his desk. He'd made the call from his car in traffic, she could hardly hear him. He said that he was going home, there'd been a turn for the worse and could she please just carry on. He would be in touch, he said, and something else that was lost in a blast of static.

She stood looking out a window for several minutes, holding her little quilted bag. The long window had a view of the black spire of the church opposite and the bare swaying tips of the churchyard trees. Below her a phone was ringing in Jonathan Fung's office. Someone with a light tread was running up the stairs. The working day had started.

There was no other message. She had a sense of abandonment which was, she knew, unreasonable. He'd left the computer on and the coffee-maker. She poured herself a cup and sat down at her desk. The air in the room was still thick with their closeness. But her feeling of well-being, of doing good in the world, had faded.

Maynard Flynn started work before anybody else in the building because he had a sick wife. She slept during the morning while their son stayed with her and Maynard left at noon to be with her when she was awake. He asked Maya at the interview if she could work from seven till three. For the time being he was in and out of the office and needed someone to hold the fort. Things had, he said, with a little grimace, got rather out of hand. That was six months ago, in summer, soon after she'd arrived.

Each morning of those first couple of weeks she took the cup of coffee he offered her and plunged straight into the messy paperwork and files. She spread them out in piles all over the seagrass matting and for a couple of hours before the phone started ringing, she crouched over them, silent and frowning. He seemed both impressed and entertained.

In this way she saved herself from the shyness that threatened to take her over whenever she was face to face with him. Shyness, she knew, had a mind of its own, chose when to strike, caused red blotches to break out on her neck, made her voice catch, her eyes fill with tears. She lived in dread of its attacks.

His wife's name was Delores. Sometimes he spoke of her as Dory. Every few days now her friends phoned to ask him how she was. He had a special tone with these women, Francine, Bernadette and Tina, women from her church. His voice dropped a note, became suave and medical. She'd had a good night, thanks, the doctor was pleased. Yes, he and Andrew were coping well. At the same time he kept tapping away at the computer. These conversations never lasted long. Maya began to understand that they were all waiting, that things were coming to an end.

She'd never got up early before in her life. This was one of her new adult acts, making herself wake before her natural span of sleep was done. She put the alarm clock out of reach, leapt from bed, pulled on her clothes, cleaned her teeth and rushed up to Victoria Street while the last stars were fading. The 6.40 tram approached just as she reached the Vietnamese deli. She liked to make the transition between sleep and work as swift and dreamlike as possible, while she was still all instinct and warmth.

As winter came on, each morning was darker than the one before. Nobody on the tram looked at one another, their faces blank and private. Some were shift-workers falling in and out of sleep on their way home. She was like a shift-worker herself, she thought, her real life happened at the other end of the day from other people's.

Leaves rolled down the pavement ahead of her as she stepped off the tram. This was when she liked the inner city most, empty and echoing, a half-world, the light seeping into the dark. Car headlights and street lamps were still on. A newsagency was open, also the espresso bar on the corner, serving the little community she was briefly part of, the dog owners and joggers and council workers in rubbish trucks. Light broke out minute by minute as she walked, pale splashes over roofs and walls. Birds were going like mad in the trees around the old church. Bells rang the hour somewhere, pink clouds streaked the sky ahead. Sometimes the experience of striding up this street – the achievement of being there – could give her a historical feeling, as if she were looking back at herself, as if these mornings were already in the past.

She thought of the sick woman lying in the dawn, listening to the birds. Her relief. Her pillow shaken, her sheets smoothed, ready at last to sleep.

She had a key to let herself into the building. Past the brass letterboxes, past Mimi's glass door with its stencilled sign, *Waxing, Peeling, Paraffin Treatments*: she still hadn't found out what Paraffin Treatments were. The stairway was in darkness. She was aware of the ticking life of the building when it was left to itself, and its particular smell, ancient wood and radiators and dust, like an old person's house. Her heart started thumping as she climbed the stairs. Her stomach felt queasy with excitement. Sometimes Dory had to have an injection and he'd arrive later than her. She could always sense if he was or wasn't there. Nearly always. With about 98.2 per cent accuracy, as her brother would say.

'I thought you were a farm girl!' he said, amused, when she arrived that first morning windswept and out of breath. 'I thought you'd be used to getting up at dawn.' She began to explain that she didn't grow up on a farm, but in a town in the wheat-belt, that her family weren't real country people, but whenever she spoke about her past she knew he wasn't really listening. He went on making jokes about her strong shoulders and legs, from all that hay baling and cow milking: if he was in a good mood he liked to tease her about her cowgirl strength. The only questions he ever asked her were about her social life in Melbourne. When she told him after the weekend that she'd walked in the Botanical Gardens, or gone for dim sum with her housemate Cecile, he seemed disbelieving, even disappointed, and quizzed her about clubs and bars and boys. She shook her head. Something froze in her when he asked her these sorts of questions.

You could tell he wasn't being looked after by a woman. The first time he held her his shirt smelt musty, as if it had been left too long in the washing machine. A bachelor smell, like some of the young male teachers at school.

It was a fatherly sort of hug that first time, an arm around her shoulder as he left for the day. The culmination of all the little taps on her arm he'd been giving her over the past couple of weeks when he was pleased with her. Just a little more lingering.

Good old country commonsense, he said that first time, his face close to hers, his arm along her shoulders. A can-do attitude, he said. This was his way of showing his approval, she told herself. It was what good employers were supposed to do. Look how it made her work even harder! All the same, all afternoon she could feel the heat of his arm at the back of her neck. It seemed like a long time since anyone had touched her.

That night she dreamt she was walking down the main street in Warton with a friend of her brother's, Ben Lester, a nice enough boy, tall, freckled, three years younger than she was, to whom she'd never given a single moment's thought. Except it wasn't Warton, it was voluptuously beautiful, it was India, it was Paradise. A grove of feathery palm trees all swayed in the same direction, like underwater plants, beside a heaving grape-green river. The light was bronze, as before a storm. Everywhere she looked was this swelling beauty, exotic and familiar at the same time. She and Ben Lester stood beneath a blossoming tree by the river and moved closer, their feelings generous and loving.

She woke with the words *of course he wants you* in her head.

The next morning as she climbed the stairs, she was suddenly aware that they were the only two people in the building. When she let herself into the office and saw him she was too shy to speak.

'There you are,' he said softly, as if he too had been dreaming of blossoms and rivers. He stretched out his hand to her. 'Maya,' he said, to her vast surprise, and yet deep down some part of her wasn't surprised at all. 'You're *tormenting* me.' His voice was husky. 'I can't stand it.' Her first thought was that she must have done something unfair to him, and she searched her mind for how she might have hurt him. He looked tired as if he hadn't slept. He must be cracking up under the strain of Dory. She took a step towards him. That was the crossing-over time.

From that moment she ceased having her own life.

When she first came here she saw an office that was too bare, that had been cheaply, hurriedly put together. It looked like he'd just moved in and could disappear overnight, though Global Imports had existed for some years. None of the furniture suited the dark wood of the old room: the flimsy pine desks, the metal filing cabinet, the plastic table for the fax and photocopier. The matting was greenish and springy as if it had only recently been grass. In the corner there was a little fold-up divan, on which, before Delores got sick, he used to take a siesta, a habit he'd picked up during his time in Asia, he said. Only the long uncurtained windows with their view of the spire were beautiful.

Now in her mind it was a room at the top of a tower, floating amongst the clouds, detached from the world. She was grateful for its unclutteredness, the space it gave them, its work functions pushed to the margins. Its bareness seemed to say that this was enough, this was all they could ever ask for. They lay on the divan's thin mattress which he placed on the seagrass. There he was fully attentive. A beam of early sun streaked across the floor, stroked their white winter ankles. It was a shock to see white flesh in the pure morning light.

Whenever she was alone, in the office, on the tram, in bed, at any time of the night or day, she would see his hands, or the flank of his cheek, relive his touch, feel the weight of his legs, hear his voice in her ear as she fell asleep. She would sense the gray light swirling around them in their wordless concentration, hear the bird cries of their endless practice, closer and closer to the brink, and a shiver would run through her all over again.

The reason she couldn't write letters was because he was everywhere and everything and he was secret.

Sometimes the phone rang, the answering machine clicked into life or a fax spewed out. He chuckled. She knew it excited him, to be lying with her at the top of this silent house of business. He liked to stalk naked across the room, and stand at the window, lightly scratching himself, with only the birds to see him.

For a short time afterwards, dressed and back at his desk, he was blinky, dopey, like a little boy woken from sleep, winking at her as he spoke on the phone, calmer, no longer *tormented*. He was very attractive to her then. 'My legs don't work,' she said as she tried to stand up from the mattress, and he'd smile but keep listening to his messages. She dressed quickly, took the little bag from her desk and set off downstairs, briefly carefree and light-headed.

He winked and joked when he was happy and had sudden bouts of fondness for her. As he passed he'd whisper in her ear that she was the best little worker he'd ever had.

Although she was proud to have made him happy, she couldn't laugh at this with him. What had happened between them seemed too large, too radical for jokes. She smiled at him but she couldn't laugh.

A *country girl*. He'd been surprised he was her first. Wasn't that unusual these days? he asked. The isolation in the bush perhaps? She shrugged, not knowing why he was so keen for news of her generation, or why he seemed so taken up with the idea of all young women as freely promiscuous. She didn't want to think about this.

She didn't say that the way he made her feel aroused a longing in her to tell him about horses and her brother and her dog and the seasons and landscapes of the wheat-belt, all the things that fed into the river of loving that flowed through her.

She knew all the tones of his voice. He had a voice for doing business with Asians and another voice for Australians. Like her father, he became more macho, jokey, his accent broader, when dealing with Australian men. He was more at ease exchanging smooth small talk with the Asians.

Then there was the way he had of talking to his mother, tucking the phone under his chin, keeping on working, rolling his eyes now and then, ironic, yet always patient. His mother lived in a retirement village and forgot things and left flustered messages late at night: *Maynard? Maynard? Are you there?* – her voice quavery with self-pity.

Who are you? she demanded, impatient if Maya answered the phone. *Oh, you're the little lass from the West, yes, yes, he's told me about you.* There were old girls like this in Warton, left over from the big landowner families, shuffling into the newsagency with their hats and walking sticks, pretending to be helpless but always getting their own way. Going on and on about something that annoyed them, while everybody else had to wait.

His nicest voice, the only time he sounded open and natural, was when he spoke to his son Andrew. He was always happy after he hung up the phone to Andrew, smiling to himself for a few minutes, in a little dream. Andrew was an agricultural science student, writing his PhD – Maynard always mentioned the PhD – who'd come back home to help look after his mother. It was when she thought of Dory Flynn as a mother that Maya was able to grasp the momentousness of the situation, the affliction that had struck this family. A mother with cancer.

The light in the house going out.

Just before she left Warton she went to say goodbye to Miriam Kershaw, the headmaster's wife. Miriam had asked for her, and at the last moment she knew she had to go. She steeled herself to step into that house, dark and stale with illness, walk down the shadowed corridor, sit beside her, and not show shock at Miriam's body, so terrifyingly shrunken in her bed. Afterwards she went to the creek and lay back on the boulders and took deep swigs of air. I'm young! I'm young! she breathed.

Her father was angry that she'd been summoned and angry that she went. Something about Miriam always made him harsh and impatient.

Maynard never spoke of Dory's illness in the office and she knew she mustn't ask him. He remained matter-of-fact, calm and cheery. He gave no sign that he was worried. She couldn't tell how much he cared. Perhaps he pretended not to care because he cared too much?

She worried that he didn't care enough.

But this morning when she came in after the weekend, the

11

face he turned to her shocked her. His eyes were sunken, his face blotchy, unshaven. For the first time she thought of him as old. He'd been up all night, he said. Things were going downhill. His voice was gruff and his hands shook a little as he shuffled papers. I shouldn't really have come in, he mumbled, looking around the room. She knew it was for her, the 'fix' he sometimes joked about. In that moment she had no suspicions of him. She went straight to him at the desk. As she held his head against her, her eyes searched out the spire in the window behind him, her point of reference. Why should she be troubled by something so simple, so generous? She bent and whispered how she'd missed him, how she'd hardly lasted the weekend. She loved him for his need of her, and for his pain at last, his redemption.

At midday there was still no word from him. She was so hungry that she closed the office and ate a hamburger and chips – taboo foods of her childhood – very quickly, sitting on a stool at the window of the espresso bar on the corner. Then a jam doughnut. She knew she ate too much to make up for being parted from him. The cafe was busy but not fashionable. She didn't feel intimidated here. It had a TV and a magazine rack and a table of pale-skinned salesmen meeting for coffee. There was a pinup board in the back corner covered with fluttery desperate-looking homemade notices, to sell, to buy, to rent. It was here that she'd noticed Cecile's *Room to Let* sign, her eye drawn to its professional graphics and its lack of chest-beating. She was still proud of this moment of good judgement, and the luck it brought her, to find Cecile. There was a new sign pinned up, a flyer for something called *The Marijuanalogues*, which made her think of her father. *An evening of hilarity you will not soon forget (unless you smoke pot of course). Spread the herb!* She remembered that her parents were coming to Melbourne to stay with her. When? It must be soon. For the past couple of months she'd deliberately wiped all thought of this visit from her mind.

She finished off with a large Diet Coke and left. The day stretched endlessly ahead.

The office was one in a row of old buildings, all joined together, two or three storeys high — a fashion agency for uniforms, a paper warehouse, a plumber's workshop — down a side street, facing the church. It was like an old-fashioned village street tucked in amongst the high-rises. Seen from a distance, it would make a good location for a film.

The city centre was only a few streets away, but she never went there, among the fashionable people. She preferred to sit in the courtyard of the church. Every day she felt the need to collect herself, by being outside, near trees. The church was nested down between the glass flanks of the high-rise on either side of it, a valley surrounded by mountains. It was built of blackened stone, as old as England. Clusters of white plastic chairs were set out hospitably beneath tall English trees. A few twittery sparrows hopped along the bare black branches. She was used to native trees full of singing birds. Sometimes it was in this courtyard that she could feel most fully a stranger. When she first came to Melbourne she was almost surprised to find the same currency. It was like another country over here.

Clouds scudded past the tops of the skyscrapers so you could think it was the buildings that were moving. A hush seemed to descend over the precinct and for a moment everything stilled. Nothing appeared, no car, no passer-by. No phone rang, no door slammed, no voice called out a greeting. On the Diet Coke billboard next to the cafe someone had scrawled *Nutra Sweet Causes Cancer*.

She understood suddenly that death meant *ending*. Her heart started to thud, for Dory.

By three o'clock she felt very bad indeed. She shut down the computer, put on her jacket, zipped it up to the chin and locked the office door. Although she had no experience of religion she went straight across the road into the old church and sat down in a pew. She had an impulse to pray for Dory, though she didn't know what for. Too late now to pray that she'd be cured.

For her forgiveness? Why hadn't she thought of this before? She'd let herself believe that to be held and caressed like this was a good thing, kind and loving, when they were both so lonely. He was more lonely than her in a way. But who knew what Dory felt or understood, lying there day after day?

She'd taken her cue from Maynard in this.

When he spoke of Delores his voice was even and controlled like a professional carer, or the parent of a special child. Once, after he'd thanked one of Dory's church friends for the curry she'd sent, he put down the phone shaking his head. 'Excellent women,' he said. 'Saints.' He sighed. 'Just like my wife.'

He spoke as if she were apart from him. He only called her 'Dory' if he was talking of the past. He said *I* when he talked of future plans. How to finance his return to Asia, probably Indonesia or Thailand. To live, for good. He spoke like a traveller who would soon be on his way.

But this morning he'd held onto her like a child does, his head against her stomach. He was breaking up inside and didn't know it. She knew she was harnessed to him now, wherever he was going.

No one had taught her how to pray. Who is God? she'd

asked her parents when she was a kid, and they had thrown their arms about and talked of trees and kindness and the way families love each other. Jason Kay's God was the Great Headmaster, watching you wherever you went. Jason lived in fear of Hell, yet when she rode past his Brethren meeting hall, it seemed to her that *it* was Hell, chocolate-brick, windowless like a big toilet block, a yard of gray sand, a high cyclone fence all around.

Churches always made her curious. What was supposed to happen there? Comfort? Inspiration? But the cold dusty light and vinegary smell inside this old church had no power to calm her.

The tram was packed with very loud schoolkids. She was only a year or so older than some of them but she shut her eyes in their midst like a middle-aged woman with worries. If she could have prayed it would have been for Cecile to be home but Cecile was in Kuala Lumpur visiting her sister. There was nobody else in Melbourne she could talk to. Her secret life with Maynard cut her off, from her own past, her own family. She belonged nowhere.

Above all do not panic, she told herself. She would buy some takeaway noodles, have a long shower and watch a rerun of *Friends*, which was like going to bed with your teddy.

The next morning he wasn't there. She strode straight through the dark office to the flickering answering machine and listened to the voice of a woman with a foreign accent telling her that Mr Flynn would not be coming in today, because unfortunately, yesterday afternoon, Mrs Flynn passed away. *Mr Flynn will be in touch*, said the woman in her precise, gentle foreign voice. Francine, Bernadette or Tina? Whoever she was, she didn't feel comfortable speaking into an answering machine. *Er – thank you. All the best . . .* Like signing off a letter.

Maya sat down in his chair. Through the window she could see the very tip of the spire, a mysterious, ornate black knob. What was it supposed to be? An acorn? A bud? She'd asked some workers at the church, but they didn't know. All that care, she thought, put into something that nobody knew about or saw. Just the birds, year after year. For some reason, this made her want to cry.

She didn't know how long she sat there. It was cold, she'd forgotten to switch on the heating. She sat sunk into her jacket, the collar turned up, the wool around her jaw. A phone rang on and on somewhere in the empty building. It felt like days since she'd spoken to another human being. What to do next? She took her little bag from the drawer of her desk and made her way down the stairs to the Ladies' Restroom.

A toilet was flushing and the black-haired beautician from Mimi's was washing her hands. She had switched on the lights and was peering critically at her skin, though her geisha-pale face looked perfect to Maya. She smiled at Maya from the mirror. All the women from Mimi's were friendly. She was wearing tight black pants and a pale-blue smock and high black platform heels. The air carried drafts of her airy, floral perfume.

'Busy day?' she said to Maya, as she reached for a paper towel. Her name, Jody, was embroidered on the pocket of her smock. Jody had a kid, Maya had watched her once on the footpath, blowing kisses to a little tear-blotched face in a car driving off up the street.

'Not really. My boss's wife died last night.'

'Oh no!' A concerned, maternal frown appeared beneath

16

Jody's dead-straight, blue-black fringe. 'Was it expected?'

'She'd been sick for a while. Cancer.' They stared at one another as Jody slowly dried her hands.

'I don't know what I'm supposed to do.' Maya heard her own voice echo, high and plaintive in the tiled room. 'I've never known anyone who died before.'

Why was she talking like this? She'd never once met Dory. And even as she spoke she remembered Miriam Kershaw.

To sound innocent.

Jody raised her perfectly plucked eyebrows. 'You could always send some flowers.'

'How do you do that?'

'There's a florist round the corner. They'll deliver them for you or you can take them yourself.' She started to edge gently around Maya. 'I'll speak to the girls. We'll send a card or something. That poor guy. Any kids?' She hesitated at the door.

'A son. Grown up.'

'You OK, sweetie? Going to close up for the day?'

'Yes, I will. I'll take the family some flowers.' She hadn't known this was what she was going to do until she heard herself say it.

Everything was speeding up. She was in a taxi holding a bouquet as big as a baby, wrapped in mauve cellophane, the stems like limbs across her knees. They were racing down a freeway, in a direction she'd never been before. Billboards, overpasses, factories stood to attention beneath a sombre sky. She was like an official mourner, sweeping past in a motorcade. The taxi was filled with the freshness of her flowers.

Why this terrible rush? She'd run into the florist's, pointing to irises and hyacinths and orchids and flowers she didn't know the name of, as long as they were purple or mauve. She'd never been in a florist shop before, and the exotic blooms, the leafy hush and tang went to her head. In Warton if people gave you flowers, they would have grown them.

She hadn't asked how much they'd cost – nearly as much, it turned out, as a really good haircut – just signed her credit card and rushed out again to hail a taxi. As if she were late. For what? To show him her support? So as not to be left out?

Her mouth was dry and she was sweating inside her coat. She caught a glimpse of her half-profile in the taxi's tinted window, and for a moment she thought she saw Dory. But Dory looked nothing like her.

She'd spotted a photo once in his wallet and made him take it out and show her. Dory with baby Andrew beside a potted palm in a studio in Jakarta, a creased little colour print, faded now, washed out. The tiny boy was fat and gingery, his face a smudge, screwed up ready to cry. In contrast, Dory was very striking, like a sixties pop-star, with a beehive of black hair, pale pink lipstick and dark, kohl-lined eyes. She was Dutch-Indonesian, Maynard said. (My father is half Dutch! Maya told him, but as usual, he didn't seem to hear.) He'd met Delores in Java in his days as a saxophonist with a touring band. She taught Indonesian in a language school. Later he went into business for a while with her father. Dory wore white gloves and a collarless mauve coat with large mauve cloth-covered buttons. Her smile was serene, her eyes shy, shining. 'She looks happy,' she said to Maynard as he slid the photo back into his wallet. He said nothing.

In her mind, as time went by, the name *Dory* came to have a sort of orchid-coloured glow.

They were off the freeway now, charging into a suburb. The

18

main street of every suburb here was a city in itself, stacked with shops and cafes, under rows of swinging wires. This was what Dory would have seen when she first came to Melbourne, looking out a taxi window over little Andrew's head.

The flowers were for Dory, of course.

The Flynns lived in a dead-end street that finished in a shallow rise of bushland. The houses were packed in, side by side, close to the road. In Melbourne everyone lived closer together. Some of the houses were modernised, with glass and timber additions and frondy landscaped gardens, but the Flynns' house was bare and treeless, like it would have been when it was built.

So this was where he came from and returned to. Winter sun shone briefly through the clouds, but the house looked dark, stricken, closed in on itself.

It was after she had paid the driver and turned towards the house with her armful of rustling cellophane and flowing purple ribbons, that she realised her offering was not only showy and over the top, it was fatally, morally *wrong*. Sweat spurted into her armpits, she swung around but the taxi had already disappeared. No shelter anywhere. Oh God, how could she get rid of it? Was anybody watching her?

The curtains in the house were drawn. There was no one on the street. Quick, she told herself, leave it on the doormat and run. Head lowered, she moved swiftly up the front path to the porch. There was no garden, just a concrete slab and some woody shrubs by the steps. Somehow she'd expected Dory to have made a beautiful garden.

Andrew opened the door as she tiptoed across the porch. He could be nobody else but Andrew, though he'd grown tall and dark and clear. The fat smudge-faced days were long gone.

How had he known she was here?

A wave of heat moved up her neck so violently that her eyes watered. 'I just wanted to . . .'

He smiled and put his arm out and firmly ushered her inside. The door closed behind her.

The hall was cold and bare as a hospital. Far down the end it opened into a room where people were talking. She caught the foreign inflection of women's voices and the clink of dishes. Francine, Bernadette and Tina no doubt, doing what women friends do. An oxygen cylinder stood in a bar of light outside an open bedroom doorway, and in the shadowy front room next to her she glimpsed a table piled high with bouquets. She could smell freesias, a cold sweetness from her own past. She had no right to be here.

'These were her favourite colours, did you know that?' Andrew said, touching Maya's flowers. She nodded, unable to speak. He had his father's hands, but more finely cast. She could see Maynard's features in the set of his face, but his skin was olive and his eyes were dark, wide-spaced, intense. Dory's son. You could tell that she'd been beautiful.

That's him, Maya thought, without quite knowing what she meant. It was as if she'd dreamt of him.

'Andy? I think you're needed.' A long-legged girl in jeans strode up the hall towards them. She was wearing a large football jumper, probably borrowed from Andrew, the way girl-friends liked to do. She put her hand on Andrew's shoulder. 'Granny's asking for you.' Perfect, cool, in charge, good skin, dark hair in a curly ponytail. She would have been a champion runner, a maths whizz, a prefect, one of the shining girls at school.

'This is Kirstin,' Andrew said. His girlfriend. The girlfriend he deserved.

There was a pause. Since Maya didn't speak, Kirstin reached for her bouquet.

'I'll take this if you like.' She whisked it into the front room with all the other flowers.

'*Maynard? Andy?*' The old girl was down the corridor of course, making sure that no one forgot her. Where was Maynard? She knew he wasn't here.

Andrew kept on looking at her. 'Were you one of Mum's students?'

Maya shook her head and backed towards the door.

'Is there anything I can do for you?' he asked. 'Anything at all?'

His dark eyes each held a drop of radiance inside them, like the gleam of water at the bottom of a well. She couldn't look too long into them. He knew something she couldn't bear to know.

'No, no. My taxi's waiting.' She opened the front door and started across the porch. Then she turned and said quickly: 'I'm Maya, from the office. I'm really sorry . . .'

'I know you are.' He stepped forward and took her hand for a moment. 'Dad's at the funeral director's. With Mum.' He looked up over Maya's head. 'What a beautiful day!' he said. 'I had no idea.' He was almost high, she saw, almost a little crazy.

'The funeral's on Thursday, nine-thirty at St Xavier's', he called out after her as she fled down the path. She nodded over her shoulder and he raised his hand to her. Fuck fuck fuck, she muttered, rushing down the street, bare, of course, of taxis. He knew. She could swear he knew. On this day Dory's son knew everything.

The bushy rise at the end of the street looked down over a football oval, a playground, a bike trail. At this hour it was spotted with retirees throwing balls for their dogs and young mothers with little kids. The embankment was floored with shredded bark and planted artistically with native grasses and shrubs. Imitation bush, city bush, not a place where you could lose yourself. Where to now? Her bladder was bursting, and without thinking, as if she were still a country kid, living out of doors, she crouched down between two bushes and pissed splashily into the bark, risking yet more exposure.

She lay awake in the dark, trying to remember when Cecile said she'd be back from Kuala Lumpur. Sometimes when Cecile came home late from her editing work, Maya got up and they talked. Could she be back tonight? Maybe Cecile would be too tired to talk, but it would be a relief just to see her, or even just to know she was in the house. She longed for Cecile's calmness. Cecile was nearly thirty, far ahead of her in everything. Her advice was always very down-to-earth.

But in the morning Cecile was still not there. What if she'd come home to get changed and then gone straight off to work? Sometimes she did that. Maya wandered in and out of rooms looking for clues to see if Cecile had been and gone. The house was dark from pouring rain. Everything was cold. She didn't know what to do next. She couldn't even think of going to the office. In the end she went back to bed.

She wished she hadn't told Andrew her name. Maynard would be angry when he heard of her visit. *You know the rules.* Would he say that to her, like a teacher? What were the rules? They'd never spoken of them, but she knew that they were there. He liked to keep all the different parts of his life separate. She knew, without anything being said, that he was afraid of demands, of being trapped, held back. If she looked away, got on with her own work, suddenly he'd come to her. Sometimes this made her laugh. It reminded her of handling Choko, the most highly strung of the horses in the Garcias' paddock. Turn your back and he'd be nuzzling in your pocket.

He was capable of sulking. He believed in his right to do what he wanted when he wanted to, and was savage if he couldn't. It had been a shock to find that out. But underneath, always, was the tug of need.

At first he joked about the matching first three letters of their names. I knew this was a good omen, he said, as soon as we met! A few weeks later she'd referred to this and his face went blank. She'd set off his alarm system: did she think that this bound them together? Was she hanging on to his every word? Nothing he tossed off to be charming could be taken as a promise.

Yet she had no dream of any future with him beyond the usual one, to spend a whole night together. She couldn't conceive of any other place in the world where they would fit, they existed as a couple only in their eyrie with the bird's-eye view of the spire. If he was offhand, became business-like and impersonal, she could cringe to think of herself on that mattress, like a creature without its shell.

He was a bit overwhelmed by her devotion, she suspected, by what he had unleashed. Sometimes he was touched by it and was tender: a small, spontaneous measuring out. Only her love kept them afloat. The creaks and sighs of the old building around them sounded like a warning. Throat-clearings of disapproval. She wondered if after this she'd ever be able to have a 'normal' relationship. If secrets and rules were part of its kick, a kick she'd got used to now.

More and more he was out of the office. This was the nature of

23

the business, he told her, a lot of running around. It was better to pick up freight yourself than deal with a customs broker. Then there was the banking and the checking of stock in the warehouse and trips to see potential customers. Sometimes a customer whom he said he was meeting rang up to speak to him. From time to time she caught him out with little lies, to her, to his mother. Why didn't she take this into account?

What did she know of him? She only had a keyhole view of him, a fixed, secret eye.

Sometimes he'd lie back and suddenly open up to her. How his widowed mother sent him to a private school where he had less money than the other boys and never learnt anything but how to gamble and play the saxophone. How when he left – he was asked to leave – he ran away to join a jazz band that was touring though Asia.

'Why were you kicked out?' she asked. These days you had to do something pretty heinous, or that was how it was at a country high. She needed to know everything about him so she could understand him.

'Got a girl pregnant,' he said briskly. 'The headmaster told my mother that she was wasting her money on me, I was a blight on the school's reputation. My God, if they only knew what was really going on there.' He was still angry about it, she could see.

'What happened to the girl?'

'She lost the baby before it was born. I was told I'd ruined her life. Girls weren't supposed to want sex in those days, you understand.'

He fell in love with Asia and married Dory and stayed there for many years. He and Dory decided to bring up Andrew in Australia, but he still went to Asia on business at least three times a year. With the contacts he'd made in Indonesia he started up Global Imports. She'd have to come with him one day to the warehouse in South Melbourne, he said, and pick out something for herself. One morning she arrived to find a large carved wooden jewellery box sitting on her desk. Not really her sort of thing, but he seemed pleased with it and she couldn't tell him that.

He couldn't remember the last time he played the sax.

He was fifty, a couple of years older than her parents though he didn't seem part of the same generation, the sixties or whatever it was. She couldn't imagine him long-haired in a protest rally. He told her he voted Liberal, and was amused at her gasp of shock. I make love with a *right-winger*, she thought. She began to explain to him what it was like being Labor in a country town, but as usual he wasn't listening. He was always dreaming, she'd come to realise, and if she asked, his dreams were always schemes for making money. If he and her parents met, they would have nothing at all to say to one another. But that must never happen. They must on no account ever meet.

'Global is never going to make my fortune,' he said, looking up at the ceiling high above them. 'I'm using some contacts to diversify.'

If he'd looked anything like her father, large, sweaty, hairy, nothing could possibly have happened between them. If he'd had the body of men in Warton of his age. But he was narrow-boned, smooth-skinned, trim. Sometimes he'd pat his belly or flex his arms and frown. 'Haven't been able to get to the gym for months now.' The stress of his current life kept his shape almost boy-like. When their two pairs of shoes lay side by side beneath the radiator, hers were the same size as his.

Her first thought when she met him was that he had the looks of an actor, an older, workaday version of, say, Kevin Spacey. His cheeks were hollow, close-shaven, with a fold on either side of his mouth like pleats in soft leather. A half-circle of creases ran up his neck and jaw if he tucked his head down. He had a habit of running his fingers back through his hair, which was cleverly cut to be pushed-up at the top where it was thinning. It was babyishly fine, a fading reddish-brown sprinkled with silver. Was he vain? At his desk he wore small, fine-rimmed tortoiseshell glasses. His eyes were quick and hard to read. In his black coat he looked like a Melbourne man.

Age didn't come into it. She registered an instant reaction to him when she saw him, a softening all through her body at the sight of his hands and wristwatch, his ivory skin, his pale shirts, his narrow, gold-buckled belt.

There was some sweetness too, a quick understanding, and sometimes a playful streak. Rarely now. He'd become more and more preoccupied.

Late morning she went downstairs and ate a bowl of Weetbix with the last of the milk. There was nothing else to eat. Neither she nor Cecile had been shopping for a couple of weeks. She ate at the kitchen bar, the big open room silent around her. The long leaves of the bamboo in the courtyard hung flat in the endless rain. She remembered the fierce rush and instant turning off of Warton rain, like a little kid's tantrum. She kept listening out for the scratch of the key turning in the lock.

When Cecile was home there was always music. As soon as she came in, even if it was very late, she went straight to her workbench next to the stairs, turned on the lamp and played music on her computer. Music was the background to everything she did. It was the same in Warton when her father or brother were home. She would never forget the feeling of relief when she first entered this house and stepped into music.

Cecile gave her the sheepskin coat a few nights after she

moved in. It had been hanging forever at the back of her cupboard, much too big for her, she said. She'd bought it from a friend who was desperate for money. The moment she put it on, Maya felt safe, embraced, protected, able to face the Melbourne streets at last. It was a perfect fit, the cream fleece tucked inside against her skin. Cecile put her head to one side and studied her as they put on their shoes at the front door. It was ten o'clock at night and they were about to go to a Vietnamese restaurant to eat a soup called pho which Cecile had a craving for.

'I knew the right person would turn up for it one day.'

Maya opened the door and set out, muttering something about being big-boned like the Dutch side of the family. At that time, before Maynard, she still hated to be looked at, and avoided looking at herself in mirrors.

After she started wearing the coat everything changed. It transformed those cold dawns, transformed her into a city girl. She began to feel at home. The house, small yet strangely spacious, had a distinct personality that in her mind she associated with Cecile. Just as, from the start, she didn't feel shy with Cecile, so she felt at ease in this house.

Melbourne started to look different to her. She got the hang of the trams. Shops and restaurants on Victoria Street became familiar. She and Cecile always ate there, or bought take-away. Restaurateurs hailed them. They never cooked at home. Cecile introduced her to Shanghai dumplings and baked pork buns and sticky rice in a twist of bamboo leaf out of the warmers in the little supermarkets. Wherever she went Cecile always looked out for quality.

She began to sense the romance of this city. One night when she and Cecile were trudging home with Thai take-away, sharing an umbrella, the lights shining on the wet road, she felt so light-hearted that she wanted to say his name.

'Maynard says Thai is the haute cuisine of Asia.'

'Maynard?'

'My boss.' She turned her head and found herself looking right into Cecile's eyes. Their gaze locked for a moment beneath the umbrella and then they looked away.

They were passing the tower blocks of Housing Commission flats that loomed above the trees in the park on the corner. Lights shone in window after window, people were home, eating together as night fell. For the first time she understood the comfort in being part of the myriad lives of a great city. Warmth spread through her from the misted-up plastic boxes she clutched. It was a relief to let her secret out even a tiny bit, ease the pressure she carried around with her every moment of the night and day.

The next day, Thursday, the day of the funeral, it was still raining. She pictured the black cars waiting outside the house, Maynard escorting his mother down the path under an umbrella, Andrew hand in hand with Kirstin, and the faithful three bringing up the rear, Francine, Bernadette and Tina. All in black clothes and dark glasses. The cars gliding off into the rain.

At midday a postcard came from her parents, in her mother's writing, but signed *T & J*, reminding her they'd be arriving next week. Her mother, always suspicious of technology, still didn't trust leaving phone messages. Typical of her, to send a postcard of the lake turned to salt, *proceeds to CALM*, from the stack on the counter in the Warton newsagency. *Can't wait to see you xx*. Maya couldn't bear to think of their familiar, expectant faces here in this house. She was a different person now.

She still hadn't cleared out the little back room under the stairs for them. Cecile said it was OK if they stayed. They planned to spend two weeks here before going to Tasmania. She'd told them she and Cecile would be at work when they arrived and where to find the key.

Her father would be blown away by Cecile's music. She felt a pang of possessiveness about her life with Cecile. It was hard-won. It was a gift.

We don't want to get in your way! If they were so anxious about that, why didn't her father take his long-service leave somewhere else?

They'd tried to persuade her to go to Perth, not the other side of the country, and study literature, acting, film, something to do with 'self-discovery'.

They had no idea of real exploration.

Nobody knew how sick she felt, those first few weeks here. She came to understand, in a way she never had before, that the city and the country were two separate worlds. She understood now the kids who grew up with her in Warton and never wanted to leave. There wasn't a person, a horse, a tree, a stretch of road or horizon in Warton that she didn't know, while here she was a stranger to everything, the beauty of the shops and cafes, the people in smart coats like Europeans, even the different brand names for homely milk and bread. The city was like a heavy mass she was trying to fight her way through. She got lost in the grid of the streets and was too self-conscious to ask for help.

She made herself sit on a high stool in a tattoo shop and have her nose pierced, which she and Jason Kay had always sworn would be the first thing they'd do when they left Warton. The first of their piercings. She wrote a postcard to Jason telling him how cool it was here, but didn't send it, it made her ashamed. She was a stranger to cool, anyone could tell that at a glance. 'Country' was written all over her, nose-stud and all.

It took her a while to realise that the sinking sensation in her stomach, the scooped-out feeling in her brain, was home-sickness. It really was an illness that she woke up with every day. She'd been unable to remember why she wanted to come here. On the other hand, she knew she couldn't possibly go back.

The only reason her parents had let her come was because it was arranged that she could stay for a while with Tod Carpenter, nephew of Forbes and Rhonda Carpenter, who owned the Warton newsagency where Maya worked after school.

'Tod is such a lovely young man, he always does his best for people, he'll look after you,' Rhonda told her. 'Why Toddy's never married . . .' She shook her head.

'Married to his own right hand most likely,' growled Forbes, waiting for Rhonda.

'Forbes!' Rhonda never let him down. Besides, a couple of years ago Rhonda had undergone a near-death experience. She had a heart attack and *saw the portals* before she was revived. It gave her a sort of moral authority.

Her father talked to Tod on the phone and arranged it all. He knew how to make a good fellow of himself, old Tod. It took her in for a while. And then mysteriously, every cell of her body seemed to shrink away from the sight of him.

It was true that Tod did his best. He played guitar, cooked

stir-fry, took a camera everywhere. When he drove his MG he wore an Italian cap to protect his head. His hair fell out ten years ago in the week before his twenty-first birthday because his girlfriend ran off with his best mate. There were photos of him at his party, hamming it up in a woman's wig. He was round-faced, snub-nosed, stocky but fit, he worked out. He'd lived in Hong Kong and London for a few years and was paying off his house, a stark home unit twenty stops out on the train. He didn't have a girlfriend just now, but lots of friends, at work – he sold insurance – and at the clubs he'd joined. He heard of the job at Global Imports from a guy at the gym.

Why, when Tod was so kind to her, showed her how the trains worked, took her on drives to the Dandenongs and to his favourite restaurants and bars – entered smiling, waving at people who didn't see him – was she, soon after she moved in with him, so desperate to get away? There was something increasingly intense about his chubby hands as he cooked and put down plates for her. Instinctively she swerved away so he wouldn't touch her when he opened the car door for her. She stopped running past him in a towel. Once she saw him bringing in her washing when it started to rain, tenderly gathering and folding her scrappy underwear. People often rang and cancelled outings with him. He chewed gum non-stop for his breath. Sometimes he was so tense he roared off in his MG for a drive. There was a devastated look in his eyes when he watched television at night, gnawing on his fingers. She wanted to write a letter about him to someone, a cruel letter about being sexually repressed. She wanted to feel free here, not trapped by pity.

Once, in the middle of the night in his spare bedroom, she woke gasping, surfacing for air. In her sleep, Miriam Kershaw's words had come back to her, in her English accent, from her bed with her eyes closed. Her last words.

Tod means death. Don't go with that boy.

After the interview with Maynard – he told her she could start straight away – she had a coffee at the corner espresso bar and copied down Cecile's phone number from the notice board. Cecile happened to be home that day and told her which tram to catch to her house. That evening Maya went back to Tod's home unit and told him she had to live closer in now, for her new job. She was starting work tomorrow. Good old Tod put her bag in the boot of the MG and, his jaw working overtime, his hi-fi turned up full blast, drove her to Cecile's.

It was night again and she was still wearing her old trackies. Was it because she was so alone that she found it hard to get a grip on things? There was nobody she could possibly write a letter to about this. If she did, where would she begin? The Flynns' house. The house of the dead.

She lay back on her bed. What sort of family lived in a house like that? A man who wasn't interested in home. A woman without joy. Why wasn't Dory happy? Miriam Kershaw said that was why you got cancer. Loss of hope. Had Dory been homesick? She was a teacher, and went to church and had friends. Why hadn't Maynard made her happy? Or she him? Maya asked him once if he'd had any affairs before Dory was sick and he couldn't help laughing. *Many* affairs? she corrected herself, hating to seem naïve, but by then he had his coat on and was blowing her a kiss.

But Dory had Andrew. *Is there anything I can do for you? Anything at all?* As if the whole world was in mourning for his mother.

Each time she thought of Andrew's face she held her breath

for a moment. The underlids of his eyes were swollen like _ ramparts to hold in grief. His dark hair had reddish glints le. over from childhood and his clothes were loose and crumpled on his tall, thin frame. He must have slept in them all night beside Dory's bed. When he smiled she saw that something which was guarded and cloudy in Maynard, in him ran clear.

He had strong, narrow fingers. She could feel them now, holding hers.

He was forever out of bounds for her. She had done something to herself which cut her off from him, as well as from her past, and most people her own age.

Perhaps she should quit, just not ever go back.

She woke late to a rainless day and the smell of something reassuring. Toast! She sniffed the air for another human presence. Cecile! She stumbled to the top of the stairs. Down in the kitchen Dieter was sitting on a stool at the bar, munching toast and sorting through Cecile's mail.

'Dieter!' She was even glad to see him. Usually they kept to the unspoken pact between them to ignore one another. 'How are you?' She came down into the kitchen.

Dieter waved his buttery knife at the open packet of bread on the bench. 'Help yourself.' He must have brought the bread with him. He kept his own jar of cherry jam in the fridge, a Swiss brand. Dieter never smiled and never had been heard to say hello or goodbye. It was restful when you got used to it. If they needed to communicate they always got straight to the point.

'Do you know when Cecile will be home?' She pulled her coat on over her stale old tracksuit. Her hair needed washing.

nlight on the bamboo leaves in the courtyard. She
away in a dark land and had just come back.
d. 'Today, I hope. We have bills to pay.'
us in the house was uncertain. He was a partner
... Cecile's company, Prodigal Films, and there were periods
when he was around for days on end, watching videos, making
phone calls, engaged in long intense discussions with Cecile.
The living room filled up with his clothes and papers, became
his personal office. He left his video collection here and a stash
of ganja in an empty 16mm canister on Cecile's desk. He stayed
up very late. Sometimes he was there in the morning, asleep in
his clothes on one of the couches.

He had thin-lidded eyes, very sharp, and a tight-closed
mouth. At first sight Maya thought he looked hostile, even
spiteful, but she soon found out that he wasn't interested in the
personal. Cecile said he was like a scientist about life. When he
was working with Cecile he despised all interruptions, as if
what he was doing was all that mattered in the world.

He had a room somewhere with a bunch of musicians.
Although, like Cecile, he had a day job at NuVision, as a tele-
cine operator, he never seemed to have any money. It was
always Cecile who bought their meals. He had the traveller's
mentality, Cecile said, unworried, he was always saving up to go
somewhere else.

So far Prodigal Films had made a music video for the band
of one of Dieter's housemates, and a corporate video for
Cecile's father which they were still editing. Cecile was the
director and Dieter the cinematographer.

'You are not at work?' Dieter said 'v' for 'w'. His 'verk' had
a driven, obsessive sound. It was a word he often used.

'My boss's wife died. It was her funeral yesterday.'

'So? You are not needed in the office?'

All at once she thought of mail spilling out of the brass letterbox, faxes scrolling across the floor, the answering machine overloaded with urgent calls. What if Maynard was too grief-stricken to work and did not come back for weeks? What would happen to Global Imports? How could she desert him at a time like this? She was not holding the fort.

She peered at the clock on the microwave. 'My God, is it really eleven?'

Coffee roared through the percolator on the stove. His arm shot out at once to turn off the gas. Fresh, perfectly timed coffee was another of Dieter's obsessions.

'Black?' Dieter said. 'You buy no milk, I think.'

It was nearly twelve o'clock by the time she hurried down the street to the office. The Global letterbox in the hall had already been cleared. Strong chemical scents seeped out from beneath Mimi's door as she passed, perhaps a Paraffin Treatment was in full swing. The dusty smell of the staircase made her heart lurch. He wouldn't have come in, she told herself, not yet.

She could see the dark shape of his head through the frosted glass of the partition. He was standing at the table and further back against the window was another shape. Somebody was with him. She hung her coat up and walked in.

He was photocopying a pile of documents. In a black suit and tie and a white shirt, as if he were still dressed for the funeral. He looked handsome, well-groomed, in control, with the little smile fixed on the corners of his lips as he turned towards her.

Standing behind him was a very short, broad Asian man in a well-cut black coat.

'This is Mr T, my good friend and new partner. His full name is much too hard for us Westerners.' There was a twinkle between the two partners, a nodding and showing of teeth. Mr T was in control, which meant he had the money, she could tell that from Maynard's readiness to please.

'And *this* is Maya.' A little pause made her wonder if he'd already spoken of her.

'Yes yes yes,' said Mr T.

'Maynard, I'm sorry . . .' Her voice went creaky. There was so much she was sorry about, Dory, the flowers, her lateness, not being there for him. 'I wasn't sure whether . . .'

'Best to carry on, I think.' He went on photocopying, quite stern, not looking at her. 'Thanks for the bouquet, by the way.' Far from being slowed by grief, he seemed energised. There was a sleek, glittering look about him that she'd never seen before. His whole presence had changed. Was he in shock? Or did he feel relief? He was pretending not to care.

He gathered up the documents, knocked them straight, slid them into a new briefcase. 'We're off to eat.' He spoke lightly, blinking, as if to bat away her gaze. 'There's going to be some changes. I'll brief you after lunch.'

There was mail to sort, a bit of filing, an invoice to prepare. She worked furiously, though her hands shook and her eyes blurred. In fifteen minutes everything was finished. It sometimes crossed her mind that there wasn't enough for her to do. If his computer skills were up to scratch he could have run the show himself. He didn't really need her. A suspicion which she'd always dismissed now came back to her. That he'd planned all that was to happen between them even before he met her and that was why he'd hired her. Office hours, the only time he had to himself. And you know what young women are like these days.

It was Tod who fixed him up.

She could hardly breathe.

He didn't need her anymore. In fact, now that she'd strayed out of the office into his private life, he wanted to get rid of her.

It was clear he was going to sack her.

Leave now, a voice kept telling her in her head, just pack up and go, but she sat rigid at her desk, looking at the spire.

She heard him let himself in. His face was a little flushed as he took his jacket off and slung it over his chair. He came towards her at her desk smiling, smelling of alcohol, loosening his tie. Swivelling her on her chair to face him, he pulled her up, and kissed her in the ear in a semi-humorous way. He was strange, she felt afraid for him. Then he was holding her close, closer and she felt his need for her, his lips cold and desperate, she tried to warm him with her mouth. She heard their breath in the silence, the little gasps from their lips. He bent her back over the desk, and they laughed a little, their eyes meeting as he ran his hands up her legs, pushing up her skirt, his hands smoothing and diving. Her whole body came alive again to meet his, soft with relief.

Something, a mouse scrape, made her eyes fly open and she turned her head a fraction and caught a movement, a glitch on the known horizon of the frosted glass of the partition, a blur that rose up and became an eye peering over the top, startled to meet hers. Mr T, on tiptoe.

If he'd just arrived, she would have heard the roll of the handle of the door from the corridor, the click of its closing. Even lying back like this, she would have registered the brief suck of new air. She knew by heart the full repertoire of sounds of this place.

They must have come in together.

'Don't look like that', Maynard was saying, smiling wide, consciously, like a celebrity, holding the glass of water for her. He helped her sit down on the chair. Everything looked different, as if the light had changed. His skin was thin and dragged across his bones. A half smile she'd never seen before hovered on his face, top teeth resting on bottom lip. Eyes flickering with nerviness and deep down knowledge of himself. He was saying something about closing the office, that he and Mr T were starting a new venture up north. 'Don't look like that', he said again in a low voice. 'I just asked him to wait while I spoke to you. Then one thing led to another. I'm sorry, I'm a bit pissed. I didn't know he'd *watch.*'

But he'd been about to make love to her. He would have.

He went into the waiting room and shut the door behind him.

She's going to pieces, she's going to make a scene.

The door to the corridor slammed closed.

Maynard came back into the office. 'He's gone, Maya. He's waiting downstairs.' He crouched down beside her. 'Listen, why don't you come with us?'

She could keep her job, he said, and have a bit of a holiday in a warm climate to boot. Whatever that old boot was, he said, trying to make her laugh as if she were a kid. Could she leave at once, was that possible? He'd call to see if there were still seats on the plane. Just come as she was. She could buy what she needed when they got there. He talked cheerfully and fast, helping her up by the elbow. And all the time, in the shine of his eyes, like tears, there was regret, that made her even sadder.

OK? he said. He fetched her coat and helped her put it on. He seemed like a friend, but he was not a friend. Everything had slowed and darkened. There was a drumming in her ears.

Strange to see the brightness outside the windows, like a world she'd just left.

He put on his jacket and picked up his briefcase. Did she want to leave a message for her housemate? Celia, was it? He wasn't very good with names. Often called her Myra in the beginning. She couldn't focus, her mind looped and slid away from something she had to remember. Something important. He ushered her out ahead of him. Her legs went one after the other as if they didn't belong to her any more.

For some reason all she could think of as she went down the stairs was the little back room that she hadn't cleared out for her parents.

2

The House

The key was under the little Buddha by the fishpond, where Maya told them it would be.

The house was a surprise, a narrow brick townhouse, wedged in between two nineteenth-century cottages. Its weathered, slatted wooden fence stood right on the footpath. Looking up, through fronds of bamboo, you could glimpse French doors opening onto a small balcony. Inside the gate was a dwarf courtyard jungled over with bamboo, and it was somehow comforting to make out, amongst the matted trunks, the little fat familiar figure meditating beside a swampy pool.

Inside, putting their suitcases down, they both said *oh* at the same time. They were looking out from a landing into one large, high-ceilinged room, set lower than the entrance, three steps down. Behind its economical façade, this house expanded into family-sized proportions, as if it had been hollowed out.

Light from the courtyard filtered in through a plate-glass window and cast a pattern of dipping bamboo over the rough brick walls.

A staircase to the floor above half-bisected the room. To the left was the kitchen, marked off by a bench and bar-stools. To the right, down a couple of shallow steps, was a sunken floor surrounded by three black built-in couches, like ringside seats at a swimming pool or theatre in the round. In the middle was a bare coffee table and on the fourth side was a TV. No mess anywhere.

What had they expected? Cramped student digs? Grungy suburbia? Not plainness as style. Not *open plan*. Although it had the stripped, shabby look of a rented house – the worn black leather of the couches was splitting in places, the varnish of the coffee table was stained with cup rings, the floorboards were dull and scratched – in the play of light and sweep of its proportions, it had a grace that still drew attention to itself. Like good bones in an old face.

'I went to parties once in rooms like this,' said Toni.

They stepped down into the living room. 'Isn't this what we used to call a *conversation pit*?' said Jacob. It reminded him of youth, sex, aspirations to sophistication. All a little dingy now. Nothing here was bright or new.

Then he spotted the gleam of contemporary hardware in the gloom beyond the kitchen. On a bench against the wall was an impressive line-up, brushed aluminium laptop, scanner, printer, a see-through perspex speaker coiled like a model of an alimentary canal. Technology he didn't know how to use. He shuffled through a wire mesh rack of CDs. Contemporary, jazz, Latin, electronic. Whose ear and eye? Most of the musicians he'd never even heard of.

'She's done well for herself,' he called out. He sank down on the black couch opposite the television. Almost by itself his hand reached for the remote control on the coffee table and began to channel-surf the afternoon programmes.

Toni went to the kitchen and filled the electric kettle. They'd left Warton at three that morning to drive to the airport and they needed a cup of tea. She found teabags and cups on the bench, but apart from a few packets of spices and noodles, the cupboards were empty. None of Maya's comfort foods. Were she and her housemate on some sort of diet? Some wrinkled apples in the fridge, a jar of jam and a packet of coffee grounds. No milk. A trail of ants was trekking across the vast white steppe of the bench.

All at once she left the teacups and ran upstairs. She opened the first door onto a still life of Maya's tracksuit and ugg boots lying tumbled on the floor. The bed was crumpled, the doona thrown back. She must have been running late. There was the usual pile of magazines and books beside the bed, and a few skeletal apple cores scattered about. Maya couldn't sleep without reading and couldn't read without eating an apple. The Chekhov paperback was on top. Jacob had given it to her, he was always trying to get the kids to read Chekhov. *The Lady with the Lapdog and Other Stories*, with a photo of Magnus and Winnie as a bookmark, just a few pages in. She wasn't doing much reading here.

The room was a lonely little tower, bare brick walls with a long thin window overlooking the roof next door. The air was cold and stale. Did Maya wake up here this morning? Toni resisted the impulse to pick up the tracksuit, pull up the doona, open the window. Maya resented anyone setting foot in her domain.

In the bathroom opposite was her towel from home, bone-dry on a rail, and another towel, more recently used. There was an expensive little pot of lemon-scented cream on the shelf beneath the mirror. Whose? Toni sniffed it, dipped her finger in and smeared it under her eyes. Her face felt dried out from the plane. What made her think she could take liberties like this in her daughter's house? Right now she'd like to curl up in Maya's bed and close her eyes.

As she came downstairs a beam of late afternoon sun shone straight from the courtyard onto the couch where Jacob slumped. Toni removed the remote control from his hand, turned the television off and sat down next to him. Within a minute she too was asleep.

This was how Cecile saw them when she came into the house. First the suitcases, then the two figures sitting side by side in the last light. She knew at once who they must be. She padded down and stood in front of the couch, studying them. The man was snoring gently, his hands across his stomach. The woman's head lolled back, her mouth slightly open and her chin squashed down in a position she probably wouldn't regard as flattering. They were just at the turning point in that process of thickening and blurring that slowly ate up people's youthful looks. In sleep, this was endearing.

They looked like they were used to sitting like this on a couch, their hands fallen down together as if at any moment they might find each other and clasp them. Cecile almost felt that *she* was the intruder. She stepped back a couple of paces.

People resented being looked at, she'd learnt that very young. Her mother – her adoptive mother – used to go red in the face and start to cry if Cecile stared at her when she was a child. She was sent to her room, but she crouched listening at the end of the hall to the inevitable phone calls that her mother would make to her friends.

To be perfectly honest she frightens me.

43

I sometimes think she isn't human.

Her mother never understood that she'd learnt to read people with her eyes from the moment she opened them because she was alone and too young to know the words their mouths were forming.

Why was Maya so offhand about her folks? When Cecile asked if they'd be OK with a mattress on the floor, Maya rolled her eyes. 'They'd love it! They're *terrified* of luxury. They're just old hippies.'

This couple didn't think of themselves as old. They both wore jeans and worn leather jackets and much-polished R.M. Williams boots, more like ageing rockers than hippies. His belt was snuggled under the gentle rise of his belly. Her long roughened fingers were scattered with silver rings. He had a pouchy jaw, a weathered face, and a mass of gray-blond hair. Her hair was dyed dark red, tucked thick and curling behind her ears. She had black arched eyebrows, clear sallow skin, a long, muscular neck. She took care of herself. Her jacket pushed out over her breasts.

You could say a sort of small-town version of Nick Nolte and Anjelica Huston. They looked right somehow in this setting. They matched the house.

She liked the way they didn't sprawl, but sat upright, self-effacing in their daughter's territory. They could be sitting in an airport lounge. There was a holiday sheen about them, they seemed to breathe a wholesome air. Good country people come to the city. Their eyelids were fluttering. People always knew when they were being watched. Cecile felt a moment's pang for what she had to tell them.

'Hi,' she said softly.

They opened their eyes at the same time and sat up blinking, wiping their mouths.

'I'm Cecile. I live here with Maya.'

Dazed, they started to struggle to their feet. Cecile held up her hand.

'First I have to tell you that Maya is not here.'

'She's at work,' said the mother, sitting back.

'She's gone away. She left a message on the phone five days ago. I wasn't here when she went.'

'Where has she gone?'

'She didn't say. She said it was for work and that she'd be in touch.'

'Did she say when she'd be back?'

Cecile shook her head.

They sat very still and solemn, their hands fallen on their laps, as if the air had gone out of them. They'd forgotten to introduce themselves. They were *sweet*.

In spite of her mother's apprehension, Cecile knew that she observed her fellow beings in a spirit of enquiry and benevolence, not to say, in some cases, with a quite disproportionate tenderness. In fact she was careful to keep a space around herself in order to retain detachment and balance. She knew, even as a child, that her distance from her adoptive mother was a kindness. Above all else she despised the exercise of power over others.

She turned on the lights and the heating and stood at the kitchen bench. 'Shall we discuss it over an aperitif?' she asked them.

'Maya and I pride ourselves on our dry martinis,' Cecile was saying, brandishing a tarnished cocktail shaker, chattering like a cooking demonstrator, aware that the parents weren't really listening, when suddenly, without a word, they rushed past her, out the front door into the courtyard. She peered up to see them illuminated by the spotlight over the fishpond, each puffing furiously on a cigarette. Smoking the way people drink when they want to get drunk, with a savage, private intensity. Like most smokers they were probably trying to give up.

How had they managed to stay together? This was the question Cecile always asked herself about couples. He was a big, pale, dreamy man. She was quite a foxy lady. What was the glue between them? Her detachment? His distraction? He was putting a packet of Drum back in his pocket. They were roll-your-own type of people.

Ever since they opened their eyes to see a tiny Chinese girl standing before them, the world had darkened and a heaviness crept over them that no martini could lift. The girl – the young woman – Cecile was very kind. Of course you must stay, she said. She was very self-possessed. She had a precise, definitive way of talking, perhaps from speaking English as a second language, or perhaps from going to an exclusive school. It was hard to tell her age, she could be nineteen or twenty-nine. Not the stereotype of the glamorous Asian girl, in her loose black clothes with her hair pulled back behind her slightly protuber-ant ears, and her bare broad face. Almost a Maoist look. Her sleeves were neatly turned back from her slender wrists, ready for work. She was a gracious host, more than she needed to be. For a few minutes she slipped out, reappearing with some sort of spicy Asian soup which normally they would have relished. She brushed aside any offer of payment. They ate, forgetting to taste it or praise it. Had Maya been unhappy? they asked. Did she have a boyfriend? Was there any sign that she was into drugs or a religious cult?

They felt shocked, like jilted lovers. Sick with disappoint-ment. They hadn't realised how much they'd been counting on seeing Maya. Now they must wait a little longer. Surely there was a good practical reason for her absence.

Or were *they* the reason?

They felt shamed, rejected, in front of this sophisticated young woman.

They must stay as long as they needed to, Cecile said. Shyly they excused themselves and made their way up to Maya's room where, like sick children, they put themselves to bed.

'It isn't like her,' Jacob said.

'Isn't it? You know how we get on her nerves.'

'That's because we still matter to her. She's very loyal, really. She's never let us down before.'

'Remember how I treated my parents?'

'We're not parents like your parents.' Right from the start, this had been an article of faith between them.

'Maybe we are, to Maya.' Toni turned her head to look out the window. They liked to think of themselves as young at heart, open-minded, but it was true, Maya hadn't seemed very pleased with them for some time.

'We *let* her go,' Jacob said.

'Perhaps we shouldn't have.'

'We had no choice, remember?' My little thundercloud, he used to call her.

'Maybe this is her way of telling us that she wants to be left alone in her new life.'

'Maybe it isn't anything to do with us. Most likely she got the date wrong and she'll be back tomorrow.'

They were silent for a while. Jacob thought of the hallfuls of parents he had faced, term after term, queuing up for his good advice. His self-righteous hints that perhaps there was something that they didn't quite get about their kid. Usually he advised easing up, letting alone, believing in the good in your child. Sometimes his palms tingled and he knew he wanted to say that the little bastard needed a strong hand.

Physician, heal thyself. Where was that from? The Bible? A line of a song or poem would often go round in his head and he wouldn't know where it came from. It generally related to where he was in his life. His unconscious sending him a message.

'Something is *keeping* her away,' he said at last.

'A love affair,' said Toni.

There were no curtains in this house. The room was lit by the glow of the sky of a great unknown city. Maya's room at home looked out onto the palm tree next to the verandah. Every day Toni stood in front of her pinup board for a few minutes to look at the photos, not for themselves, but to understand why Maya had chosen them. In Warton it would only be about eight o'clock. Magnus was probably still at the Garcias.

They'd come to bed way too early, they would never fall asleep.

They lay still, not talking. Visions crossed their eyes but they didn't share them. Both thought they were stronger than the other.

After some time Jacob decided to get up. Toni was asleep. There was no true dark here, no relief. The bed sagged and his tracksuit pants were twisted in the crotch. Usually he slept naked, but he didn't like to, somehow, in his daughter's sheets. He thought he'd sneak down to the living room and see if he could catch a late-night movie.

He heard a faint twang of music as he came down the stairs. There was no light on in the living room except for the glow of the computer screen. Cecile was sitting at it, intent. From behind she looked like a twelve-year-old schoolgirl with a ponytail. The music came from her computer, a flute, a tinkling ukelele, wailing voices, a sort of Oriental opera.

'Working late?' he called out, so as not to surprise her.

'Editing.' She kept looking at the screen. She was wearing narrow rimless glasses.

He approached. On the screen was an image of a walled courtyard with a door open to a dark interior.

'You're a *film* editor?'

'Editor, writer, director. I have my own company, Prodigal Films.'

'Why "Prodigal"?'

She turned. 'That's the name of a film I want to make. When I can work out how to do it.'

'I won't disturb you. I just need a drink of water.'

She turned back to the screen and pressed a key. 'This is just personal footage. Holiday snaps.'

He stood looking at the image over her shoulder. Light fell through a grilled window onto the solemn profile and translucent folded hands of a young Chinese girl.

'My half-sister, Clarice. In Kuala Lumpur.'

Her hand paused on the mouse and he felt he was intruding. He went and filled a glass from the tap in the kitchen and stood drinking, looking at the courtyard window. The spotlight by the fishpond was still on. Security, he supposed. The swaying bamboo reminded him of water plants streaming upwards in an aquarium. He felt he'd stumbled into an underwater workshop, a secret, nocturnal industry. Excitement churned deep in his bowels. He turned back, unable to keep away.

'You work with music?'

'For rhythm. Mood. This is a *pingtan* opera, in Cantonese.'

'What's it about?'

'The fleeting nature of love. Something like that. I don't speak Cantonese.'

She turned to face him. Strange to have such a large, solid presence in the house. Maya had the same roaming curiosity as he did, and also wore tracksuit pants to bed. It must be a family trait.

'Did Maya know about your films?'

'Of course.'

He was silent. She'd never mentioned it to him. Why did this hurt him? He'd always felt that Maya understood his passion for films.

'Have a cigarette if you like,' she said, 'I really don't mind.'

'Oh, no thanks. I'm giving up while I'm here. That was just an aberration earlier. Toni hasn't smoked for years.'

What a dag he was, in these saggy-bottomed pants, nattering, middle-aged. He lived in a dream and sometimes it cleared a little and words came to him about his life.

'Right now I feel as if I'm in a film myself,' he said.

'What kind of film?'

He considered. 'A mystery. A crime thriller? Most plots turn around a crime these days, have you noticed? It's become the norm.' All his thoughts seemed to take shape, spill out of him. 'Beautiful young women are always in danger. You're afraid for them the moment they appear . . .' He took a breath. Cecile was studying him. 'Sorry. You were working.'

'I'd better finish this tonight. I promised Clarice.'

Did she ever lose her composure?

'Goodnight Cecile.'

'Goodnight.' She gave an unexpectedly wide smile. His face loomed out of the dark like a portrait by an Old Master, an infinitely layered texture of tiny brushstrokes and lines. The sad eyes burn, self-judging.

★

To keep faith with Maya, they decided to set off the next morning to see the sights of Melbourne. Maya wished no one to worry, she wished to be left alone. They must respect that. 'We should try not to talk about her,' Toni said over the cup of green tea that was all she could find for breakfast. 'We should try to not even think about her. Our *vibes* mustn't disturb her.'

Before they left, Jacob phoned Global Imports and listened to the recorded message. *The office is currently unattended, but leave your number and we'll get back to you.* What could you learn about a man from his voice? The tone was smooth as a radio announcer going through his paces. A mature, confident, middle-class voice. What did *we* mean? Jacob took a breath and left a message, as if to answer him, man-to-man. *This is Jacob de Jong, I'm looking for my daughter Maya.* He spoke low in his throat, using what his kids called his headmaster voice. He hoped he sounded like someone to be reckoned with. As he spoke he felt increasingly aggressive. If Maya heard the message she would know he was upset.

There was no sign of Cecile. Her child-size boots were still standing by the door, but perhaps she was wearing another pair. Or was she asleep upstairs in the room next to theirs? Did she finish the holiday snaps for Clarice? Their conversation last night was a tiny lit-up room in Jacob's mind. He didn't mention it to Toni.

Out into the world they went, armed with map and camera. In the park opposite there were European trees with bare sculpted branches. Chestnut trees? Oaks? Also poplars and plane trees and unfamiliar eucalypts with tough dark leaves. The sky was gray, the gum leaves didn't shine as they did back home.

Apartment blocks towered over the park. Many of the families in the towers were refugees, Cecile had told them. It was good to think of them waking to the birds and trees, that this country had offered them a haven.

There was a playground for the kids and a set of goalposts with a large puddle in front of it. The usual man with a dog sat smoking on an ornamental rock. They passed an old Chinese couple in straw hats tied under the chin and a Vietnamese man delivering newspapers on a bicycle.

Everything was thrown into the mix here. A broken-down worker's cottage next to an up-to-the-minute converted warehouse, all weatherboard and corrugated iron. Glimpses of old-time suburbia, front fences, roses, birdsong, then an apartment block with an Asian look, tiled white balconies, wrought-iron screens. Two shops side by side, one selling newspapers, ice creams and shampoo, like a shop at a beach, the other transformed into a hip little wine bar. A Buddhist nun with a vivid homely face walked past, her burgundy robe not out of place here. In the distance were old brick factory chimneys, a spire, a civic clock, a fluttering Australian flag.

So this was what had happened to the rest of the country! Apart from camping holidays and a package trip to Bali, they hadn't lived anywhere but Warton for nearly twenty years.

What a difference a few hours' sleep made, Jacob thought. Was Maya's absence really such a catastrophe? If she had mixed up dates, arrived back a day or two late, was that the end of the world? They took their place at the crowded tram stop outside the Vietnamese supermarket, amongst tiny grandmothers in black pyjamas and smooth-faced housewives in straw hats. Some were accompanied by their daughters, patient and slender with long black hair and fashionable jeans. Maya hadn't told them this was an Asian neighbourhood, just like she hadn't mentioned that Cecile was Chinese. He could see it wouldn't seem relevant, living here. On the corner a group of Middle Eastern men were talking Arabic, doing a deal. Young people of all races milled around the shopfronts in a sort of costume of poverty, army jackets, broken-down sneakers, gelled hair. A swarm of skaters kicked their boards into their hands and swung onto a tram.

They walked across a grand old English park into legendary Carlton where Jacob had always wanted to go. Look at the trams rattling past, the rows of Victorian houses, people reading in cafes! A greengrocer played opera and sold buckets of cut flowers. They allowed themselves to be enticed by a spruiking waiter to eat spaghetti at a table on the pavement where they could study the passers-by. In this tender light all the passing faces looked intent and defined. Was it the glare at home that flattened and slowed everybody? Lovely pale-skinned girls with sensitive expressions went past, like Parisiennes on their way to a cello lesson. Young urban males walked and laughed unself-consciously together. Older women wore jagged hems and tousled hair like playful little girls. Old people were everywhere, in the bookshops and cafes, making sign language to friends through windows, as hedonistic as the young. Everybody moved fast, had somewhere to go. The elegant Melburnians. Where were the fat people? Personal beauty was rare in Warton, but here it was hard to see anyone who didn't have style. There were little specialty businesses everywhere, enterprise wherever they looked. They were used to a dying town, shops closing down one by one.

They felt slow and lumbering and, as clouds massed over the winter sun, more and more chilled. They smoked a cigarette each and then another one. What hicks they were, eating spaghetti in a tourist joint! Without their kids they didn't know how to be part of life. Unwanted, outdated, unmoored.

'The bigger the world the smaller I become,' Jacob said. There was a smudge of cappuccino foam on his lip. Toni brushed it off. She felt a moment's anger with Maya for having reduced them to this. They'd come bearing gifts and love and she'd thrown it all in their faces! She was old enough to know better.

She *did* know better.

'Something is wrong, Jacob.'

He knew at once what she meant. Pointless not to talk of Maya. They'd never stopped looking for her in the streets.

'What if she calls?' Toni said.

Suddenly they were frantic to go back. They ducked their way across a vast parade of streaming traffic, too panic-stricken to find a crossing. The heel of Jacob's boot caught in a grate by the kerb and his foot twisted as he wrenched it away. A tram came rolling down on them. He limped aboard like an old man while Toni fumbled with the ticket machine. The tram was packed and they swung close together for protection.

Toni rushed to the phone on the kitchen bench, Jacob hobbling after her. There was no message from Maya. Cecile wasn't in. She doesn't stick around much, Jacob thought. Maybe there's a lover somewhere.

From now on one of them must always be home, they said, within earshot of the phone.

They called Magnus in Warton, when they judged him to be back from school. The arrangement was that he'd eat his evening meal and sleep the night with the Garcias next door. In the daylight hours when he was not at school he could stay home with the dog. This was a compromise. It was not that Magnus wasn't comfortable with Carlos and Chris and their boys, in fact the whole family worshipped him. But he wanted the chance to have the house to himself, to live with his music. Even now, on the phone, Toni could hear the electronic thud coming from his bedroom. He'd be standing in the kitchen, looking out the long windows. All of them turned to look out the window when they spoke on the phone. The almond tree, a white radiance in spring, would be sprouting its first buds. Already there was a detached, self-sufficient note in the husky tones of Magnus's voice. The music was getting fainter, he must be walking down the hall. She saw him mooching round the house in his big sneakers, head bowed, Winnie trailing him.

'Is Winnie missing us?' She heard the smile in her voice. The whole world smiled for Magnus.

'Maybe. She won't let me out of her sight. How's Maya?'

'I don't know. She isn't here at the moment. Actually, she's been gone a few days. Something to do with work.'

'Weird.'

'Listen Magnus, where do you think she'd hang out in a city like Melbourne?'

She hadn't been going to tell him about Maya in case he worried but now she felt she couldn't risk losing the chance of a sibling insight. He and Maya were close. In fact he'd be offended if she didn't tell him.

'Music shops. Parks. Movies. Hungry Jacks. Why, don't you know where she is?'

'No.' She'd never been able to lie successfully to her children.

'Weird,' Magnus said again.

Jacob phoned Global Imports, but now the phone had been cut off.

He called the Missing Persons Bureau. A female officer with a young, out-there voice told him that to report someone missing you had to present yourself in person at a police station.

'Can I ask you something? If an eighteen-year-old girl has disappeared but left a message on the phone to say she was going away, can she be counted as missing?'

'When did she phone?'

'Five days ago. But it isn't like her. She knew her mother and I were coming to Melbourne to see her . . .'

'Perhaps she has her own reasons.' Was there a hint of suspicion in her breezy tone? Of rebuke?

'Yes. Of course. But, you know, we're a perfectly . . . *functional* family.' He realised how futile this was. It might even sound suspicious.

'Sure,' said the young constable. 'Don't hesitate to call in if there's been no word from her.'

'After how long?'

'Give it a few more days. Another week or so.'

They sat on different sides of the conversation pit but there was no need for conversation. Their daughter was missing, whatever that meant. She was out of their reach. Their worn hands lay loose on their laps as the shadows came and went across the walls.

There was a pattering of rain. They couldn't help feeling that this was it, God or fate or karma coming to meet them. If life was a test, this is what would break them. Something in the pattern of their lives, separately or together, was being worked out. Like a snake turning around to bite them. They felt that they were being punished for something, though they knew this was superstitious and irrational.

They sat very still as darkness filled the room.

3

Leaving

Once in a spring twilight, a schoolgirl was waiting for a bus on the edge of the highway between Fremantle and Perth when a stranger in a low black car pulled up and offered her a lift. And without a word, against a lifetime's warnings, the girl, Toni Parker, climbed in.

Why did she do it? She would ask herself this, off and on, for the rest of her life. A chorus of horns broke out and spread down the line of cars behind him. He was holding up the traffic, it was rush hour, he was shockingly inconsiderate. Sometimes Toni wondered if she made this split-second, life-changing decision because she'd been brought up to think of others. Because she was a nice middle-class girl who was embarrassed.

He was so calm, so matter-of-fact, that she bent down to look at him, thinking he must know her, perhaps he worked with her father. In the dim cab light she saw a youngish man, no more than thirty, with a large pale deadpan face and black eyes looking up at her, his thick eyebrows raised in query.

She saw – did she? – what could she see in those few moments? – that he was wearing black with a strip of white at the neck, like a priest. His hair was slicked back. He didn't smile, didn't try to entice her. For one moment she almost believed that this was a Christian gesture, because it was growing dark and about to rain. Could she really have been so naïve?

There was something compelling about him. And that was the truth about Cy Fisher. He always did exactly what he wanted to. In him the channel between will and action ran unusually clear and fast, unusually pure. He didn't allow himself doubts or guilt. People always obeyed him, his will was stronger than theirs. Above all else he despised fear. Fear was the only quality in others that he didn't tolerate. (Apart from disloyalty, of course.) He always tested people to find their point of fear. Did Toni sense that she was being challenged? Or was she simply thrown off-guard, like an animal caught in headlights, going forward when it should have gone back?

Attention had always come her way because she'd been born good-looking, but that evening, standing at the bus stop in her uniform, she couldn't conceive of herself as an object of desire. The bulky blazer, shapeless pleats, thick stockings that encased her had nothing to do with the expression of her body. Her hair was held back at the nape of her neck by a piece of elastic and squashed down under a beret. Even her pearly hands were encased in grubby stretch-knitted gloves. Except for her face and neck, every part of her flesh was covered. Unlike some girls, she never tried to make her uniform look seductive. Long ago she'd accepted the disguise it offered. Standing there that evening she was hardly present, numbly enduring these final days of her school life. This was probably the last time she'd ever stand at this bus stop, she thought.

She yawned, tired. The bag at her feet was heavy with books and files for the evening's revision. In three weeks' time she'd sit her Leaving exams. It was an after-school revision class in French that had made her late. French didn't much interest her, nor did any other subject. Last month she'd fallen out of love with a boy she thought she fancied. She felt no identification with her life or the future mapped out for her.

Something else happened, which she only remembered years later. As she stood there, great iron-gray clouds banked up above her, the air turned purplish, there was a hush and everything seemed to go still. And for a second's flash she saw herself standing exactly where she was, alone on the face of the earth. Then the lights changed, the cars started rolling and she forgot this vision at once.

The low black car slowed down in front of her and the door opened, just as the first drops began to fall. At once the horns started up, baying at her like the voice of public disapproval. She picked up her bag and stepped into the new that was waiting for her.

Nothing terrible happened.

No sooner had she fitted herself in, sorted out her feet in their heavy brogues, settled her bag on her knees, than the rain crashed down and it was too noisy to speak. They crawled along, enclosed by wavy walls of rain, both of them peering through the windscreen. Right away of course she realised that he wasn't any sort of man of God. A packet of cigarettes slid around on the dashboard which was streamlined, gleaming with lights like a control panel. No priest would drive a car like this. Also he had an unpriest-like five o'clock shadow.

'You can throw that into the back if you like,' he shouted, with a nod towards her bag.

'It's OK, thanks,' she shouted back, keeping it clasped to her. That way he'd know she expected to get out soon. But she took her gloves off and the ridiculous beret and stuffed them in the bag, so as to feel less at a disadvantage.

He raised his voice again to ask her where she was going. She named a street in her suburb. He'd drop her off there, he said, it wasn't far out of his way.

'Oh no thanks, if you could just drop me off at a stop further up, there's a connecting bus . . .'

He shook his head.

She decided not to press the point. Better to show trust. By car her house was only ten minutes away. Better not to offend him. But she could feel her heart beating. From the corner of her eye she checked out the door handle.

'What sort of car is this?'

'Citroën. It's French.'

'I've never seen one before.'

'There are fifteen in the whole of Perth.'

How do you know the exact number of cars like yours in a city? Why would you want to?

'What makes you so late?' he asked.

'I've just been to a French class. It's the Leaving in a couple of weeks.' It was the sort of over-information her mother gave when she was making conversation.

He didn't bother to answer. At least he didn't patronise her. He left the highway and drove deep into the heart of her leafy suburb. The rain stopped like a tap turned off and the only sound was the swish of the tyres on the wet road. He seemed preoccupied. She took the chance to sneak a look at him. He didn't resemble anyone she'd seen before. He didn't look

'Australian'. His face was too white and fleshy and his eyes too dark. His hair was long, slicked back, curling over his collar. His large nose was flattened over the bridge as if it had been broken. He wore a black suit, loose and soft from use, and pointy leather boots. A white shirt, done up to the neck. She'd never seen a suit worn with boots and without a tie before, let alone by a man with long hair. Was he fashionable or a foreigner? He was amply-built for a man not yet in middle age. A broad chest, broad thighs, a fold beneath his chin. He smelt older, humid and smoky. The black prickles along his jaw looked mature and urgent. Lips not quite closed, as if ready to speak when or if it became essential. The mouth shapely and distrustful. A heavy gold ring glinted on his right hand. He didn't come from her world.

'Which house?' They'd entered her street. She pointed, he pulled up. 'Thanks a lot,' she said as she tried the handle of the door. He leaned across her and opened it. The light came on above his head.

'*Voulez-vous sortir avec moi?*' He spoke softly, his face close to hers. She blinked, shocked. So it was a pick-up after all. His accent sounded quite authentic, a lot better than hers. There was a gleam of amusement deep down in his grape-black eyes.

'*Ce n'est pas possible. J'ai les examens.*' She was backing out of the car as swiftly as she could with her hefty bag. Safe on home ground, she bent down and bestowed a charming smile on him. '*Merci beaucoup. Au revoir.*' She shut the door.

He watched her as she set off with studied calm up the front path, a beauty got up to look like a middle-aged policewoman. Why did they do that to their girls, try to desex them? Keeping them for the right sort of marriage, he supposed. It was meant to make them all look the same of course, but nothing could hide the lines of her figure and the shape of her face. The moment

62

he'd spotted her looking up at the sky over the highway he could tell she was one for whom appearances would be everything. Arrogant. Look at the way she carried off that walk, gliding towards her house, a triple-fronter like all the others in the street, with lawn and shrubbery and stuffy parents terrified by what the neighbours think. They needn't have worried. Their spoilt, pretty daughters always scuttled back to their own kind.

Except it wasn't her house. She'd directed him to a house in the street behind hers, owned by a family she didn't even know. As soon as he drove off she doubled back down the path and hurried home around the block, exultant, breathing in the scents of wet lawns. Nothing terrible had happened!

Yet that was the start of it all.

It might have been in the same spring twilight that across the city Jacob too was rushing home late, before a downpour of rain. He was also in his last week of school, but he was late because he'd just smoked a joint — the first of his life — with his friend Beech and the Capelli boys in the back lane behind Capelli Foods. The *reefer* (as he and Beech called it, in homage to *On the Road*) was as fat as a cigar, and popped and crackled like woodfire as they handed it around. Just as they reached the lovingly constructed cardboard filter, Vito Capelli roared for his boys and after a stampede to destroy the evidence they all scattered, Beech to the Anglican rectory, Jacob to his mother's dress shop, Arlene's, two blocks further up.

The sky had turned a cinematic purple and he started to feel he was in a film. In the exhaust from the cars whizzing past him along Fitzgerald Street, his long hair blew heroically back from his face. He heard his feet ring like doom on the iron treads of the fire-escape as he made his way up to the flat on top of Arlene's. Enter Belmondo. Enter Brando. It's a bit like being drunk, Jacob thought.

His sister Kitty looked up from her homework on the kitchen table and said: 'Why are your eyes all red?' Rain started to clatter so loudly on the tin roof that he was saved from responding. The kitchen was unceilinged, a converted back verandah, walled in with louvres and weatherboard.

'She's got a fitting,' Kitty shouted, pointing to the work-room. From the kitchen you could see into the workroom through a long, broad-silled window that had once opened onto the verandah. Tonight their mother had forgotten to draw the curtains. By long institution, since childhood, he and Kitty were on their honour not to peer.

There was the familiar tableau of Arlene on her knees, worshipping at the hemline of an unknown woman whom Jacob, with the lightning eye of long experience, categorised on the spot. Late twenties, natural brunette, one of those high, pointy, possibly artificial busts, standard hips, sporty calves. Something pinched about her face. The face was important. Six out of ten. Six point five. Attractive if you passed her in the street but without that special quality that he and Beech were always on the lookout for. On the other hand she was probably tired. Some of Arlene's best-looking clients lost their sparkle at late fittings. There was something wistful about them at this hour, he thought. The client stared blankly over Arlene's head, slowly turning on the plywood platform that Arlene had once forced him to make in Manual Arts. It was a peaceful scene. In the background Chickie the canary, his and Kitty's ancient and only pet, was preening himself in his cage.

There was a crack of thunder, and the rackety tacked-on kitchen rattled and swayed.

'Kitty!' Jacob shouted, 'This is stupendous!'

Kitty peered at him suspiciously. He was four years older than her and though not actively unkind, had for most of her life acted as if she wasn't there. Her name rarely sullied his lips. She received the merest crumbs from his table. He never directly addressed her unless it was for some practical reason, usually to do with his own needs. He was the man of the house and a master at getting out of things.

'I've put the potatoes on, Jake. You've got to do the chops.'

Jacob stood blinking at her beneath the swinging light bulb. Overnight, it seemed, Kitty's jaw had deepened and her eyebrows thickened. He could see where Arlene had let out the seams of her gym tunic which was straining across the erupting islets of her breasts. Woman-sized pink legs filled the space beneath the table. Kitty was bursting out of herself. There was a glass of milk beside her books, filled with unmixed chunks of Milo. She had a chocolate smear on her downy upper lip. He saw that it was too late for his sister now, it had been decided. She was never going to be pretty.

'You're acting funny, Jake.'

Smiling mysteriously, avoiding her eyes, he navigated his way past her to the sleep-out.

There was only one bedroom in the flat, which Kitty shared with Arlene. His sleepout was another part of the enclosed verandah, next to the kitchen. It had a similar low-silled window into the workroom. He stood watching in the dark, as he always did if the curtains were open.

The client was standing at the workroom door with her back to him, putting on her coat. She reached her hands up under her brown hair and flicked it out over her collar, a female gesture which Jacob always found alluring. He heard the chorus of thanks and promises as Arlene escorted her down the inside stairs. She was nicer to her clients than to her children. How encouraging women were to one another! His mother's voice became louder when she was tired. How many hours had he spent watching the women in that room, with his light turned off, through any chance gap in the curtains?

Once when he was younger – not all that much younger, if he were honest – he'd let Beech watch a wedding party fitting. Before the appointment, he sneaked into the workroom and carefully pre-arranged the curtains. For hours Beech stayed glued, floridly describing body shapes and mouthing marks out of ten. Jacob felt glutted, soiled, somehow disloyal, which he never felt when he watched alone. He couldn't wait for Beech to go home and leave him to his private pleasures. What after all was there to see? Just a succession of female bodies in not very radical states of undress, the young and old, the misshapen, the well-formed. The soft bulks, almost comical, turning and turning on his platform, like dolls in a music box. Rarely perfect, rarely even an eight, never as yet a ten, though his and Beech's standards were exacting. An occasional bending down to reveal an entire cleavage, a bare back with the bra undone, a length of thigh, though Beech swore he'd spotted pubic hair.

Beech missed the point. His own appreciation was subtler, more specialised. It was their hands, the gentle curl, the smallness yet strength, adjusting a stocking or a fallen strap. The intimacy of their bare feet. The smoothness and tautness of their skin, over the shoulders and back, the sheen of collar-bones. The hints and glimpses, a nipple outlined, a puckered little belly button. All the versions of their underclothes, full and half-slips, bras, suspender belts, from the worn and homely to slithery shell-coloured lace and silk. Seeing who skimped and who was prepared to love herself, even with what was concealed. Their vulnerable necks, turning this way and that to examine themselves, and the private face each had when she looked at herself in Arlene's mirror. The remoteness and grace of the special ones. There was always one who was his favourite, even amongst the older women. They all had their role in his fantasies, roles that would surprise them if they knew. He felt the pain of not being able to reach them, of letting them go, again and again.

He lay down on his bed. The rain had stopped and he could hear his name – Kitty was reporting on him to their mother in the kitchen. Arlene was silent. When she came up the stairs at the end of the day she had no energy left to talk. Right now she'd be standing in her towelling scuffs at the open kitchen door smoking her end-of-work cigarette, looking out into the darkness. She'd never had any authority over Jacob, and let him off everything for the past few months because of the Leaving. All she wanted, pleaded for daily, was for him to have a haircut.

He ought to put his light on now, and start studying. He reached out, and put in the earpiece of his transistor instead. *Eleanor Rigby*. The lonely people. Everything that needed to be said came from music these days. Fat little Kitty with her books open on the table, the smear of chocolate on her mouth. Hungry. He and Kitty were always hungry. Once, years ago, he'd seen Kitty through the workroom window, dancing to the LP of *Peter and the Wolf* in the tutu Arlene had made her, throwing her solid little body around the big table, leaping on and off his platform, curtseying in front of the mirror, and he knew she was a fantasist, like him.

Insights flooded him. He, Kitty and Arlene lived together

but the real life of each of them took place elsewhere. They hid their true passions from one another. Every night he fell asleep to the whirr of the sewing machine, stopping and starting, relentless riffs going nowhere. On Saturday afternoons Arlene closed the shop and took a bath, did her nails and set her hair, ready for her night out with Joe Lanza. Joe, her friend as she called him, two feet wide and coming up to her shoulder, had put the money down for the shop. On Saturday nights she slept at Joe's house, doing what old friends do, he supposed, a grotesque thought. She came home to slap some tea together on Sunday night and put in a few hours at the sewing machine. It pays the bills, she said, but he and Kitty grew up knowing it was clothes that had her full attention, that all she really cared about was *the cut, the fit, the hang.*

Sundays in the flat were long, silent, spacious. Bells rang out from St Alban's, Beech's father's church, where Beech would be kneeling, his hair tucked inside his collar, the image of devotion. Jacob didn't know how lucky he was, Beech said. All the pretty girls in the area were Greek or Italian, and they went to the Orthodox or Catholic churches.

Everyone else in the district spent Sundays with family, with fathers, cousins, grandparents, but Arlene had no relatives here. In street after street they were eating big Sunday lunches, roasts, spaghetti, pots of cabbage. Jacob and Kitty roamed around without talking, studied themselves in mirrors, listened to their transistors, sprawled on their beds, reading. Their life was all in their heads, in dreams of the future. They made French toast and pikelets and slice after slice of grilled Kraft cheese, eating while they read.

Arlene, *couturière* before all else, took no interest in their education and yet had produced two bookish kids, always at the top of their class. From the first they had covered their own schoolbooks with brown paper and signed their own homework cards. They learnt to find the books they wanted in libraries, op shops, parish jumble sales. They were used to looking after themselves and helping out Arlene. They did things out of a kind of sorrow for her.

They never talked about Arlene's Saturday nights with Joe. Jacob had come to appreciate the freedom of his upbringing, but Kitty, he sensed, was ashamed of Arlene's unmotherly ways.

He took the earpiece out in order to enjoy his thoughts and the luminous evening light after the storm. The scene was lit up in his mind, as if he was looking down on it from very high, the flat above the shop, the miles and miles of twinkling street-lights, the dark coastline and far out, like a ship on an eternal horizon, the Flying Dutchman, the Drowned Sailor, the Lost Father. Long ago, before Kitty was born, before he could remember, their father had become an absence, soundless as the black water that had engulfed him, and like the water, always there.

His own life was a film or a book, and this was a chapter soon to be finished. He was the hero and also the writer. This was what it must be like to be a poet, one epiphany after the other!

This Capelli stuff was magic. No wonder it was catching on. A great wave was breaking, he could feel it, an extraordinary club was forming, a bright new ragged army was lining up against everything that had oppressed him about his future as a man, the nine-to-five, the mortgage, the retirement plan. Giving the finger to the old men who ran things, the government, the law, the army, and their war in Vietnam. He longed to have a draft card to burn on St George's Terrace.

The accused was lying drugged on his bed. I am lying drugged on my bed, he told himself. And he was not the only one. All across the world people were letting their hair grow, lighting up and lying down and becoming poets.

Jacob called it the Tolstoy factor, from the time when he spent the entire two weeks' swot-vac before the Leaving reading *War and Peace*. Beech had left the book on his bed, saying casually: 'This is supposed to be the greatest novel in the world.' He and Beech often exchanged books and always knew what the other was reading. There was a slightly competitive edge to it. That year they'd read, neck and neck, *Crime and Punishment, Another Country, Catch 22, Justine, The Outsider*. Beech himself hadn't read *War and Peace*, he'd bought it in a second-hand shop on his way to visit Jacob. It was the evening of their last ever day at school and they were drinking Arlene's sherry in the sleepout. From tomorrow both of them would have to study day and night if they were to get the results they needed. They agreed not to meet again until after the exams. They slapped each other around the shoulders for good luck and, mildly drunk, Beech sloped off to the rectory, *his work done*, Jacob came to think. He would never know whether Beech left the book on his bed on purpose, or whether, as he said, he just forgot it. The minister's son, instrument of the devil.

Day after day he told himself that his whole future depended on this dash to the finish line, and yet even as he ate his breakfast, stolid with panic, he found himself reaching for the book. Only Tolstoy's world was real to him. Every morning, it was as if he picked himself up out of the snow and set off again, blindly marching to his doom. This was how he wanted life to be, heightened and distilled! What were a few exams in the face of the great movements of love and history? *Why do I struggle?* he thought, with Pierre. *Why am I troubled in this narrow, cramped routine, when life, all life, with all its joys, lies open before me?* He *was* Pierre, the eye of the novel, the observer. The noble slob. He was astounded by Tolstoy's insight. Was this the story of every man's inner life, with its private hungers, its unrequited loves? With the secret desire for fame: *I want glory! I want to be beloved by people I don't know!*

And war, with the same male dilemma, whether or not to fight.

No matter how much he resolved, as he fell asleep at night, to pull himself together, take control of himself, in the morning his hands opened the book as if by themselves. He was paralysed in a bad dream. He was teetering on the edge of an abyss. He'd swum too far out of his depth. And all the time he watched himself, like a scientist observing a rat on a treadmill.

He told himself that he was caught up in the tidal wave of great literature. That all the real moments of his life had come from books or films. That he'd always preferred art to life. He even toyed with the idea – wasting ever more time – that this was his tribute to art, his sacrifice. But he knew that he was avoiding a simple truth, which was that he couldn't help himself, and all the voices of authority, teachers, ministers, headmasters, woke him in terror in the middle of the night. Why was he so weak? Because he'd never had a father to give him a good belting, like the Capelli boys? The only way he could go back to sleep was to reach for *War and Peace* and read a little more.

It was getting hot under the tin roof of the sleepout, so by day he set himself up in the workroom, at the large table where Arlene cut out her patterns. Use of this table was one of

Arlene's few prohibitions, but now she said nothing as each day he shoved aside her bolts of cloth and laid out his notes and books. She and Kitty left him alone, peeking at him through the window in the kitchen, keeping their voices low. Arlene, in a rare maternal gesture, cooked steak to keep up his strength, fish fingers to feed his brain. After school Kitty brought him cups of milky, well-sugared Nescafé. If anyone were to catch him out it would be Kitty. She was always looking over his shoulder to see what he was reading, a habit that annoyed him. Even worse, she had been known to sneak his current book out of his room and read it herself. He read Tolstoy on his knee under the table when she was home, and only grunted if she tiptoed in, to show he wasn't going to answer any questions.

Why were they being so respectful? Did the fortunes of the family rest on his shoulders, the son of the house, like Count Nikolai Rostov? He was in a nineteenth-century haze. He lifted his eyes from his book and saw the women framed by the window in the kitchen as if through Tolstoy's eyes. Kitty's desire to be good, her shy, private life of hope, related her to one of the plainer Tolstoyan heroines. There was something about Arlene, however, that resisted romanticising.

There she was, seated at the table with a towel over her shoulders while Kitty, in rubber gloves, stood behind her, dabbing at her scalp with peroxide. This was a regular household ritual, which Arlene, directing operations from a hand mirror, called 'doing my roots'. Now Kitty was checking out a pimple in the mirror. Now Arlene was telling Kitty to get a move on, Joe was picking her up at six. Everything they did was so familiar to him. They were large-boned, strong-minded modern women, managing their lives perfectly well without him. Kitty studied much harder than he did and already had plans for becoming a teacher. Arlene was a successful businesswoman who, as she said, always paid her bills. She'd never let her children prevent her from doing anything she wanted, and didn't bother to conceal the fact that she couldn't wait for them to leave.

The flat's lounge room had always been given over to Arlene's work. Only after dinner at night or on the weekends were he and Kitty allowed to reclaim the sofa from the clients, flick through the fashion magazines, listen to the radiogram which Arlene turned on when she was sewing. Apart from old Chickie sleeping in his cage by the window, the room was bare of any sign of family life. No pictures or books. No mess. No television. Arlene had read in the papers that television was bad for teenagers and had taken one of her sudden, stubborn stands on the issue. Besides she had no time to watch it herself and if she had the money she'd spend it on one of those new Japanese sewing machines.

The sigh of the pneumatic brakes of the buses at the lights on Fitzgerald Street punctured his long solitary hours, and more sporadically, the two notes of the bell above the door of Arlene's as the customers came and went. Ding-dong! Snatches of high voices and his mother's clipped professional footsteps. The distant ping! of the till. He'd never been such a witness to his mother's life before. Every morning, in lipstick, high heels, and an outfit that she might have just run up for herself the night before, Arlene went downstairs and didn't come up again until she closed the shop at six.

She took no interest in anything outside the business. Nature, the weather, the passage of time, were only seen in terms of suitable clothes. She was never happier than crawling round the hem of a client with a mouthful of pins. Best of all were those clients who 'gave her her head', an expression which caused Beech to smirk when he heard it. She looked forward to the day when she didn't have to do alterations anymore, just work on her own creations. Her greatest triumph was to be out somewhere with Joe and have a woman say to her in the ladies', *I hope you don't mind me asking, but where'd you get that dress?*

The only reading she had time for was *The Sunday Times* over breakfast at Joe's. Whoever he and Kitty had inherited their bookishness from, it wasn't Arlene.

Once, after reading the death scene of Prince Andrey, *the simple and solemn mystery of death*, where the two women who loved him wept from *the emotion and awe that filled their souls*, he looked up from the book and surveyed the bare walls around him. Wouldn't a widow want to keep something to remind her of her kids' father, a letter, a watch, a wedding portrait on the mantelpiece? Just as he couldn't remember anything about his father, he couldn't remember sensing any grief about his death.

There *was* a photograph somewhere. He'd seen it once, years ago, unless it was a dream. He went into her bedroom and rummaged through the old letters and certificates and his and Kitty's class photos and reports in Arlene's bedside drawer. He found it, a black and white Kodak snap of his parents and himself as a tiny boy on a verandah. He took it back to the living room, propped it up on the mantelpiece and studied it.

You could call it *The Sailor on Leave*. Arlene's brother Bob took it, he was also a sailor, he'd introduced Arlene to Anton de Jong. It was taken at the little wooden house in the coastal town in NSW where Bob and Arlene had grown up. Arlene stayed living there after their parents died.

Anton was in uniform, perhaps he was about to set off again. A classic sailor suit, with wide pants and a kerchief cross-tied on his chest. He was seated in a wicker chair, one foot in its huge blunt-nosed shiny shoe resting on the other knee. His head was lowered, in shadow, he was reading the newspaper that lay across his bent leg. A streak of light caught his temples, his receding hairline, his narrow-bridged nose.

Arlene, seated at the other end of the verandah with her back turned to her husband, was preoccupied, adjusting the straps of sturdy little Jacob's romper suit, which no doubt she had made herself. Her bare arms were tanned and slim and her short blonde hair was curled. He couldn't remember having a young, fresh mother. Her legs were crossed, one white high-heeled shoe peeping out from beneath the folds of her floral print dress. She would have got herself all dressed up for his visits. She might have been pregnant with Kitty. Was this Anton's last leave?

Anton was reported missing, presumed drowned, soon after his ship left Durban. There was no pension, because there was no witness to his accident and no body was ever found. Arlene, with new-born baby Kitty, had to take in sewing.

'What if he signed on and then swam back to shore?' Jacob once asked her. 'Do you believe he really drowned?'

'Of course he did! They just wanted to get out of paying me any money.' Arlene was not one for regrets or second thoughts or talk about the past.

She was vague about what happened next. There were problems with the man next door. He got a fix on me, she said, it gave me the creeps. He certainly got no encouragement. Late one night Bob drove Arlene and her kids and her Singer sewing machine to Sydney and put them on the train to Western Australia. He paid for the tickets. They left everything behind them, clothes, furniture, a dinner setting. Bob sold the house with all its contents. She had to disappear without a trace, Arlene said. There was nothing else you could do with a man like that.

If Jacob walked in the streets of South Africa and passed his father, he wouldn't recognise him. From that photo, all you could say that Anton had passed on to his kids were large feet, a love of reading and their names. At their school a Dutch name was just one of all the other non-Anglo names, Greek, Jewish, Italian, Yugoslav, Chinese. Most were not mainstream Australian. He was Jake de Jong until the Rolf Harris song, when he became Jake the Peg. After that he called himself Jacob.

But the others all had fathers. The nature of his father's disappearance was something he kept to himself.

You could almost see a line of tension between the sole of Anton's propped–up shoe and Arlene's floral back in the photograph. Had they had a fight? Did they realise they had nothing to talk about? Anton was reading the way you read when you want to forget about what is around you. If time was so short, why wasn't he playing with his little boy?

He was in the shade and Arlene was in the light. If you had to guess, you'd say she'd be the survivor. Did Anton choose death, or did he escape to another life? Was his character *weak?*

How exhausting procrastination was! He was pale and sluggish with dark rings under his eyes. He had no spirit for his old trick when he had the place to himself, of putting on the Four Tops and miming 'I'll Be There' with a fist microphone in front of the long mirror. He had no desire to arrange the curtains ready for his evening pleasures. All that was behind him now, a pervert's habit that had probably set him off on the road to mental ruin.

If he wasn't reading Tolstoy he fell asleep. On his rare excursions into the outside world, sneaking down the fire escape to the newsagent's for a packet of Columbines or a *Mad*

Magazine, he was shocked by the harshness of the light, the dust blowing down Fitzgerald Street, the banality of this desert town. He kept his head down to avoid people's eyes. He was nearly knocked over by Rosser, the science dux from school, pounding along in running shorts. 'I'm pacing myself,' Rosser panted. 'Four hours at the desk and then I run a mile.' Jacob rushed home, longing for snow, dronskies, lanterns, long rustling dresses.

It was too late for him now. All he could do was open Tolstoy, the last act of a dying man. Its effect was instantaneous, like plunging into a golden broth. Don't end, don't ever stop . . . He rang Beech to curse him for lending him the book. Beech sounded slow and distant, as if engrossed in work. Bastard! (Later it turned out that Beech had been back to the Capelli brothers, and was experimenting on his own in the rectory shed.)

'*Father! Father!*' says Prince Andrey's young son Nikolinka in the last line of the story. '*Yes, I will do something that even* he *would be content with . . .*'

But by that time, as Jacob closed the book, it was as if he were at the end of his youth, with all its happy expectations of success.

He had two days left before the Leaving started. He was washed out, devastated, purified. Almost curious now about his impending disaster, he reached for his history notes and began to memorise some dates.

His life wasn't ruined, he scraped through, though like a slap on the wrist, with only a provisional pass in English, his best subject. Without a Commonwealth Scholarship he would have to be bonded to teachers' college and study at university part-time. Beech, another star pupil, did even worse, but a parishioner of his father's helped him get a job on *The West* as a cadet journalist. Beech was called up – or as he said, 'my marble was pulled' – but failed the medical. Flat feet was the official reason, but Beech said it was because he'd told them he was looking forward to writing real-life accounts of a soldier's life in Vietnam.

Jacob was never called up. Together they plunged into the heady days of the oncoming decade. But the Tolstoy factor would remain with Jacob as a distrust of himself, a suspicion that whenever there was something he should do, something vital, he would occupy himself with something else.

Of course he found her. As she came to know him she realised that he would have sent one of the boys to find out who she was and where she lived and what her movements were. But as with most things that happened around Cy Fisher, she only saw the results, not how he achieved them. Her little trick with her address was never mentioned. Incidents in which someone got the better of Cy were rare and only meant that, sooner or later, without a word, he'd prove how futile such attempts were.

After the Leaving, she took a Christmas job at Boans, selling gloves and handbags. One day she looked up from the counter and there he was. It was a shock to see him again in daylight, his black eyes and fish-belly white face, his solidity and assurance. She felt her heart beating. Her first thought was that she hadn't really got away after all.

'How are you?' he said, with a businesslike nod, and straight away asked to look at a leather shoulder bag, the classiest, the most stylish, the one she yearned for. 'I'll take it,' he said, handing it back. She was surprised to see her hands shaking a little as she wrapped it. *'Merci'*, he said, as he gave her a cheque, and at last he smiled. He put the bag under his arm, nodded at her and walked away.

The name *Cy Fisher* was almost childishly clear in the big black writing on the cheque. Who was the bag for? she wondered.

He came back two days later, his usual span for the softening-up process. By then she'd had time to think about him. In fact, in the same way that he'd loomed over the counter, he now loomed in her mind. She felt haunted by him from the moment she woke in the morning, as if those black eyes had watched her while she slept. *Cy Fisher, Cy Fisher*, she muttered at the mirror, like a question to herself.

This time her heart lurched violently as soon as she caught sight of him, as just before closing time he threaded his way through the Christmas crowd towards her. He stood out from everybody else, in his loose black suit, with his long, groomed hair and the villainous five o'clock shadow darkening his cheeks. Hardly the answer to a mother's prayer, or a schoolgirl's dream for that matter. But then she wasn't a schoolgirl anymore. He asked her to have a drink with him after work and she accepted.

Everything that happened around Cy Fisher was swift and simple. The Citroën was parked in a loading zone at the back of Boans. He always parked wherever was closest to his mission. If a ticket found its way onto his windscreen, he crumpled it up and threw it on the ground.

He took her to The Riviera, a nightclub in the old part of the city on the other side of the railway line, where girls from her suburb never went. This is where migrants came when they first arrived in Perth, wave upon wave of them, setting up in the little dark terrace houses and shops until they could afford to move out to a quarter-acre block in the suburbs and become proper Australians. It was too early for The Riviera to be open for business but Cy knocked and was let in. He ushered her inside and as they entered he put one hand on her shoulder. To protect her or claim possession?

It was a large bare room, naked-looking as a church hall at this time of the day. From small windows near the ceiling the summer twilight fell in beams across the swept wooden floor. There was a bar near the door and a table of men playing cards. As soon as the barman saw Cy Fisher he put down two glasses and a bottle. Cy pulled out a bar stool for Toni before strolling to the table and shaking hands with each of the men. The barman filled the glasses with colourless liquid from the bottle, grappa, he told Toni, the very best. He was a small, quick man with sympathetic brown eyes and a professional manner. Cy sat down, clinked his glass against Toni's and downed it in one gulp. Toni took a sip. She felt she was being watched but when she glanced over her shoulder, the men at the table were studying their cards. They were darkly well-groomed, of all ages, in suits or laundered shirt sleeves. I could be in Europe, she thought. She took another sip. Cy and the barman, Pino, discussed soccer scores. As soon as she had drained her glass, Cy stood up. He ushered her to the door and the card-players raised their hands. She felt their eyes on her back.

In all their time together she never once saw him pick up a bill.

His timing was impeccable. He drove her to the bus stop on the avenue close to where she lived – he seemed to know that it wouldn't be a good idea for her to be seen alighting from a stranger's car in her own street – and she arrived home only a few minutes later than usual. Everything went as if to a plan.

He started to pick her up every day after work. He took her all over the city, to little restaurants where no English was spoken, or dark bars up stairways or jazz clubs in basements. She had no idea that such places existed in Perth. Mostly these establishments had not yet opened for the night, which gave a cosy family atmosphere to their visits. He knew all the owners and everybody seemed glad to see him. Doors opened before them, a table was always waiting, a bottle appeared, vodka or grappa or some other sort of ethnic brandy. The smoothness of their path, the warmth of their reception, made her feel languorous and secure. This is what grown-up life is like, she thought. There was an aura of authority around him, and within it she felt safe. Nothing was going to happen to you once you stepped into his orbit. It was clear he was some kind of leader, though she had no idea what he was a leader of, exactly. Arriving somewhere with him was like entering a ball with the captain of the rowing squad.

In all ways these excursions couldn't be more different from what she had experienced up till now. The instinct of the boys she knew was to head for open spaces, the beaches or the river or King's Park. Everything happened outside, sex, socialising, music, films. They went to drive-in cinemas, concerts on ovals or in grassy auditoriums, football games. They camped at Rottnest Island. Even at parties, everyone ended up on the porch or the terrace or the shrubbery down the back of the yard. At the end of the night their cars, or their fathers' cars, invariably headed for the beach, or parking lots overlooking the river. When summer came all the boys wore as little as possible, shorts and singlets, bare feet, a sort of native tribe.

As far as she could see, day or night, winter or summer, Cy Fisher wore the same black suit and white shirt. His only concession to the heat was to take off his jacket and roll up his sleeves to expose thick, black-haired forearms. He never exposed his legs or his feet and walked as little as possible in the street. His skin was so white it was as if the sun never reached him.

His instinct was all for dark interiors, in the north of the city, amongst people he knew, none of whom had an English name. He had no interest in nature, and actively distrusted all insects, birds, dogs. The only time she'd seen him even slightly agitated was when a bee flew around his head. He'd cursed and swiped at it and didn't rest until he'd crushed it beneath his boot. He said he wouldn't know one end of a surfboard from another. She realised she'd never known a male under thirty who didn't surf.

She began to understand that he was of another species, those who slept late and stayed up all night. She thought of him as a sort of nocturnal animal, which had, for reasons of its own, decided to bring her into its world.

He saw her for an hour or so after work each day and always delivered her home in time. Never laid a hand on her, apart from her shoulder or the base of her spine when they walked in or out of a door. She didn't know what he wanted of her. Suspense grew. She sensed it was a breaking-in process and couldn't help admiring his cool.

What did she know of him? Sometimes she told him anecdotes about her day at work when he picked her up. He listened benevolently, without comment. He drove serenely, uninterested in small talk. The smile he gave her when she got into the car was enough to warm her through the journey. Why? Because he only ever smiled if he wanted to. It seemed to signal some deep, mysterious approval that carried her past the strangeness between them.

He wasn't afraid of silence. It was as if he said, it's enough I've chosen you. I have made a decision.

Christmas passed, but she applied to keep working at Boans. The Leaving results came out, she'd passed respectably. She'd been going to stay with some classmates on Rottnest, but she had no interest in this now, nor in the backyard parties – punchbowls, coloured lights, hired music – that broke out all over the suburbs by the river. She stopped returning phone calls. Soon nobody called her anymore. It was as if she'd moved to another city.

She didn't know if she liked Cy Fisher or not, she couldn't think about it. All she knew was that these little sorties with him had a charm for her. With him, her life was suddenly exotic. In bed at home, this secret life, the places he took her to, the people she met, seemed like a fairytale.

Cy Fisher was not someone she could talk about to any of the girls she knew. Unlike them, she had no close friendships. This was not just because she was reserved by nature. Beauty isolated her. By some genetic design, all her inherited features had harmoniously come together, her father's olive colouring, her mother's fine bones, to create its own fresh, perfect form. At seventeen she was like a new star rising in the firmament, gazed upon with wonder all over her small world. Wherever she went she attracted attention. There was a hush about her if she came into a room. Old people smiled at her. It was said that she looked like Natalie Wood, that she could be a cover girl for *Seventeen*.

Girls gazed at her in class, wondering how one creature could be so blessed. They kept their distance. Face to face with some of them, it seemed to her that their eyes swam with something secret, some suspicion they were keeping to themselves. She sensed that they were on the lookout for any signs that she was pleased with herself. She had to work hard to compensate, be extra modest and nice, just to prove that she was the same as everybody else. This created tension inside her. She felt isolated, unreal, a fake. There was something unexpressed in her relationships with other girls, even those who included her. When they talked, daily, about appearances, their own or other people's, Toni had to stay silent.

And all the time she knew she was no vainer than they were. She took her beauty for granted, it had always been there, it was part of her, she enjoyed it unthinkingly, carelessly, as someone who has never been ill enjoys a healthy body.

Boys, on the other hand, were always in favour of her. In fact, the cooler she was, the more they seemed to like it. Only the confident or very daring approached her and asked her out. But this too was unreal. She felt their eyes didn't really see her when they looked at her. They didn't listen to what she said. They liked her whatever she thought or did. She lost respect for them and was bored.

In her own family, beauty was a word that was never mentioned. Her older sister Karen, with the ordinary good looks of youth, was twenty-two and soon to be married, distracted, fulfilled, lost in her own world of lists and plans and bridal magazines. They had never been close. Toni was a quiet, cool, even-tempered child, detached like her father, Beryl said. Karen was closer to Beryl. Karen's social persona was warm, poised and chatty. Karen is the *nice* one, people liked to say.

Their father, Nig (for Nigel, but also making reference to the tremendous tan he gained in the navy while on service in the topics), never seemed to really look at his daughters, as if that was taboo. He treated them both with a distant, courteous affection. Perhaps he was only too aware of the trap of appearances – during the war he was as handsome as Cary Grant in his uniform, Beryl said, he was regarded as a *catch*, all the girls were wild about him. Her marriage was a coup, the triumph of her life.

Caught, he always had the upper hand. It was as if he'd made a pact with himself, to let his marriage interfere with his private pursuits as little as possible. He resisted all of Beryl's social ambitions. When he was home he sat silent behind his newspaper, indifferent to her rants and tears. He lived for going to the pub, to the football or cricket, or card games with old navy friends. He sold insurance to rural businesses and spent one week in three staying in old pubs, going to country race meets. 'Look after your mother,' he told his daughters, smiling as he left, freshly shaved and light-hearted.

A tension grew in her as the weeks passed. Soon she would start university, the first step on the path to the future plotted out for her (an arts degree, a brief stint in the public service, a year in London. The word 'marry' hovered just where this path met the horizon). Cy Fisher was so very much not a part of that future that she didn't know how she could keep on seeing him.

But was this the future that she really wanted? And if not, what did she want? At night she lay in bed and thought about this. She felt as if there was something she had once known for herself, which now she had forgotten.

She thought about Cy Fisher. She'd never expected to find him desirable – he was hardly the ideal of an attractive man – and yet she was more and more intrigued. She thought about his self-control, his calmness, the warm dry touch of his hands. He'd never even tried to kiss her. The way he was suddenly there, filling a doorway. The way he could, just as suddenly, disappear. The way his beard grew, virile and urgent, so he had to shave twice a day. But his carefully slick-backed hair, his ring, his clean, filed nails were almost female. He cared for himself like a *woman*. What would her father think of that?

He'd left school at fourteen. He'd never read a book in his life. But this was her mother's voice in her ear. He was a king in his world. In that world, a graceful hospitality flowed around her. She could stay silent and no one said she was stuck-up. In Cy's world she felt light and simple and at ease.

By now she ought to have introduced him to her parents. Lately when she came home from work, her mother had leant forward to smell her breath. Toni was running out of friends that she'd happened to meet or invitations to drinks from workmates.

'Tell the truth,' Cy Fisher said as drove her to her bus stop. 'Tell them you're with me.' There was a glint in his eye, a half-smile on his lips.

'Then you'll have to meet them,' she said. He had no comprehension of how much they wouldn't like him. Or perhaps he did. He was throwing her a challenge.

She took a breath. 'Come home with me now.'

She knew at once that it would never be all right. Beryl and Nig were sitting in their armchairs, beneath the standard lamp, both absorbed in watching the news. Spotlit under the pleated lampshade, their old faces were bleached and sunken, fallen into worried lines. They looked up at the same time, startled by the vision of Toni in the doorway with a stranger. Nig jumped up to turn off the sound on the TV. Behind him Beryl whipped off her apron. Toni introduced Cy and the men shook hands. They all stood looking at one another. No one asked Cy to sit down.

Beryl was unable to smile. Her eyes kept returning to Cy's hair and ring. She would be thinking 'common', Toni knew, she would be thinking 'flashy'. Her father cleared his throat a couple of times.

'Do you work at Boans with Toni, er . . .?'

'I'm in business. For myself.' A small smile hovered on Cy's lips. Somewhere, deep down, he was amused. Something was happening to the room, it felt smaller, stuffier, it could hardly contain his huge unsuitability.

'What line of business would that be?' Nig ventured.

'Real estate.'

Down the hall the telephone rang and was instantly answered. Karen. Her fiancé Bevan always rang her at this time. I have never, Beryl was often heard to say, had a moment's doubt about Bevan.

'Dinner's ready,' Beryl said, looking hard at Toni, her eyes signalling. *Get rid of him.*

The two men nodded at one another, Cy bowed to Beryl and Toni saw him to the door. By the time she sat down in the dining room she knew she didn't want to be there any more.

When the university term started Cy picked her up in the Arts carpark. She hadn't realised how much freedom university life would give her. Now she could meet up with him between lectures, at any time of the day. His real estate business didn't seem to have set hours. It felt strange at first that she could come and go without having to lie or ask anyone's permission. She still looked over her shoulder before she stepped into the Citroën.

One twilight he took her back to his apartment. It was in his part of the city, on top of an old shop on the corner of

Fitzgerald Street and a road that ran along a park ringed by huge Moreton Bay fig trees. The shop had been turned into a travel agency called Park Lane Travel which his sisters ran but they had left for the day. 'I bought this building for a song a few years ago,' he said, as he led her past the counter to a staircase at the back of the room. At the top of the stairs was a door which he unlocked.

'Nobody comes up here except my mother when I let her clean.'

'No guests? Not even your sisters?'

He shook his head.

A large living room with long windows overlooked the trees in the park. He'd knocked down walls to modernise the place, he explained, he liked big spaces. The walls were painted white, there was a leather and chrome couch, a glass coffee table, polished wooden floors. She'd never been in a room like this before, and she understood at once that it was something new, contemporary.

'I really like this,' she said.

She sensed that he was keeping an eye on her reaction, standing with his arms folded. Here he was different, private, a little shy. This was a big step for him. He was letting her in.

The bedroom was bare, apart from a high, white-covered bed under a skylight. He showed her how the skylight could be opened or closed by pressing a button in the bedside table. There was a tiny spotless kitchen in a glassed-in back porch, a toy kitchen because he never ate a meal at home.

She liked best the wooden platform built out from the kitchen, right into the arms of a giant old pepper tree. You could sit out there amongst the trailing leaves and spy on Fitzgerald Street and no one would know you were there.

'Kids would love it out here,' she said.

'No kids,' he said promptly.

'What d'you mean?'

'I've taken steps. I don't want to have 'em.'

'Why not?'

He shrugged. 'I never want to do what my father did to me.'

'Why would you?'

'Violence runs in families.'

She was silent.

'Just one less thing to worry about,' he said, placing his hand affectionately behind her neck as he ushered her towards the bed. Lying back she could see the first star through the open skylight. He sat on the side of the bed and took his boots off at last. Then his watch and heavy ring. His cufflinks. He smiled thoughtfully at her and started to unbutton his shirt. He took his time. Like his flat, like everything he did, he was clean, elegant, decisive.

Later in The Riviera Cy made a great show of shaking hands with everyone in the room, like a bridegroom, Toni caught herself thinking. He was in a playful mood. He sent Pino to the jukebox, and sat listening to the strains of Wilson Pickett's 'I'll Be There', tapping with his hand on her thigh under the bar. She sat close to him, peaceful, aching all over. Pino gave him a message in front of her. Something had been decided and everybody seemed to know it. She was part of the team.

She started to spend more and more time with him, whole days if she had no lectures, in the apartment, or in Park Lane while Cy did business in a small backroom office. His sister Felice was always in the travel agency, a short, lively girl in her early twenties, quick and light on her platform heels, with a constant trill-like laugh. Her skirts were just above the knee (her mother wouldn't let her go higher), her dark hair was back-combed, her eyes ringed with white and black like a possum, but fashion couldn't disguise her good nature, or the friendliness of her gaze. She was obedient to Cy as if he were her father.

She treated Toni like a sister straight away. *We are in this together*, her laugh, her batting, clotted lashes and glowing black eyes seemed to say. They made strong black coffee in a fluted aluminium coffeepot on a hot plate – the *cafetière*, Felice called it, no Nescafé for this family – and ate pastries from the Lebanese cafe. Later in the morning the older, quieter sister Sabine came in. Sabine had domestic responsibilities, she was married to a Mauritian man in the building trade, very *traditionnel*, Felice said, laughing.

Upstairs Toni spread out her books on the coffee table, started to make notes for an essay, crept into the warm bed beneath the skylight, slept and slept. Her double life was exhausting.

She was always home for dinner, but Beryl was suspicious.

'Do you still see that chap . . .?'

'Sometimes we have coffee.' One of Beryl's friends' kids at uni might have seen her getting into the Citröen.

'What nationality is he?' Her face was screwed up, as if there was bad smell around the subject.

'His father was Australian. His mother is Mauritian French.'

'Daddy picked up some information about him in the city. Apparently he's a pretty shady customer. Some sort of *racketeer*.'

Toni started to clear the table.

'Lucky for you I've got my hands full right now.' Preparations for Karen's wedding filled every hour of Beryl's life. Her voice was high-pitched with tension. Nig was a charming man, everybody liked him, but his job had never amounted to much. As he said, and Beryl quoted to her friends, you can't predict the country sector. It was a struggle keeping up appearances. 'We will deal with this after the wedding,' Beryl told Toni.

'Come and live with me,' Cy said.

'I can't just leave.' For Beryl it would be as if the earth had opened up and swallowed her daughter in tongues of fire.

On the other hand she hated the idea of Cy thinking she was a coward.

'That's all you can do. Leave and don't look back.'

He knew this was the only course of action. He had no illusions about the wiles of the middle classes. Every group strives to keep its own level. The question really was, how long till she ran back?

'What about my degree?'

'You can still go to lectures.'

'My parents would send the police after me.'

'They can't. Not after you're eighteen.'

'They'd die if I lived in sin. They'd see it as social ruin.'

'Then we will be married.'

On the night of Karen's wedding, after the speeches and the bouquet throwing, after the bride and groom had driven off to the rattle of bumper cans, Toni slipped out of the reception in the Bowling Club and ran in soft rain, her yellow crepe bridesmaid's dress clinging to her legs, down the street to the waiting Citröen. The car was filled with the fragrance of the frangipani blossoms stuck in her damp, lacquered hair. Cy Fisher's eyes shone as he looked at her. He was enjoying himself.

They drove to her parents' house nearby where she had a suitcase packed and hidden beneath her bed. She also had a letter ready which she had written at Cy's flat. In the letter she said that she wanted to be independent. She was going to study part-time and work in a travel agency. Please don't worry about me, she wrote, I will be in touch. In an earlier draft she had written 'I'm sorry.'

'Never apologise,' Cy said, 'for something you must do.' In the next draft she wrote: 'Please don't be hurt.'

'What's the point?' said Cy. 'Of course they'll be hurt. But they'll get over it.'

She didn't turn the lights on in case the neighbours thought a thief was after the wedding presents. Moving through the dark house, clumsy with panic, she kept bumping into chairs and doors, as if they were trying to hold her back. *She's Leaving Home* . . . It's the times, she told herself, it's happening everywhere. Did she want a future like Karen's?

She couldn't change her mind, Cy was waiting for her. As she stood at the kitchen table, it was suddenly clear to her that it was he who had made all this happen, step by step as if according to a plan. She went to peer through the dining-room curtains at the long black silhouette of the car and his profile in the driving seat, not moving. *He would be hard to get away from.* Whose thought was that? Hers or Beryl's?

She went back to the kitchen, propped her letter on the table and left.

A certain light rain – at night, in summer – would always disturb her, make her feel sad, even when she'd forgotten the reason why.

Park Lane Travel was only a few blocks away from Arlene's – Toni browsed occasionally amongst Arlene's creations with Felice and Sabine – but in those years she and Jacob never caught sight of one another on Fitzgerald Street, nor at university. Jacob mostly went to evening classes after college. Toni went to lectures in the day. She didn't make friends or join in student activities. Sometimes, shopping in the city, she heard the drum beats and chants of an anti-war rally, like a dream of another life. She watched them march past and never noticed Jacob in their ranks. She felt vaguely disconcerted, left out, as if she hadn't been invited to a fashionable party. They were all around her age, and they were having the time of their lives. It must be fun to believe in something together and shout your head off about it in the street. But standing there on the footpath, a young housewife with parcels and a manicure and a whole intricate set of new relationships she had to sustain, she knew it wouldn't make anything change. Vietnam was never discussed in her world, nor politics, nor belief of any kind. That was not how the real world worked.

When Jacob was about to graduate from teachers' college a girl called Nathalie Maguire died because of him. Not out of passion – he and Nathalie had never been more than classmates all through their school years, and then for three more years at college. The Maguires lived a few streets away from Arlene's, and Nathalie often gave Jacob a lift to or from college or social events. She drove an old white Cortina that used to be her brother's. Like all the Maguire tribe, she was large-limbed, outspoken, freckled, with a mass of wiry brown hair. Their mother used to be a schoolteacher and their father was a union man on the railways. She died instantly one night when the Cortina was hit by a runaway semi-trailer soon after she'd dropped Jacob home from a party. The whole district was stunned by the news. Everybody knew Nathalie, she babysat for neighbours and coached tennis and had been a popular head girl. Kitty was in assembly at the high school when the news was announced, and a lot of the students started crying. The truck's brakes had failed just as it came to the intersection. It was all to do with split-second timing, Kitty said when she came home. Nathalie had incredible bad luck.

And then it hit Jacob. *He* had caused her to be at that intersection at that particular moment. He had kept Nathalie waiting for him at that party, even started up another conversation after he'd agreed to leave with her, until she came up to him in her straightforward way and said: 'Jacob, come or stay, but I'm leaving now.' After which he cut short his farewells and they left.

A minute – half a minute – earlier and she would have missed the truck.

He broke out in a sweat all over his body. The Tolstoy factor again, only this time it had been fatal, not to him, but because of him. He went into his room and rolled around on his bed, groaning under his breath. What was this evil fit of perversity that took him over from time to time, paralysing his will, casting him into hell? What angel of destruction had whispered in his ear?

Darkness descended on him from the moment he opened his eyes in the morning and for days he hardly left his room. He longed to die.

He forced himself to catch the train with Beech and Kitty to the funeral at Karrakatta. There were her parents, the noble lion-maned Maguires, grown old and bent overnight, and her ashen-faced siblings, their arms around the little freckled brother who couldn't stop crying. For the first time in his life Jacob heard the hollow tramp of footsteps marching behind a coffin.

He forced himself to concentrate on the Reverend Beecham's slow English voice droning the words of the service.

It was all about sin and punishment. He hadn't known that Christianity was so punitive, though Beech had warned him. (Guilt! Guilt! And More Guilt! was how Beech described it.) *For when thou art angry all our days are gone: we bring our years to an end, as it were a tale that is told.* It was grim, beautiful stuff, spot-on for his frame of mind. But what had Nathalie, that good, kind girl, done to deserve this? Why had God cut her down like a flower? And how did all this retribution stuff make the Maguires feel? *In the midst of life we are in death . . . Thou knowest, Lord, the secrets of our hearts.* Forgive me, Jacob prayed, for the first time in his life. The school choir sang 'Morning has Broken' and even Beech cried. Jacob couldn't allow himself that relief, nor could he line up to shake the family's hands.

'Your breath's horrific,' Kitty muttered, squeezing a PK into his palm. His inner putrefaction had begun to seep out through his pores.

Nobody blamed him. Nobody knew that he had kept Nathalie waiting. But it was clear he would have to do penance, he would have to pay for this. He wondered if he should confess to the Maguires. Then at least they would have a reason, a cause for why their daughter was at that intersection at that time. They would have someone to blame. The truck driver would have to stand trial but he, Jacob, was the true culprit. Surely it was the least he could do. He made a numbered list, for and against telling them. What he had done wouldn't, he supposed, put him in jail, though punishment would be a relief. He wished he had a Great Inquisitor to point the finger at him. Or a priest to confess to. At least a wise person he could talk it over with. He couldn't tell Beech, who would seize on his guilt as an existential proposition and chew it over like a dog with a bone. Besides, Beech could never be trusted to be discreet.

Beech was surprised at Jacob's grief, even faintly admiring. Had Jacob been in love with Nathalie? he wanted to know.

Jacob realised that his storm of guilt had obscured Nathalie, the girl whose living presence he had taken for granted for most of his life. He couldn't bear to think of her. His sorrow was all for himself.

Beech was too preoccupied to pursue Jacob on the matter. He was saving every cent to go overseas, partying furiously, drinking other people's booze and smoking their dope. The Last Days, he called them, in this war-mongering cultural desert. He'd booked a cheap passage on a Russian ship to Singapore. From there he was going to make his way overland to London, where he'd his sights set on a job with *Oz* magazine.

Jacob was waiting for his first posting, probably to a country school. After he'd paid off his bond to teachers' college, the plan was that he would join Beech in London, for the sophisticated life they'd always dreamt of, at the centre of the world. The nature of this life had changed over the years, from being vaguely French New Wave – writing novels in cafes, pursuing elfin girls on motor scooters through narrow streets – to something much more radical, carnivalesque, a movement so seismic it was hard to define.

But now Jacob would have settled for the simple happiness of a clear conscience. For life not in the future but as it was before. He knew he was shut out forever from the radiant world. He lacked the energy, creativity, self-belief it required. Guilt ran like poison through his veins, undermined his every thought or word. He felt sick most of the time. His face in the mirror, heavy-jawed, dull-eyed, the hopeless droop of his mouth, repelled him. Apart from his holiday job with Vito Capelli, selling olives and cheese to old ladies dressed in black, he avoided all social activity. He lay stiffly on his bed with the curtains drawn, and thought of Nathalie in her coffin. Music or reading failed to distract him. Everything led back to the same point. Obliteration. Futility. The tramp of hollow footsteps echoed in his ears.

Even Arlene remarked that he looked peaky, suggested a haircut and a run on the beach.

One hot Saturday night some instinct propelled him up from his bed. He felt he might stop breathing if he stayed another minute in his room. He went into the kitchen where Kitty was reading at the table, eating baked beans on toast. It was as if he were watching everything from a great distance. Kitty has no social life, he thought. She eats because she is depressed.

'You look terrible,' Kitty said. 'You've lost a lot of weight.'

He filled a glass of water at the sink and stood drinking. Just the two of them again, as always. They never spoke unless she was telling him off. She was his harshest critic. It occurred to him he should use this. She wouldn't let him off the hook.

He sat down at the table and laid his case before her. He asked her whether she thought he should tell the Maguires.

Kitty listened, munching on her toast. Jacob waited as she considered her verdict, brushing the crumbs from her mouth.

'What if,' she said at last, 'it was, sort of, her fate? Maybe the good do die young, like everybody said at the funeral. Maybe it was her fate to be going home with you. Like you were part of the plan.'

'Whose plan?' He'd had no idea that Kitty had a metaphysical bent.

'Well, you do keep everyone waiting, Jake. Everyone knows you're always late.'

'So I'm an instrument of fate. Or God? God *used* me.'

'On the other hand,' Kitty went on, 'maybe she was at the

97

intersection then because she stopped to buy a newspaper or Tampax or something after she dropped you off.'

Guilt rushed forward to snuff out this little spark of hope. 'She would have stopped at the shop twenty minutes earlier too if I'd left with her straight away.'

'Or she might not. She might have gone home and had to go out to the shop twenty minutes later. You can't know, Jake.'

'You shouldn't think about it anymore,' she said after a while. 'It's killing you and it won't bring her back.' She reached for another slice of bread to put in the toaster. 'If you told the Maguires they'd have to go through it all over again.'

'Don't eat so much,' Jacob said, not unkindly. Something was easing around his chest, he could breathe again. Surprise had jolted him out of himself, surprise at his sister's unexpected good sense.

Kitty rolled her eyes at him in her old way, but she pushed the slice of bread back in the packet.

Jacob went out the kitchen door and stood on the fire-escape landing. A night breeze had sprung up and blew cool in his face. He saw the gleaming lights of the district dancing amongst the trees.

He reached inside and took one of Arlene's cigarettes. As he breathed out, he saw Nathalie's face again. How she looked when she arrived somewhere and stood by the door, her frizzy hair streaming around her. Shy but taking everything in. Her eyes shining. Sometimes he'd note to himself that she was getting prettier. He'd begun to perceive something delicate about her freckled face, something fine-tuned about her presence. He liked her attentiveness, her open laugh at his ironies. He felt at home when he was with her, free to be large and reckless. But he'd never thought about this at the time. He was afraid of falling in love with her, he saw that now. One day he might have, after he'd finished chasing lots of exotic girls. Nathalie wasn't the sort of girl you could lightly let down. She read Jane Austen. She liked Bergman. She was the only girl he knew who'd read *Catch 22*. She liked *him*, Jacob. But he'd been years away from being worthy of her.

Did being in love mean seeing someone as she really was for the first time?

She was the best person he'd ever known, he saw that now. Tears spurted from his eyes.

He tried to be nicer to Kitty, to take an interest in her. When Beech came round on the weekends he sat him down in the kitchen for a while so Kitty could join in. But shyness seemed to have taken a grip on Kitty's throat. Her voice dried up. If Beech looked at her she blushed. He and Beech always ended up wandering off into his room. Once he took Kitty with them to a party. That was a disaster. He became involved in a conversation and when he looked around, Beech and Kitty had disappeared. He had to go home without her. Beech treated Kitty just the same afterwards, like a kid sister, which probably made her feel worse about herself. Where did his loyalties lie? If it fucks you up, it's good for you, Beech liked to say. Still, Jacob felt uneasy. I'm not Kitty's father, he told himself. It was none of his business.

After a while the lurch in his guts whenever he thought of Nathalie became less violent, became a tug, then an ache, then a bruise less and less sensitive to the touch. Every night after work, he went out to parties and friends' houses and as many of the festival films at the university as he could afford. But unlike Beech, he didn't fall in love every night. He still felt he was coming in from somewhere very cold and pure. It had a terrible pull, this purity, he had to work hard to distract himself.

He knew he couldn't face a year in a country town, couldn't risk too many nights alone in a rented room. He applied for leave from the Education Department, asked Vito for more work and prepared to leave the country with Beech. He wanted to forget, not about Nathalie, but about the dark sleepout, the ceaseless sewing machine, the endless passage of women through the lounge room. He wanted never to come back.

All this happened a long time ago. Long before Jacob and Toni met. Long before they became parents.

4

White Garden

It never happened when Magnus was looking. A beam of light from the setting sun came over the paddocks, through the pine trees and the window of his room, straight onto the strained shining face of Miles Davis on his trumpet in the poster on the opposite wall. Suddenly Miles was alight, every evening, and Magnus knew it was time to go. He let the last beat die away and turned off the tape. Three minutes to six on his bedside clock. He had a reputation for lateness in the family, but he could time a tape perfectly. The Garcias ate dinner on the dot of six, as his parents had reminded him several times before they left. He whistled Winnie, but she'd beat him to it and stood grinning at the door.

The de Jongs and the Garcias lived back to back on two parallel roads in the north-west corner of the town. The

Garcias on Burma Street faced west, to open paddocks stretching to the horizon. The de Jongs on India Street looked east, over a fenced reserve of scrubby bush and old bitumen which had once been the Warton drive-in. India Street ran on past the oval and the showgrounds to join the main road on its way out of town, but Burma Street ended soon after it started, curving around to join India Street. Within that curve the two backyards blended into one another, like the communal courtyard of an old farmhouse.

Right in the middle were two ancient pines, each huge trunk a massive delta of lesser trunks, their brushy arms intertwined to make a vast roof like a covered walkway between the two houses. Scattered around the block, axle-deep in the long grass, were all the spare vehicles that the Garcias had managed to accumulate, a horsefloat, a tractor, a Moke, a campervan, and the old corrugated-iron shed which Carlos still used sometimes as a workshop. Just beyond the shade of the pines was the spindly bush-pole fence of Chris Garcia's horse paddock, and her two remaining horses. She'd given up agisting a year ago, after Warton went online.

Magnus made his way along the well-worn track under the pine trees. It had its own climate under there, cool when it was hot, dry when it rained and a sound that enclosed you, wind through branches, like the sea. When they went there as kids, he and Maya and the Garcia boys, they were cut off from everything else. They made up games there that went on and on for days and took them over, like a dream. Games that they didn't talk about with other kids, wars with complex rules, pine cone munitions, lookouts, forbidden zones. Quests like *Star Wars* and *Lord of the Rings*, with clues, blindfolds, trials – leaping from one tree to another – unto death.

'What do you get up to out there?' the parents asked them.

'Nothing,' they said.

Nobody ever told them there were spirits there, yet they were always trying to call them up, daring each other to walk the path alone at night, even sleeping in a tent under the trees once, huddled together. Nothing ever happened. Perhaps the horses, with all their little moods and trots and whinnies, were the spirits. Always eating, casually looking round while chewing, aware of everything that was going on. Perhaps the magic was just in being kids, walking through the flickers of light and the giant shadows of the pine trees which they thought of as beings. To Magnus they were two friends, males, guardians, like Carlos and Jacob, who in those days used to talk and smoke for hours in the doorway of the old shed.

Nobody hung out there anymore. First Josh, then Maya started high school and the games stopped. None of the four ever talked of them again. Going to the Garcias' now was a bit like walking though ruins, crunching over the brown pine needles, past old landmarks that had lost their life, were just abandoned tyres and rolls of wire again. Only if you stopped to listen to the sound of the surf in the trees did you remember. If he shut his eyes it could still make him shiver.

He swung through the fence to the horse-paddock and the horses came trotting towards him. Granite, the old fat gray pony, the nanny ride for all of them, snorted her warm breath all over him, nudging at his pockets, while Choko stood back, cocking his soft wild eyes at him. He'd forgotten to bring them an apple or carrot. There was something edgy about them. They looked unbrushed, their thin legs restless, like kids on the loose. He couldn't see any hay lying about. Maya would have stayed with them awhile, talking and stroking and finding them some grass. Horses always made him think of Maya.

The Garcias' house looked shut down. There was no smoke

coming from the chimney and no light in the kitchen. But all the family vehicles were there, lined up down the driveway, and as he walked under Chris's hanging baskets on the patio he saw the blue glow of the television in the family room. As was the old custom between the children of the two houses, Magnus opened the back door and walked in. Winnie set up watch on the back step, she knew that was the deal.

Carlos was sitting at the kitchen table. Josh and Jordan were slumped on the couch, watching *The Simpsons* on TV. The room smelt of old wood smoke and cigarettes.

Carlos looked up. 'Magnus. Is it dinner time?' The boys didn't stir.

'Chris still on line?' Magnus sat down opposite Carlos. It was a family joke. Chris was on the computer 98.2 per cent of the time.

'Well the fact is, Magnus, Chris has left us. Gone to Florida, US of A.'

'Gone?'

'Gone to live with someone else.' Carlos was drinking whisky with a cigarette burning in an ashtray on the table. Chris never let him smoke inside. Carlos, whose features were familiar to Magnus from the earliest days of his life, had shadows like stains under bloodshot eyes and black stubble all over his face. 'She met a guy on the chat lines.' He stubbed out the cigarette and lit another. 'Funny thing is, I read about this in the paper a couple of weeks ago. A lot of people are flying off to America these days.'

One of the things Magnus loved about Carlos was the way he talked the same to everyone, young or old, friend or stranger. He never pulled rank or lied or tried to hide anything. 'She sprang it on me last night. I had no idea, if you can believe that. All I knew was that she was on that thing day and night.'

'Is she gonna come back?'

'You know Chris when she makes up her mind.'

Nobody had lit the potbelly. It was cold and there was no sign of food. The boys each held a can of beer. It hurts them too much to move, Magnus thought. They looked licked, ashamed. They needed to be private. He stood up.

'I better be going.'

Carlos roused himself. 'If you hang on a bit, matey, Josh'll go to the Lucky and get us some take-away.'

'It's OK, Carlos,' Magnus said firmly, sensing his freedom. 'I know how to cook.' He hovered at the door for a moment. He wanted to say 'Will you be all right?' but coming from him it might sound patronising. 'Don't worry about me any more, Carlos,' he said. 'I'll stay at home from now on.'

Carlos nodded with his eyes closed, and raised one finger in farewell.

Night had fallen, with a small white moon rising over the roof in India Street, but everything was different. Old Chris! Who'd have thought she'd do something so *contemporary*? He sometimes went over there early so he could chase up stuff on the net while Chris got dinner. He saw her last night. Why hadn't he noticed anything?

A thought crossed his mind: had she taken the laptop with her? No, he wasn't going to ask Carlos. Let that one go through to the keeper, as his father often said. He could still, just, live without it. When his parents came home they were bringing him a laptop.

On impulse he turned left at the end of the Garcias' patio and made his way past their shed and laundry and fruit trees, to see if the White Garden was still there. Until now he'd forgotten all about it. Everyone had. All one winter Chris had hauled white quartz in a wheelbarrow from a pile on the driveway, back and forward, day after day. He remembered her shorts and workboots, her square shoulders and bobbing blonde mullet, how serious she looked, her sweaty face and tight mouth.

She said she was making a White Garden, and Magnus had a vision of crystalline plants and snow drifts and ice ponds. When the garden was finished the two families were invited to drink champagne there at twilight. There was a sunken courtyard, with tiered banks, where you could sit, though not for very long. Everything was covered with sharp white stones. The white glow blinded you even after the sun had gone down. Jacob and Toni said it was amazing, they were genuinely surprised. Chris said she got the idea out of a magazine. Jacob and Carlos didn't make their usual jokes, because everybody knew that Chris had no sense of humour. She was so straight that Magnus often felt kind of protective of her. Chris hardly ever smiled. She was intense.

The party clinked glasses, and became quite merry, in their sunglasses, crunching around on the stones. Carlos made a barbecue and they all returned to the patio and as far as Magnus knew, never set foot in the White Garden again.

Now he followed the overgrown, quartz-edged path through the bare fruit trees and stood looking down at it. The pit was dull and streaked with murky little puddles everywhere. The quartz had grown mossy, weeds sprang out of the cracks. Some of the banks had caved in, it was half-filled with leaves. It looked like a ruined bathroom.

He dumped a bale of hay from the shed into the paddock for the horses and they came running towards it. He could hear them slathering and snorting in the darkness as he walked home under the pine trees. Alone at last, and yet he felt sad. He was walking away from his childhood. The only person who would understand this was Maya and he realised that this tug of loneliness was what was meant by 'missing' somebody.

Just as he let himself into the house the phone rang. A crackling and then a tiny voice broke though. 'Hello?'

'Maya! No kidding, I've just been thinking about you.'

'I can't talk long. Are the folks in Melbourne yet?'

'Yeah. They're staying at your place. Where are you?' He could hear her breathing as if she were walking, and traffic noise. She was on a mobile.

'On the front steps of a hotel.'

'A swanky one?

'No way. Are they pissed off?'

'The folks? With you? No.'

'Worried?'

'Yeah.'

A pause.

'Myz, why don't you call them?'

'Listen, I've got to go. Give Winnie a kiss for me.'

'A weird thing's happened to the Garcias . . .' he began, but the line was dead.

5

Country of the Young

One morning Jacob, at the top of the stairs, spotted Cecile at the front door just as she was about to leave. It was like catching sight of a rare wild animal.

'Hey! Cecile!' He sounded louder and more urgent than he'd intended. He would have tried to reach her if the foot that he'd twisted a few days ago wasn't naked, swollen and purple. His feet were exposed in rubber thongs. Boots were out of the question. It was painful even to pull his jeans on and going downstairs was hell.

'Hi,' Cecile called, her voice soft and clear. She was wearing a puffy black bomber jacket and her hair was pulled into a topknot, speared, as far as he could see, with a knitting needle. 'Any news?'

'No.' He stayed up there, not wanting the sight of his foot to repel her forever.

'I have to run . . . Jacob . . . I'm working to a deadline. I finish on Friday. See you then.'

She had nearly forgotten his name.

Another day in Melbourne. Another day in this house. He made his tortuous way downstairs, and took up his position on the couch, his swollen foot propped up on the coffee table. Rain was splashing down the window into the fishpond. Just as he reached for the remote control, Toni loomed and dumped the cordless phone into his lap.

'Telephone duty. I'll be going out soon.' It was like this every day, she couldn't wait to leave the house.

'It's raining.'

'It'll stop.'

'I'll check the weather report,' he said, seizing the chance to turn on the television.

Each morning they woke up a little more separate from each other.

He tried an old wheedling tone. 'Aren't you just a little bit sorry for me?'

'We could have done without this, Jacob.' She'd got the hang of the kitchen and was putting away last night's dishes with brisk expertise. Since his injury, perhaps because he was always having to look up at her, he saw her differently, as a sort of sister figure, eternally displeased with him.

'Why are you in a bad mood?' he said, across the room.

'I'm not.'

'Yes you are. As if everything's my fault.'

The phone rang. He grabbed it and fumbled with the button. It was for Cecile, a male with a German accent. 'She is at verk? Thank you.' The caller hung up at once without saying goodbye.

Jacob's eyes met Toni's. 'Just some rude guy for Cecile.' Her lover, he supposed. He reached back for the remote control. How much longer would they have to camp out like this in someone else's life?

They ate their breakfast on the couch, watching the news. The Olympics, the latest fiasco, a spat between officials. Some tribal war calls and chest-beating and cries of kicking ass and getting gold. He could almost feel nostalgia for the old dour ways of the Australia he grew up in, where the worst crime was to skite, to have tickets on yourself.

He was becoming old and dour himself.

The weather report was for rain continuing to fall all over Victoria, in places he'd never even heard of. He was suddenly homesick for the familiar incantation of names, the Pilbara, the Kimberly, the Eastern Goldfields, the Great Southern, the coastal waters from Bremer Bay to Israelite Bay. He was homesick for the great empty plains!

They lounged, moody and listless, flicking through *The Age*, waiting, always, for the phone to ring. For years they'd said how they couldn't wait to stop being slaves to their children's freedom and start experiencing their own, but now that they were here, with no one to look after, not even a dog, they were unable to enjoy themselves. Nurture had become a habit, not only as parents, but in their work and their life in Warton. Nurture had come to define them, it was how they related to the world. Without it they were at a loss, like soldiers out of uniform. They had nothing to talk about together.

The rain stopped and Toni went out. She'd bought a mobile

phone, so he could call her if there was word from Maya. Magnus would be pleased with this purchase.

Jacob dozed and woke up thinking about Kershaw, the retired headmaster of Warton District High. Strange how often these days he found himself thinking of Kershaw. Was he missing the old guy? Or was it because of being stranded and laid up? This was what it meant to be an old man, without wife or kids or car, without strength or any power at all.

In his early days in Warton, when he was the new cool guy on staff, he couldn't stand Kershaw, who was old school, a stickler for the rules. He never had lunch in the staffroom but walked home at midday to eat with his wife. Even on the hottest day he wore a tie to work. Formal, remote, he doggedly stayed on for five more years until he retired.

Gossip filtered down from Perth. In his past there was a thesis, a scholarship to an English university, the promise of a brilliant career. These things became known by a sort of osmosis in a country town. In England he'd met his wife, Miriam, who was a recluse, sometimes seen floating around the streets of Warton in her straw hat, her long faded plait, her distinctive, high round belly. It was generally understood that the reason he'd ended up in Warton was to provide a safe haven for mad Miriam, that she was his burden, his downfall. On the whole, the town was sympathetic to Kershaw. Unlike Jacob, they had no objection to old school.

When Maya was born, out of the blue, Miriam came to see the baby. For some reason she insisted that she and Maya had a special affinity. For a few years after that she would regularly visit Toni, but only in school hours when Jacob wasn't home. He didn't know why, but he was always infuriated to hear that she had been in the house. One day Toni spotted her coming

111

up India Street, and without thinking, in a panic, grabbed both kids and ran through the back paddocks down to the creek. She didn't know whether Miriam had seen them, but she never visited again.

After Mirim's death this year, Jacob went to visit Kershaw early one evening with a bottle of wine and sat with him on the verandah of the cottage that he and Miriam had bought for his retirement. It was on the far, flat side of town in the shadow of the great silver silos, looking out over low-lying scrappy land where horses sometimes grazed amongst shire bulldozers and piles of blue metal. When Jacob asked him if he was going to leave Warton now, Kershaw replied that he couldn't conceive of living anywhere that Miriam hadn't lived. 'I like to visit her,' he said with a smile and nod in the direction of the cemetery. Jacob understood then what nobody had ever taken into account, that Kershaw loved his difficult wife.

It was restful sitting on the verandah. Miriam had painted the house's name on the sign swinging over the gate. 'Isolation'. There was a book of Hardy's poems besides Kershaw's chair. They were not so different after all, he and Kershaw. They lived as exiles here. But Kershaw had refused to disguise himself. They listened to the bells ringing at the level crossing as the wheat train clanked past. Jacob could feel the lure of a quiescence that was all too familiar.

At midday he perched on a stool at the breakfast bar and ate some cheese and crackers that Toni had bought. He flicked through the pile of mail that Cecile must have left by the telephone and found an envelope addressed to himself, in Carlos's scrawl. On the back, Carlos had left his greeting, a round disconsolate face, with down-sloping eyebrows and a jawline dotted by villainous bristles. Inside was a postcard sent to Warton from Kitty in London. In the thick black script that always looked self-conscious to Jacob, she announced that she was coming back to live in Perth. She'd stay with Arlene and Joe for as short a time as possible – this was underlined. *'Looking forward to meeting my niece and nephew.'* Poor old Kitty. It mustn't have worked out with her fella. He noted a restless movement in his shoulder blades, the old feeling of being pursued, of Kitty dogging his steps. He didn't want to have to worry about her. Judging by the postcard's date, she'd have touched down by now.

He turned the postcard over. *Self-Portrait, Aged 51*, by Rembrandt, from the National Gallery of Scotland. Kitty was an energetic cultural tourist and liked to refer to their Dutch heritage. There was always something pointed in the images she sent. Jacob could not see that he bore any resemblance to Rembrandt, although he was nearly the same age. Rembrandt looked as if something terrible had been revealed to him which he would have to live with for the rest of his life. Jacob propped the card up behind the telephone.

The bamboo in the courtyard fluttered bright green in afternoon sun. What now?

It occurred to Jacob that he had strayed into that other country, the country of the young, the country where you still had time. Time, if nobody stopped you, to watch late-night movies and channel-surf the breakfast shows. To lie on the couch, hour after hour, thinking about yourself. To play music non-stop, everywhere, like a soundtrack to your life. Hedonism was taken for granted. It was like entering another zone. Even this vague, persistent unease was part of it, he supposed. What you forgot about being young was how unhappy you often were.

That was why young people were always on the phone. You

felt better when you were with friends. You didn't feel so perilous.

If he were in Warton now, he'd have a beer with Carlos and tell jokes about his helpless state. He'd get in the car and go and see Jerry Delano at the police station and talk over Maya's situation with him. He'd call Forbes Carpenter who always knew somebody who knew somebody. He'd have another drink with Carlos and a cigarette. All of them would try to help him.

Maya, in her last months in Warton, was always alone. She'd only ever had one friend at a time and then there was no one. Perhaps he'd missed something more serious going on? He was so used to accommodating moody adolescents and their dramas at school.

An old anxiety came back to him, that he didn't really know how to be a father, not having grown up with one.

What would Maya have done here on an afternoon like this? There was a row of unmarked videos on Cecile's desk, not, he supposed, for general use. No books to be seen. He hadn't brought anything to read from home, in anticipation of the famous bookshops of Melbourne. Maya's unread volume of Chekhov was beside the bed but he couldn't face the stairs. If he could walk, he would have gone out to the movies and lost himself in a thriller, or something warm and easy that made him believe that everything always worked out. It was one of life's exquisite pleasures, seeing a movie in a foreign town. Emerging into strangeness. Once, long ago, while he was watching *Tora! Tora! Tora!* in Calcutta, it rained so heavily that afterwards he had to wade through streets flooded up to his knees.

Sometimes on Friday nights he drove to Perth, stayed the night with Arlene and Joe, saw a movie in the morning and another in the afternoon and sped back, music blaring, through the long, menacing shadows of the drab bush along Albany Highway.

Music. He limped his way across the room to the discs on Cecile's desk. This was where he and any happy dream of contemporary living parted company. There were no familiar signposts, nothing to tell him what he felt like listening to.

'Sit down and listen,' Magnus said to him one day, when Jacob came into his room. And he had listened, really listened as Magnus played him tapes and records of Deep House, and hip hop instrumentals, and ambient jazz and the expansive dream landscapes of Detroit techno. Already Magnus was DJing at parties around the district. He'd created tapes with his own mixes, labelled *Party tunes*, *Mellow*, *Downbeat*, *Blue*. He talked of *loops* and *samples*, how producers picked out bits from other records, the funky stuff that makes you want to dance, putting it with other bits, building energies, layers, moods. There was no social message. 'It started with people playing around,' he said. 'Being experimental. Making music with machines.'

He referred to musicians called Mos Def and Recloose and Moodymann, just as Jacob had once explained Bach to him, or Pink Floyd or Dylan. Did the happiness he felt come from the slowly dawning revelation of the beauty of what he heard, or from the fact of sitting there on Magnus's bed, invited, not left out?

Sometimes Magnus came with him on his jaunts to Perth and while Jacob went to the movies, Magnus disappeared into little music shops in the back streets. His favourite was above a shop that advertised fetish and erotic underwear. 'Everything upstairs is kind of underground,' Magnus said. The owner knew Magnus and put aside records for him. He had a programme on RTR which Magnus taped.

Something new was happening. He felt as if he'd woken up from a pastoral dream and the world had changed. It was in the grip of ceaseless, relentless electronic innovation and it was just beginning. It seemed to Jacob that they were on the verge of a social revolution as great as that of his own generation in the sixties. It was no longer possible to ignore it even in Warton. When they returned and gave Magnus his computer, their life would change. Non-stop communication and information. It was like Arlene finally giving in and buying a television. After that she never turned it off.

He flicked through the mesh rack of Cecile's CDs again. The covers were elegant, delicately hip. The names were enchanting. *Sigur Ros, The Sundays, Cocteau Twins.* Some lettering was too pale and tiny for him to read without his glasses. He pressed the play button and the room filled with a rendition of 'Night and Day', just recognisable in the sad plucked chords of a solo cello. Two intermittent piano notes that broke his heart.

He'd persuaded Maya once to come to Perth with him, after the debacle with that poor young Brethren kid. He remembered listening to Lucky Oceans on *The Planet*, while Maya looked out the window into the darkness and listened to her Walkman. He wanted to tell her how often he'd fucked up when he was her age, but she wouldn't give him a chance. She never said a word to him the whole weekend.

Where was Toni? Where the hell did she go?

6

Boans

For some time she sat in the grounds of the tower blocks across the road, on a boulder amongst the trees, overlooking the little goalposts and the muddy playing field. The glowing pearl-gray air made her feel lighter and more alert. Right now the last thing she felt like was the burden of a big wounded man.

The jewellery box had upset her this morning. She was trying to shove their bags to the back of Maya's cupboard when she found it, wedged into a corner. A large, brown, clumsily carved wooden box, mass-produced for tourists. She sat on the bed and studied it, squatting on the floor like a toad. Her heart was thudding. She felt an irrational, violent antipathy to it, as if it cast a spell. Maya would never buy a thing like that. For a start, she had no jewellery. And it was ugly, dated – the sort of thing Arlene and Joe used to buy on one of their trips to Singapore. Someone who hadn't given any thought to what Maya would like had given it to her, and she had accepted it.

In the tower blocks, now that the rain had stopped, carpets were hanging out to air over the balconies and curtains were billowing in open windows. Toni caught a whiff of curry steam. No little black-haired kids and their mothers had come out yet to the playground. Yesterday she stood and watched them. When she saw parents and young children together she saw a love affair.

She walked over to the empty swings and frames in their wet bark beds. The rubber seats swung idly in a secret current of air. She dumped the jewellery box, wrapped up in a plastic bag, into the playground bin, which she hoped was emptied daily.

She wouldn't tell Jacob about this. He would say she had no right to dispose of something of Maya's. Besides, any hint of what he called 'the dark arts' always made him furious.

It was a challenge finding ordinary household goods in the Vietnamese supermarket. Where was the Vegemite amongst the chutneys, pickles, lurid syrups? The butter, in those little glass-fronted fridges with the plastic boxes of aquarium-coloured jellies? The phosphate-free laundry powder amongst the stacks of giant boxes of Omo, with instructions in Chinese? Her hand hovered over the bright green spring onions and bok choy, the mangoes and rambutans, all at no-nonsense prices. Forget about petro-chemicals, additives, sprays. No one had time for greenie scruples in this hubbub of transaction, amongst these purposeful, fast-moving people.

She was picking out mandarins from a mound on the table when from the corner of her eye she glimpsed a girl in a denim jacket with pale skin and wide cheekbones and a dark bowl-like haircut, paying at the checkout. Of course it wasn't Maya, she was nothing like her really, in her twenties, part-Asian, but after that Toni wasn't equal to the noise and clutter of these aisles any more. Coffee, she needed coffee to rev her up to the pace here. Where could she go?

She reeled down the footpath past the windows with the varnished brown corpses of ducks and chickens, the street-front GPs' clinics, the herbalists and acupuncturists, tax consultants, fishmongers and video stores. There were several Chinese and Vietnamese restaurants but she fled into the known insipidity of a franchised French Bakery. Even here fried rice and spring rolls were offered along with the croissants and baguettes, and the waitresses in their bright pink T-shirts and caps were Asian.

At a table in the back corner, facing the room, next to the exit − a habit learnt from Cy Fisher − she spooned up her cappuccino foam and listened to the old-fashioned trundle of a tram going past.

I keep thinking I see you: that's what her mother used to say when they had one of their lunches in Boans.

Beryl found her by working her way though every travel agency in the Yellow Pages until she rang Park Lane Travel and spoke to Felice. After that they met for lunch two or three times a year in Boans' cafeteria. Beryl also always sat in the furthest corner, but for a different reason, so that none of her friends would see them if, by a stroke of calamitous bad luck, one of them happened to walk past. Not that Beryl's crowd were likely to lunch there. The cafeteria was on the top floor of Boans department store, under huge meshed windows, a vast hall filled with a dusky cathedral light and the rising hum of dozens of lunching women's voices. Middle-aged waitresses in peppermint-green uniforms and nurse's caps doled out peas and mashed potato with ice cream scoops as you stood at the servery and pointed at what you wanted. Homely meat and gravy smells and the clatter of dishes issued from the kitchen. Even in the seventies it was old-fashioned.

The first time they met, Beryl talked non-stop about the same old things as if Toni had just come back from a trip and was still part of her world. Her headaches, Karen and Bevan's new house, Nig's winning team at bowls. Then she stopped, her eyes wandered and her lips trembled.

'You know, I was . . . sick . . . for a while,' she said. Toni did not respond. Of course she knew, she'd known as she crossed the Horseshoe Bridge in her bridesmaid's outfit how it would be for her mother. As if bells rang out all over the suburb, the sky darkened, war was declared. She would become hysterical and take to her bed. The doctor would be called. When she'd recovered sufficient strength to talk to her friends on the phone, she'd put it about that Toni, always independent, was off *flatting* – that was the word she'd use – with a girlfriend. But one sceptical glance, one pointed lack of enquiry, would let Beryl know the word was out. The Parker lass had run off with a common criminal, and no decent people would have anything more to do with her. A girl whose looks had gone to her head.

Toni's leather coat hung on the back of her chair, her long straight hair gleamed, her breasts had grown. She knew she was dazzling. The ease and pleasures of her life surrounded her like an aura that protected her. For the occasion, it was true, she had taken off her little diamond ring, but that was to avoid personal questions.

As they were about to leave, Beryl, hunting in her handbag for her powder compact, said in a low, deliberate voice: 'I think you should know that Daddy missed out on his promotion.' Her eyes caught Toni's. It took Toni a moment to realise. Because of you, her mother was saying, because of the scandal. 'So he still has to hawk his wares all over the country.'

Toni stood up and walked out. She'd learnt from watching Cy that you had to act quickly. You had to take the power. If people wanted to do business with you, they had to show respect.

She knew her mother would hold her tears back until she reached home. On the phone beside her bed she would tell Nig and Karen that Toni had changed, had been influenced by *him*, had become glamorous and hard. Her own daughter was a stranger.

All her life she'd known what Beryl was thinking until she couldn't stand it any more. The thoughts didn't touch her now. You never compromise, Cy said, you never look back. That way there was never any fuss.

And he was right. Beryl rang Park Lane Travel a few months later to invite Toni to lunch and never tried to blackmail her again.

She belonged to another family now. In the beginning she didn't know how to cook or even make a shopping list but it didn't matter, they ate at restaurants or in the big kitchen of Cy's mother, Régine. They sat around Régine's table with his sisters and his brother-in-law and ate vegetables from her garden, sausages she'd cured herself, chicken she'd raised on corn and killed and plucked. His mother's food made Cy supremely happy. 'Maman, you surpass yourself,' he said, each time. Régine was the only person Toni ever heard Cy praise. She welcomed Toni as if she were a waif, poorly fed, motherless, shockingly untrained in the house. After the meal, in a rush of clatter and high voices, she and her daughters would dispense with the dishes while Toni was still looking for a teatowel. But anyone Cy brought home would always be an honoured guest for Régine.

Régine stomped up the stairs to the flat to instruct Toni on how to clean it, how to make the bed in the way Cy liked. She took their washing home because Cy didn't like laundry hanging around the place. She excused this act of possessiveness, this blatant invasion of privacy, by saying she knew Toni was busy, all the young women were busy these days. Besides, wasn't she Toni's own mother now? Régine had Cy's black deep eyes, but hers were distracted, always looking for the next thing to do. She was short and dumpy with bad feet, in a wraparound coverall and fraying canvas shoes, her gray hair pulled roughly back from her white, damp face with the long, flattish nose that she had, in various versions, bequeathed to all her children. Beryl would have said that Régine had let herself go, but for her children she was an angel, who devoted every moment of her day in service to them. Even when she went to Mass, it was to pray for their *bonheur*, she said, for their luck in love and with the *monnai*.

Downstairs in Park Lane Travel, which was never very busy, her daughters made her sit down and drink coffee, and in her honour Cy would come out from his office behind the shop with whoever was with him, Johnny, Serge, Pino, and they would all drink coffee standing around Régine, laughing and teasing each other, because it made Régine so very happy.

★

Far from being the sordid, dangerous life Beryl envisioned, this new world was warm, familial, orderly and clean. Toni had never felt so lighthearted. In the mornings she worked in the travel agency – there was sometimes a booking to be made for friends or relatives, or a backpacker shopping for the cheapest deal or the odd passer-by struck by a sudden whim for the south of France. Mostly she and Felice read magazines and did each other's nails and listened to 6PR. Sabine was pregnant and kept irregular hours. In the back office, men came and went from the carpark behind the shop. It hadn't taken Toni long to realise that this was where the real business was transacted.

When Park Lane Travel was very quiet, the girls put a *back at twelve* sign on the door, took an advance on their pay from the till, and went shopping. Money, saving it, spending it, worrying about it, so large a part of Toni's upbringing, was never talked about. When Toni passed her driving test – Cy organised lessons with a driving school in which he had an interest – he gave her a car, a little red brand-new Renault that was taking up space in a yard. He said he didn't like her catching public transport.

Three times a week she drove to lectures and tutorials, and sat apart, sleek, chic, claimed. Her diamond flashed as she took notes and the tips of her hair brushed the page. She felt far older than the other students. It was as if she came from another country. After the lectures she drove straight home. Her books were set up on a table in the corner of the living room, but she found it harder and harder to summon the energy to open them. There was enough for her to learn in her new life. Besides, what use was a degree to her now? She dropped down to one subject a term, just to reassure herself that she still had a life of her own. Then there didn't seem any point and she didn't re-enrol, though she knew she ought to keep up French to talk to Régine, who kissed her on both cheeks when she tried. Something had gone soft and lazy in her.

Cy didn't like anything to seem like an effort. He was never in a hurry. In the afternoons he generally went upstairs for a siesta and he liked Toni to be there. Nobody would ever disturb them.

Since he didn't come home to sleep until the early hours of the morning, he was at his most sensuous in the afternoons. It was his Mediterranean blood, he said. Later she lay in a deep bath and dressed for the evening. When she looked in the mirror she could hardly believe her own splendour. On the nocturnal round of bars and clubs and restaurants, Cy introduced her as 'my fiancée'. It seemed to her that wherever she went she was surrounded by a circle of shining faces. She only had to pull out a cigarette packet for a lighter to appear. When she was tired and Cy wanted to gamble through the night, one of the boys drove her home, walking into the flat ahead of her, checking the rooms, snapping lights on and off.

Sometimes she paced through the flat and wondered if she was in danger of becoming spoilt, a major term of disapproval where she came from. She had acquired so easily what so many girls yearned for, a man, a house, beautiful things. But questions like this were immaterial in Cy's world. Anything that was not to do with business or pleasure was not worth another thought. She made a vague resolution to read more books and not to look too often in the mirror.

One morning she woke late, alone, in the sun-warmed bedroom and understood that she felt different. A heaviness had lifted, she could breathe more easily. The darkness and strain that had surrounded her from her earliest childhood, like the murmuring of a forest, the striving to keep up appearances, the worry about other people, the criticism, had simply dissolved.

And where it had been there was lightness, freedom, silence, an open plain.

When she sat across the table from her mother in Boans, she felt superior to her. 'I know how to live,' she thought.

Why didn't she take into account her parents' accusation that Cy was a criminal? She tossed it away as just another example of Beryl and Nig's snobbery. Criminal? What did that mean? Cy was a businessman, a successful one. It was a different way of life. What would her father know about it?

Everything was business, she was beginning to see that.

In a way which she found hard to put into words, she knew that Cy was more honest in his life than her parents were in theirs. His moral universe was more consistent. He was so honest that he made everybody nervous. In his presence you became aware of how weak you could be in your decisions, how often you lied a little, acted in bad faith. He saw no reason for lies because he always did what he wanted to. A liar was afraid of other people. If one of the team lied to him, he was out. A weak person was a dangerous person. A liar lacked respect.

More and more she suspected Cy of omniscience. There wasn't anything he didn't know about her, what she did, where she went. She discovered that he knew where she was at any hour of the day.

'So you met your mother today.'

'How do you know?'

'Deduction.'

One of the boys or one of his many contacts all over town must have seen her going into Boans. He kept an eye on everyone who belonged to him. She began to sense that beneath his smooth surface there lurked a vast possessiveness, a dark, fathomless cavern.

He was preternaturally alert. He saw, smelt and heard more than anyone else. He often prowled around the flat thinking he smelt gas, something burning or someone else's aftershave. Even when he was talking he saw things from the corners of his eyes. He was always on guard.

'I've never trusted anyone since I was four years old,' he told her. That's when he started to take his trolley round the streets of the better-off suburbs, selling fish that his grandfather had caught at the Fremantle wharf to patronising, penny-pinching, middle-class housewives.

When he was fourteen he was big enough to kick his father out. His father, Arnie Fisher, an animal, soon died, drunk, of a heart attack in a rooming house. Cy had supported the family ever since.

'How did you support them?'

'Business. Making myself useful. Running messages. Taking bets.'

He was a successful gambler not only because of his powers of observation but because of his intuition. All his decisions came from inside, he said. Especially when he was alone, he was sometimes aware of presences flickering just out of sight. Someone looked after him. Maybe his grandfather.

He was surrounded by loyal henchmen and an adoring family, but he was always apart.

After she came to live with him he didn't mention marriage again until one afternoon three years later when he came upstairs and told her to hurry, he'd made an appointment at the registry office. 'Come just as you are,' he said. Everything went very fast. They were shown straight into the office. Her documents — how did he get them? — were waiting next to his on the desk. Two clerks were called in as witnesses. There was a table waiting for them in Luis', by the window, with an ice bucket and champagne. It was raining, an early winter twilight. The champagne went to her head. 'Cyprien', she said, 'Cyprien Arnold', and she couldn't stop laughing.

'Why do you like me?' she dared to ask. She had just promised officially to love and obey him until death, but in private they rarely said the word 'love' to each other.

'Because you know how to mind your own business.' His white face had the faintest touch of colour. His mouth was twisted as if to hold back a smile, which was his way of smiling. Just this once he would indulge her: he hated questions like this. Wasn't marrying her enough of a statement? She knew that possessing her was an act of revenge against those middle-class households. For him she was as exotic as he was for her.

She looked at him across the candle on the table. He isn't really good-looking, she thought, but he's an interesting man. My husband. Even his black suits and white shirts hanging in the wardrobe looked powerful and mysterious.

He had chosen exactly the right moment to secure her, when she was at the peak of her contentment and fascination. Yet someone, a long-forgotten maiden aunt perhaps, a voice in her blood, was always whispering in her ear that it was a dangerous luxury to relinquish yourself like this.

When Beryl saw the gold band on Toni's finger, she couldn't hide the sudden bitter grimace that contorted her face. 'Now you'll never be rid of him,' she said, looking out across the tables of women.

By the time Toni met her mother for their last lunch in Boans, the rules of engagement had been long established. That is, Beryl talked on and on and Toni gave nothing away. Beryl had given up asking Toni questions about her life and acted as if it was better not to know. That silence was a curtain between them. This was how they'd managed to survive this hour together, year after year.

Beryl's injured air had been replaced by one of generalised anxiety. Her news this last time was that Karen was worried about her little boy, Lincoln. He wasn't talking or walking, he was far behind other children of his age. Karen had her hands full.

'I wish you'd give her a call,' Beryl ventured.

Toni shrugged. 'Karen never calls me.'

Toni had visited Karen in hospital after she had her baby. She went early in the morning, when she judged that she wouldn't be likely to meet up with any other visitors. Karen was in the shower. Toni stood at the nursery window and looked at the little fat red face, its mouth open, soundlessly screaming. 'I'm never going to have one of those,' she thought.

'He looks like Bevan,' she told Karen and for once they laughed together. Karen was lit up by such happiness that for a moment she could even forgive her selfish, wayward sister.

'I thought I saw you half a dozen times on my way here,' Beryl was saying.

Toni frowned and looked away. Some things were beginning to trouble her. The way she looked, like a free spirit, a flower child, when nothing could be further from the truth. There'd been a revolution in her generation and she had missed it. She wore the clothes because it was the fashion. Her life was as conservative in its way, as closed off as Karen's or Beryl's. She was restless with her easy routines. If she wasn't with Cy she was bored.

Perth had changed. There was a minerals boom, a building

boom, millionaires were born and died overnight. Wealth and travel were bringing the rest of the world closer. She and Cy went to parties in craggy brick lounge rooms in the hills, or on balconies overlooking the river, or in hotel suites hired by mining companies. Sometimes she even met girls from school there, married to stockbrokers or lawyers. All the women wore upmarket ethnic clothes, while the men's hair curled like medieval princes' onto their collars. They danced to the Beatles and the Rolling Stones, but made jokes about Whitlam and hippies and women's libbers that shocked her with their viciousness. She didn't have the words to define her position, but more and more she felt there was a war on and she was on the wrong side. She knew she was the spy in the camp.

There were drugs at these parties, and a lot of naked frolics in swimming pools. Cy didn't dance or joke or make small talk. He restricted himself to two tumblers of whisky and smoked his own cigarettes. He was there to do business. He still wore a black suit, which he certainly didn't take off. His hair was the same length it had always been.

But the village-like atmosphere of his business interests, his patch, his people, had changed. Buddha sticks and heroin were flooding in from south-east Asia. Drugs were big business, though Cy Fisher never touched them. It was the beginning of the big nightclubs. A prominent Perth madam was shot in her car, and the police investigation drew a blank. Cy told her he knew who did it. She felt the walls around her growing higher and higher.

How did people change themselves? It was as if she were waking up from a long sleep. In terms of education she was still a schoolgirl. She bought a copy of *The Female Eunuch* and read it all one night in bed alone. When Cy came home at dawn she was too angry to speak. Cy, sitting on the end of the bed, taking off his shoes, looked amused.

'What's your problem? You've got everything you want.'

'Nothing I have has been earned by me.'

'You've got a job.'

She stared him down to let him know she understood full well that Park Lane Travel was just a front for the back office, as well as a way of keeping the women of the family under his eye, in pocket money, and out of trouble. She, Felice and Sabine were no more than decorative receptionists. Suddenly she was overwhelmed with weariness. The task of converting him would be like rolling a small stone up a mountain.

'I have no power,' she said in a small voice.

'Don't you believe it.' Cy was in a genial mood. He must have won at cards.

'My little feminist,' he said, sliding into the sheets beside her, his warm dense flesh smelling of night-life. 'Who would have thought?'

She was beginning to see how many doors were closed to her. Travel, for a start. Cy didn't see the point in travelling, everything vital in his world existed around him, in the few streets which he'd known all his life. He hated being in a place where he didn't know the ropes, hated sleeping in any bed but his own. Without a real job, Toni could see she would never go to any of the places advertised in the posters around the walls in Park Lane Travel.

It would be hard to hold down a real job that fitted in with the hours required to be Cy Fisher's companion. No business in Perth would employ her unless it was answerable to Cy. And she was pretty sure that a job in the government wasn't an option for Mrs Cy Fisher.

She would never know what it was to make her own way in the world.

Boans' cafeteria hadn't changed, but its days were numbered.

'Why aren't you happy?' Beryl said.

'What do you mean?' Toni was startled. This was breaking the rules.

'You're a bundle of nerves. And you've lost weight.'

'I weigh exactly the same.'

For once Beryl did not back off. 'Something's bothering you. I'm still your mother, you know, I can tell.' Tears filled her eyes.

'Mum, if you cry I'll leave.'

But she no longer felt so invincible with her mother. She had lost her implacable faith in the rightness of her decision.

Her belief in her life with Cy Fisher had crumbled definitively one night at the Riviera when she happened to look out a back window on her way to the ladies'. There amongst the rubbish bins, in the dim light cast by the kitchen door, she saw Pino being kicked by two men. One of them she recognised as Johnny. He had taken his jacket off, rolled up his sleeves, as if to do a job. She could hear the thuds of their kicks, their panting and grunts. Pino lay curled, his arms over his face. She ran back to Cy at the bar and told him. Cy said nothing, looked her steadily in the eyes. She reached for the phone. 'I'm going to call the police.'

He put his large hand over hers.

'Then I'm calling an ambulance.'

He didn't remove his hand.

'Why?' A tear ran down her face.

'Because it's necessary.'

She began to detect an edge of cruelty in everything he did or said. His decisiveness came from ruthlessness, a belief in his own ends. When she heard him say '*Keep me updated*' or '*Yeah, go ahead*' on the phone to Johnny she was chilled.

Seeing Johnny with his sleeves rolled up, his foot swung back, shocked her, like seeing a father misbehaving. He was older than Cy, in his forties, with a short, wide body, and a bustling, determined walk. His loyalty was unquestioned. He was working as a security guard when Cy met him. Rumour had it that he was an ex-cop. His ruddy, closely shaven face was as impassive as a bodyguard's, though every now and then he'd give a short bark of laughter showing close-packed, shining, cream-coloured teeth. He wore pale suits and his hair was fine and puffy, hair-net brown. There was always a woman waiting for him at home, a series of women over the years, whom nobody ever met. Toni used to try to get a smile out of him once, but now she couldn't bear to look at him.

A new member of the team, Sam, drove her home one night from the Riviera. He was about her age, loose-limbed with long splayed fingers, a nervy jokester, anxious to please. He wore a drooping moustache, like a joke on his face, and a double-breasted, burgundy suede jacket. He'd had a stint managing some local bands and when he opened up the flat for her, he stayed talking about the music scene for twenty minutes.

'Did he touch you?' Cy asked when he came home.

'Of course not!' She didn't mention what Sam had told her,

in his exuberance, that she and Cy were known around the traps as Beauty and the Beast.

She never saw him again.

'What's happened to Sam?' she asked Cy.

'He's moved on.'

A few weeks later she read in *The West* that a young man had suffered serious injuries after being beaten up and thrown off the Horseshoe Bridge. His name was Warwick Hubble and he was twenty-seven. There was a photo of him. She showed it to Cy. 'That's Sam, isn't it?'

'Looks like it.'

After a while she said: 'Was it because of me?'

He shook his head in disbelief at her presumption.

She had become afraid of him. At night she lay beside him but she wasn't in her body. She didn't challenge him anymore because it wasn't worth it. She wanted to leave. Wanting to leave filled every moment of her days. When she was with him she tried to concentrate on what was around her, systematically noting cars, faces, advertisements, because she knew he could read people's minds. In bed she tried to remember the names of all the girls in her class, or the details of her old room so he wouldn't hear her thoughts.

Why couldn't she just say to him 'I want to leave' and walk out the door? Or tell him that she couldn't love a man with blood on his hands? Because then he would find a way to make her stay. He'd convince her that staying was what she really wanted, but after that he'd watch her, or have her watched, all the time. He'd break her, in some way. Nobody left Cy, they were kicked out.

Whenever she summoned all her strength to confront him, he didn't come home, or couldn't be found, as if he knew her plan.

For a large man, he had a startling ability to disappear. She could turn towards him in a bar and find that he was gone. Then just as magically he'd be back at her elbow. Once some detectives from the Vice Squad came to Park Lane and asked to speak to him. His sisters said he wasn't in. The detectives turned to Toni and asked to search the flat. She led them up, weak-kneed, knowing she'd left Cy asleep in bed. But when they entered, he wasn't there. His shoes were gone, even the bed was smooth. The only back exit was from the platform into the pepper tree. She couldn't envisage Cy, who hated all physical activity, launching himself into its brittle, swaying boughs. But there was no sign of accident, no broken branches. The flat was ordered, filled with tranquil leaf shadow, reminding her how quick, silent and clean he was in all his habits. She felt a moment's pride in his escape.

It turned out that at just the right moment he'd woken for a pee and seen the car turning into Park Lane. His sixth sense told him it was the wallopers. He was down the stairs and out the back door just before they walked in.

How could she ever escape him? He always knew where she was. If she holed up in a room in a distant suburb, got a job in a supermarket, changed her name, dyed her hair, he would find her. She had no money for a plane ticket to the eastern states. Besides Cy had contacts at the airport and in all the capital cities. He would chase her down.

She couldn't bear to go home to her parents. Anyway, he would have their house watched, their phone tapped.

Why wouldn't he let her go if she wanted to so much? If he loved her? But the young and beautiful can never quite trust what they're loved for. His benevolence surrounded her as one of his family. Once you left the family, you were the enemy. His sweet sisters would spy on her and betray her. Even now she suspected that Cy had asked Felice to keep an eye on her.

Régine, who kissed her all over her face and called her *my little daughter*, would throw her belongings down the stairs. There was a ruthlessness to Régine too, she had watched those old red hands wring a chicken's neck. The family would say she was ungrateful. They would say she had no respect. People who didn't understand respect, Cy said, had to be taught.

She became more and more remote. His touch was cold to her, as if it came from someone else. Cy must have noticed her withdrawal from him but he said nothing. He knew how to watch and wait.

She took to walking in the park opposite, day or night, up and down, around the dark old Moreton Bay fig trees, past the bleak little stadium, the stagnant lake. She couldn't seem to get enough fresh air. She missed nature, the suburban garden of her childhood, riding her bike along the river. Once in her childhood there had been a holiday in a beach house, way down on the south coast. In bed at night she tried to reconstruct it. Sea, sky, bush, the sound of the waves. She went for long drives alone in her car along the ocean or up to the hills.

She longed for the days when she had lain beside Cy, untroubled, content in his orbit, a child. She was emerging from a dream. Something had awoken her, her own voice again, the only voice she could trust.

She lived a half-life. A thought came to her from nowhere: *she couldn't bring a child up in this world.* She hadn't been aware that she wanted children.

It was well past lunchtime. The French Bakery had filled up and emptied again while she had sat in her corner as rigid and stony-faced as she used to be sitting opposite her mother in that great barn on top of Boans. Why had she been so hard on Beryl? *I keep thinking I see you.* Of course she did. A generation always resembles each other in dress and voice and expression.

The only other customer left was sitting at the adjoining table, a middle-aged woman with crew-cut gray hair wearing a maroon-coloured robe. In spite of her preoccupations, Toni was intrigued. A Buddhist nun, in the French Bakery, calmly drinking tea.

The nun looked up and smiled at her. She had a pink, scrubbed face traced with lines, and pixie ears. Her smile was warm and matey, almost a grin. Her clear blue-gray eyes were crinkled at the ends.

Toni indicated her long-empty cup. 'I guess I lost track of the time.' She felt washed out, as if she had been crying.

'Shopping does my head in,' the nun said agreeably. Nothing unworldly about her. She had an American accent. There was a pot of green tea in front of her. Unhurried, she turned around on her chair to face Toni.

Afterwards, Toni couldn't remember much about their conversation. She'd done most of the talking. She told her that her daughter had run away. Her companion sat very still, a look of pure interest on her face. Her eyes seemed alight. Perhaps it was her job to listen to sad people. Did the Buddhists have confession? She was afraid that her daughter had got herself into a situation that she couldn't handle, Toni found herself saying. That she had lost herself.

The nun said her name was Kesang, and as they parted she handed Toni a card. She'd said no word to reassure her yet Toni walked home lighter from the talk.

★

They phoned Magnus in the early evening, more for their sake than his. For the sheer pleasure of his calm, young voice.

Winnie had started fretting. She wouldn't eat.

'It's OK,' Magnus told Toni. 'She comes to school with me.'

'What on earth does she do there?'

'Lies outside the classroom. Everyone talks to her. She really likes the attention.'

'What do the staff say?'

'Nothing. Just make the usual pathetic jokes.'

Did all the teachers feel sorry for Magnus, abandoned by his parents?

'What about you? Is Chris feeding you up?'

'Chris isn't here any more. She's gone to America.'

'What! She never told us she was going away.'

'She didn't tell anyone. She's gone to meet some guy off the internet.'

'Jacob!' Toni called out. 'Chris has left Carlos!'

'Magnus,' she said back into the phone, 'are you still going there to eat at night?'

'Carlos is kinda out of it. I don't want to hassle him. I know how to cook.'

'What did you eat last night?'

'Can't remember. Instant noodles.'

'I'm going to phone Carlos.'

'Don't! Don't do that. Carlos doesn't want to talk about it.'

'Magnus, can you go and stay at Ben's place? Please. I'll call Beth Lester.'

'No! I can't!' For Magnus he sounded almost panicked.

'Why not?'

'They've got cats. I can't take Winnie there.'

He could hear his mother talking to Jacob.

'Magnus?' Her voice had a rising edge to it, the only

time he didn't like to hear it. 'We'll talk it over and call you back.'

After she hung up he remembered that he hadn't told her Maya had called. He hadn't made up his mind whether or not Maya wanted him to.

7

The Lucky

An Asian multimillionaire had a vision of a shift in the earth's axis which would cause earthquakes and volcanic eruptions. He bought a piece of land north of Warton, near Tumbring, because he believed that this region would be spared from a massive tidal wave which was going to hit the west coast. He saw the piece of land in a vision during meditation. In Tumbring they said that he'd spent ten million dollars on supplies to feed and house and give medical treatment for up to ten thousand refugees. He said the Buddhists believe that selfless acts would bring about a golden age of peace. He'd come to live here to get back to God.

This event might not happen, he said, but if it did it would be before the end of 2001.

Warton didn't have a mystic saviour, only the Brethren, who hadn't told anyone why they'd chosen to come here ten years ago and start a furniture business and build a church in a wheat-belt town. The Brethren never told their plans to non-Brethrens, 'the worldlies' they called them. Magnus knew this from Maya's secret ex-boyfriend, Jason Kay. But one thing was certain. If a great flood did come, God would make sure the Brethren were the first and only people to be saved.

Sometimes when Magnus set off like this, at dusk, through the empty streets, he thought about the sea water spreading across the flatness, filling up the streets and the saltpans along the creeks, turning the silted-up lake into an inland sea. He saw a great searchlight piercing through the clouds and tiny Brethren figures swirling up like dust mites, the sad, dowdy women holding down their skirts, the little nursery-rhyme girls in their headscarfs, the pale, aggressive males with their bad haircuts . . .

People would wait for rescue on roofs and the tops of trees, or make rafts and try to paddle to Tumbring to be saved. Inevitably his thoughts turned to the one he wished to save, or spend his last moments with, and here he is: leaping onto a door that is floating past and managing to reach Brooke Lester just before the chimney she is clinging to is swept away . . .

He was walking to the Lucky because he was hungry and the kitchen smelt of empty Pal tins. He'd eaten all the super-market food he'd bought, eggs, Weetbix and packet ham on white sliced bread. How did Toni do it, put together meals that made you feel good afterwards? He hadn't been to the butcher – if he bought two chops, say, everyone would know he was cooking for himself and then the Garcia situation would come out, and the mothers would get together and insist he stay with one of them . . .

Most nights he ended up going to the Lucky when all the families were inside.

He stood for a moment under the pine trees and studied the Garcias' house for signs of life. Carlos's truck was in the carport all the time now, he mustn't be going to work. When he saw Carlos putting hay out for the horses yesterday he went over and asked him how he was. Carlos said he had an almighty hangover. Magnus didn't want to look into his eyes. 'How're *you* doing Mag?' he called out after Magnus. Magnus called back that he was fine.

There were no lights on in their house again tonight, just the television, but smoke was coming out of the chimney. Josh's jeep was gone, he'd be out with his mates, it was Friday night. He must have taken Jordan with him. They'd be at the pub to watch Geelong versus Hawthorn. Carlos was probably pissed.

It was very quiet. The evening mist was swirling up from the creek. Surprising how much a house could tell you about a family's feelings if you stood and looked long enough. The horses had gone remote, back to their own horse lives again.

He was working on a tape for Carlos. He didn't know what else he could do.

The moon was rising as Magnus stood waiting for Winnie to finish sniffing around the gate of the old drive-in. To cheer her up he let her fool herself for a few minutes that she was still a young dog who could catch a lizard or a rabbit.

The drive-in was surrounded by a high cyclone fence, but from time to time a hole would appear and it would become a hang-out again, until the Shire came to fix it. When he and his friends were little kids they used to race their bikes around the cracked bitumen circuit. Last summer they sat amongst the broken glass on the steps of the projection booth drinking cans of beer stolen from home. Those who smoked had a few cigarettes or joints. He liked the feeling after a drink or a toke that you knew everything, but it didn't last. Long yellow grass grew up around the booth and the ticket box with its still decipherable sign, *Lights Out Please*. The screen and the speaker-poles had gone long ago. There was always talk that the drive-in was going to be bulldozed but it never happened. The one thing this town didn't need was space.

The drive-in had closed even before his parents came to live here. For years his father used to photograph it at different times of the day or the year, but then he lost interest. He said it had become a great Australian cliché.

For Magnus the drive-in wasn't a cliché, it was part of his life, already turning into memory. It was part of a composition. He had an idea for a video clip called *Six Thousand and One Nights in Warton*. That was about how long he would have spent here – his whole life – when he left. Everything would go into it one day. Samples of old film themes, cars horns, road trains, barking dogs, show day. Crows, crickets, the school bell, the radio in the Lucky, all the background static that you didn't notice anymore. Bits of music that his father used to play and his photos of the drive-in. The sound of bike tyres over gravel. Everything flowing together, flowing forward.

It was because he'd be leaving in two years and five months that he was able to see the drive-in as poetic. All his time here now was a sort of goodbye. One day, he knew, he'd be glad of his small-town background, it would be part of whatever he did, whatever it was that would make him famous. A hell of a lot of musicians in America came from small towns.

He whistled and Winnie rushed out to him, grinning, her snout sandy, her ears lopsided. It was like looking after a little kid.

★

Whenever he set off to town he felt a faint excitement stir deep inside him. It was sexual. There was a chance that he might see a girl he liked. That is, Brooke Lester. Even now when it was nearly dark, he had hope of seeing her. Sometimes she came home late from basketball practice. Once he walked with her some of the way. Afterwards he realised that he'd talked non-stop about himself, what he liked and didn't like. But all the time his every sense was alert to her. She had long straight blonde hair that blew in strings and she tucked it behind her ears. He liked the way she was so self-contained. Sometimes she rode her bike home, her long legs gleaming in the half-lit streets. She didn't look like a Lester, but like a visitor from Scandinavia. It seemed amazing that Warton had produced her.

The Lesters called her Brookie at home, like a toy or a baby girl. When he went there to visit Ben, she was sometimes friendly and sometimes acted as if he wasn't there. Then he knew that when she looked at him she saw one of her kid brother's friends and he couldn't talk at all.

Still, there was hope. Next year Brooke was going to Perth to become a physiotherapist. Magnus was convinced they'd meet up somewhere, Perth, London, Berlin, New York. He was beginning to think international.

He could hear his own footsteps on the gravel. This solitude, this freedom felt so natural to him that he wondered if, when he was a man, he would always live this way. If he wasn't so hungry he would have liked to keep walking, out of the town into darkness. Sometimes in the holidays he took off with Winnie into the flatness, walking towards the point where the telegraph poles joined. He felt a pull to the horizon. Old tracks and creeks led him into the bush. He carried water and a plastic box for Winnie to drink from and some muesli bars and apples. No money. He wanted to know what it felt like to be homeless, a wanderer. *Living on the long paddock*: he loved the sound of that. To sleep under a tree. To have faith that everything you needed would come your way.

He never went so far out of range that he couldn't catch the putter of a tractor somewhere or a truck passing by. If he wasn't home by dark his parents would freak out. He always ended up hitching a ride to town in a ute or truck with Winnie barking out the back the whole way.

Magnus came out of the Lucky carrying a double hamburger and there was Jason Kay on the footpath, bending down to Winnie who was stamping her feet and slobbering on his hands. She hadn't forgotten him. Jason stood up, rubbing his hands on his jeans, shuffling, his soft, smiling face looking down. At once Magnus remembered everything about him, his shyness and quietness, his naturally white teeth, long fingers and the way his yellow-brown hair flopped over his face. The feeling of liking he gave.

'So how's it going?' Jason murmured. Magnus remembered this too, how Jason hated talking face to face, yet he knew by the little dark gleaming pool in the centre of his eyes that Jason was pleased to see him.

'OK. Winnie hassles me. She's really missing Maya.' Why did he have to mention Maya straight off like that? Jason's ears went red. Magnus said quickly: 'What are you doing these days?' He hadn't seen Jason all year.

'I'm full-time at the workshop.' That meant long hours in the Brethren furniture factory behind the shop they called Warton Homeware. People came from miles around for their stuff. After Jason dropped out of school, he'd disappeared back into the Brethren world, their chocolate brick houses out on the flats and their church with a wire fence. How did a guy like

Jason, who was clever and artistic, feel about making tables and bedheads all day?

'You look pretty clean for a factory worker.'

Jason had his own style. He was wearing an ink-blue shirt buttoned up and a black waistcoat. He didn't dress like anyone else in Warton, especially not the Brethren guys. His face was smooth and pale, he was eighteen but he didn't have to shave. When you saw him up close you remembered how good-looking he was in an androgynous sort of way.

Jason laughed. 'I work in the office.' He gave a quick look over his shoulder. Brethren weren't meant to be too friendly with the worldlies. Especially not Maya's brother. Because Jason was very quick with numbers the elders had decided to let him stay on at school to study accountancy in Year 12, the only Brethren kid to go on to senior high school. He wasn't allowed to watch videos, play sport or eat from the canteen. Someone told the elders that he sat next to Maya on the school bus, and he left without sitting for his exams. Fortunately that was all the elders *were* told about.

Cannon Street was empty. Only the Lucky and the pubs were open. 'You mightn't see them,' Jason said once, 'but they're always there.'

'Like slugs,' Maya said, 'or snakes.'

Now Jason looked up under his straight fine brows and said softly: 'Heard from Maya?'

'Yeah. Have you?'

Jason shook his head. 'How is she?' He was smiling. He was always smiling. Most of the time, Magnus thought, Jason was covering up.

Magnus shrugged. Should he tell him about Maya's call? Maya and Jason used to be very close. At dinner time Maya would tell them all this stuff about the Brethren that Jason had told her. Two or three times Jason had walked around the back roads to their house and Jacob and Toni had been very friendly to him.

Jason loved everything at their place, the music, the books, Winnie. How the parents were nice to their kids. He said they all laughed a lot, which they hadn't been aware of. They showed off a bit to him like a family in a sitcom, an advertisement for the good time worldlies had at home. All the same, Jason couldn't bring himself to eat or drink with them. That was forbidden by the religion. He liked best sitting on the couch, listening to classical music through the headphones. Music saved him, he said. Magnus offered to make him a tape but Jason shook his head. 'Not allowed.'

Now Winnie was whining, pawing at Jason's leg. Jason bent down to scratch her ears. You were always aware of Jason's hands. More than anything else he would have liked to play the piano. Winnie was carrying on like this because she associated Jason with Maya. Did Jason know this? He was a sensitive guy. Soon he stood up and shuffled, murmuring goodbye. Brethren weren't supposed to touch worldlies' pets.

He ate the burger sitting on the bench next to the war memorial. It was quite dark now, there was nobody around. On the edge of town the red lights of the new mobile phone tower glared like the eyes of a giant animal. The first thing that Maya and Jason had found out about each other on the bus was that they'd both seen a flying saucer over Warton when they were ten years old. Nobody else had ever believed either of them.

Last year, a couple of weeks before the exams, Jason came to stay the night. Toni and Jacob had gone to a teacher's wedding in Perth and, by coincidence, Jason's mother and stepfather had gone to a three-day prayer meeting in another town. First of all

Maya styled Jason's hair in the bathroom, then she heated pizzas and opened a bottle of Carlos's home-brew. She had made Jason promise to eat and drink with them. Jason downed a glass and started talking very fast. He told them what would happen if he was found out here. He would be *withdrawn from*. None of the Brethren would ever look at or speak to him again. His stepfather would thrash him and throw him out. Even his mother would cross the road if she saw him.

Then he'd be free, Maya said, he could come and live with them. Her cheeks were red, she was fierce, on fire. Jason said she didn't know what being withdrawn from was like. No one ever got over it. It was like having the bone pointed at you. You went weak as a rag, you were afraid all the time. It didn't matter that you knew it was irrational, you felt damned forever. You didn't know who you were any more. You'd been brainwashed from birth. Most people begged to go back.

They had a joint. Only music told the truth, Jason said, and he put the headphones on and drank more beer. 'It's too late for me now,' he said. Then he was sick. Maya took him into her room.

In the morning when Magnus woke up, his parents were sitting at the kitchen table. They said that at the last minute they'd decided not to stay the night in Perth and drove home through the night.

'Where's Maya?' he asked and they said she was asleep. They were calm and ordinary. Last night's dishes had been washed, everything was tidy. There was no sign of Jason.

Later he went to Maya's room and asked her what had happened, but she wouldn't answer. She was lying face down on her bed. For some weeks she didn't speak to any of them. From then on she was in a bad mood most of the time, until she went away.

★

He fed the last mouthful of the hamburger to Winnie, waiting at his feet, watching every bite. Should he or shouldn't he tell the folks that Maya had called? He dropped the wrapping in the bin and Winnie stood up in one movement, ready to go.

They didn't know Maya like he did, he thought, as he and Winnie set off home. In the pine-tree games she used to swing from roofs and branches with a knife between her teeth. She could never say no to a dare. Her name was Bandit Queen. Jordan was scared of her.

8

Massage

The Garcias. If they were home now, on Friday night, Jacob would be at the Garcias, watching the first elimination final with Carlos on their plasma screen. Because of the antenna that Carlos had rigged up, the Garcias had the best reception in Warton. Sometimes Toni and Chris joined them if the Dockers or Eagles were playing, and the couples ate hotdogs on the couch together.

From their first days in Warton the two families had been friends. The Garcias had come to live there half a year before they did. Like the de Jongs, not having been born in the town, they were outsiders. Also they voted Labor and didn't belong to a church. When they were small, their kids wandered in and out of either house. The kids had grown apart now, painlessly, but they still gave each other carefully chosen gifts on their birthdays.

Very likely if the families lived next door in the city they wouldn't have had much to do with one another. But the two couples had a pleasant time together. They didn't flirt or take offence, or discuss their private lives as couples. They tended to get together to watch big occasions on television, elections, football finals, Diana's funeral, the World Cup, the millennium celebrations. No doubt, if they were home, they'd watch the opening ceremony of the Olympics with the Garcias.

Placidly, year after year, season by season, they did and said the same things. There was comfort in the rituals. It kept the loneliness at bay. Who else was there to show the photos to after you'd been on a trip? They grew sleepy early from food and wine and lack of stimulation. The women left and went off to their beds. The men stopped feeling sleepy then and stayed up talking and watching videos.

The real friendship was between the men. They liked each other. (If they didn't, it wouldn't have been possible for the couples to socialise.) *The boys*, Chris and Toni called them, and it was true, when they were alone together they shed the burden of being family men.

Carlos was easy in his skin, practical, open to a good time, like the woggy boys Jacob had grown up with. Right away Jacob felt at home with him. In the early days Carlos helped him put up shelves and build a laundry. Jacob was always trotting out to the pine trees to ask advice from Carlos in his shed. They made excursions into the bush together to cut firewood with a chainsaw. Chris had built a high stone chimney in the Garcias' new games room. She loved to keep a fire burning. 'My little white ant,' Carlos called her, which made the de Jongs laugh, thinking of Chris's busy walk, her small grim mouth.

'Why is Chris doing this?' Toni said. 'These chat-line romances never work.'

150

Chris as a romantic? Pouring her heart out in emails? The Garcias weren't people of words. Jordan, who never spoke, was like their spirit, silent and benign.

Sitting around talking made Chris restless. It was hard to remember the sound of her voice. There was always a project she was working on. She developed fierce obsessions, horses, DIY, that strange stone garden. Each new project replaced the others. When Wesfarmers closed down and she lost her job she started to spend ten hours a day on her computer. She didn't train horses any more and she never went near her garden.

'How do you know they don't work?' Jacob said. Toni's certainties could annoy him. He thought she sounded smug. 'Why not? Why not, if you start a conversation that seems to feed a private hunger? That seems to wake up a part of yourself which you thought had forever shut down?'

Chris was *in love*. What did that mean? I've forgotten, Toni thought. The notion was as foreign to her as being struck with genius. She remembered the White Garden.

'Poor old Carlos.' Jacob saw his friend sitting at his kitchen table, leaning over his paunch, which he bore as gracefully and cheerfully as a pregnant woman. He saw his dark-stubbled double chin, his small hairy fingers rolling a cigarette. His eyes downcast, his thick black lashes. His quietness. Carlos was devoted to Chris. She had saved him. He was a junkie when they met, lying beaten up in a park in Northbridge. Chris had been jogging. She'd stopped and asked if he needed help.

Chris made him go cold turkey. When you saw her with horses you understood how. A born trainer, Carlos said, proudly. She brought him to live in the country. Carlos was grateful for every moment of his life. There was something loose about him that Jacob loved. He'd been blown open and there were no defences left, no illusions about himself. He was the humblest person Jacob had ever met.

He never lied, because nothing needed to be covered up, or different from how it was. The ordinary – a wife and kids, a porch, a barbecue, his job in the workshop at the local hospital – was a miracle to him. With Carlos, Jacob felt the old longing, to give up striving to be whoever he was and give himself to the simple pleasures of the world.

One winter when the kids were small, he and Carlos cultivated a dope bush behind the Garcias' shed. After a smoke, everything in their domestic lives turned into comedy. Late at night, like bulky boys, they roamed beneath the starry sky in parkas and beanies, while the women slept, exhausted by the children. They loved escaping the intensity of living with a woman. We have to give this up, they said, guilty as lovers. They began to smoke more and more. Once, during the holidays Jacob went stoned to school, cruised down the empty corridors in his dark glasses, only just dodging Kershaw, sat at his desk, jotting down words like 'beauty' and 'cruelty'.

Chris put her foot down. Carlos was an addictive personality, he was playing with fire. Jacob could lose his job. Carlos uprooted the bush and burnt it.

They started watching videos after everyone went to bed. Seasons of Cassavetes, Fellini, Bergman, old favourites and new directors from Japan, Iran, Hungary, that he'd painstakingly taped from SBS over the years. Some of the classics he ordered through the Education Department. Carlos developed a passion for Kubrick. Jacob liked to say that it was his greatest achievement as a teacher, to turn Carlos into a film buff like himself.

He remembered a line in *War and Peace* and hunted it down. *They say men are better friends when they are utterly different.*

'Magnus has the best of intentions,' Toni said from the kitchen, 'but he doesn't have a clue how to cook. He'll never get himself to school. He won't wash his clothes.'

'He'll survive.' Jacob felt a sneaking sympathy with Magnus's desire to be alone. 'Do him good,' he added. Wasn't it a father's duty to throw his son in at the deep end?

'No, Jacob.' Toni shook her head. 'Three months is too long. If we can't sort out Magnus we'll have to go home.' It would be a relief in a way. It seemed as if their departure had upset a balance, let new, hostile forces into their world.

At that moment the front door opened and Cecile came in, followed by a skinny fellow in a dark-green pork-pie hat.

Was the whole room brighter because a young woman stood in the conversation pit in her black socks, black pants and jacket? Jacob was surprised to feel an authentic thump in his chest. Cecile seemed larger than he remembered. He forgot his invalid status and rose to his feet.

Her companion hung his hat up by the door and removed his shoes. A regular. How regular? Jacob studied him as he came down into the room. His thin ashy hair seemed to have bites taken out of it, as if he'd attacked it himself in front of a mirror. His deepset, unfriendly eyes glittered above wide Slavonic cheekbones. Jacob shook his small white hand. Dieter.

'How are you guys going?' Cecile said softly. She reached up behind her head to pull the clasp out and shook her thick hair down around her neck. She looked tired but elated in some way.

'Want to eat?' Toni said.

'Hear that, Dieter? He was ready to pass out from hunger as we came in the door. We've just worked twenty hours straight,' she told Toni. Dieter said nothing. He went over to the breakfast bar and sorted through the mail. Jacob reflected that in all his life he'd never met a man in a little hat who wasn't pretentious.

Everything seemed suddenly cheerful. It was a relief to be with other people again, young people with their buoyant self-involvement, their hearty appetites. Their powers of recovery.

Jacob hobbled into the kitchen and opened a bottle of red. Toni piled pasta into dragon bowls. They were a team again, in service. This is what they were used to and it made them feel better. Cecile and Dieter sat on one side of the bar, they sat on the other. Dieter put his head down and tucked into his spaghetti.

It turned out that Dieter was Cecile's business partner. They had just finished a project for Prodigal Films, hiring the editing suite at the company where they both had day jobs.

It was a corporate video for Cecile's parents, who owned a business in Sydney.

'My adoptive parents,' Cecile said. 'They're Australian. They came to Kuala Lumpur and adopted me when I was three.'

'You grew up in Sydney?' said Jacob.

'Yes. But I learnt everything I know in the first three years of my life.'

'Are you happy with the video?'

Cecile shrugged. 'It's a professional job. We did it to fund other projects.'

We. Dieter ate steadily, without attempting to join the conversation. Jacob remembered Joe Lanza, Arlene's 'business partner'.

'My parents commissioned the film out of guilt. As a way of making me accept some of their money. I left everything behind when I came here, car, clothes, books, watch, everything they'd ever given me. I was twenty-one. I sat my parents down and told them that I never wanted them to give me another cent. I thanked them for my education, put my key on the table and left.'

There was a faint, apricot-coloured flush on Cecile's cheeks. She's a bit high from her work, Jacob thought. But she wants to tell us this. He felt a flare of happiness. He leant across the bench and topped up her wine.

'Can I ask you why?'

'For so long it was kept in the dark. I wasn't allowed to say I wasn't happy. There is a wall of glass between me and my parents and there always has been. I have never belonged to you, I told them, and you know it. I could see in their eyes that they did. They sent me to the best schools and took me to Disneyland and put me in the will with their other kids, but I knew when I saw them at the airport, at three years old, that I couldn't be part of this family. They quickly came to regret their little fit of philanthropy.'

Dieter calmly helped himself to more pasta with the air of one who has heard it all before.

'When did you come to Melbourne?' Jacob asked.

'Nine years ago. I worked in a Chinese restaurant on Victoria Street while I finished the film course. I made a short film. I changed my name back to Wong, my mother's name.'

Cecile was suddenly weary. She put down her fork. 'Maya hasn't called?' She climbed down from her stool and stretched, her hands on her spine, her head tipped backwards. 'Editor's neck,' she explained.

'Toni can give you a massage,' Jacob said.

Toni kept on stacking dishes.

'She's the official masseur of Warton. People come from miles around to see her.' Jacob turned to Toni and recklessly went on: 'Did you bring your oils with you?'

155

Toni nodded, unsmiling.

Cecile undressed without speaking. Her room opened through French doors onto the balcony above the courtyard and was full of restless shadows from the lights of the tower blocks flickering through the trees. Everything personal was stored behind a wall of white slatted cupboards. They set out a folded sheet on the carpet next to the futon, and bent the neck of the reading lamp for the light to be discreet. It was a good space for a massage.

Toni took off her rings and boots. Loud music, jazz, was being played downstairs. Concentrate, she told herself as she rubbed her hands with almond oil. After all, she was grateful to Cecile and would like to do something for her. The small, warm body lay spread out before her, face down, torso covered with a towel. Only the legs seemed adult, with surprisingly muscular calves. She sensed an absence and knew that Cecile was falling asleep. Toni sat back on her heels, bowed her head and slowly twisted up her hair.

Why had Jacob put her up to this? He knew she didn't want to massage any more. Before they left for Melbourne she'd sent out cards informing her clients that the business was closing until further notice. Body & Soul Therapeutic Massage was no more. In fact the name made her shudder. The whole hubristic venture was over.

Tonight, without knowing it, Jacob had switched allegiances. The beam of his approval was now focused on Cecile. He'd become Cecile's knight-at-arms, Cecile's champion. It was as if an engine next to Toni's ear had been turned off, a hum of involvement was silenced.

Why don't I care? she thought. Recently a strange, primitive conviction had come over her, that to get Maya back there would have to be a sacrifice.

156

She had to clear her mind now, let her hands do the work. *The touch of a compassionate stranger.* She took a deep breath and started with a kneading movement to the feet, then, her hands rolling and pouncing like a concert pianist's, she made her way up the perimeter of the body to dig her thumbs deep into the pockets of the shoulders. Cecile sighed. Her whole upper body was ropy with tension.

This was the reason why she had gone along with Jacob's offer of her services. Because she could see Cecile was in pain. This too was why she had offered to massage Miriam Kershaw when she was dying. By the time she'd brought her up the stairs to her room on top of the community centre, she knew that Miriam was beyond any skills she had to offer. It was a shock to see how frail she was. How the poor woman had winced and cried out as Toni touched her pitifully withered body. Tears of pain gushed from Miriam's eyes.

After Toni had helped her dress and sat her on the couch to rest a little before they tackled the stairs back down, Miriam said: 'There are healers and non-healers.'

'What makes a healer?' Toni asked.

'Lack of ego.'

Toni drove her home to 'Isolation' in silence. At the door, Miriam turned to her and looked her in the eye. 'Our Lady of Warton.' She gave a broad, deliberate grin. That was the last time Toni saw her.

Toni drove off filled with a crawling shame. For the room above the community centre, with its quasi-medical, quasi-New Age aura. For her TAFE therapy certificate with its one weekend of practical accreditation, and her belief that intuition and compassion could do the rest. Above all for the clients whom she had hoodwinked into feeling better just through her attention, her aromatic oils, her rainforest music.

Miriam's massage was a humiliation she never spoke of to Jacob or any other member of the family. Perhaps it was the same for all of them. Their deepest humiliations they did not share.

Her hands kept working on the mute, tightly wound little body laid out before her, but she no longer believed they could heal.

'I've been wondering,' Jacob said to Dieter across the bar. Dieter hadn't spoken at all during dinner, just listened, his pale eyes indifferent to the point of disdain. 'Is there any way we could track Maya's phone from the message she left?' In his experience, these Teutonic types often had a technical turn of mind.

'I think no. There is no call-back on this system.' After a pause Dieter added: 'She used a mobile phone, I think.'

'You took the message?'

'Yes. You have listened to it?'

'Never thought of it. We don't have one of these . . .'

Dieter reached across to the phone. 'I will retrieve it for you.'

The voice seemed tiny, childish, far away, a historic recording. *Hi Cecile . . . a few days . . . in touch . . . send my rent . . . gotta go.* It was echoing, as if in a high wind, then something like a truck roared past. Jacob replayed it. Just as it cut out he thought he heard the first note of a chime, the sort you hear in airports before a flight announcement.

'Did Maya buy herself a mobile phone?'

Dieter shrugged. 'I didn't see her with it the last time.'

'When was that?'

'That day.' He nodded at the phone. 'At breakfast.'

'How was she?' Jacob spoke slowly so as not to show his stab of resentment that it was Dieter who had seen her last.

Again Dieter shrugged. 'OK. She slept late. I told her she should go to verk.'

Jacob wished there was another bottle of wine. So this self-righteous prick thought he could give his daughter advice. 'It's been exactly two weeks,' he said quietly, getting down from the stool and making his way back to the couch.

Dieter was sitting at Cecile's desk, rifling through her CDs. He'd put on jazz and turned up the volume, just beyond what Jacob considered to be respectful in someone else's house. The Hawks and the Cats were slogging it out and Jacob would have liked to hear the commentary. He pondered whether or not to ask Dieter to turn it down. Was Dieter, as Cecile's guest and business partner and whatever else he might be, further up the pecking order than he was, the father of an absentee housemate? After all, he and Toni were only here out of Cecile's kindness. He had no rights.

How could a girl like Cecile hang out with this guy? He was a poseur, all Jacob's instincts rushed to tell him that. Look at him, his air of detachment, his pale blue nylon shirt that he must have found in an op shop after some old guy had died. Was he a cheapskate, or very fashionable? The way he listened when you spoke with an air of containing himself, no doubt ready to pounce on any sign of the mindless, the conservative. Well, he used to be a bit like that himself in his revolutionary phase. A pain in the neck. But this guy had no sense of humour. Jacob knew the type from his travelling days. The sense of entitlement. The reluctance to part with his money.

Dieter sat down on the other side of the conversation pit. He placed a film canister and tobacco on the coffee table. 'You like a smoke, I think?'

'What? Oh, well, why not?' My God, there was nothing he'd like more.

They stood in the sharp night air out by the fishpond and shared Dieter's immaculate joint. Smoking has become an outdoor activity, Jacob thought. At home he smoked an after-dinner rollie in the doorway of his shed. He loved to watch the house beneath its peaceful curl of smoke, while the family members passed by its windows and the brilliant stars swirled overhead.

He looked up to the sky above the courtyard. 'You can hardly see the stars in Melbourne.'

Dieter made a barking noise. 'You guys are so cosmic with your drugs.'

'What do you mean "you guys"?'

'Your generation. *The Doors of Perception.* Did you read that? Did you read Timothy Leary?' Dieter's shoulders shook up and down. This stuff made him more forthcoming. But no more likeable.

'Why do you smoke then?' In the spotlight over the fishpond he could see that Dieter was well into his thirties, a Generation X-er, a natural enemy.

Dieter shrugged. 'To relax. Watch porn on the internet. Get into music. It's too cold out here I think.' He threw the butt into the fishpond and went inside. Through the window Jacob watched him glide back to the CD player.

Did any generation ever get a worse press than his? Why sneer? Why give that grating laugh? Maybe it was jealousy. Because who wouldn't have liked to believe that they were revolutionaries when they were young? To forget the problem of who you were and throw yourself into the collective? For better or worse it was his true education.

He hadn't thought of it for years. God knows he groaned as much as anyone now if he happened to get stuck on Albany Highway behind a slow-moving 'hey what's the hurry, man?' hand-painted Kombi. A revolution always leaves its relics. No doubt that was how Dieter saw *him*. Fresh from the deeps of the country.

The air felt soft and fresh out here. *The bamboo gives off more oxygen than any other plant on the planet.* Who told him that? Minty Brown, Beech's aunt in Sri Lanka. That was why he liked passing through this courtyard. The inside-outside feel of it, the little Buddha, the air of having seen better days, reminded him of the time he stayed on Minty Brown's tea plantation at the end of 1980.

He was heading home, travelling overland. He made his way from India to Ceylon, as it was still called then, and sat in a planter's chair on Minty's verandah, reading. With the last of his money he'd bought a passage on a boat from Colombo to Fremantle, due to depart in three weeks. He still felt the shadow of the great sub-continent, still trod lightly, as he had through the teeming vibrant streets, the eternal Indian villages. For a little while he had lived in a world without time, without anxiety. It seemed to him that those he passed amongst, peasants with hardly a rupee to their name, were in harmony with their surroundings. He felt an ever-growing imperative: to live differently, simply and in peace.

He'd been away for seven years. It was, as he told Minty, a turning point. She was a person you said those sort of things to as you drank gin and tonic and chain-smoked cigarettes with her. From her perspective, in her sixties, nothing interested her more than what she called 'the long view'. Nothing, she said in her lilting, upper-class voice, seemed quite so serious any more. She was like someone out of *A Dance to the Music of Time*.

He was mortally tired of travelling, he wanted to find a place where he belonged. In his years away there'd been wars, coups, the three-day week, the five-day war, the IRA. Even now bombs were going off in London. There was an apocalyptic feel to the old world. And Kitty was coming to London, as if his past was catching up with him, his feelings of responsibility and guilt.

But he dreaded the thought of Perth with its sprawl of suburbs, its white midday glare.

He slept a lot in Minty's house. Eight hours at night lulled by the rhythmic thud of the fan. He woke to the smell of Minty's cigarette smoke as she wrote letters in bed and the croaky sound of her voice giving the day's orders to the sixty-year-old houseboy when he brought her tea. Once the servants had opened the giant wooden shutters it was a house without doors or glass in the windows, floating on its promontory above the valley.

In the mornings he sat in a deckchair on the verandah and read, the Russians again, Chekhov, Tolstoy with his 'problem of the self', *The Brothers Karamazov*. He felt like a nineteenth-century gentleman himself, surveying his country estate.

Minty was a painter, trained in the thirties at the Slade. She spent the mornings in her studio, a thatched-roofed, open-sided pavilion with a view down to the valley, where tiny figures in sarongs rode bicycles along the banks of a winding river. She was working on a series of paintings of the coconut palm. The life cycle of a coconut palm was similar to that of a woman, she told Jacob. It didn't produce fruit for twelve or fifteen years, stopped production at forty-five and died at seventy.

In the afternoons everybody slept again, he and Minty in their net coffins, the servants slumped on benches in the outhouse kitchen, the dogs under the trees. Servants were a fact of life here, Minty said briskly, an essential source of employment, but Jacob believed all men should be as brothers, and felt guilty at allowing himself to be waited on.

At dusk Minty liked to have a drink or two on the verandah and play a hand of patience on a little rattan table before she dressed for dinner. Egrets and crows rose in great white or black flocks from an island far up the river. The Tamil tea-pickers filed their way home through the thick green bushes down the hill. A light breeze stirred the tips of the coconut palms and the frangipani blossom fell. In spite of the colonialism, he played with the idea of staying here forever.

Minty laughed. 'You're too serious a young man,' she told Jacob at dinner. 'My nephew now, he could live here. Mind you, there'd be havoc with the local gels. He's like me, not serious, it's in the blood, a strain in the family. Some of us are decadents, and some, like my brother, go into the Church.' They ate by candlelight on the verandah, curries served by the houseboy in a white sarong. 'Experience taught me not to get involved with serious men,' Minty said. 'They think they'll reform you. They want you to be good.'

'Then what happens?'

'Then I can't paint any more.'

She'd had three husbands and many more lovers. She came to Ceylon with her second husband, a colonial administrator. He lived in the mountains now with a horde of children. Fell in love with a local gel, Minty said. After the death of her third husband, Mr Brown the tea-planter, she decided it was time to live alone and give herself to painting. To grow old as naturally

163

as a palm tree. The only thing that saddened her was the thought that she would never fall in love again. One of life's loveliest experiences, she said, like an unexpected guest arriving on a summer night.

'Have you ever been in love?' she asked Jacob.

'All the time.'

'Then you haven't, really. It only happens once or twice in a life.'

He was haunted by traces of her beauty, like a half-obscured painting, by the gestures of faded glamour, the elegant stained fingers, the way she uncurled her long thin leathery brown legs from a chair, her ability to study him through half-closed eyes and stay silent. In her bedroom was a self-portrait she had painted when she was twenty, wide-spaced brown eyes, pale hair flowing back from a broad, tanned forehead, the same earthy, intense gaze. He could have fallen in love with that girl.

One morning Jacob sat on the verandah trying to finish a letter to Beech in London. The world-weary tone he and Beech adopted with each other bored him. He was sick of cynicism, of trying to impress. Sunlight had just dissolved the mist and now the hillside of tea bushes, the village in the valley, the river winding to the sea, were shining like a dream revealed. Eden, Minty called it, the world before the Fall.

Behind him he could hear the steady raking of leaves across the gravel in the courtyard, the beating of a rug, laughter in the cook-house. Squirrels flicked like shadows in the corner of his eye.

Suddenly the two came together, the long view and the domestic, the grandeur of nature and the fellowship of simple toil, and he had a vision of how he wanted to live. A communal life on the land. Houses with a verandah and open windows and doors. In his own egalitarian country. Eden in the bush.

A lot of people were doing this now, he knew, dropping out, but he hadn't paid it much attention. He thought he was a city boy. They even had their own bible in America, *The Whole Earth Catalogue*, and suddenly he understood what they were about. He had a sense of blinding truth. He sat quietly without reading, watching everything, and all the time he was planning, planning, how he was going to live. As he dressed for lunch, his eyes looked different to him in the mirror. He felt the call came from deep inside him. The moment was, he thought, Tolstoyan.

He thought of the bowl of frangipani blossom left each morning in front of a little stone Buddha in the courtyard. A life of devotion to the spirit.

The two women were sitting on the end of the futon. Cecile was wearing a red silk dressing gown. Like strangers after an intimate but soulless assignation in a motel room, there seemed to be nothing to say.

'You're very strong,' Cecile said, as Toni squeezed her rings back onto her fingers. But why does she wait hand and foot on her man? she thought.

I'm glad she doesn't fake her reactions, Toni thought. There'd been no release, no rhythm between them. Deep down, she is resisting me. Because of Maya? Because she knows more than she's letting on? Because she doesn't trust middle-aged Australian mothers?

'Cecile, did Maya know anybody else in Melbourne?'

'There was the guy she used to board with. Tod.'

'Tod Carpenter. We know about him. Nobody else?'

'She worked pretty closely with her boss. Maynard. I don't know his surname.'

'How did they get along?'

Cecile shrugged. 'Half her life was spent with him.'

'Do you think she might be with him now?'

Cecile shrugged again. Maya must have reasons for her silence.

The air was warm and smelt of almond and lavender oil mingled with the scents released from their bodies. Toni couldn't quite bring herself to leave.

'Do your parents miss you?' she asked Cecile.

'How can you miss a child who always held herself apart? I never let them near me. I think they were relieved when I left.' Cecile lay back on the bed and spoke to the ceiling. 'Don't get me wrong, they're not bad people. Though not as good as they think. They bought me with their money because they wanted to *do* something. They had three kids of their own and they thought it would be good for their education. They had a name all ready for the cute little Asian girl – Kiki – but I wouldn't answer to it. The nuns at the orphanage had told me I was named after Saint Cecile. The family didn't understand that I was already a fully conscious person, with memories and affections. I didn't want to be carried around by their kids like a doll, I was used to being independent. I don't hate them, not at all. I just couldn't go on pretending that everything was OK. People have to be what they are meant to be.'

Just as the cold in the courtyard defeated him and he was

166

entering the house, Jacob remembered another homecoming. He smacked his forehead, looked at his watch and hobbled fast to the phone.

9

Kitty

The first thing Kitty saw when she stepped off the bus into Cannon Street was the window display in Take Five Fashion, two life-sized models, male and female, outfitted in pyjamas and dressing gowns, bent into sitting positions on a couch, in front of an ancient TV. On the coffee table at their knees were two mugs and a plate of varnished Anzac biscuits which resembled a pile of turds. *New winter sleepware! Don't be late!* was handwritten on a yellowed sign over the window. Kitty stood with her suitcase in front of this cosy still-life for some minutes. It could have been an installation in a gallery. She couldn't believe it was for real.

The street seemed deserted. There was a row of turn-of-the-century pubs and shops, run-down but picturesque. Everything modern was banal and ugly. Warton Homeware, Billabong

Crafts, Ezi Plus, Warton Meats, Melissa Hair. She bought herself a bottle of water from The Lucky Tearooms, a great dark barn-like place smelling of hot fat.

Kitty was not in a good mood. The bus trip had been spoiled by piped talk-back radio, and then just as the landscape became interesting, a video started up, an American high-school comedy which, as there were no headphones, you had no choice but to hear. Since she'd been gone, this country had become colonised. In Arlene and Joe's home-unit the TV blared non-stop, mostly American shows. That was a blast, to come home to *Lakeside*, pre-grown palms, an artificial lake, retirees buzzing around in shopping buggies. She shared the spare room with Arlene's sewing-machine, which seemed somehow symbolic.

Up Cannon, left into Trench, she read, her own scrawl on Arlene's telephone pad. A twelve-minute walk, Jacob said. Her suitcase rumbled over the gravel footpaths. A small black pull-along. Over the years she'd become an expert packer. She'd learnt by now how little you really need.

Where was everyone? The emptiness after years in crowded streets was almost frightening.

The sky was a vast, white desert. It was a mild afternoon in late winter, but she wore sunglasses and a black polyester parka zipped up to the chin. She felt like a spy come to town.

She could have taken Jacob's car, parked in Arlene's carport, but she didn't have the confidence for a long drive into unknown country. She hadn't driven for years. Once she arrived, Jacob said, his neighbour Carlos would lend her a car – he had a yardful of cars – and she could build up her confidence. Normally he would have asked Carlos to meet her at the bus, but the poor guy had been incommunicado since his wife left.

Hence this invitation, much sooner and keener than if Jacob himself was in Warton. Some things hadn't changed. Her brother never had been slow to ask if he needed something. She hadn't seen him for twenty-seven years.

From Trench, veer left into Shotgun Avenue. She passed a small war memorial. You could see what had obsessed Warton's founding fathers. It was like going back fifty years. So many things she hadn't seen since childhood, garden gnomes, swan-shaped planters, lion griffins on gateposts. Beach umbrellas over hydrangeas, pink hibiscus, paperbark hanging baskets. How could Jacob do this to himself?

Or was her eye sharper now than his, her view more worldly?

Come on, she told herself. After all, she was going to meet a nephew she had never seen. Didn't a gypsy on the beach in France last year tell her that a child was going to come into her life? (They always tell you what you want to hear, Tim had said.) It was a long time since she'd had a family to have Christmas with. She took a breath. The air was beautiful, soft and clean, smelling of honey and eucalypts and dung. Cars were parked under trees. Every second house seemed to have a yard of horses. Dogs barked as she rattled past. There were giant gums with ochre-streaked trunks and clumps of leaves like broccoli heads. What species were they? She knew nothing about Australian plants because of her urban childhood. Arlene had never taken her kids on so much as a picnic.

How long country roads were! A city block between houses. Everything so flat and bare. She was on the edge of town. The road went on and vanished into paddocks on the horizon. On one side was a scrubby enclosure which must be the old drive-in that Jacob had mentioned. Facing it was a stone settler's cottage with a red corrugated-iron roof and a deep verandah.

Jacob's house. There was a stretch of weedy lawn out the front and one of those ancient emblematic palms that she associated with Australian army badges. Behind the house loomed two giant pine trees. Jacob wouldn't have been able to resist the drive-in.

Where else in the world could you leave a house unlocked these days? The shadowy hallway ended in a large back room with a wall of windows, a kitchen at one side, a television, hi-fi and sagging couch at the other. Books, videos and newspapers were piled up on plank shelves around the couch. Pale sunlight streaked across the dusty slate floor. School notices, flyers, bills, sprouted from magnets on the fridge. This was where Jacob's children had grown up. A house like an old shoe, so habitual that you no longer saw how down-at-heel it was.

How quiet it was. The silence of old stone rooms and trees in the wind. Out the back door was a line-up of wellingtons and rubber thongs and a huge pair of rotting sneakers. A breeze set off some wooden wind-chimes swaying from a rickety pergola. Jacob never had been a very convincing handyman. By the back shed an almond tree was breaking into early blossom. The yard was streaked with shadows from the pine trees.

She peered into rooms, which like those where famous people once lived (Rodmell, Garsington) appeared too small and crowded for the fabulous lives that had passed there. So this was Jacob's great idealistic venture. All these years she'd thought of them as a sort of Holy Family, leading a radical spiritual life, a reproach to her frantic worldly pursuits.

Now she saw the ordinary muddle of people everywhere, bringing up children without a great deal of money. By the looks of it they'd built this back addition themselves. Off one side was a bedroom crammed with electronic equipment and a poster of Miles Davis. The boy's room. She'd known houses like this in Bayswater, in Islington.

Rain started to patter on the iron roof. The fridge was empty apart from an open tin of dog food. She was reminded of the astounding domestic absent-mindedness of adolescent boys. The benches were greasy, and the floors were awash with dog hair. She parked her suitcase in the master bedroom, took off her coat and pushed up the sleeves of her black cashmere sweater.

A hooded figure passed by the kitchen window. An ancient bulldog was suddenly barking in the doorway, quivering with outrage, and a boy in a sodden brown windcheater nudged her gently inside, pulling the string of a Walkman from his ear. He looked like a young Franciscan in a cowl.

Kitty embraced him, and felt his thin strong arms courteously attempt to return the gesture, while his body stayed back, private, resistant. He smelt of the classroom, socks, bananas and one of those pungent deodorants adolescents use. He pulled his hood back and crouched down to the dog and she saw dark blonde curling hair like his father and the tilt of his mother's eyes. She knew better than to say this to Magnus. His smile was pure, his skin was olive. After years of teaching adolescent boys she could guess that only a short while ago he would have been beautiful as an angel, but now was lump-necked, thick-nosed, croaky, a young bird. In a few years' time he'd be beautiful again, but as a man.

He stood gangly, a little at a loss. 'He's not a big talker,' Jacob had said on the phone. 'In fact this year he just about gave up talking altogether.'

We'll see about that, Kitty thought.

When she first came to teach in London she was given the lowliest, most refractory of classes. All boys. She found she liked it. Year after year she was form mistress to successive groups of inner-London boys, classified more or less officially as unteachable. She still received Christmas cards from some of them. Some had become teachers themselves. Even as she climbed the ranks, adolescent boys remained her speciality. She knew it had started years ago, a little fat girl's infatuation with her brother and his friend.

The first thing to remember about boys was that they were always hungry. Food was an overture offered to savages. It smoothed negotiations, established trust. She'd bribed her way into classes with lavish rewards of Belgian chocolates, French pastries, pancake breakfasts at McDonald's. A food angle kept a class happy. The smell or promise of food seemed to trigger associations of peace in some of her students, so that their true charm could emerge.

'Want to come shopping, Magnus?' There was a touch of wanness about him as the old dog pawed at his leg. The poor boy was clearly starving. 'You can show me what you like to eat.'

'I've got money,' Magnus said, quick to uphold family honour. 'They left me plenty. I meant to buy some stuff, I just kept running out of time.'

A nice boy, intelligent, sensitive, she could see at a glance. There was no company she enjoyed more. He probably hadn't liked being alone as much as he thought. They would have a good time together.

'Listen, I need to cook. I have to do a little cooking every day. It's the greatest — no second greatest — pleasure in my life.'

'What's the first?' Magnus was genuinely interested.

'Don't ask,' said Kitty, putting her coat back on with a swagger.

That was the other thing about boys. Don't be a goody-goody. Flirt a little. Be yourself.

Magnus took Kitty through the pine trees to pick up a car from Carlos. Large black cockatoos swooped and squawked overhead, hunting for pine nuts. The Garcias' house was silent. Magnus knocked. After a while Carlos came to the door, a little dark Mediterranean man, unshaved and overweight. He nodded at Kitty when Magnus introduced her but didn't try to smile. His eyes were bloodshot and he'd just put out a cigarette. Without a word he led them across the yard to the old yellow Moke. He wore thongs, a baggy pullover unravelling over workman's pants. There was a stillness about him, as if to look anywhere but straight ahead would hurt. Kitty, veteran of heartbreak, didn't try to make conversation but trod softly beside him.

Late that night, lying in the parental bed, she heard the horses whinny and she thought about the man lying in the dark next door. Over and over you cry out and there's nobody there. You take a pill and sleep for exactly four hours. In the morning, ghost-faced, you have a shower and go to work. On the weekends you make sure to take yourself off on a programme of expensive cultural events. You feel obliged to remind yourself that this pain is nothing compared to that of most of the people in the news. You go through the motions and then after a few weeks of paralysis you realise one day that you've lost weight, and you go shopping for a size smaller jeans . . . Then you understand that the stiffness is going out of your body, you were able to smile at the assistant, you're on the mend.

The phone rang in the kitchen and Magnus padded out to

answer it from his bed. Who could be calling at this hour? She heard him talking quietly as he walked back to his room, and then his door closed.

10

Retrace

They were watching Lateline when the phone rang.

'Magnus! Everything all right?'

'Yep.'

'How's Kitty?'

'Good.' Surprisingly emphatic for Magnus.

'Is she looking after you?' Too late Toni remembered Magnus didn't think he needed looking after.

'Actually she's a really great cook. She cooks international dishes. Tonight we had an Iranian soup.'

'What's that like?'

'You make it with spinach and yoghurt.'

'I didn't think you ate spinach or yoghurt.'

'It's different, cooked like that.'

'You'll have to give me the recipe.'

They were silent for a moment.

'Maya rang,' Magnus said casually.

'*What!* When?'

'Bout a week ago. Then again last night.' Suddenly at school today he knew he had to let them know.

'How is she?' *Why didn't you . . . ?* Pointless to ask.

'OK.'

'What did you talk about?'

'Nothing much. We've both been having dreams about Winnie lately.'

'Listen, Magnus, did she say who she's with or where she's staying?'

'No.'

'If she rings again could you ask her, *please*?'

'I don't think she wants to tell me. She's on a mobile, in a city. She only talks for a little while.'

'How do you think she is?'

A pause. 'Not happy.'

'Could you let us know when she calls again, *straight away*? Doesn't matter how late. We were about to go to the police.'

'OK.'

'Does she know we're in Melbourne? Does she know we're *very worried*?'

'She knows.' She wanted me to tell them, he thought.

Everyone is replaceable, Toni thought on the tram. If she died or disappeared, all the family would find substitutes. Less than a year after her mother died, Nig married a divorcee called Mavis Kearns, fifteen years younger than him, and retired to the

Gold Coast. All creatures acted from self-interest. The last and greatest vanity was to think you were essential.

The sky was dour outside the window. Last night she'd hardly slept.

The tram was not the early one that Maya would have caught but it followed the same route. At this hour it was filled with schoolkids swinging on poles and gossiping. Maybe Maya would have been happier growing up here. When she left Warton she had no real friends.

Odd lonely people were taking their first ride for the day. An ageing man with black teeth and an airline bag sat opposite and tried to catch her eye. Did he sense she was now one of them, homeless, adrift on the streets?

But she was on a mission, resolved in the bleak dawn light, to retrace Maya's route to the office, look for clues to her state of mind. She had to focus now, try to see this city through the eyes of an eighteen-year-old country girl. A young woman descended from the tram ahead of her and strode down Russell Street. She had wide shoulders and a free swinging walk, and she wore a red hooded jacket which reminded Toni of a red windcheater that Maya used to wear. She could almost think it was Maya, a city version, grown sophisticated and purposeful, head bowed listening to her Walkman. This girl had magenta streaks in her hair and that indefinable big-city chic.

As if she were leading her, the girl turned into the street that Toni was looking for, a little road of nineteenth-century offices and factories tucked in amongst the high-rises. Toni's boots clipped along after her, a brisk, leggy countrywoman, out of place here. The girl turned up a laneway and disappeared.

A *For Sale* sign swung high from a window on the top floor of the narrow building which housed Global Imports. This panicked Toni for a moment, as if all evidence of Maya's life in

178

this little fairytale canyon might also disappear. The front door next to Mimi's salon was open. She went in. Through the glass salon door she could see a pretty, black-haired beautician smiling as she spoke on the phone. From the dingy hallway Mimi's world glowed, soft, female, maternal. That was why women came to these places, to be comforted.

The treads of the dusty stairs creaked as she made her way past Jonathan Fung Barrister, up to the top floor. Global Imports, handwritten in biro on a card, was slipped into an antique cardholder on the door. She knocked. The door was locked.

She walked out onto the fire escape and stood looking at the tunnels of pale sky between the blind glittering walls of the modern buildings, the rusting roofs and fire escapes of the old. There, one floor lower, in a warehouse across the laneway, was the girl with magenta hair, helping to move a screen. Large colourful canvases were leaning against the walls. The girl had removed her red coat and was wearing a lime-green shirt. For a moment Toni was filled with longing for Maya to be like that girl, laughing with workmates in a big bright space. Why did Maya always have to pursue the dark and solitary, the creaking stairs and narrow passageways, like this Dickensian building?

She went to the ladies' restroom on Jonathan Fung's floor. It reminded her of the toilets in Boans in the seventies where she used to rush for respite from Beryl. In the mirror she saw the shadows fall across her face. The heaviness like a stone inside her had dragged down the corners of her mouth.

The pretty receptionist in Mimi's shook her head. 'The office closed a couple of weeks ago after the guy's wife died. He's never even been back to pick up his mail.' She indicated one of the letterboxes out in the hall, overflowing with flyers.

'I'm looking for my daughter. She used to work here.'

'The young girl with short hair?' She frowned in sympathy. 'I saw her on the day they closed. She left with him and another man. We didn't know it was the last time.'

Toni thanked her and turned to leave. She turned back.

'How old was he? The boss?'

'Late forties. Fiftyish.'

'What did his wife die of? Do you know?'

'Cancer, I believe.' She gave a sober nod as she spoke, woman to woman. With a small farewelling smile she answered the phone.

She isn't just pretty, Toni thought, as she pulled the sheaf of flyers from the mailbox, she's the Beauty around here. So where was the Beast? An envelope slipped out, addressed to Mr Maynard Flynn, Global Imports. She stuffed the flyers back and put the letter in her bag.

She opened it in the corner lunch-bar as she waited for her coffee. A bill for goods sent from a company in Thailand. No huge sums involved. At least she knew his name now.

A man whose wife had died. Some men couldn't stand it. Like Nig. They rushed for consolation.

Yesterday she'd rung Karen. Maya loved her cousin Lincoln and sometimes stayed with Karen to give her a hand. She was much closer to Karen than Toni was.

'Nuh, not a word,' Karen said in the blunt way she had these days. As if she didn't have much patience for fuss over trivial matters. As if nothing more was ever going to upset her. 'She promised to send us a postcard, but Linc and I are still waiting . . .'

'That's not like Maya.'

'Ah, you know how it is at her age.' Karen wouldn't hear a word against Maya. 'You fall in lurve and can't think of anything else.'

If anyone was going to say *history repeats itself* to Toni, it would have been Karen. But she didn't. Conventional life, its small disruptions, was far behind her now. When the kids were small, Toni was ashamed of their health and boisterousness if they visited Karen and Lincoln.

Bevan had left when Lincoln was two. He said that he was sorry, but he couldn't take it. At that time the house was full of a team of round-the-clock volunteers which Karen had organised for one of Lincoln's therapies. As soon as the divorce came through Bevan married his secretary. He proved to be tight with maintenance payments. Karen cared for Lincoln full time. She kept her hair cut very short and wore tracksuits. They lived in an old home unit and had few luxuries, but Karen said they were better off by themselves. 'I'm not sorry,' she said once. 'Everything I know about life I've learnt from having Lincoln.'

'Maybe she's taking care of someone,' Karen said before she hung up. 'Got sucked in. She's all heart, that girl.'

The coffee was good, the sunlight was pleasant in the window, there were newspapers to read, but Toni was unable to feel the ordinary contentment of things anymore.

This morning Jacob had stood at the kitchen sink drinking a glass of water. 'Lovely!' he said.

'What's lovely?'

'Water, when you're thirsty. Melbourne water's really quite good.'

All his observations of this city were positive, while she thought of it as dark and hostile. But Jacob, she could see, was still alive to life's joys. He was able to be distracted.

It wasn't a death, after all. It wasn't an abduction. Not even a missing person case, since Maya couldn't quite give up

Magnus. But now, as clearly as if she were watching through Mimi's glass door, Toni saw Maya pass down the dingy hallway, her head bowed, following two men.

According to family myth, Jacob had rescued her from a dangerous criminal. Did she fall in love with him in Cy Fisher's kitchen? She couldn't remember. Or did she – unconsciously – seize on him as a means of escape?

She wondered if she'd ever really been in love with anyone apart from her kids.

On the first day she and Felice watched the painters troop up the back stairs with their ladders and trestles, the handsome, hung-over Capelli brothers – their father owed Cy a favour – and a friend they introduced as Dutchie. All of them had cigarettes in their mouths. She registered Dutchie as different from the brothers, quieter, more introverted, as thin as a teenager in his outsized borrowed overalls. Unlike the Capellis' lustrous black curls – to the base of the neck, the longest their father would allow – his rough tawny hair was cropped short. All day she could hear their footsteps and radio and the scrape of ladders on the ceiling overhead. They were still working when she closed Park Lane. She and Cy were staying with Régine while the flat was painted.

One slow, hot afternoon when everyone else was out, she slipped upstairs to check the painters' progress. Only Dutchie was there, high on a ladder, slapping a roller back and forwards over the kitchen ceiling like a robot, like a kid playing games to relieve the boredom. A paint-spattered transistor tuned to 6PR was blaring on the scaffold beside him.

'Hi,' she called.

He swung around, knocking transistor and paint tray onto the tarpaulin covering the floor. They watched while a wave of white paint spread across the canvas. He scrambled down and tried to block its progress with rags. His face was red. 'I've got no aptitude for this sort of thing,' he said. It was so hot up there, with the sun through bare windows bouncing off the white walls, that he had to shade his eyes when he looked at her. She invited him downstairs for a cold drink.

'Coke? Beer?' she said as she opened the little fridge.

'Water will do,' he said, then gave a short, self-conscious laugh. 'He was about her age but of the other camp. A hippie. At last she had a chance to talk to one of them.

What man could ever resist the opportunity to explain himself to a receptive woman? He seated his paint-spattered rump on her desk, and talked for two hours. Political activism was all but over since Vietnam, he said. It had been replaced with a non-violent, non-materialist movement that was spreading across the world.

As soon as he had enough to buy a Kombi he was heading down south to find himself a commune.

Upstairs the puddle of spilt paint hardened on the tarpaulin.

'Am I boring you?' he asked. By now the sun was shining low through the trees in the park and light seemed to outline his body. He renounced his meditation session for the evening and accompanied her in a second gin and tonic. They sat facing each other on opposite desks.

'I think about this stuff night and day,' he said, half to himself. There was something melancholy about his long cheeks, their fullness around the jaw, but his mouth was firm, obdurate. His eyes were wide-spaced, idealist's eyes. He had a wispy beard and moustache that you didn't notice.

He ran his hand through his rough hair. 'I got a fever in

Ceylon before I came back. They made me cut this off.' He laughed again. 'They said my head had to cool. I was thinking too much.' Everything about the men she knew, it seemed to her, he had eliminated. The gestures of aggression and defence, the hard presence, the air of humorous patience if a woman spoke . . . He was gentle, open. Could this be a new sort of man? It was deliberate, she thought, something larger than himself was at stake. She felt the pull and strangeness of his conviction. A spattered paperback stuck out of the pocket of his overalls. The late sun caught on the silver Sikh's bangle on his thin brown arm. She thought of the word *light* when she saw him.

He was a good storyteller. Already a vision had been transmitted and was taking form in her head, a strange mixture of the tropics and the bush. Torchlit processions, bare feet on dirt tracks, the sound of drums and singing. Cooking fires all over the valley, lamplit tables, rain through trees. Children's laughter.

Any moment they could be disturbed but they kept sitting there on the desks, swinging their legs as the light softened and their faces glowed in the shadows. Already, if they only knew it, he had crossed the peak of zealotry and was on the other side, going down. Later he was to say — with some irony — that this was his true moment. Never had he been so articulate, his mind more agile and creative. This was what he'd been waiting for. His ideas had finally served their true evolutionary purpose, that is, to attract to himself the faith of a good-looking woman.

His eyes suddenly shifted beyond her. Cy Fisher was standing in the doorway. How had he managed to materialise without so much as a creak on the floor? A smooth exchange followed about the speed of drying paint in the heat. But that was it, Toni understood. The next day Romano Capelli came to finish off the painting. She knew better than to make any comment.

That night she lay beside Cy on Régine's feather pillow and went to a place in her mind, a small house, a clearing, sheets snapping in the wind. A tank for water with a pipe running into it. The sound of children playing. Was it somewhere in her own childhood she wanted to return to?

She knew he was lost to her forever. She tried not to think of him in case Cy picked it up. She was consumed with fear that the hippie painter would suffer some mysterious injury. One thing was certain, his career wouldn't prosper in this town.

She wanted to warn him, tell him to leave for that commune of his or at least lie low. He'd mentioned that he was living with an old friend who'd come back from London. She couldn't risk sending a note via the Capellis. You never knew who was an insider. Any further sign of interest on her part could be fatal. This sounded like a joke in the morning light. *But I'm not joking,* she said to herself.

She remembered Jacob telling her that he grew up a few blocks away from the Capellis, above that funny dress shop on Fitzgerald Street. While Cy was in a meeting out the back, she told Felice she'd buy Greek cakes for morning tea and fled down Fitzgerald Street. She entered Arlene's to a peal of jangling bells and, trying to calm herself, rifled through her awful frocks.

Arlene was with a customer. *Guipure lace to soften the neck,* she was saying, *off-the-shoulder Thai silk. Sand-coloured or bone.* She had a broader accent than her son, a low-pitched, relentless voice.

She had glimpsed Arlene before, in brief sorties to the shop with Felice and Sabine, but now she looked at her with new eyes. Strange to recognise his features in this large, professional woman, like landmarks overlaid with time and change. Already there was a sense of familiarity about her. Her gray eyes were his, though very slightly bulbous. Her hair was silvery-gold, back-teased in the style of the sixties, but with Jacob's widow's peak. All the time she was talking she was taking garments off the racks to display to the customer and hanging them up again, straightening and smoothing with expert twitches of her plump wrists, as if each were a piece of art. She herself was costumed in traditional saleswoman black, though the ruffled skirt was not flattering.

'Can I help you with anything?' Arlene called, once the customer had left.

Toni asked for Jacob's phone number. She had her excuse ready, but the bell rang again and Arlene scribbled the number down and handed it to Toni without speaking, hardly looking at her. Toni stayed a few minutes more, browsing politely, listening to Arlene's spiel. It wasn't that Arlene was unfriendly, she thought. She couldn't tune in to anything that wasn't to do with clothes.

She rang Jacob from a public phone box in the early evening before Cy came home. He sounded dozy and friendly, he said he'd been asleep in front of the telly after a long day's painting. So the Capellis hadn't been instructed to sack him. Cy must have wanted him to stay where he could keep an eye on him.

'Have you told the Capellis about your commune plans?'

He laughed. 'The Capellis think all drop-outs are just uni kids.'

'Have you told anyone else?'

'Only my ole pal Beech.'

'Can you trust him to keep his mouth shut?'

'Well that depends,' Jacob started to be humorous, but he sensed her urgency. 'Sure, if I ask him to . . .'

'I think you should head off down south right now.'

'Hey,' Jacob said gently, 'that just isn't possible. Not until I get some cash together.'

'Then *please* lie low for a few weeks. Watch your back. Go away as soon as possible. And don't talk about where you're going.'

He was silent. Did he understand why she was telling him this? No doubt the Capellis had given him the lowdown on Cy. But how to explain the speed, the thoroughness of his revenge? Jacob might think this was strangely intense after what was, after all, one casual conversation, but it didn't matter. Yet she couldn't quite bring herself to say: keep away from me.

'I liked talking to you,' he said.

'Do you want to talk some more?' she heard herself asking. Suddenly, as if she'd been planning this all along, she told him of a lonely little burger joint on the ocean road to the north. She'd noticed it on one of her drives a few months ago and must have stored it away in her mind, as a place that no one she knew would ever go to.

'Tuesday, 2.30,' she said, amazed at herself. 'Or the following Tuesday, if I'm not there.'

That'll test him, she thought as she hung up. She ripped up Arlene's piece of paper and threw it down a drain. Better to forget that number. Now to buy those cakes. She was suddenly shaking with fear.

Strange how the traditional shape of a church, the upward reach of its spire, like a lightning rod to God, seemed to promise comfort. Toni, wandering back into the street, felt herself drawn to the old, black-bricked church opposite Maya's office, as if to a place where she might ask for help.

But as soon as she sat down in a back pew she remembered the school chapel. The same smell of wood and mustiness and incense. The same punitive hush. *Lighten our darkness, we beseech thee O Lord, and save us from the perils of the night.* She could almost hear the nun-like chant of adolescent girls. The clap of their skirts as they fell to their knees, like birds landing.

She went to sit outside in the courtyard on a plastic chair beneath the trees. Maya would have sat here, she was sure of it, at home each one of the family liked to sit outside alone in the sun with the birds and the wind in the trees. She felt closer to Maya here than in Cecile's house.

The sun disappeared and for a moment all went quiet. A chill came over her spirit. All her life, wherever she lived, it seemed to her that each street, block by block, had a different presence and character that affected her, so that she chose certain routes according to her mood. Here, in the middle of this city street, in spite of the soaring glass buildings around it, it was the old black church and its courtyard that presided. There was something uncanny about this little precinct.

What was it that had trapped her daughter?

Fear, she was forgetting fear, the way it made you do things.

Where to now? Not back to another day of waiting to hear from Maya. Not back to Jacob on his couch. What more could she do? She stood up, tightened her scarf, dug her hands into the pockets of her jacket. Her fingers grasped a card. Suddenly, clear as a photograph, she remembered Kesang and the kindness of her face. She hadn't really stopped thinking of her.

The card was deep blue, with a stylised white lotus. Beneath it, *The Maha Institute* was written in fine white lettering. *We work to relieve all beings from suffering in all its forms.* On the back was scribbled a mobile phone number.

11

Warton

'Is she pretty?'

'Stylish. Her hair's sort of red and her skin's really white and she wears red lipstick every day. She looks like someone from London. She talks like a Pom.'

'What are her clothes like?'

'Black.'

'Is she nice?'

'Pretty much. She's taken Winnie off my hands. And she cooks really amazing meals . . .'

Maya interrupted him. 'I gotta go now.' The line went dead.

Kitty won Winnie's heart in her usual way, through food. She bought big meaty bones for her from Warton Meats and slipped her snacks when she was cooking. Within a day Winnie had given up school, too busy following Kitty everywhere. They went on long walks together, sniffing out the town. Kitty was still trying to understand how Jacob could have buried himself here for so many years.

Even mid-morning the main street looked uninhabited. The shops were vast barns half-lit by fluoro strips, the sparsely stocked shelves reminded her of Prague in ninety-one. Plastic streamers flapped in the doors. In the newsagency she ordered *The Guardian Weekly* and the woman behind the counter put on the glasses which hung from a chain across her bulging tracksuit top and introduced herself. Rhonda Carpenter.

'We didn't know Jacob had a sister! If there's anything you need, just sing out . . .' Her eyes, enlarged behind the glasses, bored into Kitty.

'Thank you.' Kitty heard her voice sounding plummy and English. 'We seem to be doing quite well.'

Jacob mustn't have told her about me, Rhonda thought.

She sensed that everyone knew who she was. Trailed by Winnie, all in black, she pursued her research, picking up leaflets on the town's history from the Shire office, stalking in and out of Warton Real Estate, Billabong Crafts and Warton Homeware, run by some funny-looking sect. She hated the ugliness of everything. If she lived here she'd be like one of Chekhov's angry, yearning provincial spinsters.

Four-storey truckloads of sheep thundered past. Bells rang, a bar came down across the wide street. All traffic stopped while an endless wheat train trundled its way towards the distant silver towers of the silos that melded into the whiteness of the horizon.

It was a tame world Jacob had chosen. There was so much

you didn't have to deal with here, noise, queues, strangers, crime. Urban life seemed very far away. Yet when he was a boy, it was cities her brother had wanted, like her, great cities that promised to save them. They were both, after all, half European.

Eighteen years in this town: perhaps you got attached to it, as prisoners do. Perhaps it got so you were afraid to leave.

She explored the oval, the showground, the cemetery, the bleak Shire picnic grounds beside a creek as brown and sluggish as a drain. The township was a frail grid placed over the landscape. So quickly, after the stage set of the main street, it dissolved into paddocks and bush. One day, she thought, when all the farms are owned by corporations, Warton will be a ghost town, absorbed back into the land.

In the Moke with Magnus, testing out her driving skills, she drove to the lake, ten kilometres to the east. They parked at the top of a hill and looked across a silver-white expanse, edged with dead black stick-like trees. It stretched as far as the eye could see, like a Russian snowfield. When he was just a little kid, Magnus told her, everyone used to come here to picnic and swim. Gradually the lake salted up till swimming in it stung your skin. Now beneath the white crust was a thick mud with a terrible stench. Everything was silent out there, even the birds. She could see rings of salt surf, like petrified time.

Each morning, she woke Magnus to an *international breakfast*, pancakes or hash browns like the Americans, or English bacon and eggs, French toast or Israeli fruit salad and yoghurt, even chops and grilled tomatoes like Australians used to have. Lots of coffee, her fresh lipstick smearing the mug as she read her *Guardian* and left him to eat in silence. Then she whisked him off to school in the Moke, Winnie grinning in the back. He croaked 'Bye', and loped inside just before the bell.

The school was of the model of the school of her childhood, red brick with an iron roof and white-rimmed, twelve-paned windows, one of hundreds that the government erected in the fifties to cope with the baby boom.

Wonderful trees grew all around, immense gums with pink trunks and thick leaves that caught the morning sun. The kids she'd taught, shivering in dark ancient courtyards, would think this was paradise. She watched some teenagers in a line throwing a basketball, healthy-looking boys and girls in high spirits, showing off to one another. No mobile phones. Mist was rising above a distant playing field where tiny boys playing soccer were dwarfed by giant trees. An Aboriginal mother dropped off a carload of small kids. A group of girls from another era, wearing long skirts and headscarves over waist-length hair went through the school gate, the older ones ushering the small ones ahead. It wouldn't be a hard life, teaching here.

Like an echo of the past, she heard a handbell clang, the scrape of chairs, sing-song greetings breaking out in classrooms. Then the old-fashioned chortling of magpies in an emptied playground.

The back shed was Jacob's study, Magnus said. Of course he'd have to have a place for himself, like her, they'd grown up living secret lives in separate rooms. There was a battered wooden school table beneath the window and a cheap office chair. Except for an old tape deck, the table was bare. Spidery stacks of boxes took up one wall: he'd never got around to making shelves. She sat down in his chair. The view was straight across the terrace into the kitchen window. The fridge light came on and there was Magnus pouring himself a glass of milk. A yellowed teaching timetable was blu-tacked to the wall and a fly-spotted photo of a little thatched pavilion under a coconut palm. No sign of teaching notes or research, but then how much preparation would you need, year after year in a country junior high?

Jacob's room: it was as if the young man she knew had died.

In the drawer of the table were two bound folders, each with a title. *How Much Land Does a Man Need? – A Screenplay adapted from Tolstoy* by Chickie Fitzgerald. And *Glad Rags – A Screenplay* by Chickie Fitzgerald. This one had a received date stamped on it, 29 June 1994. From what she could read, flicking hastily through the yellowed script, it was a kind of slasher movie set in a country town. By Jacob? No, not Jacob, *Chickie Fitzgerald.*

'What does he do out there?' she asked Magnus.

'Stares out the window. Plays music. Falls asleep. Has a smoke when he thinks we're not looking.'

'Sounds like when he was a boy.'

'No kidding! He's always telling me to get my act together.'

'Nobody ever told Jacob to do anything. Maybe you're lucky.'

Chickie Fitzgerald. So this was the person she'd been trying to prove herself to all these years. The big brother who was always her superior. When she was teaching she made herself go to bed early, no matter what the hours of her current lover, to have enough energy for all she tried to do in the classroom the next day. She counted each lesson a failure if she did not see some light of interest or ease on every student's face. She had to take care she slept enough or she became exhausted.

Slowly she'd climbed the ladder from teacher to policymaker. By this time, nobody even knew she was Australian. She couldn't have carried on teaching the way she did, but she came to look back on her teaching years sadly, like an artist appreciating the vitality of early work. By the end of her time in London, she was just another bureaucrat slowly burning out.

Meanwhile Jacob had disappointments of his own. *Chickie Fitzgerald.*

But he did have beautiful children.

Best of all she liked Maya's room. She fell into the habit of taking an afternoon nap on Maya's bed. At that hour the sun lay in a streak of warmth across the quilt, and the walls were patterned with palm tree shadows. No posters, no trinket boxes, no childhood teddy bears. A packed-away emptiness that declared life in this room was over. All that she'd left were the photos on a pin-up board above the desk. Every day Kitty studied them. An enlarged, arty shot of the neighbour's horses in mist, probably for a school assignment. Maya and Magnus as little snaggle-haired kids, arms wrapped around an ecstatic bulldog pup. A frail teenage boy in a wheelchair with a drooping head. A snap of Jacob and Toni slumped asleep in sarongs on their bed, slightly turned away from each other, yet somehow fitting together. Even asleep Toni was photogenic. Arlene and Joe getting married in those terrible matching white Thai silk suits. And the famous photo, The Sailor on Leave, Anton de Jong reading the paper on the verandah, ignoring his family. How had Maya got hold of that? There was even a faded Polaroid of Aunt Kitty in the snow, sent one Christmas years ago.

Kitty was touched. Why had Maya left them this shrine? Didn't it show, at the very least, strong affections? It was a sort of farewell to childhood and its cast of characters. To one's sleeping parents. In the top right-hand corner was a tiny mug-shot cut out of a school magazine, of a self-conscious, delicate face that at first sight Kitty took to be a girl.

'Was Maya happy here?'

Magnus shook his head.

'Why not?'

Magnus considered. 'It's like, there's some kids in Warton who can't wait to get away. And there's some who never wanna leave.'

'Was she hard to live with?'

He shrugged. 'She just wanted to do things her way.'

They were talking after dinner, when Magnus was at his most communicative. Kitty had excelled herself again. Like an old-fashioned French housewife, each day she relied on inspiration, seeing what vegetables were fresh, what cuts in the butcher's took her fancy. She bought wine from the pub, trying out different Australian reds. She fed Magnus huge meals, food she remembered from London dinner parties in the eighties, coq-au-vin and pot-au-feu, recipes from Elizabeth David. Keep good food on the table was one of her life rules, she told Magnus. She never forgot how hungry she was in adolescence, how she and Jacob had prowled around the kitchen, how the empty cupboards affected them like the hollowness of fate. She shuddered at the thought of those comfortless plates of chops and peas and mash.

Parenthood fascinated Kitty. What would she have been like if she hadn't always had to be on the alert for herself? If as a little child she hadn't been put to bed with the door shut and the light firmly out? She had cried, even screamed, but nobody came to her. She'd had to teach herself how to be alone, how to console herself with plans for what she would do tomorrow, or when she grew up. How to live for the light in the morning and have hope.

Arlene had work to do. No point in complaining to Arlene.

At first Magnus stayed in his room, padding out for meals or snacks and going back again. Kitty left him alone. She didn't even ask him how school was that day: her students used to tell her how much they hated that question. Now after dinner, full of rich consoling flavours and a small glass of wine, Magnus stayed at the table and talked. She could see that he lived in a dream of his future. How did she rank London as a place to live, he asked, compared to New York, Tokyo or Berlin? Had she been to any good concerts? Had she seen Sting? Did she go to clubs? Why had she left London?

You don't have to shield kids from your truth, she believed. Let him know she was a woman who'd been through things, with men. She topped up her glass and told Magnus the story that was still white-hot inside her. One night at a party she overheard Tim – Tim Lees-Walshe, the poet she'd lived with for seven years – asking a lawyer friend whether he could put in a claim on her flat if they parted. 'After all,' Tim said, 'it is my place of work.'

'Do you pay rent?' the lawyer asked. 'Do you share expenses for its upkeep?'

'How would anybody know if I didn't?' Tim said.

She left the party at once and rang an estate agent first thing in the morning. Tim, she knew, without her, always missed the last train, and would still be asleep on the living room floor of the party. She took a taxi to a shipping agent and brought home a dozen boxes. Then she rang in sick at work and packed up her London life. Useful household things, kettles, doonas, she took to Oxfam, the rest she dumped in a skip at a nearby building site. She packed up Tim's stuff too and left it in the corridor. It was all she could do not to dump his manuscripts and notebooks in the skip. But that would give Tim an excuse for his lack of productivity for years to come, how he'd lost his best work, his essential material, because of her jealousy. There is nothing, Tim often used to say, like the ambition of a small-town colonial girl. It would be a gift to him.

At last she could admit to herself that his poems, so rare, so erudite, so minutely dissected with his friends at the kitchen table, these poems that had required her to support him body and soul for seven years, had never given her one moment's joy or insight and never seemed to be about anything of the slightest importance.

By midday, the flat, with furniture, had been sold unseen to a wealthy, desperate immigrant family. She booked her ticket home, moved out to a cheap hotel, and stayed there for two weeks until she'd finished up at work. She never saw or spoke to Tim again.

After years of therapy – and thousands of pounds – she knew that everything we are, why we do what we do, is formed in childhood. 'It was instinctual,' she told Magnus, 'I couldn't talk myself out of it. I needed to come home.'

She felt it was the end of one part of her life, the part with men. This she didn't say to Magnus.

Magnus told Kitty about one of his ideas, to set up a business called Living Sounds, different music for different places and occasions. Not muzak but real music, custom made, for restaurants and shops, buses, trains, hospitals, schools. If they played different music all through the day at school, for example, they'd really change the feeling of the place. It would be like music for movies, the movies of ordinary lives. People would order music for their houses and cars, or for things they were going through, like studying for exams or a love affair or feeling sad. For each client he'd make a special compilation. It was the sequencing that was important. In music it was mood that really interested him.

Pretty soon it would all happen on computer, he said. Meanwhile he offered to make her a tape.

'How will you know what to choose for me?'

'It's intuitive. I can't start till I sort of hear the music, or see a scene when I say your name.'

It was Magnus's room off the kitchen, with its artery of wires and stacks of tapes and decks, that was the real creative centre of this house.

On the handle of his door was glued a tiny piece of newsprint that said *hello*.

Kitty felt a prickle of professional excitement. She recognised talent when she saw it. A Gifted Child. Her mind raced in the old way, with challenges, strategies, possibilities.

He was one of the ones who were dying to leave, like his sister. Where would be the best place for him to go? He had to consider the options. She took care to leave *The Guardian Weekly* on the kitchen table where Magnus could read it. The shyness, the slovenliness of speech, would drop away by itself, as hers had. It was important to give him the right sort of support now. So that he didn't make some self-destructive decision like Maya probably had. Above all, he had to learn self-discipline. She'd known a lot of disappointed men who'd once been gifted boys. Starting with Beech.

The quintessential golden schoolboy. Who can transgress

more gloriously than the son of a minister of the Church? For years she'd brush her hair after school and do her homework in the kitchen, in case Beech visited. Sometimes he'd wink at her, call her Miz Kitty. Sometimes he didn't notice her, too busy announcing himself to Jacob. She listened to their non-stop voices in the sleepout, the shouts of laughter in bass tones. If Jacob was out, she sneaked into his room, picked up the books they lent each other, took them to her room and read them, turning the pages that Beech had touched.

She was sixteen when Beech, for lack of any other amusement, turned his attention on her and whisked her off to a bedroom at a party. It was better that she lost her virginity now, got it over and done with, he said, with an old family friend. It was a real handicap these days. 'For a girl like you, Kit, it could be years and then you'll get a complex.' He was sharply intuitive, it got him what he wanted. It got her every time. In those days he half meant well. People hammered on the door, she lay wincing amongst other people's coats, while he hissed commands. It hurt. There couldn't have been a less romantic deflowering.

Then came the early London years when Beech, peripatetic journalist, would arrive begging floor space for a night. One thing always led to another, especially as you couldn't spend time with Beech without drinking or getting stoned. She could never resist the violence of her physical reaction to him, a sixteen-year-old again. His eyes like a bright shrewd kid's, *show me a good time.* His tiny, thin-lipped smile: *Rien ne me surprise.* He was the only person in London who knew where she came from and, as if he were some wild, childish part of her, she was unable to give him up. Eventually he got a job in Bangkok and never came back. By then she'd begun her long career of sleeping recklessly, hopefully, with men she knew didn't love her. Beech had taught her how to throw caution to the winds, broken down some basic instinct for self-protection. Like a good disciple she adopted her master's bravado. There was anger too. Why couldn't she act as men did? Anger but also, always, shy hope.

One year she had three abortions. After that she didn't get pregnant any more.

She'd never had so little to do. Time at last for the Great Books. She started reading Jacob's old copy of *War and Peace*. There were no distractions at all, except for a restless need to walk, as if she'd grown addicted to the air. Her shins ached from walking over the gravel roads.

At night under Magnus's direction she embarked on a season of his favourite videos. Magnus considered Hitchcock was a good way to start.

She slept long and deep, as if she was learning to breathe again. Looking after Magnus was a sort of cure.

On Saturday morning Magnus wandered out in his pyjamas to the backyard where Kitty stood looking up at a pair of black cockatoos dive-bombing for pine nuts. The air was full of their screeching.

Kitty pointed to the pine trees. 'I can't help seeing them as a couple.' One was larger, bushier, the other smaller, better shaped. 'Jacob and Toni, keeping an eye on us.'

'Really?' Magnus stared at her. She continually surprised him. 'I've always thought of them as Jacob and Carlos.' The giants of his childhood. Now they made him feel a bit sad.

'Have you seen Carlos?'

'No. But his ute's there all the time. I don't think he goes to work.'

'Magnus, let's ask them to dinner tonight.'

'The boys'll be going out.'

'Then just ask Carlos.'

I hope I don't have to spend the whole night listening to his problems, she thought.

12

Music for Carlos

It was interesting, Magnus thought, to live in a house with another woman. Everything about her was different, not just her clothes and the smell of her products in the bathroom, but her amazing white skin and her sad, shining eyes and her long jaw, a female version of Jacob's. There was an aloneness about her wherever she went. It made her dramatic. Everybody noticed her.

He made her scream by walking soundlessly right up behind her, just like he did with his mother and Maya. What was it with women? They were always thinking about something else.

As soon as he'd returned from inviting Carlos, Magnus went straight to his room to finish working on the tape for him. Carlos had shocked him by his appearance, puffy and red-eyed, stinking of cigarettes.

'Oh mate . . .' Carlos stumbled round for an excuse. But he wouldn't refuse him, Magnus knew. When they were all kids and he was the littlest, Carlos used to carry him around on his shoulders. They'd always been close.

Carlos arrived with a bottle of wine, his hair wet, in a clean shirt. One that Chris would have washed. It had the Garcia smell, the smell of childhood, when Magnus used to inherit the Garcia boys' clothes. There was a red nick on his chin where he'd mown into his fierce black stubble. He'd made an effort, Magnus could tell. While Kitty poured them all a glass of wine, Magnus started the tape. A little friendly spat of jazz filled the room, as if they'd walked into a bar. By the time she put the big pot on the table Patsy Cline was singing, Carlos's favourite, and everything felt more natural.

'If this is music for ordinary lives,' Kitty said, 'I want to put in an order for each day of the week.' She lifted up the lid of the pot with a flourish and steam rushed out. Lamb with white beans. She'd told Magnus she was going to make a dish to warm the heart.

After they were onto the second bottle of wine, and Tom Waits – Kitty told them a funny story about seeing him perform in London – Magnus knew it was going to be OK. The food had made them all feel better. He could see that Kitty would be a good teacher – she made people join in. Carlos was sitting the way he'd seen him sit a thousand times at this table, with his legs and arms crossed and his whole body shaking as he laughed. The Four Tops started up and they reminisced about rock festivals. Kitty did a Wild Thing demonstration, a bit pissed, showing off.

Magnus took his plate to the sink and told them he was going to jam at his friend Ben's house now and would probably stay the night.

'But you haven't had any chocolate cake!' Kitty looked upset.

'I'll have it for breakfast.' He started putting on his backpack. Kitty had a right to a good time but he hated watching old people dance. He edged to the door. 'Thanks a lot, Kitty.' They both stared at him, but he didn't relent. Everybody knew that on Saturday night you had to be with your friends or you got depressed. 'There's still some really good stuff to come,' he said. Some Spanish guitar, mellow after-dinner music. It was an eighty-minute tape.

'Look,' Kitty said to Carlos a little desperately, 'don't feel you have to stay.' She started to clear away the dishes. 'It can be hard being with other people. I know what you're going through.'

'You do?' Carlos looked shocked.

'Bye,' Magnus called as he shut the door behind him. There was Leonard Cohen to finish up. Leonard always sent that generation wild.

Rain started beating on the tin roof, so loud they could hardly hear the courtly Andalusian ripples as they drank their coffee. Carlos laid his head back on the couch, closed his eyes and stretched out his legs. All over Spain she'd seen profiles like this, fine aquiline nose, receding curling hair, small pointed chin with a sad little bristling fold beneath it. His hands were neat and square, hairy-backed, with a wedding ring.

In a little while I'll stoke the fire and start reading my book if I want to, Kitty thought. She felt sleepy and at ease. Why? *There was no need to talk.* How long since she'd sat with someone in a room without speaking? She was getting used to silence here. What were these familiar doleful chords? *Bird on the wire* . . . Oh Magnus. The melancholy was almost orgasmic. She and Carlos turned and laughed at one another.

'D'you think Magnus knows what he's doing?'

'You bet he does.'

They were equally proud of him. They put their cups down on the floor at the same time.

Suddenly Carlos looked at her. 'You've got really beautiful skin,' he said, as if he could no longer keep it to himself. She felt the purity of his good nature rising like an evanescence beside her.

'All those years without sun.' Her eyes fell on the cover of the tape lying beside the stereo. *Music for Carlos* was written in Texta on the spine. Why did Magnus love this funny little guy? Why did he trust him? Their eyes met.

Eighty minutes. That was all that it took.

He stood in the bedroom doorway, water dripping off his parka, Winnie butting against his legs.

Kitty hardly moved when she slept, a kid-sized parcel deep in his parents' bed. Winnie pattered over to her and licked her face.

A little yelp from the pillow. 'Magnus! What's the time?'

'Dunno. Maybe eight.'

'But it's dark outside.' She'd left the curtains undrawn. 'Usually the birds wake me.'

'It's been pissing down. There's going to be a storm.'

'Why didn't you wait till it was over?'

'I always come home first thing when I sleep at someone's place. I'm gonna have a shower.'

He lost track of time under the hot water. He especially didn't want to hang around the Lesters' this morning because he didn't want to see Brooke. Last night an amazing thing had happened and he had to get his head around it. Brooke came home a little high from a party and as she went past him in the kitchen doorway she kissed him hard on the lips, her body right up against his, and ran off laughing to bed. He hadn't slept all night. He couldn't bear to see her now in case she patronised him.

An iron-gray luminescence filled the house. Kitty came into the kitchen wrapped in Toni's old blue kimono, looking like his mother did sometimes, private, distant, pale and young. She stood looking out the big window in silence. Old Jacob and Carlos were pitching back and forward as if gearing up for a fight. The wind-chimes were going frantic. Somewhere a tinnie was rolling on gravel. Winnie whimpered at his ankles.

Carlos suddenly rushed past the window. In he burst with the cold air, full of words about battening down, turning off appliances, keeping away from windows. Bring in some wood, mate, he said to Magnus. Heavy drops started up like a spray of pebbles on the roof, thunder growled. Carlos's eyes flashed warmth at both of them. 'I gotta check the horses.' He ran off, as fast as a man in solid middle-age can run.

Rain crashed on the roof and doused the windows like ocean waves. Lightning turned on and off. Winnie cowered in the bathroom. The music from Magnus's room cut out. The clocks jammed. It was too dark even to read. They roamed separately from room to room, staring out the windows.

Late that night, in the post-storm quiet, Magnus, in bed, thought he heard footsteps on the verandah. Winnie's ears twitched but she didn't bark. He could swear there was a soft knock on the window of the front bedroom, the discreet scrape of a sash. Then the quiet thud of footsteps retreating.

The phone rang. Magnus ran out to answer it and carried the phone back to bed.

'Were you asleep?'

'No. What's the time where you are?'

'Never mind. I have to phone when I can. How's it going with Kitty?'

A conviction suddenly broke over him. 'I think Kitty and Carlos are fucking.'

'What! Now?'

'No, last night when I was at Ben's.'

'How do you feel about it?'

'Weird. Like it's incest or something.'

'Except it isn't.'

'I guess it's the shock. That people can . . .'

'What?'

'Move on.'

Maya was silent.

'Anyway it kind of leaves me free. They can look after each other.'

'Free for what?'

After a moment Magnus said hoarsely: 'Would you kiss someone you thought was repellent?'

'That depends.'

'On what?'

'Whether or not you have to.'

'They better be careful,' she said, before she hung up. 'Or the whole of fuckin' Warton'll know.'

Kitty walked and walked, further than ever before. She walked to the far corners of the town, to every point of the compass.

To the silos, the hospital, the flat scrubby outlands where the Brethren had built their windowless meeting hall and their bare ranch-style houses. To the swampy parts near the river with the few desolate Aboriginal cottages, the underclass that nobody talked about. She was aware of layers and layers here that would take years to fathom.

She walked out of restlessness when she couldn't be with Carlos. To keep her passion in check, her expectations from blooming. Sometimes Winnie was too tired to go with her. Her whole body felt toned, every cell aerated.

Willy Wagtails whizzed past her at calf level. The breeze embraced her face. 'Hi, how're you going?' a woman said as she passed. Everybody said hello. She smiled at little kids playing on the wide gravel kerbs and they smiled back, unafraid.

It broke upon her, the magic of the place, spreading itself around her, its spaciousness and slowness. The sky met the paddocks behind a delicate line of windblown trees. There was an edge of sadness to every vista, like the landscapes in great paintings.

She'd had affairs in London, Paris, on the trans-Siberian train, the Greek islands. Even in Birmingham once. But Warton! City of Love?

One day she came upon a little wooden house out near the silos and stood staring at it for several minutes. She read the hand-painted sign swinging over the verandah: 'Isolation'. It was all she could do not to open the gate and make her way up the path. It drew her in, like a gate at the end of the world. A stooped, white-haired man shuffled out to a line and pegged up a pair of underpants. His hands shook, the underpants were baggy from perished elastic. This was prying: she made herself walk on. The wind was sharp out there, a barren wasteland with scrappy trees.

Sometimes with a trick of her eye that she'd learnt in Europe, she had a flash of the streets as they were, a hundred or more years ago. The past wasn't far away. She saw herself in a bonnet, rolling into town on the back of a bullock dray. With a brood of kids, a semi-arranged marriage and years of hard drudge ahead of her. A happier life than the one she'd had.

If she taught at the school, she would focus on Warton, make every element of it come alive. The narrative of a town, history, ecology, sociology: she'd treat it as a microcosm of Australia. The students would never forget what it meant to come from here.

There'd been classes that she had turned around. Energy spreads through a school . . . she might introduce herself to the Warton headmaster.

No, Kitty! she told herself. No plans! Visions, plans had been her undoing.

Last night she'd said to Carlos: 'Most of these internet romances come unstuck.'

He shook his head. 'You don't know Chris when she makes up her mind.'

Twenty happy years and two kids. Jordan. Jordie can speak, Carlos told her, he just can't see the point. After Jordan had some experience at the meatworks, Carlos was going to take him into the workshop, train him up so he could be independent.

Asperger's, she'd bet, there was a programme . . . *leave it, Kitty!*

If Chris came back, she thought, I wouldn't have a chance. It wouldn't be the first marriage she'd helped.

The town at night! The brilliant stars, the scattering moon, the cold fragrant air . . . She set off each night after dinner. People went to bed early here. Already some houses were in darkness, the town seemed to disappear. It was easy to misjudge the length of the roads and she took note of landmarks so she could find her way home. The air was full of the static of crickets, the croak of frogs, now and then the distant rumble of road trains. She walked towards the few lights on Cannon Street. The Lucky was still open, one light high above the counter in the vast darkness of its interior. A man was leaning over the counter talking to a waitress as she wrapped his hamburger. Pure Hopper.

Most of her life with Carlos was in the daytime. Sometimes Carlos stayed at home until she returned from driving Magnus to school. They drank coffee outside if there was sun. Or he came back for lunch, something light and spicy she had dreamed up for him, which always turned out to be exactly what he felt like. Saturday nights were theirs, when the three boys went out. Always, any time they were alone, they ended up in the De Jongs' big shadowy parental bed.

Why did they feel they had to be secret? Carlos was a little ashamed at how quickly he'd found love again. It would upset the boys. He still couldn't believe this had happened to him. And what would Jacob and Toni think? Their boy's appointed guardian gets off with the man next door. Who knew what twinge of jealousy Jacob might feel. He had discovered Carlos first! Years ago he understood how unique, how simpatico Carlos was. Once more, she was following in his steps.

If Carlos hadn't seen her since morning he'd knock late on the bedroom window to squeeze her breasts and kiss her goodnight.

One night he didn't come and she went out to find him. He was there, under the pine trees, waiting for her. They pressed together against one of the great rough trunks, Carlos's army coat opened around them. There was a thrill to it, the secret life.

Daily she gave up a bit more of the need to be a performer. It got in the way, it prevented them from going further. She had to be naked and braver. She started to tell Carlos this but he wouldn't hear a word against her, not even from herself.

13

Balcony

Jacob woke to see Toni fully dressed, placing folded underwear into a carry bag.

'Are you going to tell me where you're going?'

'To a Buddhist retreat. In the country.' She put a brochure
on his chest. 'It's for two weeks, but I'll take the phone
with me. I can always come back if I'm needed.' Her voice
was a calm, deliberate monotone. She sounded Buddhist
already.

The pamphlet was blue with a white lotus on the cover.
There was a misty photograph of an old ivy-covered house.
'*Thirty kilometres from Melbourne, tranquil, secluded, with fantastic
birdlife and radiant sunsets,*' he read out. '*Beautiful vegetarian food.*'
Purification came at a price, he noted, but when he looked up
at Toni he decided not to mention it. *If I'm needed* . . . as once

she always was. It was worse for her, he thought suddenly. When had he last seen her smile?

'Spiritual tourism.' He spoke lightly. 'Well, it doesn't look as if we'll be doing any other sort of travelling.'

'The truth is, Jacob, I can't stand another day waiting in this house. I never stop thinking about Maya.' Last night beside him she spoke into the dark. Should they have gone, years ago, to live in the city? Maya was an outsider in Warton, as in truth, they were. Was their life a sort of lie? Warton had provided an *idyllic* childhood, he'd said firmly. This was always their way. When one went down, the other rallied, became strong.

Toni picked up her bag. She hesitated. 'It might be good for us to be apart for a while.'

'D'you think so?' A little squirm of what – excitement? apprehension? – started up deep in his guts.

'Cecile will look after you,' Toni said, without irony as far as he could see. She bent down to kiss him, her lips warm on his. Her thick hair brushed across his face, as it always did.

'I think Maya is with her boss, Jacob,' she said from the door. 'See if you can find any leads.'

He felt as if he'd been cut free from a twin, a shadow, a mother he had to report to. He could sense the space around him, hear the silence. He stood under the shower and wondered if this was how he used to feel, before Toni.

Cecile was in the kitchen when he came downstairs. He stopped mid-step, hardly believing his eyes. Since the night of the massage he'd only spotted her at odd times, rushing in or out, like a delicate bat in her dark, strangely chic proletarian clothes. Sometimes it was just the bang of the front door closing that told them she'd been home, that she must have returned very late and slept a few hours in her bed. But here she was in a beam of morning light, standing at the kitchen bench reading yesterday's *Age* and eating rice porridge.

'Classic executive eating habits,' Jacob called out. How many years ago did he adopt that jocular tone? The tone of a teacher, a father.

'Hi, Jacob.' Her glasses glinted up at him as she smiled. Why was the sight of her always so reassuring? 'Hey, your foot's better!'

'Almost better,' he agreed. He stood at the end of the bench. 'What's keeping you so busy?'

She was doing a lot of overtime, she said, so she could have a couple of weeks off to get on with her own project. Every spare moment was spent working on the script.

'*The Prodigal?*'

'You remember!'

He reached over and poured himself a cup of tea from the little fat iron pot in front of her. 'How's it going?'

'Slowly.' She sighed. 'It's about being Chinese in Australia. Dieter wants to turn it into a road movie documenting every Chinese restaurant around the continent. He thinks he could probably get funding.'

'And you?' He realised he smiled when he looked at her. What was the expression? She was *light on the eye.*

'Whenever I think of it, for some reason an immense weariness comes over me.'

'I know the feeling.'

But already she'd taken her glasses off and was folding the newspaper. 'I must go, Jacob. We'll talk some more another time.'

'Toni's off at some Buddhist outfit for a couple of weeks,' he called after her as she rushed to the door. 'So I'm holding the fort.' She kept on tugging at her boots.

'If that's OK with you,' he added, suddenly apprehensive.

'Of course it is.' She grabbed her backpack, smiled at him and left.

Her smile always surprised him, so warm and sudden, in someone so self-possessed.

He poured himself another cup of tea. *We'll talk some more.* Was this out of kindness? Or was it an acknowledgement that they had things to say? Some conversations that didn't bore him to death, he found himself thinking.

Part of him had died in Warton, or gone into a sleep so deep that he'd forgotten what it was to be energised. Moods of restlessness or despondency could always be traced back to ego, lust, the greed that was the source of Western discontent. According to Hindu philosophy, he was living out his Householder stage and must submit to its responsibilities.

Beneath the surface of his life lay a substructure of belief, long neglected but never quite forgotten, like the music from adolescence, an ideology made up of bits of Eastern religions and the theories of his youth. A spiritual quest that he still turned to for consolation, but which he no longer believed had the power to change the world. It contained the secret hope that through the simple life you become enlightened. That something numinous was waiting at the end of the road.

Gradually he'd stopped thinking of himself as a revolutionary in exile. The revolution hadn't happened, instead there was *economic rationalism.* The movement he belonged to, so careless and playful and ragged, had barely lasted ten years. Its gurus were discredited. A gear-change in history had swallowed it up.

One night as he sat at his desk in the shed marking Year 10 essays, he wrote: *He was just one of the world's millions of poets who stay silent.*

A few months ago, Magnus had asked him: 'How old are you?'

'Forty-eight.'

'You don't have much time left, do you?'

'Time for what, my boy!'

'You know what I mean.'

For all his dreaminess, Magnus could display a surprisingly practical streak.

How beautiful this house was. Its elegance grew on you. The bareness was soothing, it matched the austerity of his mood. At this hour, the light pouring through the glass wall of the courtyard filled every corner of the room. A house of glass, he thought, an airy leafspace that enclosed him. A house with its sleeves rolled up, its decks cleared, ready for work. As alluring to him as a loft in New York, a studio in Paris.

Upstairs he shaved and slicked back his hair, searched out a clean black T-shirt to wear under his leather jacket. It seemed like a long time since he had really looked at himself in a mirror. His face was paler than it had been in Warton, and there was a new, sad puffiness under his eyes. He wasn't fat but he was amazed to see in old photos how much more slender he used to be. Sometime in the past few weeks he'd crossed a line, he thought. He could never again be taken for a man younger than his age.

He liked being alone. His thoughts were sharper.

As he opened the front door he felt a pang of sadness, as if, by getting on with their lives, he and Toni were moving further away from Maya.

Who knows? he thought, tucking the key under the little Buddha, perhaps she needed us to change.

★

He saw the spot of light pulsing like an eye in the shadows as soon as he came in. Cecile's laptop, left sleeping all day by itself on her desk: he hadn't noticed it in the light. It was late afternoon, he was about to pour himself a glass of red and read his newspaper, and then, before he thought about it, he was opening the laptop lid.

An image filled the screen that he recognised, of the sulky young Chinese girl sitting by a grilled window. Cecile's sister, Clarice, in Kuala Lumpur. He scrolled down. All the images were of Clarice. Some were old photos out of an album, Clarice as toddler with bowl haircut, Clarice as schoolgirl in white socks and sailor collar. Clarice as teenager, her hair crinkly from plaits, talking to a parakeet on her finger. Clarice nearly grown-up, in posed shots, legs too thin in high heels, torso too slight in a bikini. He scrolled down to the end. Clarice posing at the top of a set of steps. Wasn't that the Melbourne Town Hall? Clarice crouched by the fishpond, eye to eye with the Buddha. Model thin, her face blank, watching television in the conversation pit. Clarice had lived here for a while and she hadn't been happy. She must have gone back to KL.

Was Cecile compiling this for Clarice, or for herself? Was she in love with her half-sister? She was clearly obsessed by her. He scrolled back, looking for clues. The calculated intensity with which Clarice stared back at the camera began to chill him.

Suddenly he saw himself bent over, squinting, pressing the keys with large intrusive fingers. An old man peering at a young woman. A modern form of voyeurism, though that wasn't why he kept on looking. Clarice the girl left him cold. It was because of Cecile, because he wanted to understand her. Did he hope to catch a spark from her creative fire? All at once he was struck with a deep yearning for her. He shut the laptop with a click and turned away.

A shadow which had followed him all day crept up on him. *How old was Maya's boss?*

He poured himself a glass of wine. This evening he'd start phoning all the Flynns in the book. When people came home for dinner.

He caught sight of Dieter's silver film canister tucked behind the speakers and couldn't help smiling: exactly where you used to find it in one of those freewheeling shared households in the seventies. He opened it and sniffed the secret nostalgic aroma. Once it had been regarded as a holy weed, a short cut to revelation . . . Like a whisper in his ear he heard the words *Why not?* The merest pinch . . . he'd tell Dieter when he next saw him. With a smoothness that shocked him, he found himself sitting on the couch rolling a quite passable little number. He hadn't lost his touch, he told himself grimly.

On the balcony upstairs you looked down over the traffic passing in the street, and into the upper branches of the trees in the park opposite. Leaves on the evergreens swayed in lush, rustling armfuls. He'd come up here with his wine and his joint to enjoy a change of vista. The only access was through the French doors in Cecile's room, but he presumed the balcony wasn't private. He walked swiftly through her room without looking. No more prying! No more trying to work the poor girl out.

It was a bit like being on the top deck of a ship. He lit up, inhaled and was flooded with well-being. Inhaling again, he saw a sharp wind run in a wave towards him through the tops of the trees. It blew the smoke into his eyes and slammed the door behind him and when he turned he saw there was no handle on the door. He threw the butt down into the fishpond and tried to fit his little finger into the hole where the handle used to be. He ran his nails down the edges of the doors. He looked around for a stick, a piece of wire that he could insert in the lock, but the balcony was without furniture, a bare slab of concrete. He peered down over the iron balustrade and his eyes met those of little old Mrs Chen next door, sweeping her spotless white-tiled porch. She was frowning up at him, one hand on her hip, the other on her broom.

'I know wha' you do!' she shouted. 'Drug addick!'

Jacob leapt back, an accused man. Guilt made him panic. He looked around for escape.

The walls on either side were wedged up against the neighbours' walls. If he held onto the top of the balustrade and let himself drop, he would land, heavily, onto the rocks and slime of the fishpond. He was only wearing socks: in the custom of the house he'd left his boots by the front door. His sprained foot was still tender. He'd certainly damage some part of himself, worst of all his spine. In boots and with two sound feet – or if he were younger and lighter – he might have had a crack at a Tarzan leap from the balustrade onto Mrs Chen's verandah roof. The roof might collapse. Mrs Chen, now gone inside, would call the police. She would tell them about 'the drugs'. She would sue him for damages, for giving her a heart attack.

If she came out again, would she listen to him while he begged her to find the key under the Buddha, let herself in and come upstairs to release him?

He could hail a passer-by. Though he'd have to make a quick judgement about the person. Otherwise it could be an invitation to ransack the place while he was stuck up here. But as far as he could see there was no one on the street or in the park opposite. The six o'clock traffic sped past.

He could break one of the glass doors, using his shoulder or fist. Then he would have to find an afterhours glazier to come straight out and secure Cecile's room before nightfall. He couldn't bear the thought of her coming home and finding the room strewn with splintered glass.

He decided to wait for Cecile to return. Take a chance that she wouldn't be too late. Wait it out until he couldn't bear it any more. Hadn't she implied that the job she was working on was nearly finished? He sat down on the concrete, his back against the wall and stretched out his long legs. It was in postures like this that the skeletons of explorers were often found, after they'd died of thirst and exposure . . .

He tried to remember if he'd scrolled right back to the beginning of the Clarice file. Had he put the canister back? He'd left his leather jacket slung over the back of her chair, incriminating evidence. What would Cecile think if, after discovering these intrusions, she came upstairs and saw his large shape crouched outside her bedroom door?

Windows lit up one after the other across the apartment blocks. Sunday night. Cars braked over and over at the lights on the corner. He heard the distant rumble of a tram, metal on metal. There was no sign of Mrs Chen, and no one out on the street to shout to. It reminded him of twilights when he was a little kid, looking down from the flat at the rush-hour traffic, the sinking feeling in the pit of his stomach that he called 'homesickness', even though he was at home.

How had he got himself into this situation? There was a hunger inside him that he couldn't even name. How undignified it was! A man of his age, who regarded himself as being, in his own way, honourable. (He couldn't think of any man he knew who didn't think that of himself.) What would his family say if they saw him now?

He pictured them standing on the footpath opposite, pointing up at him, the kids bent double with laughter, Toni shaking her head. She always had been the more grown-up of the two of them.

This was how he'd watched them, night after night, year after year, from his desk in the shed. A family in dumb show, passing to and fro across the kitchen windows, lit up as they argued or snacked or talked on the phone. Leaves from the vines over the terrace framed the scene: they looked as natural and self-centred as animals prowling in their lair.

Once, after one of his annual declarations that he was giving up cigarettes, he was standing at the shed door smoking, when suddenly a loud knocking started up on the glass of the kitchen window and he saw his children frowning and shaking their fists at him. Even Magnus, who generally minded his own business. For a moment he couldn't move, gripped by shame and panic. Then they burst out laughing and disappeared.

He cut himself off from family life with his desire to create. He used to toil in his shed all during the long summer breaks, trying to write screenplays. One hot evening when he was at his desk, his plastic fan whirring, Maya burst in, panting, her face alight. She was in the middle of one of the wild, terrifying games the kids used to play with the Garcia boys in the dark. She'd come to him for refuge. For a few minutes she stood beside him, her elbow on his shoulder, watching him type. Her breath on his cheek was warm and sweet like the scent of the long dry summer grasses and he didn't turn or speak, so as not to break the effortless bond between them. She took a sip of water from his glass, tapped a farewell on his arm and ran off again into the night.

He could still feel the confiding touch of her fingers and he groaned aloud. He hadn't been able to protect her. In this, the most primary of responsibilities, he had failed.

Always looking through windows. Arlene's boy, peering through the chink in the curtains. At the Garcias' millennium party, a few long months ago, he slipped outside to smoke a cigarette. His last for the old century, he'd told Toni, though it was well past midnight by then, the older guests had gone home. The hot lounge room was empty except for Magnus, absorbed in playing Carlos's old LPs.

He stood on the porch and surveyed the street. The Garcias' verge was lined with cars, old bombs, utes, four-wheel drives. He could name the owner of each of them, even the history of purchase and maintenance of most of them. As he knew the history of the dent in the Garcias' brown striped roller door, and of the *Forbes Carpenter Real Estate* sign on the block opposite, which had been there for fifteen years. He stubbed out his cigarette and took a walk around the house, skirting Chris's strange white mildewed pit. For some reason it had always embarrassed him. The horses were awake, shying and snorting, taking off in little nervy spurts around the yard. There'd been fireworks at the showgrounds, and from time to time a spray of stars still broke out in a bang over the roofs of Warton. All the livestock in town would be awake. Through the arch of the pine trees he saw the shape of his own roof. He caught the echo of one of Winnie's mournful howls.

In the Garcias' backyard a group of very drunk young men and a few girls, Josh's friends, were standing around the barbecue, staggering and laughing, slapping each other with frozen steaks. They'd come back from the bash at the show-grounds, his own kids with them, Maya looking distant and bored. None of the social events on offer in Warton held interest for her any more. He couldn't see her now. Had she gone home?

He lurked in the shadows, looking into the kitchen. He could see Toni standing by the window, wearing a sarong, the fall of her hair on her bare brown shoulders, her strong arms crossed, a drink in one hand. Tom Gabbelich, the Phys Ed teacher, new last year to the school, was reaching out to top up her glass. Were they flirting?

The first time Tom met Toni, as a dinner guest at their place, he blurted out to her: 'You look like Elizabeth Hurley.'

(I don't think young Gabbo's got much between the ears, he said to Toni later when they were washing up.)

Suddenly he made out Maya's pale young face against the far wall, deep in observation of her mother. He was swept with relief that she was still at the party, that his family was starting the new era together. He couldn't quite read her expression. Toni, without trying to, without *wanting* to, somehow took the light in a room. Usually, he thought, it was the other way round, the mother kept her eye on the daughter.

They both watched as Toni, smiling at Gabbo, put her hand over her glass and shook her head.

It was nearly dark. If the sky wasn't so opaque he'd see the first stars. The tower blocks loomed, lit up festive as ships moored in a harbour. The tossing trees seemed like the only things alive on the street, he almost felt neighbourly with them. It was getting dangerously cold but he couldn't afford to think about that, or regret his jacket and his boots. The cold of the concrete slab seemed to spear through his buttocks and he sat on his hands for a while. He was locked up in a fresh-air prison.

He hadn't felt this bad about himself for many years. The grief over Nathalie Maguire had long gone, but the black hole, once known, always lurked ready to open up again before him and now, with Maya's defection, he knew he must take himself in hand. Focus on something, follow a train of thought or memory. To prevent madness a prisoner had to discipline the mind.

At least it isn't raining, he thought, and then the first sprinkles blew onto his face.

It was raining on the morning that he went to pick up Toni and drive down south to the commune. There would be no coming back, at least not to Perth, Toni warned him, Cy Fisher had a long memory. Who'd want to come back here anyway, he thought, as he crawled in thick traffic past the tatty warehouses and budget shops along Albany Highway. True to form, he was running late. That was because, when he was due to leave, he couldn't stop rubbing at the blu-tack left on the walls of his bedroom.

Beech peered around the door. 'Got cold feet?'

He kept on rubbing. He suspected it was a case of the Tolstoy factor and yet he couldn't stop.

'I don't blame you. You wouldn't catch me running off with a gangster's moll.' Beech advanced into the room, comfortably scratching his stomach.

'His wife, actually.'

Beech whistled. 'And you haven't even porked her.' Naturally that had been his first question.

'That's not what it's about.' Or was it? If it was the Tolstoy factor, then it meant that there was something he was avoiding. Deep down, all those years ago, he'd been afraid of becoming involved with Nathalie. After her death he made a pact with himself, that he'd never let another woman down.

'I wouldn't worry about the walls,' Beech was saying. 'This place'll be knocked down soon by some big crook developer. Probably her husband.'

Jacob picked up his kitbag, made a thumbs-up sign to Beech, and left. 'Rather you than me, old boy,' Beech called out after him. There would be the occasional letter, but they never saw each again.

Beech was the only person to know where he was going. He'd had to tell him when he bought his scrapyard VW for two hundred dollars. Beech himself, only in Perth to spend some time with his old, ailing parents, was going to stay at the rectory before he went back to London in a few days. He could probably manage to keep his mouth shut till then.

He'd warned Beech not to spend another night in this house. Fear was a virus. Now he was always looking over his shoulder.

Everything had been planned down to the last detail. Toni was to leave her house at ten, after Cy had left, without taking anything more than a shopping bag. At eleven he would pick her up at the train station in Armadale. By now she'd have left her car keys and jewellery and chequebook in the top drawer in the bedroom, with a signed note saying she relinquished all rights to her account. In the shopping bag was a change of underwear and a toothbrush and her housekeeping money for the week.

Timing was essential. The longer Toni stood around Armadale station, the more chance there was that she'd be seen.

She couldn't wait more than half an hour. On the two or three occasions that Toni had ever been significantly late Cy traced her within the hour. Their best chance of staying undetected was in the wilds down south, she said, because of Cy's nature phobia and general aversion to the country. But they couldn't afford to make any contact with banks, hospitals, families. They had to drop out of the known world.

He didn't know how it had got to this point. They had never even kissed, not so much as held hands. Each time they met she suggested another rendezvous the next week. Surely this only increased the danger, which was the reason she'd contacted him in the first place? But he always agreed to meet. He drove miles out to the backlands, to sandwich bars in industrial areas, a tacky Devonshire teahouse in the foothills, fish and chip shops overlooking bleak suburban coasts. Toni seemed to take pleasure in the unlikeliness of these places. She found them on the long drives she took when she wanted to be alone.

Their meetings quickly became a ritual, a secret part of each week, and then they became its focus, its romance.

Summer ended, autumn rain fell down greasy windows, they wore coats and blew their noses and left umbrellas hanging over plastic chairs. Each time they met she seemed more beautiful. He breathed in her perfume and tried to read the mood in her soft eyes. Once she came to meet him at a drop-in centre in an outer-suburban church hall, dressed in a long black coat like a Cossack's and knee-high tooled leather boots. She was on her way to another appointment. He could hardly look at her as they queued up at the urn for their tea, her pale winter face emerging from her fur collar, the little diamond flash on her hand. Like Anna Karenina, like Natasha . . . Sometimes she turned up in a duffle coat and beanie, but nothing could disguise her fineness, her radiance. Everybody looked at her. In spite of the danger, he was proud to be seen with her.

Afterwards the meetings seemed dreamlike, a sort of fairytale.

They talked of one thing only, the commune movement, the quiet revolution, the alternative society. What else did he have to offer but his ideals? He was nervily aware that he was nearly thirty with nothing to his name, back in the town he'd vowed to leave forever. Utopian fervour, pastoral dreams gave him power. They were all that saved him from despair. He believed that the whole of his moral and political education of the past decade had led him to this. All that was left to him now was to take the step. It was the great adventure, the last frontier. Forty years ago this energy would have been consumed in fighting Hitler's war: fifty years earlier he would have been a communist.

Toni learnt quickly. She was his first and only convert. One by one he lent her the books he'd bought in London, on Findhorn, subsistence living, folk medicine. She read them whenever Cy Fisher wasn't around and returned them the next time they met. Talk of monastic-style rituals, harmony with nature, mystical things, made her lower her eyes and slowly nod her head. She spoke very little about herself, but said she'd wanted a different way of life for a long time. They talked only of the future and gradually it became their future.

Communes were springing up all over the south, he told her. Groups of people raised the money for the land, or leased it from a struggling farmer, and then lived on the dole until they were self-sufficient. That was the goal. He thought of them as pioneers in a new way, an elite network that would eventually have its own schools, and bands and poetry, its own trading arrangements. He'd made contact with a couple he'd met in India, who were starting out on a piece of land in the forest on the south coast. It was all planned. There was work in the local timber industry so that after a few months they could buy materials to build their houses and put in a cash crop, nut trees or avocados. They'd called the commune 'Karma'. Even he had to grin when he told Toni this.

He caught himself talking to her in his mind all the time, which always happened when he was going to get involved with a girl. He wanted to tell her everything about himself. Who was she? It seemed amazing that she'd grown up at the same time as him in Perth and yet their paths had never crossed. He tried not to think of her in a carnal way. She was a married woman with movie-star looks – ten out of ten – way out of his class. He borrowed Arlene's car or Beech's VW for these appointments and, like her, always parked at least a street away.

They were sprung when the brother-in-law of Cy Fisher's sister Sabine walked into the roadhouse on the Great Eastern Highway where they were eating eggs and chips. 'Don't look around,' Toni hissed at Jacob, her head bent over her plate. 'It's René.' The young man made no sign that he'd seen her, paid for his petrol and left. But that was enough, Toni said. It was only a matter of time now.

'You've got to leave town as soon as possible. Tomorrow. *Please* Jacob.' He felt a stab of pleasure at her concern for him, her voice catching in her throat, her lovely brows knotted in a frown. She fixed her eyes on his.

'I want to come with you,' she said.

As he drove through the rain to Armadale, he could no longer avoid the thought which had lurked at the back of his mind for some time. That all along she'd been planning this, she'd been laying a trail in which to trap an unsuspecting man. Beautiful women always found a man to save them. They got men to do what they wanted. And she was desperate to be saved.

If he told her at the station that he'd changed his mind, would there still be time for her to catch the train back home, go to the top drawer, screw up the note, put her jewellery on again?

By now he was nearly half an hour late. Another minute and Toni would have left. He had pushed fate to teeter for a moment, to see which side it would fall. A minute could decide his future, could even mean life or death. By the time he reached Armadale his blood was thumping in his throat and his eyes had blurred. When he caught sight of her standing just inside the station entrance he was flooded with relief as if she had become his only friend in the world. He realised suddenly how tired he was of himself, how he could no longer face going on alone.

For the first half of the trip they did not speak. The VW's heater didn't work, the windscreen misted up and Toni sat shivering. She still smelt of perfume, of the city. The car had no radio or tape deck and shuddered violently if pushed past ninety ks. They sat stiff and cold and silent, checking behind them every few minutes. Without ceremony they had become a couple, making their bid for survival.

They turned inland, towards the wheat-belt, and the rain stopped. According to their plan, to put Cy off their scent, they didn't drive directly to 'Karma', but headed for a bay on a remote part of the south coast, to a beach house where Toni had once stayed as a child. It was owned by an old couple from her parents' church, the Richardsons, who couldn't often make the long trip there. At this time of the year the house would be empty and they could stay for a night or two. Toni said she knew the way. She had never forgotten that holiday.

It was understood between them, though neither said this, that before they started their great communal venture they needed some time alone. Were they committing themselves to it separately or as a couple? When he glanced at Toni she looked serious and self-contained. They knew nothing of each other in the everyday. Yet this commitment was, for the time being, final.

They stopped in Warton for petrol and for Toni to phone her mother. She was directed to a coin phone in the bar of the Federal Hotel. Nig answered, to her relief. She told him she was driving north to Broome for a long holiday and would be in touch when she came back. 'Right you are, lovey,' said Nig cheerfully. No questions. No hurt feelings. Year after year, in this way, they rang each other on birthdays. He was probably running late for bowls.

So much for Daddy's broken heart, she said as she sat on a barstool next to Jacob, but brighter nevertheless. They each ordered a pie and a beer.

The Federal was empty, apart from the barman, a surprisingly exotic man, slim and tanned with a head as bald and shining as Yul Brynner's and a manner so cool and ironic that he didn't even take a second look at Toni. It was a great brown dusty room, once grand, now cluttered with pool tables and coin-machines, reeking of cigarettes. They saw their faces in the tarnished mirror over the bar, small and smudged like newsprint. Did it stick out all over them, they wondered, that they were on the run? The beer went to their heads and for a moment they felt daring and glamorous like heroes in a movie, safe because heroes always won through in the end. Even the enigmatic barman, now reading the paper, seemed part of this, their great adventure.

They had to stop for a train that was crawling across the main road towards the silos with an interminable clanging of bells. A good scene for an outback thriller, he thought. The barrier lifted and they drove off without a backward glance. There was no hint or omen that it would be here, in this sleepy town, that their real future lay. (By that time the bald barman had gone, leaving no trace in the town's memory.)

As soon as they left Warton the land grew flatter, the sky larger. On one side was a low silver lake, its shoreline lapping around the ankles of dead trees. A road sign announced: *You are now entering the Great Southern.*

'The Great Southern what?' Jacob asked. Toni didn't answer and he saw she was asleep.

For a while he was alone with nothing for company but the sad pop-pop of insects hitting the windscreen and the disturbing little rattles and missed breaths of the car. The horizon rose up out of the flatness. They passed through a grove of trees he'd never seen before, the slender white trunks splashed with orange as if stained by gravel dust, their branches tapering into broccoli clusters of waving, gleaming leaves.

He became aware of a shadow lurking in the corner of his eye, a tracery in smoke-coloured pencil along the right-hand horizon, that as the miles passed, like a theme in music, grew ever more present, until there it was in full symphonic impact, a range of mountains towering above the plains. He slowed down to study the humps and turrets of its outline, sharp as a paper cut-out against the sky.

'The Stirlings,' Toni said, awake.

'I didn't know.' He meant he had no idea about the landscape of his own country. He'd trekked mountains in Nepal, crossed deserts in Afghanistan, jungles in Sri Lanka, but he'd never been past the hills around his home town. There'd been no bush holidays in his childhood, no picnics, no relatives on farms. Rural Australia never entered his consciousness. He wondered what the Aboriginals called this range.

And now it was as if they'd entered another zone, an airy land of space and sky, with silver lakes and long-grassed roadsides and plains in great clean sweeps shadowed by clouds as big as airships. Sheep were grazing right up to the foot of the mountains and a trembling line of birds hovered over the vast horizon, stretching and shrinking like the tail of a kite.

Something lifted in his spirits. It felt so far away. There was no other car on the road. The few houses they saw were small and lonely, fibro bungalows with a shed and water tank. One sat with its back turned, its tiny verandah facing the mountains. What would it be like growing up here, he thought, in this magical, Tolkienesque land?

There was a flock of parrots on the road ahead. Toni reached over to sound the horn and just in time they rose in a green cloud. But a wedgetail eagle, busy with something brown and fluffy on the tarmac, stared them down with eyes so vengeful that Jacob wound his window up and took a wide berth around it. The sun was sinking. Light speared under the clouds, and the roadside scrub glowed emerald.

'We've got to be on the lookout now.'

'Why?'

'Kangaroos.' She was an old hand compared to him.

They took a turnoff onto a gravel road. The VW began a valiant course of bumping and bucking. If it can just make it to the house, he prayed, in dread of having to expose his total lack of mechanical competence to this unknown woman. There were no houses anymore, no help if they broke down. Just acres of shining bush as far as the eye could see, the land as once it would have been. The mountains loomed huge, in the shape of a resting lion. They raced through bush-covered cuttings, ripe for ambush.

And then the road rose up, there was a lightness on the horizon, a flash of white desert hills far in the distance, the dunes of the coast. It was dusk now, the sky was a deep religious blue. They stopped to pee, leaving the doors open, the engine running for fear it wouldn't start again. He stood at the front of the car, Toni crouched at the back. He remembered hippie girls on his travels squatting in the dust beside him, hitching up their long skirts.

In the last light they bumped up a white track to the beach house. It stood remote, a dark shape on a headland overlooking unseen water. They stepped out into the great hollow murmur of the sea. A fumbling of matches in the wind, Toni crouched under the water tank, emerging triumphant. The spare key was still there on a stump, as it had been all those years ago.

Nature had found protection in this empty house from the storms of winter. Like a warning to keep out, a spider web fell onto Toni's face as soon as she opened the door, so that she stood gasping and swiping at sticky threads in her hair. Inside was pitch black, with the stale reek of mice. They shuffled in, feeling their way. They hadn't thought to bring a torch, and now as they stood in the kitchen, they realised they'd neglected the matter of food. The deep chill in the place seemed to be lying in wait for them. They struck matches and found candles on the kitchen bench. The light flickered over armchairs covered in sheets, drawn curtains, a Tilley lamp on a table, a kerosene fridge with its door ajar. They felt a primitive need for fire, to keep the devils out. There was a basket of kindling and newspapers beside the potbelly stove. They achieved a small blaze for half an hour. There was a woodpile at the back of the house, Toni said, but − her voice trailed − snakes could be hibernating there.

The house creaked in the wind, windows rattled, creatures scrabbled in the roof-beams. A bleak loneliness took them over so that they couldn't speak. What else did fate have up its sleeve for them? They knew too little of each other to offer comfort. They took a swig each from an old bottle of sherry and ate some stale digestive biscuits sealed in a tin in the mouse-riddled cupboards.

Beneath the green chenille cover of the Richardsons' bed, mice had made a nest in the hollow of the mattress. Toni screamed, Jacob quickly pulled the cover up again over the frenzy of scattered kapok. There remained the bunk-beds in the loft, left over from the young Richardsons' childhood. Zipped up to the chin in Jacob's sleeping bags, on separate narrow berths, they blew out the candle and hastened to fall asleep.

The town was ten kilometres away, along a gravel track that wound around the escarpment, past the bluffs and bays, the heave and sparkle of the Southern Ocean, the miles of white beaches where nobody went. It was no more than a handful of buildings scattered around an inlet, some modest houses, a fishermen's co-op, a general store with petrol pump. A caravan park overlooked the ocean, empty until summer. Surely Cy Fisher's long arm didn't extend this far. They bought what provisions were available, eggs and bacon, Weetbix, milk, chocolate, tins of baked beans. The newspapers were five days old. They fell on the chocolate as soon as they sat in the car.

The ocean was the dominating presence, the reason for everything here. From the first morning when he pulled back the living room curtains to the shock of it, the great turquoise bay spreading out below him, he was conscious of it, its moods and colours changing hour by hour. Across the water was a long headland that led out to the open sea. Beyond was the Antarctic. They used Doug Richardson's binoculars to see the headland's yellow cliffs lashed by cruel waves.

The Richardsons had built the house themselves out of concrete blocks. Outside it looked rough, rustic, amateur: inside it had all the trimmings of genteel housekeeping, old floral armchairs, crocheted runners, vases of everlastings, little machine-woven rugs strewn over the floors. Everything spoke of the old couple's rigour and industriousness. Polite instructions were written on a kitchen pad in an upright spidery script. *Note to Visitors! Firewood at back of house. Please replenish!* Biscuit tins with pictures of Highland dancers were labelled *First Aid* and *Sewing Kit*.

The bookshelves were a time warp, bestsellers from past generations, *A Town Like Alice, East of Eden, The Grapes of Wrath*, a whole series of cowboy tales in paper covers.

Nothing at all had changed, Toni said. She went from object to object with cries of recognition, as if she were still twelve years old.

On the bookshelves was a snap of the Richardsons, Doug and Rosemary in overalls, huge and craggy-faced as the Whitlams, standing over the foundations of this house brandishing their trowels. Good Christian people, Toni said, pillars of their church, with a grown-up family who'd all done well in life. When she was a kid she was rather frightened of them. But a few years ago Rosemary came walking towards her on St George's Terrace and, unlike others from her mother's circle, didn't purse her lips, or toss her head and look away, but greeted Toni warmly and asked her how she was and seemed genuinely pleased when Toni said that she was well. The Richardsons had always stood apart. They weren't interested in social life, but were loners who did everything together. They loved driving off to this bay at the bottom of the world.

One summer Beryl must have confided in Rosemary that they couldn't afford a holiday. Beryl would have been in one of her states. She must have trusted Rosemary a great deal to speak like this, without fear of losing face. Rosemary offered them the house.

Here, Toni explained, for a short time, the first and only time she could remember, her family was happy. Nig sat smoking and drinking beer, reading cowboy stories one after the other. He teased his women all the time about sharks and mice and snakes. Beryl didn't wear lipstick or set her hair, but slapped around in rubber thongs, bare-legged, showing her veins. At night they played Cheat in the light of the lamp, yelling and laughing and throwing down cards. They ate grapes on the verandah and spat their pips out into the bush. Something had melted between them all. Even Karen told her a disgusting joke from the upper bunk, and they lay chortling on their lumpy mattresses. They fell asleep listening to the sound of the waves. She had never felt so safe.

On the drive back, Beryl snapped at Nig and then, miles further on, apologised. Nig went silent. They all froze up again.

She often dreamt about this place, Toni said. She lost her reserve when she spoke of it, became warm and intense. He wanted to touch her.

They passed a third night separate in their sleeping bags, even though he'd poured them each a large glass of the Richardsons' sherry and suggested a game of Cheat, when he hated card games. He lay awake for ten minutes in a drunken rage. The wind whistled around the house and the sea pounded discouragingly.

The issue was palpable between them. It was a stalemate, a standoff. Their voices creaked in their throats, they could no longer talk naturally to one another. They were no closer than they had been eating pies in one of her roadhouses. If anything, they were growing further apart. What did he really know about her? She was so silent. What was he to her, some sort of sexless knight errant? Had he outgrown his use now?

Don't think I will automatically sleep with you, her silence seemed to say.

What makes you think I want to? he silently answered. Like all beautiful women, however disingenuous, at heart, he detected, she was vain.

They went for walks alone and came back hours later, their faces freshened and hopeful from the air. All day they went in and out, separately. Outside, stepping off the verandah, all was wild, ramshackle, vivid in the light. The dizzying play of sun and wind was like childhood.

Everything seemed to be in a perpetual state of motion. All along the limestone track to the bay pods snapped, crows called, the wind rustled in the peppermint trees. The sun glinted on the shot-silk surface of the sea as it shifted in invisible currents. The sky came right down into the bush, filled in all the gaps, and rose up, a wall of royal blue above the line of the olive green escarpment.

Clouds passed overhead as he stood on the beach, their shadows racing towards him, dimming everything for a moment and then releasing him into light. The sand squeaked under his feet, so white he was snowblind. Only he seemed to be in stasis.

Sometimes he struck off along weedy tracks where nobody went. Myriad birds chattered amongst the trees, like the occupants of a thousand miniature tenements. If he could turn the sound up he would be deafened. He sat on a fallen log. Dense bush crowded in on him. He felt watched by creatures he would never see.

He was a stranger here, a stranger to nature, and yet it seemed to accept him. He tried to listen to the voice of the wind as it ran across the trees, each gust a variation of a theme. What did it say? Something he could never decipher.

That evening the little niggle of rage started up again as he stalked home along the track. He was going to speak. He was going to have it out with her. One more night and they would drift past each other forever. All they had between them was a dream.

Toni was hanging out her towel on the line between two verandah poles. The bay lay before her at its loveliest, all pastel shimmer, the coastguard lights twinkling like diamonds. The air was luminescent gray. A giant yellow rim was rising up behind the escarpment.

Her long hair was wet and she was barefoot, in his sarong. She looked like a hippie or a gypsy, but in fact, he reflected bitterly, she was anything but.

He walked straight up to her.

'It's OK, Jacob,' she said. 'It really is.'

They sat down on the plastic chairs overlooking the ocean. He folded his hands on the rickety table.

'You have lovely hands,' she said, as if this was a matter of record.

One thing he'd learnt about women, they always knew who they did or didn't want to touch them.

Darkness was flowing in and at that moment they heard the hum of a motor. A pair of headlights came swerving up the track. They rushed into the house, locked the door, closed the curtains and spied through the gaps. The car wavered to a halt at the water tank, but left its headlights shining on the house. Luckily the VW was parked amongst the peppermint trees out the back.

'Dear?' they heard a woman's voice calling in the stillness, 'did we leave our towels out all this time?' In the car light they saw a big woman in a headscarf like the Queen's, standing at the driver's side, looking towards the house. Stiffly, a little stooped, she made her way around the car to the passenger's door. Inch by inch, a little old man emerged, and stood shaking, bent and helpless, gripping onto his wife. Toni gasped. 'Something terrible's happened to Doug.'

She turned to Jacob. 'I can't face them,' she whispered.

'It'll take them a while to get to the door,' he said, watching. Now Rosemary was propping Doug's back against the car as he fumbled with his fly. The poor old guy must have been at bursting point. Rosemary bent down to help him.

They rushed around collecting their possessions. They had so little that there was even time to sweep the crumbs off the bench and shove their cups and plates back into the cupboard. He tipped apples out of a bowl into a sleeping bag, Toni threw the dust sheets back over the chairs. Just as they were letting themselves out onto the verandah, they heard the feeble scrabble of the key in the front door. Stooped over their bundles, they ran around the other side of the house.

Now there was nowhere else to go but 'Karma'. They drove tensely, on kangaroo watch. All they could see was the stretch of gravel ahead in the VW's weak lights. Something about the quality of silence made him aware that Toni was crying. He didn't dare look at her but put one hand for a moment on her knee. That made her burst out.

'It was terrible not to have gone to help them. Those poor old good people. Did you see Doug's shaking hands?'

'They must have been confident they could cope or they wouldn't have come.'

'I feel like a thief. I feel like I stole from them.'

'We hardly used anything except a bit of kerosene. We replaced the firewood. They won't even know.' He suddenly remembered the sherry.

'Of course they will! What about the towel? Bit by bit they'll discover little things. Our ashes are still warm. They'll smell my shampoo. We stole their privacy. They'll never feel secure there again.'

'Old people don't have much of a sense of smell,' he said, trying to joke. He couldn't help feeling a secret exultation that she trusted him enough to show herself to him at last. She sobbed bitterly, her cheeks wet with tears.

'That makes it worse! We took advantage of their age.'

'Toni, they gave us shelter and I'm grateful to them. Does a few days' squatting in a house that's hardly used really matter?' He was surprised to see what a stern moralist she was. Years of travelling, camping in other people's houses, had made him casual about possession, he supposed.

'I'm always running away from things,' she said drearily, blowing her nose. 'I want to be honourable. I want to be *good*.'

He drove into a track leading off the road into the bush and pulled up in the dark. They listened to the ticking silence for a moment as the moonlight found its way into the car and then at last, like a pair of teenagers they lowered their seat backs and wound their legs and arms together. Orphans, fugitives, outsiders in a landscape: already the pattern of their future life was set.

After the rain a low sharp wind had started up that blew across the balcony straight onto his body in its sodden clothes. He sat against the wall with his arms around his knees, trying to control spasms of shivers. What time was it? The light flickered so busily through the tossing trees that he couldn't read the face of his watch. It must be ten o'clock at least. He ought to get up, stamp his feet, wave his arms around, but he was too stiff to take any action at all.

He hadn't thought about this journey for many years. He used to tell it as a comic story from the crazy seventies. Funny, what remained most vivid in his memory now was the glimpse in the twilight of the old couple at their car, Rosemary helping Doug with his fly.

Soon, like old Doug, he wouldn't be able to wait any more, he was going to have to pollute the fishpond. It was that or desecrate Mrs Chen's porch. Was it possible to die of exposure on a Melbourne balcony?

He dozed and woke to hear voices passing in the street, talking in a foreign language. '*Um-ber-to!*' someone called, plaintive and musical. Perhaps he'd caught pneumonia and was delirious. If he died, one of the things he'd miss would be the soft voices calling out in Fellini movies.

The light came on in the bedroom behind him.

He started to gather up his legs but when he tried to stand he fell forward. He slowly turned himself around and looked through the glass door on his hands and knees.

Cecile was putting one arm into the sleeve of a cardigan and then the other arm. It was the tiny purple cardigan he liked, the one that subtly mocked home-knitted cardigans. She was doing up the buttons like a little girl, slowly, her head bowed.

It was clear to him now that such simple, ordered movements came from strength of mind. She was fending off sadness. Why hadn't he seen before how sad she was? *The heart within me burns.* Who said that? His thoughts were looping, as if he had gone crazy. All his being was waiting to be recognised by this marvellous girl. With his last strength he reared up like Frankenstein and knocked on the glass door. Her face coming towards him was at once familiar and yet changed, as if he'd been away for many years. Oh no, not this, he thought.

He felt her fingers, fine as chicken bones, grasping the purple slabs of his hands.

After he'd stood for a while under hot stinging water and put on clean clothes, he went to find her. It was nearly midnight but she was sitting at her laptop. She swivelled around to smile at him.

'How do you feel?'

'Extremely humble.'

'That handle! I should have warned you. Someone tried to break in once and I never had it fixed.'

'I wasn't snooping in your room, by the way.' When she stood up, he'd quietly reclaim his jacket from the back of her chair.

'Of course not.'

'I went out there to have a smoke and see the view.' He felt wild and simple, a man come in from the desert. Past fear, past hope.

She sat studying him with full, thoughtful attentiveness. 'Are you hungry, Jacob?'

243

'I need a drink, first of all.'

'There's a little late-night place around the corner where you can get a good soup and a glass of red wine. How does that sound to you?'

He wanted to tell her that nothing much mattered except to be with her, but he couldn't find the words.

14

Karma

If happiness was so simple, so natural, how come it was so hard to achieve? She thought this as she sat cross-legged in the meditation hall, trying to concentrate on her breathing. For thousands of years people had been striving to follow this path. A whole religion had been built on this belief in inner peace, millions of lives devoted to its disciplines. All this, the house, the monks and nuns, the humble students, the chants and talks, was a product of a vast ancient project to teach humans how to be happy.

For some years now Toni had thought that she'd be 'good at' Buddhism, a natural. She had a little book of the Dalai Lama's sayings which she often referred to, and after reading a page or two she always felt more serene. She'd allowed herself the fantasy that the Buddha was waiting for her. Each time she passed the chubby little statue in Cecile's courtyard she smiled at him as if they had a private understanding. Sooner or later, she thought, she would be called.

In her current state of uncertainty and worry, the sight of Kesang's plain clean face gleaming at her with loving kindness was enough to make her want to throw herself into the Buddha's arms.

But now that she was here, dressed in the gray coarse-woven cotton of the novice, under a rule of silence, she was discovering that far from being comforting and maternal, the Buddha's embrace was hard-edged and austere. She saw that years of gruelling discipline and practice lay ahead of her if she were ever to still her racing mind. Gongs rang, instructions were given, candles lit, and there she was, left stranded in her own unquiet heart. The more she tried to leave the world behind, the more it seemed to crowd in on her.

Without words, did you see more? Or was it the clarity of the air? In the first meditation session in the hall, as she closed her eyes and mindfully breathed in and out, she was startled by a technicolour, large-screen vision of Maya, Maya as a little, wild, big-toothed, tangle-haired girl, galloping towards her through the trees, in the days when her greatest wish was to be a horse. Her face loomed into close up, until she saw the pale skin still faintly pitted here and there from her teenage years, like scars, like sensitivity.

While the other novices breathed softly around her, lost in their devotions, Toni was consumed with longing for her, so acute that she could have groaned out loud. Nobody knew you like your girl-child, your stony watch-dog. Your fellow female. The one who always brought you to account. Right from Maya's birth this had been a secret tension in the household.

★

The ashram sat on the crest of an escarpment, an old stone mansion built in the twenties as a country retreat for a wealthy family. One of the heirs had endowed it to the Centre. Now temple bells and gongs echoed through the wide hallways, robed figures glided up and down the grand wooden staircase, chanting lifted the cold air. The rooms had been cleared of carpets, paintings and furniture, the floorboards stripped and polished, the walls painted white. The old stables across the courtyard had been converted into sleeping cells.

Nobody knew each other's names. There were two male novices and six women, whose soft worn faces reminded her of those women in Warton who filled the congregations in the churches, made the cakes for the stalls, ran the charity drives. Each night as she lay on her canvas futon, she heard their solitary rustlings and sighs, women on their own, released at last from looking after everyone.

The robes made all their figures look bulky. They walked slowly, like brides or girls in evening gowns. Toni wore a sweater underneath. Some mornings they rose to mist winding itself around the courtyard and the valley was obscured. At night a modest fire barely warmed the hall while they sat cross-legged, listening to the evening talk. She was always a little cold.

There wasn't a mirror in the bathroom, or anywhere in the house. The fall of her hair on her shoulders was probably inappropriate: she half-expected to be told to pin it back.

Meals were served at a refectory table in the grand old kitchen. Two tall young nuns, their bare heads revealing swan-like necks and dainty ears, their beetroot robes unable to conceal a loose-limbed slenderness, were the cooks for the ashram. Pearly-faced, serene, they dished out porridge in the mornings, thin yellow dhal and vegetables and rice at other meals. The servings were not large and needed more salt. Toni was always a little hungry. The novices didn't look at one another as they ate, but attempted to concentrate, as instructed, on who had grown and made the food and the interdependence of all things.

At six in the morning when the meditation gong sounded, she had an impulse to pull her thin white quilt over her head, like a naughty girl at boarding school.

Wherever it was that Maya phoned Magnus from, she wasn't happy.

Breathe in the pain of a specific person, they were instructed at morning meditation. Toni saw Maya's bowed head. *Breathe out the white cool light of compassion*. Toni breathed in and out, in and out, but still Maya's head did not lift.

Extend your practice to all who are suffering in the world. Maya pushed Lincoln around in his chair. He knows everything, Maya said. He's full of feelings. She sent him drawings of horses. He used to cry for her if it had been too long since he had seen her.

One night in her cell, when everyone else was asleep, she phoned Magnus and in a low rapid voice instructed him to tell Maya what she had omitted to say in every other call. That they loved her and nothing else mattered. That if she needed money she must let Magnus know.

The youngest woman amongst the novices was in her early thirties, short and buxom with a distorted walk. There was something wrong with her hips, she had to sit in a chair in the Hall. She had soft dark troubled eyes and black curling hair. Italian perhaps, or Greek or Maltese. She was very conscientious in her devotions. Her affliction burdened her,

Toni thought, she was trying to get relief. One day during walking meditation, as the girl made her torturous, lurching way on the bush track that ran along the top of the escarpment, Toni, coming from the opposite direction, broke the rules and looked her in the eyes, smiling at her. The girl, surprised, smiled back. The sweet, obliging smile of a strictly-brought-up girl in a patriarchial household. Suddenly she understood that she was drawn to this young woman because she reminded her of Felice. Sweet Felice, her long-lost sister-in-law.

She'd thought it was quiet in Warton, but not compared to this. There were no other buildings nearby, no cows or chooks or dogs, no road. The meditation pathway looped through the bush and turned back on itself. Far below a small road snaked through the valley, with a scattering of houses beside it. One afternoon she saw an orange schoolbus pull up and five tiny kids swarmed out and ran off into separate houses. She felt a longing to go down there, to be amongst the life of children and houses.

Karma. A word once so familiar that it had its own meaning for her and Jacob now, as a sort of joke, a joke against themselves. Here it was again, the subject of an evening talk from a big-shouldered, bespectacled Australian monk in his mid-thirties, delivered in the matter-of-fact, boyish way of a sports teacher. *If you're unhappy or in a poor situation, it's due to actions you yourself have committed in the past, including past lifetimes.*

The only escape from this endless cycle was mindfulness. She breathed in, she breathed out.

★

One night she could not sleep. As she lay listening to the snores of the other novices she saw light falling soft and sparkling through a roof of leaf shadow into a forest clearing, as if she were standing there. She saw the two old railway carriages parked on blocks parallel to each other, and between them the cooking fire. There was the big iron pot hanging from its tripod, the battered kettle on the embers inside the ring of blackened stones. She saw the stumps for seats arranged around the fire in their companionable circle, and then the wider circle around the clearing, the great soaring trunks of the tinglewood trees. A line of tatty T-shirts and jeans was strung between the two nearest trees and a canvas bag, hoisted by a rope and pulley, was hanging from the lowest branch. They called this the shower tree. Prem had invented the pulley. Now she could see the white naked bodies of the communards, Prem and Wanda and Jacob, gasping and bobbing under the precious gush of water, one after the other. After a shower, if the evening was mild, Prem and Wanda liked to stroll around for a while with the air on their skin, chatting, bending to stir the pot, hanging out their towels. She could still see in detail, as if the sight had shocked itself onto her retina, Wanda's deep-clefted, indented womanly flesh, Prem's neat muscly buttocks as he crouched to stoke the fire. She looked away when he stood up.

Jacob's turn at the shower tree was theatrical, baritone warblings, soap in a lather. She found a way of dousing herself with a bucket of hot water behind the carriage. She said she'd have a shower when summer came.

The trees were so high that the sun only started to light up the clearing at the end of the morning. If it was overcast, or raining, they walked around all day in twilight. At certain hours, between certain trees, the light penetrated in cathedral beams. The ground was strewn with leaves and nuts and fallen logs and tufts of bright green grass. Around the camp the ground was trodden into gray-black earth that quickly turned to mud.

From the moment they arrived, she realised that she was unprepared for the grubbiness and scrappiness, the dingy half-light. Prem and Wanda's greeting was so cool as to be offhand. Each morning she woke to darkness and shut her eyes again. She prayed that today she'd begin to like it. There was nothing else to do but to try to make it better, because there was nowhere else to go.

Prem and Wanda had been there for some months now and could give them the lowdown on the weather, the wildlife, the open suspicion and contempt of the locals. The lack of sunlight in the clearing was proving to be a problem for growing vegetables but soon they hoped to clear another acre at the northern end of the block. They counted on attracting followers to help with the felling and milling of the trees and the building of houses. Perhaps because the block was so far south, and the giant forests so daunting, up until now only Jacob and she had turned up. Prem and Wanda weren't from the west and had no contacts here. They'd come because they heard the land was cheap. Prem was from Melbourne. He worked in the family foundry before he dropped out. He had mechanical skills and was used to the bush. His whole family used to go camping together all around the peninsula.

Prem was small and wiry, snub-nosed with a wispy beard. He'd travelled for several years and ended up with a guru in northern India. That was where he and Wanda met. Wanda was American, and an old hand at communes. A long time ago she had been married to a businessman, but she ran away to San Francisco to join the flower kids. The block and ute and railway carriages had all been paid for by her marriage settlement. She reminisced about communal living in California after dinner as they passed around one of Prem's huge, home-grown joints. 'Sure, everybody balled each other all the time. There was no possessiveness. It was *wild*.'

Toni and Jacob slept on a mattress in the second carriage, which also served as the communal storehouse. They shared it with a happy company of country mice, who partied furiously all through the night. Jacob talked of traps but Wanda was horrified that he could even think of taking any living creature's life. At least the snakes were in hibernation now. As summer came on moths hatched in the sacks of rice and flour and lentils and beat against the windows to go out. If they tried to read in bed, the moths hit and sizzled against the kerosene lamp. There was no flywire if they opened the windows to the night air where the mosquitoes hovered, waiting to come in. In the end they daubed themselves with citronella oil and pulled the sheet right over their heads.

In spite of brotherly love, they had fallen into a natural alliance against the other two.

'Where did you meet them?' she whispered.

'On a houseboat in Kashmir. I have to admit we were all pretty stoned at the time.'

Prem and Wanda weren't bad people. It was just, she thought, they weren't her people. It was almost biochemical, the way kids in a playground chose or rejected each other. Meeting them, she knew at once deep down it was never going to work. Did they also whisper about her and Jacob in the other carriage? Somehow she thought they were too pure.

Above all was the worry about money. When they arrived at the commune they were down to their last twenty dollars. In the one-store town, all they could afford was a little petrol, soap and tampons, not even toothpaste or a newspaper or a bag of mixed lollies to console themselves. There was no question of credit. The woman behind the counter, Mrs Skinner, rang up their scanty purchases without speaking or looking at them. To her, Prem told them, they were the vanguard of a plague that was advancing south, across the honest rural world. There were shops in some little towns in the south-west with signs that said: *No hippies served here.*

For the time being they had to share Prem and Wanda's provisions, but that was cool, Prem said, his eyes narrowed, he was keeping a tally, which included rent for the carriage and instalments for their share of the land. The money trip wasn't what it was about, he said. All the same it put Jacob and Toni at a disadvantage. They saw Prem looking at them if they took second helpings, and they felt like bludging guests. Wanda gave them each a special twig from India to clean their teeth.

Thrift and its grim little satisfactions came naturally to her, as it did to all of them, children of parents who had grown up in the Depression and set up house after the war. She remembered Beryl's bargain hunting and penny-pinching. Even in the midst of a fight with Nig, she would stalk around the house snapping off lights. But now they felt the exertion of poverty, the time and energy it took to make do, mend, barter, plan, go without. Time and energy were all they had. She remembered with wonder the shopping sprees she used to go on in her old life with Felice and Sabine.

They heard there was work at a sawmill, a small temporary outfit called a spot mill, set up amongst the lighter trees at the edge of the forest. Jacob tied his hair back and went off with Prem. He returned exhausted and very quiet. The great whirling saws scared him to death, he told her in the carriage, as she massaged his back and rubbed some of Wanda's herbs on his cuts and bruises. Machinery had always been his natural enemy. Prem, on the other hand, had even fixed a broken roller for the boss.

Jacob was given the job of loading the nonstop spew of milled blocks onto trolleys, and soon he was the butt of all their jokes. It reminded him of playing football when he was kid, he was never in the right place at the right time. The other workers were a very rough lot. Some of them were on the run from the law. They told stories during smoko about the tricks they played on fellow workers. There were a lot of missed digits and stumps amongst them. It was only a matter of time before it was his turn. Already they called him Jake the Peg. You have no idea, he groaned. The infernal noise, the smoke from burning piles of sawdust . . . it was purgatory, it was Gomorrah, probably Sodom too if he didn't watch out, the stories of nights drinking in the shed were bloodcurdling . . . his voice croaked on and on, like a little boy's. But the next morning, without speaking, wincing from his injuries, he set off again with Prem. The work was casual, he didn't need papers. They paid in cash.

They treated themselves to a tin of tuna, eaten on their own in the car. Jacob bought tobacco and a bottle of port. She bought a pair of workman's bib-and-brace overalls, and canvas sandshoes, all that the store stocked in the way of clothes. Her single pair of city jeans was threadbare, her boots in holes.

She and Wanda dug compost into the vegetable patch, hauled water from the creek, picked bugs off stunted silver-green cabbages. When Prem had time, he was going to make a special pit to process their shit as fertiliser. The natural interdependence of people with the land, Wanda said. They used to have chooks to eat the bugs, but the foxes soon got them. She was hanging out for a couple of angora goats to raise, but they'd have to build a strong pen.

Inside her carriage, which she'd made cosy with Afghan rugs and woven Indian hangings, was a spinning wheel and loom bought by mail order from America. She had a thriving herb farm in a collection of old paint tins and saucepans she'd found in a dump. For relaxation she sat on a stump talking and sewing herb pillows made from cut-up flour bags to sell at the Nannup fair. Her hands were never still.

Wanda had a rosy face, flat-cheeked like a Tibetan, with waist-length, graying chestnut hair. She wore long Indian skirts, faded beyond pattern, hitched up above her rubber boots. All day her slow flat vowels washed over Toni.

It turned out that she had left a child behind with his father in San Diego. A boy, Otto, now nine years old. Now all she wanted was to have a baby. She was obsessed with moon cycles, fertility herbs, propitious times according to the I Ching. She told Toni endless stories of home births, children born on the floor of a tepee while everyone sat around chanting and holding hands.

The clearing was claustrophobic. Toni walked for miles along the road looking for a horizon, but apart from an occasional set of ringbarked karri, there was nothing but the black-green walls of trees. The only solace was to sit by the creek that ran across one corner of the block, and listen to the quiet brown water, eternally leaving, going somewhere. To join the inlet, she supposed, to lose itself in the great Southern Ocean.

Clouds moved in overhead, ready to pour down rain. It was a sodden, remote place and the farmers were hard-pressed. There was a darkness everywhere.

★

A slow, dishonourable nostalgia took hold of her, not for Cy Fisher, but for the ease of her life with him. How simple everything had been! Without Cy she was back in the real world, fumbling along like everybody else. With Jacob, no doors opened for her, no tables were waiting, no respectful space cleared around her.

It wasn't that she wanted to go back. But she began to realise how much Cy Fisher had formed her. Because she'd been so young when she met him, he had commandeered every part of her. She was still haunted by his judgements. She couldn't help seeing the clearing though his eyes, the mud, the musty carriages, the pathetic garden, the hole dug in the bush with the toilet paper stuck on a twig beside it. She could almost see the black car pulling up in the clearing and Cy, with henchmen, stepping out and calmly giving orders. What would he think of Wanda wafting through the trees, putting her ear against their trunks, calling out that she could hear the sap rising? He would say she was a lady who'd taken too many drugs. Prem, on the other hand, he would recognise as a serious player. He always liked to use talent and application if he saw it: he might offer him a place on the team. But if he caught Prem watching her the way he sometimes did, the next day there'd be a nasty accident at the sawmill. Wanda would find herself on a plane back to America. Bulldozers would roll in. The carriages would go up in flames. Her imagination balked at what would happen to Jacob.

What she missed most were the mornings in the travel agency, coming downstairs to drink fresh coffee with Felice. Tuning the radio, discussing their dreams or the state of their hair. The sun shone in the park through the clear window and the boys walked past them to the back room, joking and winking at them, smelling of aftershave. Sabine might drop by with pastries and her new baby. All of them laughing, making plans to entertain themselves that day. However sinister some of Cy's activities were, everyone was strangely lighthearted around him.

Yet if she walked down a street now and saw her, Felice would turn her face away. She would find the nearest phone and call her brother.

Had she grown too soft for any other way of life? She felt tired and listless all the time. She could hardly face the relentless beans and rice. The hole in the bush repelled her. She hated being dirty. The others got on her nerves. She ached to be alone, for light and space, a bath, an end, a future.

The spot mill closed down. For the time being work had finished. Prem went on the dole, which he collected from the post office in the store. Jacob witnessed Mrs Skinner's open disgust as Prem signed for it. Prem remained serene, a prophet misunderstood in his own time. Jacob noted Prem's real name: Gregory Payne.

It was too much of a risk for Jacob to go on the dole. They tried to think of jobs where they wouldn't have to register. Cabbage picking in Manjimup? Waitressing in Albany? They couldn't even afford the petrol to get there. Soon they would have to sell the VW, then they'd really be holed up here. Cy Fisher had got them well and truly trapped.

Already she knew more about Jacob than she ever had about Cy. She noticed how he changed with Prem and Wanda, using the right language, 'man' and 'trippy' and 'bummer'. To hear him you would think he had no personal past, no experiences that weren't political or psychedelic. He reinvented himself as one of the new breed.

It hurt her somehow, the way he changed. To see him as the outsider, trying to get in.

In private he was ironic, and had a rather literary turn of phrase. He missed books and described his favourites in detail to her. He missed music and films too. 'What were you like as a little girl?' he asked her. 'What sort of books did you read?' He said he couldn't live with a woman without knowing about her childhood.

It was a crash course in living with each other. Now that they'd bridged the distance between them, Jacob came right up close. When they were alone together he couldn't stop touching her. He slept with his arm or leg or hand on her. He said he couldn't believe what had happened to him. To wake every morning to such loveliness beside him. The carriage rattled on its blocks. It was gritty and sticky, it was teenage passion. It was their test site, their honeymoon. She woke tired, as if even asleep, being with Jacob was intense.

Outside the mornings were dreamlike. His dazed crumpled face across the fire seemed to her to be her own face. He had become her familiar, at her shoulder, always with her, watching out for her, muttering his point of view. He was always telling stories of his life, trying to work it out. *We*, Jacob said. She wasn't used to *we*. She'd never known a man to make himself so vulnerable.

It was like living in a new country, learning its customs and history. But it gave her back her youth, a lightness, an open-endedness. I'm not the slightest bit afraid of him, she thought.

He wasn't a man of action. Before every task he liked to sit down and have a cup of tea and a smoke. She noticed that he always started with the least important thing first. If it was his turn to light the fire, he took so long spreading cold ashes methodically on the garden that Prem, impatient, jumped up and chopped the wood.

Jacob didn't know how to work. She'd learnt from Cy Fisher

about men and work. Cy would have said he was useless and sacked him.

As time passed Jacob became more and more morose. With no prospect of money they were stymied, stalemated everywhere they turned. He spent hours in the carriage, lying on the mattress with his eyes open. It made her brisk and practical. She tried to curb her impatience. After all, he was in this situation because of her. She was in his debt, a fact he never mentioned.

Sometimes they fought, their lovers' faces spiteful and ugly, glistening in the dark with sweat and citronella. At heart she blamed him for not getting his act together, even though she wasn't doing any better. He called her a spoilt middle-class girl, which was too close to the truth, and she didn't talk to him all the next day. But they always made up, they had to, they had no choice. Under their sheet they clung to one another, grubby and slippery and desperate, not knowing how to save themselves.

One night she dreamt that she was walking through her parents' house. She had never been back since she left, but now she saw everything with detailed accuracy, the bakelite switches, the ceiling roses, the varnished skirting boards. All the doors were open, swinging in the wind. She went from room to room and nobody was there.

In the morning she told Jacob that she wanted to go to the store and ring Beryl. The last time she'd phoned had been from the hotel in the wheat-belt. How many months ago was that?

Nig answered the phone. 'Toni! We've been trying to find you. We've had the police out looking for you all over the north-west.' Then he told her that last Friday Beryl had a heart attack.

'She didn't make it, sweetheart. The funeral's at twelve tomorrow.

'She was watching TV after dinner,' he said into the silence. 'I went to the club for a couple of hours and when I came back she was still in her chair. I thought she was asleep.'

My mother died alone, she told Jacob. She saw the empty chair in the lounge room under the standard lamp.

She stood still while everything moved around her. All at once, even as a grubby hippie in overalls, she had human status. Mrs Skinner's son was about to drive the truck to Perth, Jacob told her. He held her hand.

'Brad'll give you a lift, love,' Mrs Skinner called out.

Jacob gave her all the money he had, six dollars. 'How will you get back?' he asked, suddenly panicking, as she climbed up next to Brad.

'I'll ask my father for the bus fare,' she called out the window as the truck roared into life.

Brad Skinner left her to her thoughts. He was a bulky country boy who lived with his mother behind the store and served petrol. She couldn't recall ever hearing him speak. Now he squinted at the road, too shy to look at her. They drove down the winding shadowy roads of the forest into farmland, through miles of rolling tender paddocks. Everywhere she looked she saw light shimmering, at the tips of the trees they were passing, in the haze lying over low hills. The air seemed charged with energy. Is this where her mother had gone?

The closer they were to Perth, the warmer it became. Brad bought her a Coke and a cheeseburger from a roadhouse. She took one bite so as not to hurt his feelings and slipped it into her bag. Maybe later she'd be able to eat. She hated waste now, her mother's daughter after all.

Brad dropped her off in the city. She caught the same green MTT bus from St Georges Terrace. It was dark by the time she walked down the familiar streets, the gardens luminous with spring blossom. Inside the old house was one thin yellow light. Nig opened the door, wearing worn slippers and wiping his mouth from his widower's supper, sardines on toast. Still the gentleman, lean and handsome and courteous, though his eyes were very dark like an animal in shock. He showed no surprise at seeing her, but acted like a host, a little at a loss. 'Help yourself to anything you want,' he said. There was a bright jerkiness to all his movements. He was just enduring this. She left him to go back to his chair in front of the news while she walked through the rooms.

Already the life seemed to have been snuffed out of the place. The furniture huddled together in the crowded rooms. A large bouquet of white roses was dumped in the kitchen sink. Nig obviously hadn't known what to do with it. The flowers were wilting, the water had seeped out. In one movement, without thinking, she took a vase from the cupboard, filled it with water and stuffed the roses in it. As she did she saw her mother's hands. In the fridge were Beryl's little bowls of left-overs with elasticised plastic covers. Days old now. She emptied them into the bin. Everything was older and smaller than she remembered.

But the bathroom looked luxurious to her. Taps! A toilet! A cupboard full of soothing creams. A mirror. She hadn't looked at herself for months. Now she saw she wasn't a city person any more. She was lighter, thinner, burnished by weather and air. She seemed too vivid for the mirror. Her hair fell below her shoulders in wild curls. She stood under the hot shower for half an hour, her overalls and sandshoes a grubby pile on the tiles. It was as if her life in the forest had been nothing but a gigantic children's game and now she'd been called inside again. She reached for the old blue candlewick dressing gown hanging behind the door and then drew back. It was so much a part of Beryl that to wear it would be like putting on her mother's skin. She found a big flannel shirt of her father's to wear.

'Think I'll turn in now,' Nig said. 'Big day tomorrow.' He gave her a fixed look, rueful, almost humorous. He smelt of whisky. The funeral represented everything he dreaded. Fuss. Emotion. Pity.

She lay on her narrow bed and listened to the creaking joints of the house. She remembered lying here as a child, home from school with a temperature, listening out for her mother's sounds, tracking her around the rooms. Her high heels clattering to and from the bathroom sounded panicky when she was dressing for bridge. Her perfume was so strong it smelled chemical when Beryl kissed her, off to the field of battle up the street, an afternoon of fierce gossip and appraisal. Even as a child she knew her mother feared the judgement of women, as of a flock of pecking birds and ripping claws. There were feuds, stand-offs, hurt feelings.

The air changed with Beryl's moods. Sometimes she sang as she dusted, and the sound was like morning sunshine. Sometimes, after a fight with Nig, she lay on the bed and cried violently and the house went dark.

When she grew up she had to cut that bond, she was ruthless and her mother was afraid of her. What she didn't understand at the time, couldn't afford to understand, was that in running away from her mother she was running away from grief.

★

Karen walked into the bedroom where Toni and Nig were inspecting themselves in Beryl's long mirror. 'So you turned up,' Karen said. 'Your hair's got very long.' She went over to her father and straightened his tie. Her eye was caught by the dress Toni was wearing. 'I see you've been through Mum's things.'

It was the dress Beryl always called 'my good silk', navy-blue, tailored along matronly lines, but Toni pulled it in with an old leather belt. Her legs were bare and she wore flat leather sandals, the only shoes of her mother's which fitted her. She'd coiled her hair up but she looked like a gypsy. She had to admit she enjoyed the swish of silk against her legs.

'Go ahead, take what you want. It's all going to the op shop in a few days,' Karen said.

'I don't want anything.'

Something had happened to Karen. Her face had tightened across the cheekbones and her eyes were screwed up with tension. Her lips had shrunk. She was gaunt.

'How's Lincoln?'

'Haven't you heard? We finally got a diagnosis. He's never going to walk or speak or sit up by himself.' She turned her head away for a moment. 'I think it was the last straw for Mum.'

Bevan filled the doorway. 'The car's come for us.' As if to balance Karen, he'd grown fuller everywhere. Toni followed him down the hall and saw a little roll of fat spilling over the back of his white collar.

There was no wake afterwards. Nig couldn't wait to go home. After Karen and Bevan had driven off, he disappeared into the bedroom to reappear in casual clothes, a polo shirt and crumpled gaberdine trousers and worn soft shoes that Beryl would have tried to throw out. He swung his car keys, ready to leave.

'You're welcome to stay as long as you like, of course, but I have to tell you that I'm putting the house on the market as soon as possible. I'd like a little flat overlooking the city. I might even move into a hotel.' He spoke rapidly but firmly, knowing this could be taken as cold-hearted.

She knew he couldn't help himself. He couldn't wait to be alone, to come and go, unaccountable. He'd waited too long for his freedom. Then the poor girl died, by herself, just as she'd always feared. Far from being cold, he was exploding with emotion.

'I'm ready to go,' she said. 'There's a bus I can catch.' Beryl's daughter, she ought to have murmured something like *if I'm not needed here*, but alone at last, there was an instant understanding between them. He didn't demand hypocrisy. She wasn't sure there would be a bus, but like him she had to get out of there.

A retired bishop had listed Beryl's virtues, service in the WAAF, work for charities, above all commitment to husband and family. Dates and names were confused, but he was too bland and professional to care. Another funeral was waiting to come in one door as they left out the other. Outside, all her mother's well-dressed, sharp-eyed friends clustered around Nig, murmuring that he mustn't cut himself off, he would have to come to dinner very soon. He was so distant and handsome in his dark suit that they didn't quite dare to kiss him. Soon they would be match-making for him. Beryl's worst fears would be realised.

The field of battle had come to honour Beryl, or at least look over what remained. They stared openly at Toni as if she were Patty Hearst returned from robbing banks with the Symbionese Liberation Army. If the Richardsons were there, they would have spoken to her, held her hand, and she would have had the chance to look them in the eye. To say without words that she was sorry. Perhaps Doug was too frail to come, or perhaps they were at the beach house now, far away where nobody could reach them.

Where was Beryl in all this? Toni looked up at the sun shining through the well-groomed trees, and tried to recall her conviction in Brad Skinner's truck, that Beryl was in the light around the edges everywhere, that she knew something different now and was free.

She slipped away from the line-up to wait for Nig and Karen in the memorial garden. She realised she missed the silence. The silence that wasn't silence, wind through leaves, bird calls, nuts falling. The space it gave her. She'd thought she was running away to the country, but in fact she was running towards something she had wanted all her life. She couldn't wait to go back.

But not to the commune. She paced up and down the lawn.

She didn't offer her father any explanation about where or how she lived and he didn't ask any questions. Except one, just as they were about to depart. He stopped and looked at her in the hall as she waited for him, in her mother's dress, her overalls and sandshoes in a plastic bag.

'Anything you need?' he asked.

'Yes. My bus fare. About twenty dollars.' She hated having to admit this.

He went straight to the bedroom. She heard a drawer scrape. The sock drawer, where he and Beryl always hid their cash. He put a roll of notes in her hand.

'Here you are.'

'That's far too much.'

He pushed her hand away. 'If you need a bus fare, you need

more than a bus fare,' he said, moving to the front door. 'Let's go.' He was dropping her off in the city. He had never changed towards her. She would never know if he was very wise or just indifferent. '*Daddy can't bear to see you.*' Perhaps Beryl hadn't wanted her to see Daddy.

'Where are you going now?' she asked as Nig dropped her off at the Perth station.

'To a pub where nobody knows me.' He caught her eye. 'To play pool and drink myself silly.'

They laughed.

He kissed her affectionately and drove off in a great hurry.

Within a year he'd be snapped up by Mavis and living on the Gold Coast. It was his curse to have sex appeal. It turned out that Mavis and her ex-husband used to run a pub in the country. Mavis had been on the scene for years.

There wasn't a bus until seven the next morning. She sat at the table in Boans' cafeteria where she and Beryl used to sit. With the roll of notes she could afford to buy a meal but she wasn't hungry. She bought a cup of tea. There was something consoling about being amongst the clatter of strangers. Ordinary people, eating decadent Western food, meat pies, ham sandwiches, jelly trifle. This was what people wanted and who could blame them? Who wants to eat beans in a forest? The clearing was a little lit scene at the back of her mind, tragic, biblical, the thin smoke, the tiny long-haired figures toiling like peasants. How amateurish and make-do everything seemed. That was the whole *point*, Jacob said.

Why all the fuss about the way you lived? It was over in a flash.

She was in a strange state. Being close to a death was a bit like being high. She hadn't counted the money but it would be enough for her and Jacob to drive away from the commune for good. There was still the matter of Cy Fisher's long arm. Just a street away, across the railway line, was his territory. Someone would see her here, she found herself thinking. And then what would happen?

Nothing at all.

She realised her fear had started to lift a few weeks ago after a dream about him. She was at some sort of family reunion, a party or wedding in a little suburban house, and Cy Fisher appeared. He brushed against her in the crowded kitchen, and to her amazement she felt a beautiful warmth from the contact with his large body. She tried to find him again to say goodbye, but he never reappeared.

Was this a sign that Cy had moved on? Cut your losses, he used to say. It was almost his motto. Business as usual. He was above all a business man.

Everything comes to an end, she knew that now. She stood up from the table and went straight to the public phone in the ladies' restroom and dialled the familiar number.

He was there waiting for her at six o'clock in the bar of the old hotel beside the railway line, a five-minute walk across the Horseshoe Bridge. How smooth he looked to her now, a well-groomed city man. The blue shadow was just beginning to creep up his jawline, and his glass of whisky was on the bar in front of him. He hadn't given any sign of shock to hear her voice on the phone but now, after years of reading him, she knew he was affected by the sight of her. He sat very still and his eyes went dense with calculation. As she climbed onto the stool next to his, he lifted a finger and her standard drink, brandy and dry, was put down in front of her. They didn't look at one another for a while. Her eyes roamed the room as if it was of almost scientific interest to her. In fact it was a blur of jumpy light and smoke, and end-of-the-day cracked male voices. She noticed that her hand shook a little as she lifted her glass. Yet she hadn't thought she was nervous.

She'd never been to this pub with him. It opened straight off an asphalt carpark, where cars pulled up and drivers rushed in out of the day's last heat to down a glass, and then another one before they went home. There was a line-up of skinny, livid-faced old regulars at the far end of the bar. Not Cy's usual sort of place. Not the sort of place you'd take a woman to. The barman didn't look at her. He was generous with the brandy though and because she was unused to alcohol now and hadn't eaten for two days, its effect swept over her.

They looked at one another via the mirror behind the bar. She asked after Régine, the essential courtesy. He replied that his mother was well. She couldn't bring herself to ask about Felice and Sabine.

She'd forgotten his stillness. He didn't speak or move, apart from taking an occasional sip of whisky. The barman was suddenly there, filling his empty glass.

'My mother died last week.'

He bowed his head in acknowledgement. She could tell he knew already. He would have read the notice in the paper: he kept a hawk-like watch on *The West*. His expression was grave. Anyone in his employ could rely on his respect for a death in the family, especially of a mother.

Then she understood that she was there because *she wanted to tell him*.

'The funeral was today. It was awful.' She suddenly wondered if he'd had the proceedings watched.

The elegant little collar of Beryl's *good silk* caught her eye in the mirror and she started to cry. She made no sound, but watched her mouth drop open and her eyes scrunch up, until like a storm outside a window, everything was obscured. Cy Fisher put one of his large, Régine-laundered handkerchiefs into her hand.

Still she cried. She had the funny feeling that this at last was real and that everything else, Jacob, the commune, the forest, was a dream. 'I am so tired,' she said at last, blowing her nose.

Cy Fisher made a sign to the barman who handed him a key. He put his arm lightly around Toni's back and ushered her through a door behind the bar, up a flight of dusty stairs, along a green corridor smelling of old bathrooms.

The room's window was open and a yellowing lace curtain billowed in the hot evening breeze from the carpark. Cy sat her on the bed and took off her sandals. She lay back on the threadbare cotton bedspread, her plastic bag beside her. You could hear the trains rumbling in and out of the station.

A no man's land. 'It's nice here,' she said. He always got it right. She felt as light and scorched and inconsequential as the blowing curtain.

He lay down on the other side of the bed and put his hands behind his head. 'You like it? I've bought the place. We'll modernise next year.' He sniffed the clothes inside her plastic bag and cocked an eye at her. 'Now why can I smell wood smoke?'

'You smell the same as you always did,' she said. She yawned. Her eyes closed.

He was gone when she woke. It was early morning. The curtain hung still in the gray light. He must have folded the bedspread over her and her plastic bag. *Just keep out of my sight.* Did he whisper that before he left or did she dream it? Could she take it as a promise?

She made her way down through the dark empty pub, unlocked the door into the carpark and went to buy a cup of tea at the station before she caught the bus.

She saw Jacob's sad, soft face from the bus window, waiting for her in the dusk outside the store. She could smell the leaf-mould damp of the air.

If she hadn't been on this bus, he said, he would have come for the next one in two days' time, or the one after that. 'It's terrible here without you.' He couldn't even smile. 'I was afraid you wouldn't come back.' Because in the silence between bird calls, in the emptiness of the carriage, it had become clear to him that the whole meaning of life was centred, not on the clearing, but on her, being with her, having her with him.

As they drove through the forest she told him they could leave the commune now. She showed him the roll of notes. But for the time being, she said, they should lie low, stay in the country. Keep out of sight.

'You seem different.'

'Do I?' she said lightly. 'I suppose you only go to your mother's funeral once in your life.'

During the interminable bus trip down Albany Highway, the long wait in the terminus, the local bus's crawl along the edge of the forest, she had packed up the hotel room, the blowing curtain, the sound of the trains, and stowed it firmly at the back of her mind.

Jacob went to the store and rang the Education Department next morning and accepted a post as temporary teacher at Warton Junior High, starting as soon as possible.

Accommodation provided. They went back to the commune and packed.

Prem and Wanda waved them off. No one had much to say. Jacob promised to start sending the money owed as soon as he was paid. Who knows, we might turn up again, he said cheerfully, once we've saved up a bit. But they all knew there was no going back. To leave meant they had lost faith. They were deserters, their will was too weak, they were abashed and shamefaced.

They drove in silence until they hit the open road.

'I don't want to hear the words *self-sufficient* again for a very long time,' Jacob said.

'Or *compost toilet*,' she said.

'*Wind power*'.

'*Findhorn*'.

They laughed like naughty children, the wind on their faces.

But it had marked them.

They would continue to live by their ideals, they told each other – simply, not wasting the world's resources – but they would stay quiet about it. For some time they kept themselves apart in Warton. The values of the town were conservative, while they felt they occupied a natural position of dissent. They thought of themselves as more enlightened, more radical, more contemporary than the local inhabitants. They took care however to be seen as respectable, paid their bills, helped out if called upon, wary of the hippie label. In all sorts of small ways they tried to be good.

They retained a long-term distrust of luxury, viewing dishwashers, microwaves, air-con, the latest toys, with an almost moral distaste. They were suspicious of synthetics, additives, technology, material extravagance of any kind. They debated whether or not to have TV or a telephone. They had a hatred of formality, 'good china', clothes 'for best', any sign of bourgeois display. Their relationship with nature was more romantic than their neighbours'. Discreetly, alone or together, they would head off into a sunset, a moonlit night, the aftermath of a storm.

Slowly they came back into the world. They forgot that they had ever thought they were different. After all, their children were natives here. Over time they were accepted. They were helped in this by Toni's appearance. Babies, dogs, shop owners were always drawn to her gleam and fragrance, the symmetry of her features. Men kept an eye on her. Women were suspicious of her, but everybody enjoyed looking at her. There was the story of the truck that veered into the kerb, smashing a verandah post, one hot afternoon when Toni pushed her pram down Cannon Street in a pair of small denim shorts. But she was modest and helpful, a devoted mother, and never flirtatious. In the end the town was proud of her. A world-class beauty, they said.

Jacob was well-liked by many of the students, and being with Toni, he suspected, gave him extra clout.

Soon after they came to Warton Toni discovered she was pregnant and after that there was no question that they would stay together. She must have been pregnant when her mother died, when she went to the city. Sometimes she wondered if unconsciously she'd known, and that was why she phoned Cy Fisher from Boans. To make a home for a child.

And so they had another shared project, one that called on their innermost resources, which they could not desert, or afford to fail. Everything served that purpose, and in its relentlessness they were grateful to discover each other's constancy and diligence and were satisfied with the simple joys of their life. For many years they were busy, their arms full, their hands occupied. Jacob at last learnt how to work. Apart from his sporadic little trips to Perth, he stuck around. His kids were going to know what it was to have a father.

Toni never asked him to do anything he didn't want to, as if deep down she felt she owed him. She gave him space, the greatest gift, which she herself required. They never married because to divorce Cy Fisher would not be keeping out of sight. Anyway, as they told their kids, they didn't believe relationships needed official sanction. After a while they forgot about lying low. Toni never spoke of her former life. The years with Cy Fisher were like a silent movie. She couldn't remember the words.

They ended up with a house, a dog, a TV and video, a four-wheel drive. They grumbled about bills and teachers' pay. Like the farmers around them, they had good and bad seasons. They went to funerals and weddings and quiz nights, just like everybody else. The values they'd aspired to, sharing, hospitality, community, turned out to be country values, not radical at all.

Jacob sent three instalments of money to Prem, and then he let it slide. With a baby there were new expenses. A dilapidated cottage opposite the drive-in had come up for sale. He was sure that by now he'd reimbursed Prem for their share in the meagre meals and the occasional jerry can of petrol. He wasn't going to run his family short to pay back rent for a mouldy mattress on a carriage floor.

Some years later they met a visiting teacher who'd taught for a term in the one-room school in the forest. He told them that Prem and Wanda had stuck it out, built up a seed business, gained respect with the locals. That is, Prem did. Wanda was always regarded as not being the full quid. Did they have kids?

Toni asked. The teacher thought not. But there were always people and kids hanging out there. Then a few summers ago they got burnt out. Houses, trees, plant, everything went. Uninsured of course. Prem and Wanda went to join the Orange movement in Poona and never came back

15

Tod and Clarice

Most nights now, when Cecile came home late, they went to the little wine bar around the corner. She was always hungry after work, and though exhausted, not yet ready to sleep. It was the time she liked to talk. In the house they had a whole conversation pit to themselves, and yet they seemed to need this neutral territory – with a couple of glasses of red wine for Jacob, a steaming bowl of noodles for Cecile – in order to sit face to face across a table and speak about whatever came into their minds. He liked to think of it as *their* place, but he kept that to himself.

He made sure that he was always downstairs and dressed ready to go out when she came in the door. All day he saved up things to tell her in the bar. He even went to places so he could report on them to her, caught trams all over Melbourne.

Once he went to see a Russian film she recommended in an old art-house cinema in the city and waited for her afterwards in Chinatown amongst ferociously fashionable young Asians. It was a warm night, every shop and bar was open, the trams swung along under their canopies, and he began to feel alive to this city.

He worried that she kept meeting with him because she felt sorry for him, deserted and adrift in Melbourne. After all, she had seen him at his lowest point. But the ordeal on the balcony was like a wound he couldn't even bear to think about, he had to leave it alone to heal. He felt he'd died out there and been reborn, delivered into her arms.

Each evening he was taken over by a sense of urgency. Another day gone without news of Maya. He'd worked through all the Flynns now, even had genealogical conversations with a few of the old ones, and at this hour, after a drink or two, braced himself to retry the last few unanswered numbers.

He had a sense of time running out. Time for what? To save Maya, save her soul from peril? To save his own? Alone and restless all day, he knew he had to guard against spilling over to Cecile in the wine bar, telling her too much about himself, more than she would want to know.

Like the way, in a burst of confidence, he found himself telling her about *Glad Rags*, by Chickie Fitzgerald, and the whole glorious frenzied summer he'd spent writing a screenplay about a dressmaker's son who goes berserk in a small country town. Being Chickie Fitzgerald seemed to help.

He'd had the idea for years, ever since the day, soon after he came to Warton, that he heard the whirring of a sewing machine at the back of the newsagency, and poked his head around the door. And there was old Nora Carpenter, a spinster

276

aunt of Forbes's, feeding a hem through the foot of an antique treadle Singer with spotted arthritic hands. She used to be the dressmaker for the whole district in its heyday and she still worked a little in this room lent to her by Forbes. Everything was so familiar to him, the cutting table and ironing board, the ghostly tissue-paper patterns, the mirror, the magazines, the bent, devout head of the dressmaker. Her heavy, lethal scissors. In a flash he had his story. Her son, an ageing biker, spies on her clients, gets fixated on the town beauty, kidnaps her and goes around stabbing his rivals. It was supposed to be black comedy, he explained to Cecile, in which small town morality, hypocrisy etc is exposed. He hoped he sounded suitably ironic.

Cecile remained serious. 'Did you sell the script? I've a feeling I've heard of a film like that.'

'Because it's like everyone's idea for an Australian film! The tragic outsider. The country town. Sending it all up. Of course he ends up letting the girl go. She's enraged and sets fire to his house. He dies in the blaze.' Even now, as he spoke, his heart sank at his lack of originality. Why turn everything into a farce? Like a smirking adolescent, wanting the laughter of the crowd. Why didn't he take himself seriously? Sometimes Warton blazed into poetry before his eyes. He saw stories all around him, real stories, beautiful stories. Nora Carpenter lay amongst the long grass of the cemetery now.

After it was rejected – with not even the suggestion of re-submission – he saw Chickie's work for what it was, false, derivative, Hollywood generic. He couldn't believe how he'd deceived himself. Up until then he still had faith he could do it, produce the great work, from a back shed in a country town. He blamed his failure on the time he gave to teaching, fatherhood, being a good citizen of Warton. But the truth was he'd turned away from the harder labour, the labour of thought.

277

'Why Chickie Fitzgerald?'

'It's the name of my first pet and the first street I lived in. An old friend once told me that's how you get your porn name. I'm not into porn, but I liked the name, it sounded like a jazz musician. For Chickie the words came more easily.'

'I think your work should always carry your own name.'

In one stroke, Chickie Fitzgerald, hired Hollywood hack, morphed back into a canary and a stretch of tarmac. *Glad Rags*, with its trail of failure, was finally laid to rest.

Cecile spoke of her conviction that everything would change in the film industry, with handheld cameras, high-grade video, internet distribution. 'I think film will become more eclectic, more personally expressive. I see a new sort of cinema, closer to the grain of life.'

She talked about her favourite directors. He swallowed his despair that he'd never heard of any of them and asked if she'd select some videos for him to watch out of her collection.

'If it is her boss, he must be away,' he told Toni when she called him. 'I've spoken to every other Flynn in Melbourne.' An M Flynn with an Indian accent. A snobby old lady Flynn who told him to mind his own business. Kiddy Flynns who hung up when he asked if they knew a man called Maynard. The only one left on his list was the number of M&D Flynn. He tried it whenever he thought of it, at every hour of the day. The number leered at him from the notepad by the phone.

Toni was silent. They were distant but gentle with one another.

'Why can I hear birds singing?'

'I'm on my walking meditation,' she said, her voice lowered.

'Jacob, I've been thinking. Didn't Tod Carpenter get her the job? Maybe he knows where the boss is.'

At the last minute Cecile said she would come with him. It was Sunday afternoon, and she didn't have to start work till five. She felt like walking. They could walk through the Fitzroy Gardens to Kafka's, the cafe where Tod Carpenter said he would meet Jacob. It was near Tod's gym.

Tod, on the phone, though he had no news of Maya, had been full of bonhomie and eager to help. 'Yes, Jacob, what can I do for you?' he said. 'Look forward to meeting you, Jacob.' That was the way with Tod's generation, Jacob supposed. Everything was public relations. They called you by your first name at every opportunity, the salesman, the manager in the bank. The personal touch. It was a relief to take action, though he doubted that this Tod could tell him much.

But as he set off with Cecile he felt his spirits soaring to a dangerous, an inappropriate degree, the sheer happiness that he remembered feeling sometimes as a young traveller, for no better reason than having the freedom to please himself, and a girl he liked beside him, and the world spread out before him.

He stood on Wellington Parade and surveyed the three modes of public transport, tram, bus, train, running smoothly side by side. What organisation! There was a civic long-sightedness about it here that intrigued and pleased him. The Melburnians made their way easily amongst each other. These people had a belief in their city, a pride, a history. Melbourne was confident of itself.

Toni had said that the Melbourne air was filthy, the trams threw up a fine black dust that got into her hair and eyes and skin. This had annoyed him. It seemed to him that it was this fussy search for purity that had kept them out in the cow paddocks under the gum trees. Too easy to blame Toni, he thought now, generous in his freedom. Just for now he wanted to pretend that he belonged here.

'I'm beginning to get the hang of this place,' he told Cecile, a little breathless as they strode across the park. Though her legs were so much shorter than his, they always walked in step with one another. She set a city pace.

They passed through velvet theatre curtains into Kafka's interior, dim and intimate, a stage-set lit by ornate wall lamps, with plush armchairs set around little tables, and polished wooden racks of newspapers and magazines. Old-world Prague. Mid-afternoon, most of the tables were empty.

They sat down and ordered double espressos. A short, broad man in a zippy black tracksuit and baseball cap stepped through the curtain and peered into the shadows, screwing up his eyes. This could only be Tod. He had the fresh pink look of one who has recently showered, and a shaven head beneath his cap. Mid-thirties, Jacob thought. Baby-faced, but getting jowly.

'Isn't this place insane?' Tod said as he shook Jacob's hand, in a cloud of aftershave. He smelt like the boys in Warton on Saturday night. 'I love the ambience.' He pulled up a chair and parked his sports bag underneath it. 'Had a girlfriend once who used to work here. Have you eaten? The cakes are sensational.'

Jacob introduced Cecile as Maya's housemate.

Tod took Cecile's hand with a quick keen look at her. His eyes flicked between the two of them for a moment with a half-smile.

Jacob stared at him coldly. He's a creep, he thought, but all the same he felt a warmth rising up his neck. He'd never considered how much he and Cecile must look like that classic pair, older man and young Asian woman. He glanced at Cecile, mortified for her. As if to celebrate the afternoon's outing, she was wearing a boxy black hat, like a miniature priest. Her hair was parted severely in the middle and drawn back. Her black high-collared coat was plain as a uniform. Couldn't Tod see how unique she was? He didn't think of her as being of any race, but as a sort of angel, far more grown-up than him.

'Ludo!' Tod hailed the waiter. 'They know me,' he explained to Jacob, 'I come here after the gym. Mind if I eat? They have real food – European. I'm always starving after a workout. I recommend the strudel. No? Not hungry? You won't join me in a glass of red?' He turned to the waiter and called out, 'The usual, Ludo.'

He turned to Cecile. 'I'm off on a business trip to Asia next week. Where are you from?'

'Sydney.'

'No, where are you really from?'

'I was born in Kuala Lumpur.'

The waiter, as pale and gaunt as a tubercular poet, brought Tod a dish of golden cutlets, the slender bones paper-ringed and fan-shaped around the plate. 'Schnitzel,' Tod said with satisfaction. 'Best in town.' He chomped into the cutlets one after the other, holding the bone in his hand. The meat was pink, like his rosy tongue and mouth.

'No vegetables?' said Jacob.

'I only eat protein. These are cut by a Viennese butcher.' Tod went on picking at a bone. 'What line of work are you in, Jacob?'

'Teaching. English and Communications.'

'Ah ha, a highbrow.'

'Hardly. I'm a teacher at a country district high.'

'English teachers are terribly important,' Cecile said. 'I had a teacher once who fed me books. Reading saved my life when I was a kid.'

'I love reading myself,' Tod said, wiping his hands and picking up a toothpick. 'Have you read *The Alchemist*?' he asked Jacob.

Being with another person gave Jacob a chance to watch Cecile. Tod threw her into relief. Everything about her was simple, natural, and did not call attention to itself. And yet the more he saw her, the more he understood that she was, in every way, supremely elegant. Her face, when she looked at Tod, was without expression. But her eyes were alive. They saw things in the same way, he believed. As scenes, as an unfolding narrative. Perhaps it came from reading as a child. Was that why they'd always been at ease with one another? Or was that her gift? Maya had sounded happy when she moved into that house. All at once he was flooded with relaxation and warmth. He would have liked to squeeze her hand. He felt close to her, united against Tod.

On the other hand, after years of watching classroom politics, he would say that Tod probably had this effect on a lot of people.

He had an instinct to get her away from Tod.

'I wonder what you know about Maynard Flynn?' The table was cleared, more coffee ordered.

'Ah. Maynard.' Behind one hand Tod was busy with his teeth. 'Haven't seen him for yonks.'

'Do you know him?'

'He started off as a client – I'm in insurance – then it turned out he went to the same gym. So we used to talk, yeah, you know, on the treadmill, in the shower.'

'What sort of guy is he?'

'Maynard? Your average small businessman.'

'What does that mean?'

'Works hard. Always trying to get ahead. Having a bit of a struggle financially.'

'Did he chase after women?'

'Huh!' Tod took the toothpick out of his mouth and half-laughed, glancing at Cecile. 'To be honest, we didn't go that deep, mate. We talked business. Anyway he stopped coming to the club when his wife got really sick. The last time I saw him he told me he needed someone to hold the fort in the office. That's when I sent him Maya and they took it from there.'

'The office is closed up.'

'I heard that, yeah. His wife passed away.'

'He doesn't answer his home phone. This number.' Jacob jotted it down on a serviette. 'Is this right?'

'No idea, mate.'

'Do you know where he might be?'

'Like I said, it's been a while. He used to talk about moving back to Asia, Jakarta, maybe, or was it Bangkok.'

'Could Maya be with him? Is he that sort of guy?'

Tod shrugged. 'To be honest with you, Maya's a pretty strong-minded little lady. She does what she wants to.'

Why did he have to keep on declaring his honesty? You couldn't doubt that he was fit, but there was something about him that wasn't healthy. He never stopped acting the man. His voice was too loud, his eyes flickered, watchful. He was angry, he could easily explode. No wonder Maya left his place as soon as possible. Did he resent her for this? Was he capable of spite? What did he really know?

Jacob decided to order a glass of wine, and another one for Tod. Cecile left for work. As soon as the velvet curtain swung behind her childlike hatted figure, Tod dropped his voice and leaned across the table.

'They've got something, haven't they?'

'Who?'

'The Asian girls.'

Jacob stared at him.

'To be honest, I did hear that Maynard had a bit of a taste in that direction.'

'What do you mean?'

Tod shrugged and shook his head. He drained his glass and hailed the waiter for the bill.

He couldn't help himself, Jacob thought, he had to show he's in the know. Now he regrets it.

'So Tod,' Jacob said, leaning forward, man to man, 'if you had to make an educated guess, would you say there's a pretty good chance Maya is with him?'

Forbes's nephew, the man to whom he'd entrusted his daughter. Because of him, he and Toni had let Maya come to Melbourne. Did the bastard set her up? How could he ever make him talk? Jacob repressed an impulse to toss his wine into Tod's sly, disingenuous face.

But Tod was already standing up, reaching for his sports bag, rummaging inside it. He slapped an envelope onto the table. 'Nearly forgot! Here's a couple of tickets for the grand final next week. Turns out I'll be in Bangkok. On me, for old Forbes's sake. Just don't ask me how I got 'em.' He was backing out through the curtains. 'No teams from the West this year, but they're good seats. You can take your missus. Or your girlfriend!'

'Let me know if you hear anything,' Jacob yelled after him, but the curtains had swung closed.

It was a relief to be outside again, breathe in the innocent air. Tod was someone you felt you wanted to wipe off you after being with him. There was something disturbing about what he'd said. What was it? It seemed to have a grip on Jacob's body, clutched his heart, made his legs turn heavy. He suddenly remembered watching Forbes once in the newsagency serve a Chinese family that was passing through the town. After the family left, Forbes pushed the corners of his eyes up and grinned at Jacob. Jacob had shaken his head at him and turned away. He was only friendly with Forbes, he'd told himself, because of the smallness of the town.

To calm himself now he tried to concentrate on what he was seeing, shutting out everything else. He was walking through a Melbourne twilight, down laneways between the back walls of shops and foundries. Every view was picturesque. He saw a poplar, a church spire, a full moon rising over roofs. An old tree in a yard with its arms lifted, laden with blossom. A solitary nineteenth-century streetlamp came suddenly alight. It was bewitching. He felt a pang of pleasurable sadness that he used to feel as a boy, roaming the back lanes around Arlene's at this hour. Or looking out the flat's front window at the lights coming on along Fitzgerald Street, dreaming of making his way to great cities. He used to feel he came alive in urban twilights, as if that was his natural territory.

What had happened to that boy? He belonged here, or in some other city's streets. What had stopped him following his rightful course?

Ideology. All his primal energy, his youthful virility had gone into an idealistic movement that had simply petered out, been subsumed by new imperatives, by the world grinding on. The great wave of his times had swept him up and dumped him in a country town, left him stranded, washed-up, a dinosaur. No wonder his kids wanted to get away as soon as possible. This must be how an old commie feels, he thought.

285

The counter-culture was the father he never had. Fatherless boys need something to belong to. Hadn't he offered this advice at countless parent nights? Something to believe in.

Once in his travelling days when he found himself in Holland, he'd tried to trace his father's family. He knew from his own birth certificate that Anton de Jong was born in Utrecht in 1927. He set himself up with a pile of coins by the telephone in a sleazy Amsterdam hostel and in the end he found a second cousin, Grete.

He took a train through the flat, wet landscape to what she called her summer house, a little makeshift hut on an allotment by a canal. Grete was a large-boned, pleasant-faced, intelligent woman in her late sixties, undaunted by this long-lost, long-haired foreign relative. She spoke good English, like so many of the Dutch. Anton was a nice boy, she said, quiet, much younger than her, whom she sometimes saw at family weddings. There was a little sister who died as a child. Anton's own father, Jacob, her cousin, was a tailor. It was said that Anton did well at school. He would have been a schoolboy in the war years. She lost all contact with his family during the Occupation. His father died. After the war she heard that Anton had joined the merchant navy. She would have said he wasn't the type but conditions in Holland were terrible then, no jobs, no money. Perhaps, she said with a gracious smile, he was looking for adventure, like you. Later she heard that he had drowned. She never knew that he had an Australian family.

'Do you think he really did drown?' Jacob asked her. He told her of his speculations when he was a kid, that perhaps his father had jumped ship and swum ashore to South Africa. His mother had, after all, never received a penny of his pension.

Grete stared at him. 'Why would he do that?'

He shrugged. 'To start a new life.' Too hard to explain something so shadowy, based on the length of a verandah between his parents in an old photograph. On the shadowiness of his own memory.

Two men came, noisy, enormous, the house was filled with deep voices, heavy treads, he was picked up and thrown in the air, but by whom? His father or Uncle Bob? In his memory it happened only once and was as exciting as Christmas. He didn't want to go to bed but Arlene shut the door. She never showed any grief or nostalgia for Anton. Far too hard to explain Arlene.

'I can't believe that.' Grete shook her head. 'He wouldn't have walked out on you. He was – how can I explain? – he was like his father, a sensitive boy.'

'Do I look like him?' More than once in the streets of Amsterdam he'd passed an older man and saw, in his build and colouring and features, his own future.

'Perhaps in your expression . . .'

'What?' He had to persist. This was his last, his only chance.

'The look in your eyes.'

For years he and Grete exchanged Christmas cards. Then one year hers stopped coming.

To start a new life. To jump ship. The moment of decision. The plunge into cold waters. Because you had no choice, you couldn't stay any longer, you were dying. Then the new shore, starting again, knowing there was no going back. Did you sometimes wake up thinking you were in your old bed? Did you carry a shadow-life with you, the smell of a hot country twilight, your wife's face when she was sad, your little children wanting to play with you and not go to bed?

★

As soon as he opened the door by the fishpond his thoughts turned to Cecile. He stepped down into the conversation pit and everything about the room spoke so strongly of her that it was like a face with an expression. Even though he knew she was going straight to work from the cafe, he moved swiftly, compulsively through the house, checking out the food in the fridge, the cups on the sink, the CDs that had been played. He saw what he was doing, but he couldn't stop himself. He was always waiting for her. He never knew when she'd be home. Sometimes in the early morning he woke to hear the toilet flushing, the discreet rush of the shower. Her footsteps were too light to hear. If he didn't leap out of bed at once, all he'd find would be a warm teapot, an open newspaper, a load of clothes swirling in the washing machine.

He didn't check her bedroom. Since the night she'd rescued him from the balcony, he'd never entered her bedroom or opened her laptop again.

He went to the bathroom (her towel was dry) and looked in the mirror as he washed his hands. Why had this happened to him now, at the end of his life, just as his jaw was sagging, his gut loosening, his hands turning red and knobbly? Just as he really knew how to love. Toni and the children had taught him.

Meanwhile Beech, arch-seducer, had, according to occasional brief despatches, retired from the field. After years of living the expat life in different cities in Asia, drink, drugs and women, he had caught malaria and nearly died. Now he lived at a different pace. He was married to a wealthy Thai business-woman and had three children. He drove them to school and helped out in the business. 'It's a family tradition,' he wrote. 'Asia suits us. It's anti-romantic, anti-guilt.' A photo fluttered out from his last letter, of three bright-eyed little Eurasian kids. On the back of the photo Beech had written 'The Golden Birdcage'.

He hated this prowling obsession that had taken him over, like an old man in a boarding house. He wondered if their daily, unspoken intimacy was driving him mad. It recalled the climate of his mother's house, the haunting presences, the scents and voices, the women in the lounge room taking off and putting on their clothes. He fell in love from afar, over and over again. That was the real story of *Glad Rags*. The making of a voyeur. The dressmaker's son going mad.

He marched downstairs again and stood in the empty kitchen. Enough of this, he was hungry, soon he would go out and buy some noodles, double-serve. Meanwhile he poured himself a glass of wine. He stood drinking, staring into the dark living room lit only by the spotlight over the fishpond. His mood grew sombre. He felt the shadow of Maya's boss creeping back. Meeting Tod seemed to make Maynard Flynn all too credible. He could almost feel Maya's fingers tapping a reminder on his arm. As if in some way this stubborn absence of hers was telling them something. What?

He picked up the phone and once again tried M&D Flynn's number.

After *Glad Rags*, he didn't write any more. He had a feeling of emptiness that stretched into the plains around him. There were times of a free-ranging hunger, a sense of missing out. It was probably only the extremely limited field in Warton that had restricted his passions over the years, shallow crushes in comparison with this. There was Lisa, the Norwegian physiotherapist in Tumbring with the severe, polished planes to her face that made him fumble for similes with ice floes, fjords, northern light. He emerged from her graceful but efficient ministrations into the waiting room and there was Forbes Carpenter grinning at him. 'You too?' said Forbes. 'A lot of guys are having back problems right now.' It wasn't long before Lisa's enormous Latvian husband got a transfer and whisked her away.

Once when the kids were small, he nearly stayed the night at an English and drama teachers' conference in Perth with a Canadian exchange teacher, Hilary Mosel, who had spent a term in Warton. She was in her mid-thirties, short and dark and buxom, passionate about her work. The whole school fell in love with her. Warton in spring erupted around him, magpies carolled in gleaming trees, the wattles were heavy with blossom. As soon as he walked out the door in the morning, he started to whistle. Each class Hilary took erupted into laughter, shouts, crashes, thumps, songs. He was aware of exactly where she was at any given time around the school. After a while they could hardly meet each others' eyes. She was a serious woman in spite of her bright jokiness, honest about her emotions. For years they talked in Warton about the play Hilary's students wrote and performed on her last day there.

But then at the conference he found himself drawing back. Away from her work, there was something anxious and intense about Hilary that was like a warning to him. She reminded him of Kitty! Why hadn't he seen this before? Her professionalism covered a yawning loneliness, a lack of self-esteem. He was overcome by a shameful archaic terror of being swallowed up. One more step and he would feel responsible for her forever.

He still remembered the look in her eyes when he said he had to leave, made some excuse and drove home recklessly through the night, half-hoping he'd be hit by a kangaroo.

He decided to ring Magnus.

'How are you, matey?' Strange the comfort that the sound of your child's voice could give.

'Good. Kitty made soup out of beetroots for lunch. It's Russian.'

'Bortsch.'

'Yeah, that's what Kitty called it. Tonight we're having duck cooked in a Chinese way.'

'I didn't know you could buy ducks in Warton.'

'Carlos knows someone who raises them.'

'How is Carlos these days?'

'Good. He's coming to dinner. Right now he's giving Kitty a driving lesson at the lake.'

'Sounds like you're all having a great time.' Jacob was surprised to feel a little pang. 'Heard from Maya?'

'No.' Magnus hesitated. 'Kitty answered the phone the other night and she heard beeps but then the person didn't speak.'

'Was it Maya, d'you think?'

'Kitty could hear cars, like when Maya calls. Now I always answer the phone.'

They both went silent.

'How's Winnie?'

'Getting fat. Kitty gives her snacks all the time. She follows Kitty everywhere.'

Occasionally he and Magnus forgot themselves, Jacob as life-coach, Magnus as son always fending off the threat of advice, and for a few minutes they talked freely in a way they couldn't quite do with anyone else, which might be the poor form of the Dockers, the politics of the Olympics or their deepest feelings about a piece of music or a film. Magnus's revelations, the maturity of his insights, always surprised him. They never spoke of school: neither of his kids had ever allowed him to discuss their school work with them.

He was just about ready, Jacob thought, as soon as Magnus finished school, to drop the parental role altogether, and reveal himself, his doubts, his truth, his past.

Along with his fear that he was going to die, or almost as bad, become a tracksuited, impotent senior citizen, was the fear of dying without ever having been able to give expression to what it meant to live.

It had got to the point when, if he woke at night, he knew at once whether or not she was in the house. Subliminal signals, the click of a switch, a faint luminescence beneath his door, seeped their way into his dark room and alerted his sleeping consciousness. He must be waiting for her even in his dreams.

At once, without thinking, he pulled on his jeans and went out towards the light below the stairs. In spite of his resolutions, he was flooded with happiness as he looked down on her, the slight black-clad figure at the desk, sitting very still, intent on something on her screen.

'I can't sleep,' he said as she looked up at him, though he was instantly aware that he must be the image of someone just woken, blinking and puffy-faced. 'Still at work?' he said throatily, descending. 'Aren't you tired?'

She turned back to the screen, but not before he noticed that her eyes and cheeks were wet.

'I never finished this piece on Clarice.' Her voice was very flat and quiet. There was no music playing a sound track for her. 'I had an email from her tonight.'

'She wants it soon?'

'She doesn't want it at all. She doesn't want anything more to do with me.' To his horror he saw a small tear roll over her cheekbone. He stood behind her, clenching his hands.

'A cup of tea? I'm making one for myself.' As quietly as he could he filled the kettle, sprinkled the green leaves into the black pot in the way she'd taught him, all the time alert to her every move. Years in a pastoral role had taught him to approach on the oblique. He stirred a loaded teaspoon of honey into her cup, the way she sometimes liked it, and put it on her desk. He pulled a chair up, not too close, for himself. She was slightly shaking.

'Are you cold?'

'No. It's shock.'

He went to turn up the heating. Cecile sipped her tea and after a while she sat back and looked at him.

'How's the script going for *The Prodigal*?'

'Without Clarice, it isn't going.'

'How come?'

'I began to see I had to go back to the roots of it all. To the personal. My true passion is the story of my mother, an unmarried Chinese girl, a double outcast in her own society. Which of course leads to the story of Clarice and me. I planned to use everything to tell this story, interviews and photos, archival footage from the KL anti-Chinese riots in 1969.'

'How does it start?'

'With a return to the orphanage. My mother left me there when I was born. She had no choice. I remember a beautiful young woman who used to visit me sometimes before I was adopted, and of course it would have been my mother. And I loved her, I remember loving her with a passion. Her name was Phyllis Wong. I think my adoptive parents paid her money to let me go. About the same time that I came to Australia, she bought a little hairdressing business. She would have thought it was for the best, for me. A few years later Clarice was born. But this time she was married and after her husband left, there was Auntie to look after Clarice while she worked. In a way, Clarice was raised on the money paid for me.'

'How did you meet Clarice?'

'When I came to Melbourne I started to try to find my mother. I went to KL and found out she had died three years before, and that I had a half-sister. We met. Clarice's English wasn't good, but she told me she lived with an old aunt of her father's and worked in a department store to support them. She'd left school young and wanted to work as a model. She had photographs of herself. Last year I finally persuaded her to fly out here and live with me. I enrolled her in an English course and a drawing course and promised her that next year she could try out for fashion design. I sent money to KL for Auntie.'

Cecile sat with her shoulders hunched, her hands clasped in her lap, like a little old lady herself. 'But she hated it here! She was so homesick. She hated the English classes and the weather and she thought the people were rude. She missed Auntie and felt guilty for leaving her. She missed her friends and their outings. I couldn't make her happy. In fact she was angry with me. I saw her getting thinner and paler like a dying plant. I told her of all the opportunities for her here. I told her that I couldn't bear to live without her. She was brutally honest and told me that I'd done to her what had been done to me. For selfish reasons. I put her on the plane home. A few weeks ago I went to visit her, as you know. I thought we were building our relationship. I felt hope. Then tonight, this email.'

She sat shivering, not looking at him.

'You talk of her as if she is a lover,' Jacob said.

'Because I do love her! Apart from that tiny memory of my mother, I've never loved anyone before. From the moment I met Clarice I loved everything about her. I feel I understand her, that no one else sees her as I do. Isn't that how a lover feels?'

'Yes.' Jacob stood up and went to the cocktail cabinet. Over the weeks he'd familiarised himself with its contents and now he poured them each a shot of ancient saki into little green porcelain cups and put one down on the desk in front of her. He wanted to put his arms around her and brush her hair with his lips. He could feel her small sad body tucked into his. He sat down again.

'You're good at looking after people, Jacob.'

'Am I? Years of living in a family.'

'I have friends whom I understand, like Dieter, but I don't have intimate attachments. I've tried, but I lose concentration.'

Was she warning him off? If so, he was almost flattered.

'When I visited Clarice and Auntie in their little house, and saw how close they were, I envied them. But they don't want me. Clarice has made that very clear. If it was just about the film, I'd gladly give it up. She said some pretty nasty things. She told me to leave her alone, called me a lesbo – she must have picked that up in Australia.'

Jacob sat back, sipping his saki. He was suddenly on safer territory. Saving a woman again.

'In my experience – as a teacher – some young women, especially pretty ones who want to be models, are extremely interested in celebrity, in the lucky break, in being noticed and given their chance.' He wondered if it would be obvious to her that he had peeked at Clarice's poses and fantasies on her computer.

'If I were you,' he went on, 'I'd mention contracts, agents, publicity, Cannes and Venice, Sundance, LA . . . It's a gamble of course, but I'd hint you had a beautiful young actress who was begging to play the half-sister.'

Cecile sat very still. He couldn't tell what she was thinking.

'All this is not, after all, outside the realm of possibility. It may very well come to pass. Isn't the Prodigal story about redemption? Doesn't it have a happy ending?'

16

The Vision on the Highway

She was growing accustomed to a simple, regimented life. She would have done quite well in the army. Five o'clock reveille. Tidy barracks. Assemble on parade ground. The ashram regime, so quiet, so calm, was no less authoritarian. Life arranged around fixed points. Tasks. Practice. The covert pleasure in small things: meals, walking alone. But the strict rhythm of the days was doing its work. She was no longer missing Maya or anyone. The outside world seemed very far away.

Each of the evening talks had a title. The Four Noble Truths. The Six Perfections. The Seven Point Mind Training. The Eight Steps to Happiness. Buddhists were very numerical. She'd become fond of the young Venerable, his black horn-rims, his shawl thrown casually across his broad shoulders. His Aussie voice intoning Tibetan words was rather pleasing, like the promise of some cross-cultural fusion.

But when the old Tibetan Geshele, with his small round head, bright eyes, and crooked, haunting smile arrived to address them one evening, his words opened up vistas of peace, like long avenues in a garden. Happiness was very simple, he said, a transformation in the mind. She felt dazed, on the verge of making that transformation. Afterwards, crossing the melancholy courtyard back to her room, it was hard to remember exactly what was said. All the lights in the house went out. The moon was very high, a moving glow behind the clouds. She watched it, lying awake in her little cell.

To be happy, the Geshele said, you have to break attachment to life. *I know*, she thought, lying in her little moonlit cell, *I've always known what that meant*. It was how she felt looking out her bedroom window at the cold lonely beauty of the paddock running down to the creek. Pushing her babies along bumpy country roads, she had heard the wind run through the trees like a parallel energy rushing past her. It was the strange, intense satisfaction of observing something quite ordinary, grass along a wire fence, the weeds around the broken-paned projection booth, the gravel back lane behind the shops on Cannon Street with their clusters of rusting iron sheds. As if for a moment a light came on inside the scene. And when it happened she was reminded that these little fits had been part of her since childhood. Then she forgot them again.

For many years she had forgotten the moment on the highway, when she was a schoolgirl waiting for a bus, just before a storm. Yet now it seemed to her that all the other experiences were mere precursors to or aftershocks from this, the defining moment. What had happened? First the silence, the stillness, the unhooking of the everyday. Then came the will-less spaciousness of it, the calm understanding that everything was in its place.

Then Cy Fisher came along and interrupted her and her life as a woman began. How long had she been waiting for that to be over?

She lived with silence now.

Was all this breathing in and breathing out just another way to be good? A sort of insurance policy? *Above all else be good.* What you've been taught in childhood always comes back. After Cy Fisher she'd craved purity. She'd scrubbed and ordered, saved water, recycled, visited the sick. Not just to be good, to be *seen* to be good.

What if Maya decided not to see them again? What was it she thought they could never understand?

Out of the worry and self-doubt since Maya's defection, something new was emerging. She saw more, Toni thought, now she was outside her life. Now that she was not so pleased with herself. Gradually this was becoming her compensation.

Did she really need bells and gongs and robes? What she wanted was an even more extreme modesty, an anonymity, a lightness on the face of the earth. She wanted to apply herself to this, give it her whole life.

A small, a very small place. Trees, bush, but not too far from the plains. She'd grown used to the wide vista over the years. A verandah where she could sleep. To be closer to the drama of weather, the stars, the pure cold air.

You could eat the air. You could live on air. The sounds – a single bird call across the valley, then another by the track. So clear in the silence it made you attend. You became more present. Getting closer to what? To that which she sought.

You become addicted to noise, radio, TV, telephone. It was threatening to be alone. She was just at the beginning.

She thought of the lone ones who sometimes came into town. Old shearers, or jobbers who lived out on a back block. Miriam Kershaw, walking the streets, was called the town witch. Solitude was not much approved of in Warton. It was related to madness.

To live apart. Even as a child, at the Richardsons' beach house, she had thought this was a better way to live. For her that possibility – when Magnus left – was far more thrilling than a trip to Paris, say, or Istanbul, or the world which she had never seen.

She wondered if Jacob, always faithful to her wishes, would grant her this.

No news from either of the children.

'I've seen Tod Carpenter.' Jacob sounded cheerful, even breezy. 'No leads. But he's given us a couple of tickets to the Grand Final next Saturday.'

'I leave the retreat that morning. Ask someone else. Ask Cecile.'

'I want *you* to come,' Jacob lied. To take Cecile to a Grand Final, to see this great Australian ritual through her eyes, was his idea of heaven, but Cecile worked every day of the week.

'It might be a bit much . . . it's not really my . . .' But her voice failed. She knew this was a dream of his.

'It's a once-in-a-lifetime chance. These tickets are gold.' He produced his trump card. 'Magnus would never forgive you.' Though he wasn't sure – who could ever be sure about anything with that boy? – that Magnus would care at all.

They agreed that he would mail her ticket to her, and they would meet at the seats.

'Do you good. Bring you back to reality.' He made the smack of a kiss before he hung up, sounding false and debonair. He was possibly a little stoned. She supposed he'd fallen in love with Cecile.

She was crossing the courtyard when she came across the young nuns in a sunny corner, shaving each other's heads. They were chattering and laughing as one sat in a chair with a towel around her shoulders and the other sheared her downy skull with battery-powered clippers. Toni enjoyed standing there in the sun with them. Suddenly she asked if they would cut her hair.

'How much off?' they asked when Toni had sat down and put the towel over her shoulders. They pulled back Toni's heavy mane into their hands. Others gathered around.

'Like you,' said Toni.

17

The Mimosa

'What's the time where you are? It's really late here.' It didn't sound as if she was speaking out in the street this time. He could hear her yawning. Moonlight splashed across the cold kitchen floor. He took the phone back to bed with him. For some reason he felt it was warm where she was.

'Why are *you* up so late?' She never gave any information.

'Talking with Kitty. Playing music for her. That's all we do these days.'

'Are Kitty and Carlos still going strong?'

'Yeah. They think it's a secret though . . . I've just remembered something. I saw Jason the other day.'

'Jason Kay? Is he still around?'

'I saw him outside the Lucky. We talked.'

They were silent for a while.

'Myz? Are you still there?'

'That fuckin' weak wimp Jason.' She broke into Warton High lingo when she was upset. 'When's he gonna get his shit together and leave that fuckin' town?'

'Also Ma sends her love. She said to let me know if you need money or anything.'

'You told them I called you?'

'They were gonna get the cops.'

Silence. This time he didn't try to break it.

'Are they still in Melbourne?'

'Yeah.'

'Weren't they going to Tasmania?'

'I guess they're waiting for you.'

He couldn't hear her in the silence but he sensed she had started to cry.

She'd been dreaming. She was walking up a hill towards some sort of celebration, loud music and bonfires. It was night-time, the path was lit by burning torches stuck into the earth, the flames streaming in the wind. He was ahead of her, holding his little son Andrew's hand. Then she saw he was also carrying a tiny girl, with flying strands of thin dark hair, who suddenly jumped down and ran to cling to her, Maya, walking behind them. She picked the child up and started carrying her. The dream was dark and urgent, black and red.

She woke into thick darkness and for a little while she didn't know where she was. Then she became aware of the familiar rattle of the air-con, and saw the faint glimmer from a street light around the edges of the sealed frosted-glass window. He had gone out earlier in the evening, and she must have fallen asleep.

It wasn't till she turned on the light that she saw he'd forgotten to take his phone with him. It was lying on the table on his side of the bed.

The only person she wanted to speak to was Magnus. The only one she could bear. Because he wouldn't be shocked or worried, and he wouldn't ask questions. He knew she did what she did because she had to. Kids growing up together got to know each other in a deep, realistic way. He was the one she told the truth to, because with him there was no need to lie.

Sometimes the desire to speak to him was so strong that she'd take the phone from Maynard's jacket when he was asleep or in the shower and go out onto the street to phone him.

It was the straightness of his voice, the pureness of his tone, without probing or put-downs, that made her want to cry. As if a clean breeze had blown into the sealed air of this room. She looked at the clock. 3.34 am. That meant 1.34 over there. It was pretty cheeky of her to call so late, yet he'd shown no shock. She lay back on her pillow and thought of him at this moment, across the continent, falling asleep in his room off the kitchen, the moonlight flickering over the long hump of his body, and the wallful of looping wires and dials that was beginning to define him.

His room was the centre of the house. All the purest channels of the family ran towards him.

What would happen to him if there was something that he really wanted? Would he change? Would he compromise? Would his heart get broken if he was betrayed?

In the way that she and Magnus were different, she and Jason

Kay were the same. She'd sensed this from the moment she first saw him but hadn't liked to admit it. Every morning when she saw his face on the school bus she had the feeling she was looking at herself.

She sat next to him the first time because it was the only empty seat left. He radiated difference, like a halo around him. Sitting next to a Brethren was like sitting next to someone who didn't exist. You never talked. They weren't supposed to talk to worldlies. She hated school and didn't want to talk to anyone. It was restful, with him, a little island amongst all the action around them. They both looked out the window – flat paddocks, scrub, the big water pipe – and left each other alone. She sat next to him on the way back.

They started to talk. He was doing maths and economics, tech drawing and accountancy. He wasn't allowed to do sport or English Lit, history, biology or religious studies. He couldn't socialise or buy food. He went to the library every lunchtime, the first Brethren kid here who had gone to senior high school. She began to notice how beautiful he was, in his own way. Brown eyes, shining brown-blond hair, white teeth, eyebrows as delicate as fishbones. Long fingers, long torso, with a way of wearing his school clothes that made him look as if he were going to an office.

How was it they discovered they had both seen the UFO, back when they were ten? Jason had never told anybody. His stepfather Grant would beat him for telling lies, he said. When his mother Valda married Grant, they moved into the community in Warton. She picked out Valda amongst the Brethren women, meek-looking like all of them, but prettier, fine and pale like Jason, with long blonde hair under her headscarf.

Even her parents told her she must have been dreaming. They told her it was better not to talk about it. No one else

305

reported seeing it. Something made her mention it to Jason on the bus. It turned out that on the same night, at the same time, they were both woken by a bright light coming through their windows. They each described it – long, glowing, cigar-shaped, hanging in the northern sky – nodding excitedly at one another. It was silent, yet alive, like an animal. After this, how could they not be bound together? They were a club of two. They felt they'd been in some way chosen.

They started to meet during the holidays, on the afternoons when Jason's mother helped out at Warton Homeware. Sometimes he came to her place. They met in the cemetery along the Perth road if they wanted to be alone. Jason walked from his side of town and she walked from hers. They had to take care nobody saw them. This made them a little tense. It was exciting. They walked around the graves reading out the epitaphs. They lay down in the shade and talked about school and everyone they knew and how sick of Warton they were and what they would do when they left. He'd like to work in a music shop in a big city, he said. She had it all worked out for him. Every week he had to put away a little money until he had a bus fare to Perth. Once there he could stay with Arlene and Joe, get a job and save his fare to Melbourne and join her. Surely the elders would never find him in a gated retirement village in an outer suburb? Jason raised his eyebrows but said nothing.

By mid-year they were kissing. She thought she was in love. She had to fall in love with *someone* and he was the only one who came near being possible. When the chance finally came, with both sets of parents out of town, even Jason said it felt God-sent.

She didn't think of Jason as male but as a fellow being. When they lay side by side under her doona, naked, his smoothness against hers, it hadn't felt sexy, but natural. She thought of animals in dark burrows, insects beneath leaves, earthworms rubbing together.

'Try! Try!' she said sternly as she held him. He'd sneaked out of the Brethren enclave under cover of darkness. First she made him smoke a joint that she'd got from Josh Garcia and drink a glass of Carlos's beer. Then came the ultimate test. Something about him made her want to rip her clothes off and confront him.

'I can't.' A clamminess had broken out over his skin.

'Why not?' They were whispering so Magnus wouldn't hear them.

'It's a sin.'

'What sin?'

'Lust and fornication. If you sin you have to stand out the front of Chapel and be judged by the elders. I'd be withdrawn from.'

'But *you* don't think it's a sin.'

'It's in the Bible. The bottomless pit. The lake of fire.'

'The Bible was written by *old men* like the elders. Anyway, they can't see you.'

'God can.' He was shivering all over his body.

'Your God's like a surveillance camera.'

'This is the Devil's country.' He was groaning.

'You have to give that stuff up.'

'I can't! I can't!' He was rocking back and forwards, on the edge of her bed, his fists in his eyes. 'It's like a virus. It's like AIDS, once you get it, it's always with you.'

It was a pretend world they'd made, she'd turned him into her pretend lover. Now she saw he didn't really want her. He was crying. He sickened her a little, filled her with sadness.

Then her parents walked in. She went under the doona and stayed there while her mother sat down on the bed and put her arm around him. 'It's OK, Jason, it really is, just put some clothes on and go home. Nobody need ever know.' They lectured her through the doona after he was gone. She didn't know what she was up against, etc, how she could harm him, cause irreparable psychological damage.

When she came to Melbourne, she'd wanted a lover. A real man. To prove herself.

Jason was pulled out of school and started working in the furniture factory. It was as if he'd moved to another town.

One evening just before she left, when she'd been working late in the newsagency, she went to the dunny out the back and stepped into the lane to look at the moon. And there was Jason, standing further up the lane behind Homeware. Quietly they approached each other and stood talking in the shadows for five minutes. She told him her plans for Melbourne and he listened, looking down and shuffling, a little smile on his face. She carefully didn't ask him any questions, except one, just as they parted.

'Why did you come out into the lane just then?'

'I wanted to look at the moon.'

At ten, he'd come back to the room with a pizza which they'd eaten sitting on the bed watching TV. He drank a couple of cans of Fourex beer and was almost asleep when there was a call on his mobile and he'd gone into the bathroom to talk, sliding the door closed. Then he said he had to go out. Maybe this time I'll come too, she said from the bed. To test him. And because of the long night ahead.

He frowned. 'I have to meet some people. You're not dressed.'

She was wearing the short denim skirt she'd left Melbourne in, her legs bare for the heat. He must know there wasn't anything else.

'Get some sleep,' he said, deftly slipping a handful of coins into the fruit bowl. She knew this was for her breakfast in the morning. He wouldn't be back tonight. Any hint of complaint on her part turned him to ice, to acid. All her problems, he'd tell her, were in her own head. What's happened to the old, spunky Maya? he'd say, if he was in a good mood. Nothing was too hard for that girl! He liked her sparky, 'cute' like she used to be in the office. What he called 'this droopiness of yours' annoyed him. As if she was still a paid employee and falling down on the job.

They stayed in a different hotel at first when they came here, a modern, LA type of place where the rooms all opened onto a central pool. Mr T was on a higher floor. After Mr T went to Bangkok, they moved to the Mimosa, to this room. It was so small that they had to turn sideways to walk past the bed. The bathroom was a closet. The shower wet the toilet. The frosted-glass windows were sealed shut.

'Why did you bring me here?' she asked, sitting on the bed.

'Just until a deal comes through,' he said. He looked around the room and pulled a face. 'Then we'll upgrade.'

'But *why* did you bring me to Brisbane?'

'I thought it might be fun.' He turned away coldly to hang a shirt up in the narrow cupboard. It was empty apart from her sheepskin jacket.

'This isn't fun.' Her heart was thumping. She had to fight her fear of him these days, fear of his temper.

'Well, all right, because you were so upset! And I'm fond of you, I can't help being fond of you for some reason.'

He moved quickly, snatching up his keys and slinging his jacket over his shoulder, unable to bear even the threat of a scene. 'You know you can leave whenever you want to,' he said, as he stood by the door.

'I can't afford to buy a ticket.' She'd spent the last fifty dollars on her Visa card on underclothes and a T-shirt and a pair of Indian sandals so she didn't have to wear her boots. She couldn't bring herself to mention pay because what would he be paying her for? Two words she was unable to say to him were *money* and *love*, just as she was no longer able to smile at him or call him by name.

He rolled his eyes. 'Oh for God's sake, I'm sure we can scrounge you up a fare!' But he didn't bring the matter up again and neither did she.

After that he started the habit of emptying the coins out of his pockets into the plastic fruit bowl on top of the bar-fridge if he was going out somewhere. Sometimes he was gone for a whole night and the next day. She had no choice but to use the money to buy coffee or food. It was another of the things they didn't speak about.

Fond of you for some reason. She let that warm her for a while. How little she made do with these days! She sensed it wasn't a lie. He rarely spoke of his real feelings except in irritation. Trying to shave in the bathroom, he swore under his breath. He knocked her nose-stud – *that damned thing* – down the drain. She heard the finicky clipping of his nails. He had to bend down to spike up the tufts on top of his head in the mirror. She knew he hated losing his hair. Sometimes the traces he left, beard flecks, nail clippings, swirling hairs, made her feel strange. His snores woke her when he came back here to sleep. Would she feel like this with a boy of her own age?

She lay on the bed and turned the TV up loud to block out his sounds and give him privacy.

What had happened to the high room, the lonely tower? To that girl walking towards her lover through the city streets at dawn? She was a different person then, going to a different lover.

Why couldn't she leave? This was where the thinking stopped. He rushed in and out, distracted, sweating, anxious. *You're not yourself*, her mother used to say when she was grumpy. Sometimes in bed he'd turn to her and clutch her and breathe her warm body into his.

Devotion. Devotion had brought her here.

'He's all right, just got some funny little habits,' Maynard said to her on the plane here, after he'd had a gin and tonic. Mr T was in business class.

'Like voyeurism.'

He tapped her hand half in praise of her vocabulary. 'Maya, I didn't think you'd be like this . . . He's my business partner now.'

In her on-going, non-stop thinking, she was sometimes occupied by thoughts of strange people. Miriam Kershaw, Dory. How brave they were facing death. Rhonda Carpenter, famous for taking a look and *coming back*.

She woke to the toy-like ring of his mobile somewhere in the bed. Morning light filled the frosted glass of the window. In a panic she searched amongst the sheets and found it.

'Andy here!' A young man's voice. Andrew. He sounded phony-cheerful. After a moment he said, 'Dad?'

'He's not here.'

'Who's this?'

'Maya.'

'You're with Dad?' The line crackled with his surprise.

Accused, she looked around and saw all the evidence around her, the jumble of bedclothes and newspapers and tissues, last night's pizza carton and empty cans, their pathetic, make-do life together. No point in pretending this was an office. She had no energy for lies.

'He went out last night.'

'Are you expecting him back?'

'I guess so.'

The phone beeped dead in her ear.

She had to get out of this room. She rushed into the tiny bathroom, showered and dressed. Just as she was scraping up the coins in the fruit bowl, the phone rang again.

'Maya? I'm sorry.'

She was silent.

'Dad still not back?'

'No.'

'Maya, it's OK, it really is. I know what he's like. My mother knew.'

She was unable to speak.

'Talk to me,' he said gently.

'What about?'

'Do you like it there?'

'No.'

'Why don't you leave?'

Silence.

'My father used to talk about you. He said you were a country girl and nothing was too much for you.'

Silence.

'I remember your face, Maya. Your flowers.'

She remembered his face too and the long, grieving tower of his body in the doorway. She cleared her throat. 'Do you miss your mother?'

Silence, this time from his end of the phone.

'I thought I was prepared. She tried to prepare me.'

'Were you very close?'

'My mother was special. Close isn't the word for how she was with people. Sort of a saint, really. Maybe too much for poor old Dad.'

'Do you love your father?'

He half-laughed. 'You certainly get straight to the point.'

'There isn't much time.' She was shaking. Any moment Maynard could walk in the door. He would be furious to find her talking to his son. He would be tempted to slap her. But from the moment she'd heard his voice, she knew that Andrew, like Magnus, was someone she could talk to. For some reason she knew he'd tell the truth.

'Of course I do,' he said.

'Do you think he's a good man?'

He hesitated. 'We knew about his trips to Thailand and everything, my mother and I. But that's only one side of him. I mean, he thought the world of her. He couldn't stand it when she got sick. She was his heart and soul.'

She said nothing. He's worse than you know, she thought.

'How is he? I'm worried about him.'

So that's why he'd rung back. 'Dunno.' Her voice went harsh again. 'How's Kirstin?'

'Kirstin?'

'Your girlfriend.'

'Kirstin's the daughter of Mum's oldest friend, Francine. She's the closest I've got to a sister. She's just got engaged.'

★

Out into the narrow white-tiled corridors that criss-crossed the Mimosa, an identical map upstairs and down. Past the rows of numbered doors, the growly coughs of the morning, the talk-back and TVs of the permanent residents. Through every door now she could hear the muffled voices of the morning shows.

The woman who cleaned the hotel was so thin that she almost seemed suspended from the wings of her shoulder-blades as she bent over a mop at the end of the corridor. She nodded as Maya walked past. Her name was Helga. Close up you saw she wasn't very old but had the lined face of a smoker and a weary flickering kindness.

There was a sign above the manager's desk: *Rooms not serviced daily.* She'd forgotten to bring the pizza box and beer cans out of the room: it would smell when she returned. The Mimosa smell, mould, cigarettes, cheap room freshener, clung to her wherever she went. *Neat dress and shoes required for the dining room at all times.* The dining room, glimpsed through a glass door, with its chairs turned up on the tables, looked as if it had been closed for several years. Beside the office was a set of shallow steps with a sign above it, *Kitchen Facilities Provided.* Beyond was a dark cubbyhole with an electric stove and sink and a door opening onto the carpark out the back. Men sat around the doorway, smoking and talking at all hours of the day. Even in the morning someone would be drinking beer. *Special weekly tariffs & long term tenancy rate available.*

There was something grimly homelike about the place, with its regulars and its rules. But it was not a place you stayed in unless you had to.

Across the desk she could see the manager reading the paper at a table in his private quarters. Strange to see a normal living room, a couch, a cat, a television. The manager's name was

Terry, a Pom with a shaven head and a T-shirt which showed his biceps. Polite, brisk, uncurious: he wanted to get back as quickly as possible to his life in the living room. Sometimes he shouted for Helga who lived with him. He didn't seem to have made her happy.

From the outside the Mimosa was a three-storey, redbrick façade with rows of frosted-glass windows, each with an air-conditioner protruding out of it. It was a masterpiece of ugliness. The first sign you saw was beside the front door. *No Charities.*

The Corner Cafe was next door to the Mimosa, up another set of steps from the footpath. It had a little terrace with an iron-grill fence around it and two white plastic tables set out beneath dusty umbrellas advertising coffee. In the middle of the terrace was a tall palm tree but if you looked up you saw its leaves were just a bunch of brutally pruned brown stalks.

Inside were more plastic tables in a dark bare space and a glass-fronted counter filled with rows of bains-marie. There were all sorts of Asian food, noodles, rice-paper rolls, couscous, curries, tagines. Or you could have chips and sausage rolls and toasted sandwiches. Today's special, written on the blackboard, was chicken korma. The owners, a young couple called Ali and Rita, seemed to live out the back, and their relatives and children came and went through a bead curtain behind the counter. Business was steady, Maya noted, with a professional eye from her days in the newsagency, but it was seldom busy.

She was unable to eat. Sometimes she ordered fried rice or a toasted cheese sandwich, but more and more she wasn't hungry. Her denim skirt had sunk dangerously low on her hips, soon she'd have to improvise a belt. 'Are you trying to look like a model?' he said one night. 'You're becoming gaunt.' She even had to tighten the watchband on her wrist. Funny how you got

315

what you thought you wanted – travel, living with your lover, being thin – when you no longer cared. Perhaps this was the secret to life? Maynard should stop *wanting* to be rich.

She ordered a cappuccino and took up her daily position at one of the tables outside. They were just beyond the city centre, on a wide, windy, indifferent street about to be reclaimed from seediness. Businesses were moving in amongst the cheap hotels, old flats and boarding houses, a Persian Rug Centre, a Hair Concept Salon, a Flight Centre. A single flight to Perth cost $450. The lunch bars and newsagents and chemists were for the office workers. Men passed in white shirts and ties, and women in high heels.

There were trees along the street she'd never seen before, with long green leaves hanging from their stems like the teeth of a comb. Birds dived in and out of them. Around the corner was a jacaranda tree, catching the blue of the sky. Every day she went and looked at it. Her mother would do this, she caught herself thinking.

Rita brought the cappuccino to her table. They smiled, both too shy to speak. Rita was neat and quick with beautiful rosy brown hands. Today she wore her hair back, twisted up into a spout with a tortoiseshell clip, the way Cecile sometimes did. Rita made her long for Cecile.

Maynard didn't like her talking to people. 'Speak to anyone today?' he'd ask casually, his only question to her. He even frowned when she said hello to Helga. He didn't want anyone knowing their business, he said, there were some sensitive deals in the pipeline. They'd be moving on soon. When a day's nego-tiations went well he was happier, gentler, like he used to be after sex.

She went walking. If she had more energy she would have liked to head for the hills, where she glimpsed parks tumbling down slopes, old timber houses, pylons, switchback roads. Maybe there'd be some bush to disappear into.

She walked around a bit in the city, the food courts, the war memorials and parks. She went to the Mall and walked amongst people of her own age. She felt cut off from everybody. Each day she bought a juice from the Boost Bar, an Energy Lift or a Stress Relief, so cold it made her head ache and her heart constrict. No food. If she could save a dollar or two she could buy Magnus a CD. The air was warm, there were tropical blooms appearing on the trees, she liked the dips and valleys, the frontier freedom of the streets after Melbourne. But she didn't have the spirit to tackle a new city.

Mostly she sat in the Corner Cafe or on the fire escape at the back of the Mimosa, or lay on the bed in their room, trying to read. Cheap magazines with their tips for ideal bodies and lovers, and pages of celebrity pics. She slept.

She moved like a sleepwalker. A dull anxiety had taken her over and she didn't like to go too far from the Mimosa. He didn't have to worry about her talking. Days could pass without her speaking to anyone.

Except now there was Andrew.

She kept the phone with her. 'Speak to you soon,' Andrew had said, at the end of their conversation. She knew he was programmed into the top left-hand key. Number One in Maynard's life. Just one little press of the button.

How much could she trust him? How much was he on his father's side? Would he tell Maynard that she'd spoken on his phone?

He was right to be worried about Maynard. Dreams woke him, drenched with sweat. He was plagued by what he called 'nasal problems' with the spring pollens, so that he sat up in bed blowing his nose, lost in misery. His face jumped in and out of focus as she stared at it, like a mask pulled on and off, and sometimes for a moment a face she didn't know peered out at her, wary, calculating, the eyes cold as stones. Yet his touch still had love in it.

A pale fat man in his thirties had come to sit at the other table on the terrace. He was wearing a sagging knit T-shirt and enormous moulded maroon suede sneakers. He had the air, like her, of having nowhere else to go. Rita brought him his breakfast, two sausage rolls and a cup of chips.

If this was a letter who would it be to?

It was coming back, a little shoot breaking through, the instinct to note the grit of details. If she had a notebook she would describe the man at the next table, and the private school girls who had just walked past in round hats and tartan skirts. A little gold chain swung out from Rita's blouse as she took away her cup and she wanted to write that down too. Ever since she spoke to Andrew she'd started recording again. Was this a letter to him? Images came to her. She saw her father talking films with Carlos at the kitchen table. Her father at his desk in the back shed, his mournful eyes staring through the window. Sometimes with his kids he gave a harsh shout. *Don't tell me you were taken in by that!* As if something in his past had hurt him or tricked him. She missed his crumpled, honest face.

The phone rang. 'Hi. Dad?'

'No. Maya again.'

'Where are you? I can hear traffic.'

'In a cafe, sitting outside.'

'He's not back?'

'No.'

'When he comes in can you tell him to phone Granny? She calls up every hour about him. She's driving me mad.'

'She's a terrible old woman.' Why was she so un-shy with him? The truth lay around her, a devastated plain. He knew everything, the only other person in the world who did. She had nothing more to lose.

He burst out laughing. 'Are all you country folk so straight-forward?

'Not that country girl stuff again. I didn't deliver dead calves or anything.'

'What was it like growing up in all that space? Did you feel free?'

She considered. 'I felt safe. Every single thing, trees and rocks and hills, kind of had a character. You felt they knew you. There were these pine trees that were like people. We had a whole world in the trees and down by the creek. The horses used to pretend not to watch us. Horses are mystical creatures, did you know that? I saw a UFO when I was ten. Do you think there are such things as UFOs?'

'If people see them. Maybe they exist in the unconscious.' He paused. 'Do your folks know where you are?'

'I don't want them to.'

A hire car – *No Birds* – had pulled up on the opposite side of the street. Maynard got out, carrying his jacket and crossed quickly to the Mimosa. The car drove past and she saw the toady hunch of Mr T at the wheel and the glint of his glasses. She thought there was an Asian girl sitting in the back.

'I gotta go now. Bye.'

She turned the phone off and hid it at the bottom of her bag.

18

Andrew

Cecile was waiting for him at the wine bar. She'd called him and arranged to meet him straight after work. There was a silver bucket with a bottle of French champagne on their table. He loved the way she did things. If he were meeting any other woman he would have ritually kissed her. Her face glowed up at him as he sat down, her hair crow-black, her skin like liquid. He knew what she would tell him. Clarice had agreed to be in *The Prodigal*.

'I admit I was unscrupulous,' she said. 'I emailed her yesterday and told her that with a topic like this there was a good chance of festival screenings around the world and potential for a large Asian audience. Cannes was not out of the question, or for sure some place in Europe, and I promised to take her with me wherever I was invited. It didn't take her long to make up her mind. Today she emailed back.'

A waiter opened the champagne and poured it for them. She lifted her glass in a toast to Jacob.

'You look happy,' he said. Strands of hair fell around her face, her eyes were bright.

'Maybe this is the best time, at the beginning. I have new ideas every hour. I'm too excited to sleep.'

'And you'll be with Clarice.' She didn't see Clarice as he did, vain and wilful and self-centred. 'Is Dieter enthusiastic?'

'Dieter's going to California. He wants to get involved in more commercial projects.'

Need someone to carry the camera? he wanted to ask. Book flights and hotels? Handle your temperamental leading lady? Hail taxis, order meals? Let me be your *grip*, your *best boy*. They were always mentioned in the credits but he never had found out what they did. How could he help her raise some money for this film? Capelli Brothers was now a multimillion-dollar business, you saw their name on building sites and trucks all over Perth. If he gave them a call? He sat very still for some minutes.

'What are you thinking?' Cecile asked.

'I'm thinking that everything I thought was bad — capitalism, materialism — is now seen as good. And everything I thought was good has turned out to be . . . ineffective.'

'But you know, Jacob, everything creates its opposite. Being creates nonbeing. Absence creates presence.' She smiled, out of general happiness. 'It's the Tao.'

He decided to go to the house of M&D Flynn who never answered their phone. Action after non-action, he supposed.

On the tram he tried to focus on Maynard Flynn. Middle-aged, a struggling businessman. Did he have kids?

This Flynn was the person Maya was *last seen with* . . . A man walking down a street, little Maya skipping beside him, holding his hand. No, not little Maya. His grown-up daughter. A law unto herself. But still with a sweetness of touch, a loving heart. What sort of older man would lightly take that for himself?

He knocked decisively on the Flynns' front door. Modest, but on the way up, he thought, surveying the street as he waited. Looked like couples with young children were moving in. There was some sort of park down the end.

The Flynns' house was bleak, the curtains drawn, the concrete front yard covered with fallen leaves. Unoccupied, he'd say, the life all gone out of it. This is how he'd report it to Toni.

But when he knocked again, he detected through the door's coloured-glass panels an answering glimmer deep within the house. Footsteps. A tall thin young man opened the door.

'I'm looking for a Maynard Flynn. Does he live here?'

'He's away at the moment. Can I help you? I'm his son.'

'Any idea how I can get in contact with him?'

The young man stared at him. Early twenties. Unusual coloring, not Anglo-Celt. Pale olive skin, almost greenish, red glints in the hair, dark eyes. Shadows under the eyes. A quietness about him. Of course. He'd just lost his mother.

'My name's Jacob de Jong. My daughter Maya used to work for your father.'

'I'm Andrew. Come in.'

Jacob followed him down a long corridor to a living room dark from overgrown vines on a pergola outside the windows. Cheerless, unlived in, filled with the sort of antique-style teak furniture that you could buy in import stores.

'Sit down.' Andrew indicated a chair at the table. 'Would you

322

like a drink? I always help myself to my father's whisky when I call in.' He took down two cut-glass tumblers and a decanter from the dresser. 'It's lucky you caught me. My father's put the place on the market. I'm packing up my kid stuff.' He indicated an open door into a small bedroom. 'You know, hockey trophies, *Asterix*, *Tintin*. Cheers.' He sat down opposite Jacob and took a sip of whisky. He kept his eyes on Jacob. The place was cold, Jacob was glad of his coat. But he sensed that at last he was getting closer to the heart of the matter. Because why was this son so willing to engage?

'I'm sorry to disturb you . . .' Jacob began.

'I'm glad of company. I don't like coming here.' Andrew threw his head back and swallowed the whole shot. 'I reward myself with whisky. I find it helps.'

He seemed like a nice young guy or was he being disarming? Of course he'd want to protect his father. (Would Magnus protect *him* if he knew he was in the wrong?) Maybe it was *him*, Jacob, that Andrew wanted to check out? He remembered the attitude of the sergeant at the Missing Persons Bureau. What, after all, might a girl be running away from? Fathers were suspicious people these days.

'The fact is, Andrew, we don't know where Maya is. We haven't been able to contact her. Perhaps your father could help. Are you in contact with him?'

'We talk occasionally on the phone.'

'Do you know where he is?'

Andrew shrugged. 'He travels all over. I call his mobile.'

'Could I ask you for his number?'

'I'm sorry, he never gives it out.'

'Then could you do something for me? Next time you speak to your father could you ask him to give me a call? Here's my number.'

'OK.'

'Can I also ask you to call me if you hear anything about Maya, anything at all?'

Andrew bowed his head, a signal of acquiescence, if only to Jacob's right to ask. His deep brown eyes were full of thoughts, sad and grown-up. Already his high forehead was faintly lined. When he wasn't smiling there was something ascetic about his face. He wouldn't want to lie. Toni would approve of him, Jacob thought, unexpectedly. She loved sensitive young men.

Jacob put down his glass and stood up. 'Thanks Andrew.' He hesitated, then looked him steadily in the eye. 'The thing about Maya is, she's a very special girl. We think she is. She's very intense, very loyal. Once she commits to someone or something . . .'

The two men shook hands.

19

Grand Final

Toni was late and for a while Jacob was glad to be able to give himself to the experience, to the rumble of anticipation that was building up in the stadium, to be part of things for once, lifted up and carried along by the energy waiting to be released.

Tod had good connections. Seats in the middle tier of the stadium, mid-field. Next to Jacob were two men in their mid-thirties, friends, Demons supporters, like him. He'd decided to back Melbourne, the dark horse, the desperate, you never knew what they'd pull out of the bag. He could shout and swear along with them, throw his arms around. Here he was allowed to be male. If he had a mobile phone he would have called Carlos. *Guess where I am, mate!* They'd made a tradition of setting up for the big match at the Garcias', stacking the fridge with beer, wearing team scarves. Chris made everyone hot dogs. He thought of the streets of Warton, silent and empty, the whole country gone into retreat, everyone hunkered down in darkened rooms before the telly, as if war had been declared.

A massed choir assembled on the emerald field and belted out a medley culminating in 'I Still Call Australia Home'. Schoolkids did some aerobic dancing to indulgent cheers. Smoke and balloons went up, jet fighters circled overhead. Then the national anthem, the young gladiators burst out and a hundred thousand people stood and roared for blood. Then the toss, the grapple for the ball, the break. Everyone started calling out, as if the stakes were personal now, screaming his or her advice. Strange transformations materialised around him. 'Get it out! Get it out!' screamed the genteel middle-aged woman in front of him, in a sort of a tantrum. For a moment he was dizzy with the occasion of it all. This was his culture! His country!

But where was Toni?

Suddenly he was on his feet. '*Holding the ball, ya mongrel,*' he roared, showing off to the guys next to him, who laughed and stamped their feet.

Then for a little while Jacob forgot about his women, and his sense of having in some way failed them, and settled into his habitual meditation on the players as warriors, symbols, losers and winners on life's playing field.

The world was more changed than she had expected. Mile after mile it displayed itself to her in a hotchpotch of detail, factories, warehouses, car yards, rows of matching houses disappearing into the haze. It had never been clearer to her, what the world

326

cared about. Her gaze seemed more acute, as if a blast of air had passed through her head.

The bus moved slowly in the city traffic. Jacob would freak out if she was late. In the ashram they would be having the pre-lunch meditation. She never had improved at meditation, but already she missed it, like you miss regular exercise. She wanted to keep this calm, this clarity and purpose. One day during meditation it had occurred to her that Maya must be *persuaded* to come back.

The game had started and she passed easily through the ticket gate. She was glad she was late. If she'd had to fight her way through throngs of people she might have turned back. From the moment she'd put on her jeans and black leather jacket this morning, the world seemed heavy and dark and animal again. As she stood on the first step at the bottom of the gigantic concourse, a roar broke out and filled the stadium, like chaos amplified. She should never have agreed to this. Stay in the moment, she told herself, but the moment was exploding, volatile, aggressive. She had an impulse to cower and cover her head.

She went to the ladies', and looked in the mirror and saw herself at last, the graying stubble of her hair, her ears puckish and alert, her brown skin faded to sallow, her valiant neck, her whole face carved into a new angularity. She caught a glimpse, like a ghost, of the hawkish features of Beryl. Her hand rose to her head. Her heart thumped in her chest. She wrapped her scarf tighter around her neck.

She took a breath and went to buy a bottle of water from the kiosk before she battled her way to her seat. The large man in front of her at the counter turned and she was face to face with Cy Fisher.

They stood silent for some moments while the hollow massed

roar of the stadium rolled all around them.

'Come over here,' Cy Fisher said. She followed his black back with its gray-streaked hair to a square of wall beside the fire escape. The stadium held its breath again and everything went still. In quiet voices, they began to speak.

'So you follow Australian Rules.'

'Just dropped in for a while. I've got some money on this game.'

'Who's going to win?'

He snorted. 'Essendon.'

'You couldn't stand sport once.' He'd hated exercise of any kind, but had that changed? He was trimmer and more youthful looking than he used to be. All these years he'd loomed giant-like at the back of her memory but he seemed lesser here, on a more human scale. Something had relaxed in his face. A little baggy around the jawline, and there were swirls of violet skin under his eyes, but they were still black and shining. He was dressed casually, in a black T-shirt and zip-up jacket. His hair beneath the gray streaks was still dark, pushed back from a receding hairline. He must be nearly sixty. She hadn't expected that he'd age this well.

'Didn't used to have the time. Now I've retired.'

'Retired! What happened?'

'I've had Death Therapy.' He treated her to one of his sudden teeth-baring grins. 'Heart attack. At a wedding! Triple bypass, three years ago. Someone looks after me . . . but I do things differently now. Had to get out of Perth.'

'You live here?'

'Melbourne's an interesting town. Tons of *culture*.'

'How's your mother?'

'Lives with Sabine these days. I fly her over a couple of times a year.'

'What do you do with yourself?' Obviously he couldn't show his face in Perth.

'Work out. Walk. Cook healthy food. Go to concerts. Would you believe it, I'm learning French!'

'No business?' But there would always be business . . .

He looked amused. 'I've got my finger in a few pies. But I was winding down in Perth. The big conglomerates moved in from the eastern states. No fun any more. I was always on my guard . . . Anyway, what's happened to you?'

His eyes skimmed across her baldness but he refrained from comment. She noticed the interest, even affection in his eyes.

'Oh Cy, we've lost our daughter.' What did anything else matter? She was an old woman in black scuttling down the road, wailing and waving her hands.

'Lost her?' He looked around as if for a child.

'She's eighteen. She came to Melbourne and then she disappeared.' She felt relieved to be telling him, as if he were a policeman or a doctor. Like handing over to a professional.

'She do drugs?'

'Not that we know.'

He stood looking down at her. 'We'd better go somewhere and talk.'

'After the game?'

'Now. You don't want to watch this, do you?'

'No. If you don't mind missing it.'

He shook his head and set off towards the stairs.

She ought to tell Jacob. But she couldn't risk losing Cy in the crowd. Once Cy decided on action, he took it. If stalled, he could change his mind. And what would Jacob say if she told him she was going off with Cy?

As she followed him the siren sounded. It must be half-time. The crowd instantly spilled out all around her on the stairwell, pushing her against the wall. She could only just keep track of Cy's head bobbing further and further down.

She felt the old luxurious pull of relinquishment to him, of putting herself in his hands. Though she rarely thought of him now, she sometimes still had dreams of him in which he showed pain, even vulnerability, and she woke feeling tender towards him. Suddenly she remembered what it was like to be with him. How you saw things differently. Anything seemed possible.

A light rain started to fall. It had rained like this when he spirited her away from Karen's wedding, and in the restaurant after he took her to be married. When he asserted his powers.

Maya would be found.

He was the reason for everything, Jacob, their children, the way they lived.

She and Jacob were small and ordinary, she thought, as she made her way towards him, tiny figures in the roaring crowd. Winds of change blew around them, wars broke out, plagues ran rampant across continents, children died. Still they trudged on. Long ago they opted for the small life, for safety and peace and a home for their children. They kept their heads down, their fingers crossed.

There was Cy, leaning against a railing, at ease, missing nothing, a little space around him. Retired? He would never retire.

Essendon had it in the bag. Jacob sat drinking beer morosely beside his fellow Demons supporters as the slaughter ground its way to the final goal. A losing game resembled those dead ends in life when you can't do anything right. Hird was chaired off the ground to a roar of adulation. Wasn't that every man's secret dream?

His neighbours stood up to leave.

'Looks like I've lost my wife now,' Jacob said. 'First my daughter, then my wife.'

But their moment of fellowship had passed. The men slunk off towards the exit without even saying goodbye.

20

The Devil's Country

This morning it was raining. The street was empty, swept by sheets of rain. She sprinted between the doorways of the Mimosa and the Corner Cafe to sit at an inside table. Through the open door she watched some doves sheltering beneath the tables on the terrace, pecking at crumbs, as diligent as ever, their feathers fluffed up against the weather. A summer storm. Leaves parted and hung dripping off the tree by the road. She thought of the manes of horses in the rain. A gust of wind set them shivering and tossing. Next time maybe she'd be born as a horse. Or a bird. She didn't want to be a person any more.

Something had woken her, a mauve light through the frosted-glass windows that seeped in under her eyelids. Or was it a dream? In the dream she was moving through the Flynns' house between sliding doors that opened to reveal Dory lying on a couch in a glowing mauve dressing gown, propped up on her side, her hand beneath her cheek. He was kneeling beside her. Go, just go, a voice said.

She had a burning thirst and drank from the tap in the bathroom. She noticed she was still dressed. Her sandals were by the door and she pushed her feet into them. Her bag was by the bed. She felt deep inside it and the mobile was still there. *Seen my phone anywhere?* He was asleep on his back with his mouth open, like a corpse in this strange light. She let herself out.

The smell of this place made her stomach clench. She must have slept but she was exhausted, as if she'd just done a full day's work. Sore everywhere, but she had no time for a shower. Behind the desk at the entrance Helga was yawning, pinning up a strand of hair. Helga too was tired.

Running in the rain to the cafe woke her up a bit. But when she came to order she found she didn't have enough money for coffee. Just enough for a camomile tea. Even Rita seemed distant this morning when she brought the cup to the table. The tea had a dusty clover smell that reminded her of her mother. If she were home she would stay in bed today and let her mother take over. When she was sick, her mother, with her natural cures, her herbs and soups, kept the world at bay. She made you a child again. A vision crossed her mind from long ago, her mother's hands, tanned and strong, wrinkled at the joints, the shiny oval nails clipped short for service.

When she was a little girl, the word 'mother' sounded dark and velvety and sheltering, like flowers in the rain. She hated sleeping over at other people's houses, even the Garcias. She didn't like to be too far away from Toni.

The fat man was inside too, stolidly eating his breakfast, his maroon suede sneakers splotched with mud. Salty chips and

Coke gave him a little hit, so he could forget his misery for a moment.

A big man at the table by the door was tucking into the kind of breakfast her father liked to have in cafes on his jaunts to Perth. Poached eggs and spinach and tomatoes, while he read a newspaper. It made him feel like a city man.

Ali and Rita came and went through the bead curtain, not speaking. Ali's mother shuffled out with bains-marie of fresh-cooked food. A baby was crying out the back.

'Here's a drink for you, baby.' A memory flash, the sort you get after you've been drunk. She gasped, opened *The Courier-Mail* lying on her table. She couldn't read the words. Something had happened to her brain.

There was a party. *We're going to a party.* He was actually smiling at her. A taxi, a white high-rise block of flats. A lift with a dim mirror reflecting the two of them going up, side by side, not touching, like a father and a daughter. A living room furnished like a hotel, generic paintings, wall-lights turned low, a smoked-glass table covered with bottles. Everyone was out on the balcony, smoking and admiring the view.

'Here's a drink for you, baby.' She thought there was a gunshot down below but it was just a car backfiring. Everyone laughs, thinks she's being funny. Her own voice, the 'cute' voice, exclaiming at the coloured tracery of headlights. He puts his arm around her. He's pleased with her, even though she's still wearing her denim skirt and T-shirt, like a schoolgirl, and everyone else is dressed up. Why didn't he care how she looked tonight? She knows she's becoming too excited. The balcony is dangerously high. Mr T is there, back from Bangkok, but keeps his back turned to her. She speaks with an Asian girl, beautiful as a model. My home is far away, the girl says. She gives a little shivery laugh after everything she says.

★

The fat man was standing at the counter, ordering take-away. Sweet and sour. Probably for his morning tea. Ali's mother brought out a bain-marie of steaming rice. He pointed to it. She scooped up a large spoonful for him and dumped it in the foil container. You could smell it, the sweet bready smell of hot rice. She watched the fat man lumber across the terrace carrying his take-away in a white plastic bag. The rain had stopped, the doves had flown away. Her heart was pounding and the sweat spurted into her armpits.

Baby, have a drink. Like a father wanting to help. He's never called her baby before. Then the need to go horizontal, to close her eyes, she's about to curl up on the floor. But she's falling back onto a bed in a dark room and he's lying on top of her, kissing her, touching her, his face so close she can't see it anymore. She sees behind him the stocky silhouette against the light in the window. She tries to kick and buck but she can't move. She's pinned down. 'Wait,' he hisses in her ear. She gasps but he puts his mouth on hers. She's going under. This is the Devil's country, she thinks.

She's sitting on a bathroom floor, being sick in a toilet.

You promised. Never again.

'Pull yourself together. You've been dreaming.'

Was it a dream? She couldn't remember how she came back to the Mimosa.

The need for coffee was so strong that she thought of asking Rita for credit. But everyone was strange today, tired and sad, even Rita.

She pulled the phone out of her bag and pressed One.

'Andy here. Hello?'

'Just to let you know, I've taken over the phone.'

'Maya? What's the time?'

'Did I wake you?'

'No.'

'What were you doing?'

'Well . . . I was praying.'

'*Praying!*' For once he shocked her.

'I pray every morning.'

'How long have you been doing this?'

'It sort of started by itself when Mum got sick.'

'Fat lot of good it did.' She didn't know why this made her so hostile.

'Maya!'

'Well she *died*.' A screw had dropped out, she was running loose and wild, out of control, faster and faster.

'That's not exactly what prayer does.'

'Pretty funny in a scientist.'

'They don't exclude each other. But I'm thinking of giving up science and going into the priesthood.'

'*No! No!*' Her voice went hoarse. '*That's asking too much!*'

'Maya, what are you talking about?'

'It's her, you're doing it for her. She wants to keep you for herself.'

'Who does?'

'Dory. She's very powerful.'

He said nothing for a while. 'Why are you so upset? Is it Dad?'

This time she was silent.

'He wants you to hate him, Maya. He hates himself so much. You shouldn't be loyal to him, it will only make it worse.'

After a while he said: '*Your* father came to see me last week. I don't think he trusted me, but he seemed like a good guy. Pretty worried though. Maya, why don't you . . .'

She hung up.

★

She sat very still, her elbows on the table, her hands over her eyes. She didn't want to see her father's face, the way it looked when he was hurt, pale and hollow-cheeked, his lips moving stiffly. An injury to one of them was felt by all of them. In their family they tried not to harm people.

'Excuse me.'

She parted her hands and saw the big man from the table by the door looking down at her.

'Mind if I sit here?' He sat anyway, the light behind him.

She wanted to tell him to go away, she couldn't stand having any man near her. He started talking.

'My name's Cy Fisher. I'm an old friend of your mother's.' He put his hands on the table. He wore a thick gold ring. His hands were large and dry and so white it was as if they'd been dusted with flour.

'Coffee?' He gestured to Ali, who came over at once. 'The usual,' he said, with a little flick of his fingers between them. How did he know she had a usual? How long had he been coming here? They sat in silence.

A cappuccino was put in front of her, a short black for him. 'Just a mouthful or two,' he said to her in a low voice, 'before it goes cold.'

There were teachers like this, that you find yourself obeying. She took a sip.

'Milky coffee. Best thing for you. Big night?'

She mumbled something about a few drinks.

'And the rest.' He was looking in her eyes.

'What d'you mean?'

'By the look of your pupils.'

'No,' she said, at the same moment as she realised he was right. She gulped some coffee.

'Your mother asked me to find you.'

'It's none of her business.'

'She gave me two names. One I traced. Tod Carpenter.'

She covered her face again.

'They aren't nice people, Maya. Your friends.'

His eyes were black like marbles, shining, smiling. She kept looking down. 'Are you the crim my mother was married to?'

'Still is, I think.' He gave a suave smile. 'I think of myself as an ex-businessman.'

Ali came to the table, hovered, respectful.

'Two more of the same,' Cy said, keeping his eyes on Maya. Ali went away.

'Time to leave, Maya.'

'Where would I go?'

'Back to Melbourne.'

'I've got no money.'

'I drove up from Melbourne. Come back with me.'

She stared at him coldly. 'How do I know I can trust you?' She saw a sort of purity, firm, clean-lined, that reminded her of her mother. Did lovers always leave an imprint on each other?

'What do you want? Toni's birthday? Sixth of March. Her mother's name was Beryl. How's that? She's cut all her hair off, by the way.' He turned around and gestured at some point beyond the terrace. 'That's my car, over there.'

The rain had stopped, the sun came out. She saw gold specks of dust floating around him. 'You're happy.'

'Why do you say that?'

'I always know if people are happy or unhappy.'

He smiled. 'You are so like your mother.'

Maya looked away. She knew what he'd be thinking. Everybody always thought it. Kids came out with it. *Is that your mother? No kidding! But she's so pretty . . .*

'You are more beautiful,' Cy Fisher said. 'You have more passion.'

She was startled into looking at him. Could he read thoughts?

'You can't help him, Maya.'

She sat very still.

'Where is he now?'

'In the room, asleep.'

'Do you have to go back for anything?'

She thought for a moment. 'My fur coat.'

'You don't need it anymore.'

He went to the counter to pay.

She reached into her bag for the phone and pressed button One.

'Maya?'

'I've got a chance of a lift to Melbourne.'

'Who with?'

'A friend of my mother's. I don't know what to do.'

'You should leave.'

'Will I still be able to speak to you?'

'You will.'

'Promise?'

'I promise.'

21

Departure

They left at eight the next morning, buttoned up in coats. Carlos offered his Toyota, but Kitty said she felt more confident in the Moke. He waved them off with a smile on his face, that little fleeting disbelieving smile that she knew was for her. They hadn't made love for two days because Jordan was home with a cold. Winnie howled inside the house. As soon as she dropped Magnus off at the airport, she was turning round and coming straight back.

As they drove down India Street Magnus slipped a disc into the player, an electronic piece, spare and hushed like the trees etched against the horizon and the lean bare hills.

'What's this called?'

'*Music for Airports.* Brian Eno.'

Last night, after Jacob's phone call, they had floated round

340

the house, laughing and calling out. Carlos and Jordan came over for a celebratory drink. Magnus stayed up past midnight, his music full on while he packed. Maya was coming back tomorrow night. Their parents wanted them all to be together again. They'd managed to get him on a flight. He was going to miss several weeks of school. Winnie slumped, one eye propped open to watch his every movement.

'Once you've delivered him to the airport your duties are over, Kit,' Jacob said on the phone. 'According to Magnus you've done a fabulous job. You'll have to come to Warton often and stay with us.' He was expansive with relief.

'I think I'll stay here with Winnie while I follow up some options,' she said. 'If that's all right with you.'

They entered the last stretch of the highway before the start of the metropolitan area, a dark region shadowed by dense pine plantations and miles of tall unfriendly bush. 'Dad calls this body-dumping land,' Magnus said. Kitty put her foot down and let the little rattling Moke tear into the overtaking lane.

A tinny red *No Birds* hire car flashed past. She glimpsed its driver, a blonde in sunglasses with a tight determined mouth.

'Chris!' Magnus said. 'That was Chris Garcia.' He leaned out of the Moke and waved, just in case she recognised the Moke and was looking in her rear vision window. Then he remembered Kitty.

The overtaking lane dissolved and Kitty veered suddenly into a truck lay-by, pulled up, fell out of the car and leaned over into the bush making harsh coughing sounds. Magnus climbed out in sympathy, but walked a little way down a gravel track. It always made him feel sick when someone puked.

Once you were walking through it, the bush was actually quite beautiful. The sun sparkled through the rustling trees and

341

shadows flickered across the gravel. There were ferns and fat grass trees with fresh green spears. Without thinking, he cracked off a fistful and swished them round like a kid. He looked back at Kitty, bent over, all in black, the strings of red hair falling across her face and he felt very sorry for her.

What would happen now? Carlos would have to choose.

She stood up, wiping her mouth and he walked back to her.

'It's OK Magnus,' Kitty said, though a moment ago she'd thought she was dying. Good old Kitty, once again, the sacrifice at the feast. She wanted to scream *God!* and run into the path of the oncoming traffic. Only the thought of the young male psyche in her care held her back.

She took a swig from her water bottle and sat down on a picnic bench. 'It must be all the rich food we've been eating. I often feel a bit sick when I wake up.' After all, wasn't there one rule in her life that she could depend on – she always paid.

'Morning sickness,' Magnus said, unexpectedly. He didn't know what that was, but he'd heard his mother say it. He was trying to be sympathetic.

Kitty turned her head away to hide a sudden stab of tears.

'Just give me a few moments and then I'll get you to that plane,' she said. Already there was colour in her face. Magnus strolled off down the track, head bent in thought, idly swishing his spears. It was this question of luck again, or not, in your life.

No plans, Kitty, she told herself. *No plans.* All her life she'd planned and she was always disappointed. But she couldn't stop herself gathering evidence. Three weeks of good, daily, loving sex. Even twice daily. Relaxation, happiness, no stress. Fresh air.

They drove off, her thoughts racing ahead. As soon as she left Magnus she'd find a pharmacy and pick up a test.

She'd keep the Moke for the time being. The family could pack her things when they came back.

First a house. Inner city, near Fitzgerald Street. Go back to what she knew. Near a park and a school. A simple teaching job where she could go part-time. She'd need some help for a while.

One thing was sure, she wouldn't call on Arlene.

No secrets, no mysteries, no dark rooms with shut doors.

'Are you all right now?' Magnus asked. She nodded, her eyes on the road.

By the time they reached the outskirts of the city and took the turnoff for the airport, her beautiful dark-haired child was born, named, educated, lovingly reared.

22

Arrival

Here they were again, passing under the playful red arms of the Melbourne Gateway, but going the other way now, seasoned by the city it promised, a thicket of glitter left behind them. It was rush hour, the taxi edged its way along the last stretch to the airport. The dark gray walls beside the road were dissolving into the dusk. Beyond was a glimpse of suburban roofs. They sat side by side on the back seat, lost in separate dreams.

Last night after Cy Fisher's phone call, he left a note for Cecile on the kitchen bench. He found it this morning, with a row of exclamation marks scrawled on the bottom of it, surrounded by radiant hearts and clouds with the number 9 inside them. *I'll be home early for the champagne*, she wrote.

She was leaving for KL next week. He had an image of her disappearing through a series of arched doorways.

The taxi wasn't moving. It smelt of their anticipation, their clean, scented bodies, the fresh clothes they'd put on to meet their children.

He glanced at Toni. There was something touching about her ears, like a boy's after a haircut. She was smaller all over, less ripe and luxuriant. Yet more approachable somehow.

Women survived without him. It was a mistake to think that you were indispensable.

At first Jacob had been furiously disbelieving that she could entrust Maya to Cy Fisher. They slept soundly beside each other from long habit, but did not touch. He'd barely spoken to her.

She wasn't used to this dailyness now, living your life next to another being. This big tortured man with his heavy tread, forever requiring her attention.

Once when they had just moved into the house in Warton, she came upon him standing in the dark front room, pale and shaking. Something about the shadows reminded him of the death of a girl he knew years ago, he said. As soon as he opened this door he'd felt it again, the black hole yawning before him. She put her arms around him and held him tight. 'Whatever it is, I won't let it harm you,' she said. 'I won't let you go down.'

The traffic had started moving.

She looked at her watch. 'Magnus will land before we get there.'

'There's nothing he'd like better.'

From the moment of their birth, her pure, fierce devotion to their children had filled him with wonder and respect.

Yet a short while ago how lightly he'd been prepared, at least in his mind, to put her to one side.

★

345

After they left the MCG Cy Fisher drove her across town to an unpretentious little cafe where – of course – they knew him and the coffee was excellent. She sat across the table from him and told him about Maya and their life in Warton. How dull it sounded, even to her. It occurred to her that for all these years what she'd called 'good' was no more than fear and guilt and prudence.

This was the effect he'd always had on her. He overturned you. He woke you up.

She still didn't know what 'good' was.

To go further out.

When he drove her home from the cafe, she saw an old terrace cottage with a row of ragged Tibetan flags waving across its porch. Who lived there? she wondered. Was it an ashram or a hippie house? Decoration, or a frail reminder of the spirit?

A rhythm had started up in his head. Da dum da dum . . . *They hand in hand* . . . What was it? *Paradise Lost.* Adam and Eve banished forever. The last two lines.

> *They hand in hand with wand'ring steps and slow,*
> *Through Eden took their solitary way.*

The airport was lit up like a theatre, a gala occasion. The taxis filed in one after another, they were suddenly in the midst of a panic of people lugging their baggage in and out of cars. A huge plane was lowering overhead, coming in to land.

Jacob paid the driver, they called out their thanks and slammed the taxi door. Now he took her hand and they ran.

23

The Call

He asked her if she minded opera and then played the whole of *Don Giovanni*, disc after disc. There was no expectation of talk. She slept and woke, slept and woke. He stopped for petrol in a town called Goondiwindi and she walked a little way into the sun and shut her eyes to smell the dust and feel the warmth on her face. Cy Fisher came out of the service station carrying snacks and drinks. She saw how exotic he looked out here, black clothes, black car, white face.

He bought them each a bottle of water and an apple and what he called a passable foccacia. She felt like a kid.

He drove and took fast bites of the foccacia lying unwrapped on his knees. He had sharp teeth for an old person. 'Usually for lunch I eat Japanese,' he said. She could tell he liked food.

There was endless scrub, trees with thin black trunks and fresh green leaves and yellow wattles everywhere. Her body had stopped aching. She started to come awake. She opened the window and took a breath.

As the road fell into shadow she put herself on roo watch: she wasn't sure he'd know about kangaroos. A full white moon was rising.

'Do you believe in the supernatural?'

'Someone looks after me, no doubt about it. I've got a first-rate guardian angel.'

Then she told him about the flying saucer and Jason Kay and the Brethren, and all her life right up to the office and the flowers.

The lights of Dubbo appeared on the horizon.

He cruised the streets looking for a motel.

'Do we have to stop?'

'I don't know about you, but I'm not up to another ten hours' driving. I promised your mother I'd bring you home safely.'

It was early evening when the black car pulled up outside Cecile's wooden slatted fence. The plane trees across the street had broken out in pale green leaves. The courtyard light was on. Maya sat very still. The car was warm and cosy, littered with pistachio shells, a capsule outside time. It felt like home.

'Would you like to come in?'

'Not this time. But you have my number.'

'What am I going to do?' she said, almost to herself, as she opened the car door.

'Something amazing, no doubt.' He smiled at her.

The car slipped back into the traffic.

★

The key was in its place under the little Buddha. She stalked from room to room, snapping on lights. Where were they? She saw the discreet flash on Cecile's closed laptop. In her room the bed was made and the floor was cleared and there were clothes she recognised from long ago hanging in the cupboard, her father's red cowboy shirt, her mother's best black pants.

She looked in the bathroom mirror and saw her face was thinner, paler, almost translucent. *You have more passion.* What did that mean?

She went downstairs and paced around the conversation pit, strangely bereft. Something was missing, she was filled with nostalgia, but for what? They were all here and yet it wasn't enough.

Deep in her bag, the telephone rang. Her hands shook as she scrabbled for it. She saw the number and pressed the green button.

'Hello Andy,' she said.

Acknowledgements

My thanks to Drusilla Modjeska for her generosity and encouragement.

And for their help in various ways with this book, my thanks to Priscilla Alderton, Peter Bahen, Christophe Bourguedieu, Derek and Julia Carruthers, John de Hoog, Bob Hewitt and FotoFreo, Ruth and Kerry Hill, Giles Hohnen, Gail Jones, Eveline Kotai, Robert Riddell, Bob Shields, Clancy White, Terri-Ann White and Morgan Campbell.

About the Author

Joan London is the author of two prize-winning collections of stories, *Sister Ships*, which won the *Age* Book of the Year in 1986, and *Letter to Constantine*, which in 1994 won the Steele Rudd Award and the WA Premier's Award for Fiction. These collections were published in one volume by Picador in 2004 as *The New Dark Age*. In 2001 her first novel, *Gilgamesh*, was published, shortlisted for the Miles Franklin, as well as a host of other awards, and chosen as the *Age* Book of the Year for Fiction in 2002. It was also longlisted for the Orange Prize and the Dublin Impac.

Gilgamesh has been published in Europe, the UK and the US, where it was a *NY Times* Notable Book in 2003 and an Editor's Choice Book.